Dickenson

Dr. Heather J. Lyall

ISBN: 978-1-959700-15-9

Victoria Fletcher
hootbookspublishing.biz
vfletcher56@gmail.com

Dedication

This book is dedicated to all of the residents of Clinchco, Haysi, Clintwood, and Dickenson County. Through Facebook posts, private messaging, and public meetings, each of you has helped create this book. Your personalities, your skills, your knowledge, and your quirks have developed characters that are easily loved, and for that I thank you from the bottom of my heart. I hope this book helps you, and many others, realize how wonderful and unique our people truly are.

Acknowledgments

Other special thanks should go to the Dickenson County Sheriff's office. The deputies and office staff were always willing to help by answering the (occasionally dumb) questions I would ask during the writing stages.

A special thanks to my editor, Cappi Gibbs. Based out of Nashville, Tennessee, Cappi worked tirelessly to teach me how to use commas correctly. Even though she failed at her attempt, we should all be thankful to her for making the book readable.

Lastly, a special thanks to my three daughters (Kim, age 13; Cassidy, age 12; and Lydia, age 10) and my husband. Over the past year, getting away with murder has become a family discussion. The good news is that Rodney and I no longer worry about someone mistreating our daughters.

Table of Contents

Chapter 1

Sometimes our memories are involuntarily summoned from the mind's deepest recesses. Memories seldom fail to emerge in the presence of familiar smells, colors, circumstances, or surroundings. Today was not uncommon nor unfamiliar to Jacob McKinney. He parked on the street directly in front of a two-story brick colonial completed in 1905. He was accustomed to parking his sheriff's vehicle where he could quickly leave if he were called out for an emergency. He sat momentarily admiring the architecture and bracing himself for yet another occasion where he would see family and friends in mourning.

Jacob gazed at the four white pillars stretching from the porch's base to the roof above the second story of the building. Directly above the main entry door, the brick was interrupted by a stone lentil that beautifully contrasted with the brick and formed the entryway. A solitary light swung from a chain above the doorway from the second-story ceiling. The light-housing looked antique, and the wind caused the light to swing like a pendulum above the entrance each time the wind blew.

A unique aspect of the former Skeen family home was the second-story door directly above the main entryway with no ladder, steps, or stairwell and no small deck to stand upon. Most people would have never noticed the odd doorway, but it had always stuck out in Jacob's mind. Trivial images that were out of place and unordinary would take hold. The thoughts were like a splinter stuck in his mind that could not be removed. Those trivial images would occasionally distract him and interrupt regular thought patterns with what could be described as disturbing mental pain. Jacob often wondered if he had a touch of obsessive-compulsive disorder that made him notice odd things that were out of place with greater intensity.

Jacob sighed and stepped from the vehicle. He crossed the sidewalk and walked through the wrought iron gate into the neatly manicured yard. On each side of the walkway were trees that shaded and protected the walkway. As he approached the main door, he noticed a small plaque on the right side of the entryway for the first time. Jacob knew the sign had probably been located in that very spot for years, but the doorway with no steps above the main door had always drawn his attention, so he had never noticed the small sign with white letters and trim that read, "Open to sunshine, friends, and God."

Dickenson County is tucked deep inside the Appalachian Mountain range and has only three incorporated towns: Haysi, Clinchco, and Clintwood. Clintwood is the county seat. Clinchco is the center of the county, and Haysi sits on the Russell Fork River near the Breaks Interstate Park. The county has a little over fourteen thousand residents, and most are related within four generations. Dickenson County was the last county to be formed in Virginia and was nicknamed "Virginia's Baby." The small population of people and the county's heritage, culture, and history made Dickenson County one of the best places in the world for Jacob to live. The economy and lack of housing options made it one of the worst. But it was home to Jacob, who loved the people and the mountains.

Jacob made a habit of going to every funeral in the county. There are only three funeral homes in the county, and two were located down the street from the courthouse, so stopping by for a quick visit was not difficult. Jacob was elected to the Sheriff's office last year and was the youngest ever to be elected to the office. Jacob had made a name for himself while playing football for the county high school as a running back. After graduating, he spent eight years in the Army and completed a bachelor's degree. Jacob had then decided to return home and work with the county sheriff's office. When the older sheriff, Tom Linkard, retired, Jacob ran for office and won the election. Jacob had always felt like it wasn't because of his education, background, or experience but because he was distantly related to almost everyone in the county.

As Jacob stepped through the entryway, the familiarity of his surroundings made him feel comforted. Jacob had always loved the old building. The funeral home had once been the home of the Skeens family in the early 1900s. During the process of updating, many of the old features had been refurbished to keep their historical value, while other features had changed due to the commercialization of the property. Entering the foyer, Jacob looked down at the tile flooring and beautiful rug covering the original hardwood floors.

While shaking hands and speaking with friends and family, his eyes wandered around the room to the beautiful, exposed beams, chandeliers, ten-foot ceilings, the rounded stairwell, hand-built fireplaces, and the furnishings from the early 1900s. The building confused the senses. Almost everything was over a hundred years old, yet the air was crisp, fresh, and clean. The building itself could transport you back in time, and you could imagine ladies in chiffon dresses with high lace collars, long sleeves, and beautifully embellished wide-brimmed hats. The men wore black coats and trousers with starched shirts, low-cut waistcoats, and derby hats while they smoked in the parlor during the funeral.

Proudly displayed on the antique furniture and around the walls were photos of family, friends, and neighbors from days gone by. He momentarily stopped and looked at a picture of his grandparents. He smiled while looking at the photo of his grandmother smiling proudly beside his grandfather. She was a petite woman wearing a chevron knit dress that was stylish in the day for the younger generation, and the glow on her face told the story of a happy marriage. His grandmother had placed her left hand on his grandfather's shoulder and her right hand on his forearm. She leaned in towards him with her right leg bent at the knee, holding her foot suspended in the air playfully behind her. They had been married for over fifty years when the photo was taken, and Jacob hoped that one day a woman would smile like that while standing beside him. But so far, it had not happened.

Jacob had served in the Army for eight years before returning to his hometown. During his time in service, he attended funerals all over the country. Jacob was glad that most of the funerals he attended were not the funerals of his brothers and sisters in arms but of their elderly family members. Jacob was good-looking, intelligent, friendly, and single. Apparently, that meant everyone with a deceased family member brought him to the funeral. Funerals were different all over the country, but Jacob would be the first to say that an Appalachian funeral was different from all others. Depending on the religion, an Appalachian funeral could last up to six hours. Baptists were prominent in the area and were known to have several preachers for one funeral. Each would take their turn talking about God, the deceased, and anything else the Holy Spirit would lay on their heart.

Jacob walked into the chapel of the funeral home. On each side of the aisle, wooden pews lined with red cushions sat welcomingly on a burgundy-colored carpet. At the front of the room sat a brown casket with ornate trim and gold arms holding the bars around the sides. Concealed inside the coffin was twenty-nine-year-old Hunter Raynott.

Jacob had attended high school with Hunter, but the two had never been close friends. It was not uncommon for Hunter to drink with friends and go to parties. Hunter enjoyed his freedom and would prefer to spend his hard-earned money restoring his old muscle car than providing for a family. Hunter was not known as a mature and civic-minded person, and weekends were usually filled with parties and alcohol.

Last weekend, Hunter had attended a party with friends and drank excessively. The four friends dropped Hunter off at home later that evening, and he was drunker than they had ever seen him. He had been groggy with slurred speech and vomiting. The friends explained that Hunter had fallen out of the truck when they arrived at his home and that they were all laughing joyfully as they helped him up the front steps. None of the friends had a second thought about Hunter after they dropped him off at home. The drinking buddies also couldn't remember how many drinks Hunter had consumed during the evening when they were later interviewed by law enforcement. The next evening Hunter was found dead by a neighbor. An autopsy found an alcohol level of .25%. Alcohol poisoning had been deemed the cause of death.

Jacob sat down in the fifth pew from the front. He was directly behind the family. He recognized Hunter's parents and grandparents. The entire family looked tired and distraught. Hunter's younger brother and a few cousins sat in the second pew. Two unfamiliar faces also sat with the family. Jacob assumed that the woman beside Hunter's grandfather was a woman Hunter had been dating from the next county over and her seven-year-old daughter. As the first preacher took his place behind the pulpit, Jacob began thinking about his own family.

Jacob understood that his family was unique. His parents were Jack McKinney and Sara Lester. Jacob's mother and father were high school sweethearts and had a long courtship before marriage. They were an adorable couple because his father was over six feet tall, and his mother was only a little over five feet. After graduation, Jack worked as a coal miner in the small county and stayed in the area to watch over his aging parents. Sara went to college and earned a teaching degree. Jack was twenty-four, and Sara was twenty-two years old on their wedding day.

Jacob's father had an older brother, Calvin, who had joined the Army and learned to be an electrician. During most of his little brother's courtship, Calvin had been serving overseas and had only met Sara on holidays. Calvin did manage to return home for his little brother's wedding in the spring of 1992. At the wedding, Calvin met Sara's younger sister Helen for the first time. Calvin had spent eight years of his life in the Army but fell in love with Helen almost instantly.

After an incredibly short courtship, Calvin asked for her hand in marriage. The only complaint from Helen's parents was that they didn't want him moving their daughter far away. It was an easy decision for Calvin, and he left the Army that fall. After a short engagement, the two brothers were married to the sisters within the same year. Calvin was twenty-seven, and Helen had just turned a very mature nineteen years old. Calvin worked as an electrician and part-time officer for the county sheriff's office.

Jacob always laughed when someone mentioned the marriages and made jokes about being "inbred" because two sisters married two brothers, and the sisters had given birth within a year of each other. Jacob was born in 1993 to Jack and Sara, and Katie in 1994 to Calvin and Helen. Lastly,

Isaac, the second son of Jack and Sara, was born in 1999. Katie wasn't only Jacob and Isaac's first cousin but their double first cousin and emotionally closer than most siblings.

Jacob returned from his thoughts and watched the funeral procession. As one preacher sat down, another took his place behind the pulpit, and Jacob allowed his mind to drift to another childhood memory. He was again a six-year-old boy watching Saturday morning cartoons. His mother, Sara, was in the kitchen. His father, Jack, had just finished breakfast and was putting on his boots. Jack intended to complete a few jobs around the house that had fallen behind from working so many hours in the mines the previous week. The phone rang, and Jacob watched his father walk over to pick up the receiver. Jacob remembered the older style phone was mounted on the wall near the end of the couch when Jacob was a child. Jack picked up the receiver and said, "Hello?"

Jacob remembered hearing a distraught female voice on the other end and his father dropping the receiver onto the floor, running out the back door, and driving away in his truck without saying a word. Sara entered the living room, lifted the receiver to her ear, and said, "Hello?" Jacob's childhood mind was afraid that his mother would have the same response as his father and that he would be left alone, but after listening for a few moments to the female voice, his mother calmly said, "It's okay, sis. Jack is on his way. I'll stay on the phone with you until he gets there. Where is Katie? Is she okay?" Jacob remembered realizing that his mother was speaking to her sister. He wondered what Aunt Helen could have said to his daddy to make him run out of the house and drive away as he did.

"I will call Ms. Travis and ask if Cat can stay with Jacob and Isaac. I'll be up in a little bit. We can bring Katie down here to be with Jacob and Isaac to get her out of the house, okay?" Jacob listened as his mother calmly planned. Jacob allowed himself to stop the memory momentarily and think of the situation as an adult. Until now, he had never realized the strength his mother had shown that day. She was forcing herself to be calm and handle a horrible situation.

Jacob's memory from over twenty years ago was foggy. Flashes of memories surrounding the events of that day and the following weeks were sporadic. Jacob remembers Cat Travis coming to his house and staying in the guest bedroom for a week. Cat's real name was Catherine, but everyone called her Cat. In Jacob's mind, Cat was the greatest babysitter ever. She was only fifteen, but she was smart and taught Jacob new games. Cat would also let him conduct science projects in the kitchen when making snacks or lunch as long as Jacob promised to eat his project. Jacob's childhood mind remembered her with big hair, big earrings, and big makeup. Cat's mom had given her an old bedazzler, and everything Cat owned had been bedazzled. Even a few of Jacob's jeans had fallen victim to the fashion trend that Cat so admired from the seventies.

Cat had turned forty years old recently, and she still had big hair, big earrings, and big makeup. Cat had been married three times over the years. Cat was a sweet and giving person who somehow managed to always choose men who were not worthy of her genuine kindness. Cat had been born with a caregiving personality that particular men would use to their advantage. She had been trained as a cosmetologist in high school, and she married her high school sweetheart two months after graduation. They had been married a little over a year when he passed away in a car accident while driving to work one morning. She restarted her life by opening a hair salon with the insurance money he had left her.

Two years after the death of her first husband, she remarried. The second choice was not as wise as the first, and Jacob remembered sitting on his bunk in the barracks when his mother called to tell him about visiting Cat in the ICU. His mother told him that Cat had a friend sitting by her bed day and night. The friend made Jacob's mother feel safer about leaving Cat at the hospital. It was one occasion that Jacob was happy to be stationed so far away. He wasn't able to hop in the car and visit immediately. He was angered beyond words, and, given the opportunity, he may have killed the man for hurting his sweet friend. After Cat recovered and was discharged from the hospital, she moved in with her mother and went through a divorce.

The third husband was the friendliest and most charming man anyone had ever met. He lived two counties away and was always doting on Cat. The problem with the third husband was that he was also doting on two other women in two other counties. This time Cat didn't have to go through a divorce because bigotry was a criminal offense, and her marriage wasn't legal.

After the third husband, Cat started working part-time at the sheriff's office. The older sheriff was not good with what he called "that new-fangled internet stuff." So, Cat would come in a few hours a day and on weekends to help out by answering emails and doing small bits of research for the aging sheriff. She had stayed on when Jacob took office and was currently dating one of the part-time deputies under Jacob's command. Jacob felt a little safer with her choice this time. Everyone who knew Jacob thought of Cat as an older sister and loved her very much.

A loud voice jolted Jacob away from his memories when the third preacher began shouting, but it didn't take long before memories from the past flooded Jacob's mind once more.

Cat was standing on the back porch, holding Isaac in her arms and feeding him a bottle while he and Katie played on the tree swing his father had built.

Another memory flashed, and he saw Cat and Isaac lying on a blanket in the yard while he and Katie played with the water hose. Isaac was working desperately to crawl off the blanket into the grass but was too young to move anything but his arms and legs. He remembered Cat trying to protect the baby and Isaac's laugh when he was accidentally splashed with water from the hose. When the water hose had made a mud puddle, he and Katie used the opportunity to paint themselves with mud. He remembers Cat hosing them off before they were allowed to go inside.

Only then, as an adult, Jacob realized that the week was very purposeful. Cat had been sent to do a job. Cat was to cause distraction and allow the children in the family not to be engrossed in the circumstances the family was dealing with at the time, and she had done a fantastic job.

Jacob then allowed the darker memories to erode his mind. He remembers being in the hallway after awakening early one morning and witnessing his Aunt Helen uncontrollably sobbing on his mother's shoulder. He remembered not sleeping well because he could hear his father's footsteps as he paced through the house late at night when his father couldn't sleep. He remembered everyone wearing dark clothing and neighbor after neighbor from all over the county bringing enough food to fill his and Katie's house. He'd never seen so much food and was excited to try all the desserts, but the adults seemed disinterested in eating anything.

Sitting in the pew of the funeral home, he allowed himself to remember the conversation when they told him and Katie what had happened. After the police and ambulances had left that fateful Saturday, Cat excused herself from the living room. Jacob remembered his father sitting on the couch and pulling him close. Helen, Katie's mother, sat in a chair across the room and pulled Katie into her arms. Jacob's mother explained to the children that Katie's father and Jacob's uncle had died that morning. Jacob's father had lost his big brother, Katie had lost her father, Helen had lost her husband, and Jacob had lost an uncle all in one fatal moment.

Jacob was accustomed to being hugged by his father, but the hug his father gave him that evening was different. It wasn't a hug that expressed compassion and love, but a longer hug that expressed to Jacob how much his father needed him. Jack broke down with his son in his arms, and for the first time in Jacob's young life, he saw his father cry. It was the same with Katie and Helen, but the tears and the hug lasted even longer. Katie reached up and petted her mother's hair, and said, "Mommy, it's okay. Pastor Mark said that heaven is nice, and daddy is waiting on us." With those words, Helen began to sob uncontrollably and clung to her daughter as if it was the last hug she would ever give her.

Jacob remembered that he and Katie had cried during the hugs, too. They were both too young to fully comprehend death. In later years, Jacob realized that the tears were not linked to the death of his uncle but were brought on by witnessing the sadness of his father. Jacob and Katie discussed it when they were teenagers; she had felt the same. Seeing her mother cry hurt more than anything else that happened that week. Later in life, tears came for the uncle and father they had never really gotten to know.

The funeral flashed through Jacob's mind. It was much like the funeral he was currently attending, but it was his family in the front row. He remembered his grandparents sitting with his father, mother, and Aunt Helen in the front row. They passed away in a plane crash in 2014, fifteen years after losing their firstborn son. But it was the death of his uncle that caused Jacob to want to go into the Army. At the age of six, Jacob watched the military funeral honors ceremony. The sharply dressed soldiers, the salutes at the coffin, the folding and presentation of the United States burial flag, the playing of Taps, and the twenty-one-gun salute made quite an impression on the six-year-old boy. He also watched as the Sherriff's department honored the part-time officer with salutes and watched how they all offered their services and help to Aunt Helen and his father. Jacob made the decision right then to become a part of it. It was a defining moment that shaped his life.

It wasn't until he was older that Jacob finally asked his mother what had killed his uncle. Jacob's mother explained that a storm had hit the area the night before. They awoke the following day to find that the basement of Calvin and Helen's home had gathered about six inches of water. Calvin opened the basement door and saw the water. In a hurry to turn on the sump pump, Calvin had not bothered to put on his shoes. He walked barefoot down the stairwell and stepped into the water. Calvin had no idea that the cord running to the electric dryer was frayed and was lying in the water. The surge of electricity caused his body to tense, and he fell forward into less than six inches of water, where he drowned before his brother could arrive. The former Army electrician died from electric shock drowning in his own basement.

Jacob realized that his memories had grown quite dark, and he forced himself to think about how their life changed after his uncle's death. His Aunt Helen had gone back to school and became a registered nurse. His uncle had a life insurance policy that had paid off the house and gave them money to live on until his aunt could return to work. Helen quickly found work at Dr. Reynold's office. Dr. Reynolds had moved here from Kentucky because he saw that no one in the county treated children, and he was an exceptional pediatrician.

But the best part Jacob remembered was that he and Katie were nearly inseparable now. She was his best friend, and his mom watched them while his father worked in the mines. Jacob's mother, Sara, had decided to temporarily stop teaching and stay home with Isaac until he was school age, so the situation was perfect. Every day they would eat breakfast at his house, get on the school bus, and then eat dinner together. Since Jacob was almost a year older, he helped Katie with her homework. They would play outside every day until the sun went down, and Katie went home to sleep.

The situation was ideal until they reached dating age. Katie was beautiful, and the other boys noticed. Jacob had both given and received several black eyes and bloody noses fighting for his cousin's honor as a teenage boy. Many times, Sara and Helen would talk about the kids being teenagers together, and Helen would always say, "We thought him helping her with homework would get her into college, but we should have known that it would be him beating up the other boys that did it in the end!" Katie had graduated at the top of her class, gone to college, and then to Harvard Medical School. She returned to her childhood home as an emergency room physician last year. Jacob had never been happier in his life. He was the sheriff, and his best friend was back home. It had been a long ten years, but they were finally reunited.

Aunt Helen never remarried. She could have easily found someone. Aunt Helen was a beautiful lady, so it wasn't because of a lack of options. She was a petite, five-foot-two-inch woman who weighed no more than a hundred and ten pounds with beautiful black hair and startling blue eyes. But something had changed in her the day that Calvin died. Jacob and Katie noticed the change in her through family albums. Aunt Helen had been what Sara referred to as "the girl of the family." While Sara was a tomboy growing up, Helen always wore dresses. While Sara was never a "makeup and hairspray kind of girl," Helen made up for it. Helen had been a high school cheerleader and loved the newest fashions, while Sara wore jeans and a tee shirt.

After Calvin died, everything changed. Helen most commonly would be seen with her hair pulled into a tight bun that sat directly on the top of her head, a long sleeve shirt, baggy skirt, and tennis shoes, none of which matched. Helen wore long sleeves even during the hottest summers and refused to wear makeup for any occasion. Another quirk she had developed over the years was distrust for doctors. No one ever understood how a registered nurse whose daughter was an emergency room physician refused to see a doctor. Helen claimed that it was because she preferred natural remedies. But the natural remedies often included poultices with very loud and distinct odors. There was a definite difference between the woman in the photographs and the woman that they knew and loved, and it began the day her husband died.

Jacob was so deep in thought that the vibration on his hip startled him. He immediately reached down to turn off his phone attached to his belt. Two other officers in the room also reached down to their belts and began to walk toward the exit. Out of respect for the grieving family, they reached the foyer before the conversation began.

"Were you focusing that hard on the preaching, Jake?" Scott laughed.

"Just thinking," replied Jacob.

"You were thinking so hard that I thought you were gonna get rebaptized at a funeral!" They both laughed at the absurdity as they walked out the door.

On the short drive to the courthouse, Jacob thought about his friend and colleague, Scott Travers. Scott was a veteran officer and was ten years older than Jacob. When Jacob joined the department, it was Scott that had shown him the ropes of the job. They had become fast friends and maintained the relationship after Jacob had won the election. In the sheriff's office, no one was trusted more.

Scott towered over most men in the county and would have been intimidating if you didn't know him. He stood six-foot-five and two hundred and twenty pounds of muscle. Scott was an incredibly handsome man. Scott had never been married, but he was sought after by many eligible women in the county. In all honesty, he was sought after by quite a few of the married women in the county too. Scott's mother, Maribeth Travers, was a dispatcher. When there were issues surrounding race or domestic violence, you would hear an older feminine voice over the radio saying, "Scottie, fix it but don't end it." That was an order directly from Scott's mother, telling him to control his temper.

Scott had grown up in Clinchco. Scott was mixed race, but you couldn't tell because he looked so much like his beautiful mother. His height was the only thing inherited from his white father. Jacob had only gotten to know Scott since joining the sheriff's office but had heard the story of Scott's past and knew there had been a shooting in Clinchco when he was about a year old. Scott had a rough childhood. His father, Bernard Travers, was an alcoholic that became violent with his mother and Scott many times in Scott's youth.

When neighbors would hear the violence, they would call the police. Time after time, the police visited the home. Neighbors and officers offered help to Maribeth consistently, but Maribeth always refused. She was determined to keep her family together. But she wanted to keep her son safe more than anything. Thinking ahead of time, Maribeth had taught her son that if she ever told him to go to his room with a wink, he was to climb out the window and sneak to the neighbors across the street. If the neighbors were not home, he was told to hide under the front porch until she came for him. She explained that he was the most important thing in her life, and she couldn't live if something happened to him. She made her son promise that he'd stay beneath the porch until she came for him.

When Scott was eleven, his father started binge drinking and had a small pistol. His mother pretended to be bothered by something Scott did and said, "Scott, go to your room!" with a wink of her eye. Scott knew what he was supposed to do. Eleven-year-old Scott went into his room and out the window. The neighbors across the street were not home, so he crawled beneath the porch and watched through the lattice. From inside the house, Scott heard crashing noises and his father yelling as he sat beneath the porch and cried.

The crying gave way to shock when he heard the gunshot. He started to run from underneath the porch to check on his mother, but Maribeth thought quickly and yelled, "Stop shootin' in my house!" She knew she'd receive another beating for screaming at her husband, but she also knew that she needed to alleviate her son's fear and keep him under the porch across the street.

The call came in from the neighbors, but this time they reported hearing a shot fired from inside the house. When the police arrived, they could hear a man shouting and loud noises coming from inside. They prompted Scott's father to come outside using a bullhorn instead of knocking on the door. When Scott's father opened the door, he used Maribeth's bruised and broken body as a human shield and held the gun to her head. Maribeth could barely walk. You could see that she had two black eyes that were nearly swollen shut. Her lips were swollen and bleeding from the beating, and the officers could see from the street that she had a broken arm. Her clothing was ripped, and she was walking with a limp.

An effort was made to de-escalate the situation, but Bernard wasn't listening. He kept shouting profanities at the officers and saying, "This is my bitch! You go get your own!" Bernard held the officers at bay, screaming, "She's mine, and I'll kill her if you come into my damn yard." The attempt to calm the situation was made for almost an hour. Bernard had a whiskey bottle and kept drinking throughout the confrontation, so the chance for him to become sober and calm down was not happening. In the end, to protect Maribeth, the previous sheriff, Tom Linkard, took the shot.

Tom had been a sharpshooter in his younger days, and when the shot rang out from his pistol, it landed true. Within an instant, Bernard lay dead on the porch with a single bullet hole in the center of his forehead. Maribeth, covered in her husband's blood, screamed at the sound of the gun and the sight of her husband lying dead beside her. Limping through the pain and holding her broken arm, she ran into the yard towards the officers standing in the street, screaming Scott's name.

The officers were shocked when Scott came from behind them toward his mother. The officers did not know that Scott was watching the entire time. When Scott reached his mother at the yard gate, they clung to each other in an embrace as Maribeth collapsed to her knees, and they cried in each other's arms. Sheriff Tom walked over to Scott and knelt to face the young man, and with tears in his eyes, said, "I'm so sorry." Scott released his hold on his mother and embraced Tom's neck with both of his small arms and whispered into Tom's ear, "I'm not. Thank you for saving my momma." Hearing his words, Sheriff Linkard's lip trembled before he raised his hand to cover his emotions and wipe the tears as they escaped his eyes and rolled down both cheeks.

After a stay in the hospital, Maribeth took a job as a dispatcher for the same deputies and sheriff that had saved her that day. When Scott decided to become an officer, Maribeth worried that the trauma her son had suffered in his childhood would cause him to make an emotional rather than a rational decision regarding domestic violence or racial situations. Her words over the radio, "Fix it but don't end it," to her son were a reminder. If it had to be done, she wanted another officer to take the shot.

Scott never had to take the shot. His height and raw strength were intimidating enough to stop almost any domestic violence situation. Luckily, they had never had a call when a woman was the perpetrator of a domestic violence dispute. Everyone knew Scott wouldn't help much if a woman were hitting her husband. The deputies would laugh and say that they'd still send Scott because he'd charm and flirt with her until she just packed up and left her husband. Scott would smile and say, "You're just jealous because I'd still get the job done!"

Jacob and Scott arrived at the office within five minutes of leaving the funeral. Walking into the office, Jacob asked, "What's going on, Maribeth?"

Maribeth looked up in surprise, "Why didn't you just call instead of coming in? There's an emergency, and you could have left from the funeral home." Without giving an opportunity to answer, she continued, "You boys better head to Haysi pretty quick. Someone called and said there's a body floating near Haysi Beach, and if you don't get on the move, you'll be looking for it in Kentucky." Maribeth replied.

Chapter 2

Haysi Beach isn't a beach. Years ago, a local businessman paid to have steps built down to the Russell Fork River in the center of Haysi. The steps lead from a parking lot in the center of town to a sandy area where people can fish and enjoy the river. Haysi Beach is small but beautiful. It is located where the Russell Fork and McClure Rivers combine and flow toward Kentucky through the Breaks Interstate Park. That someone had called to say a body was floating in that area was unusual but not impossible.

Two hours later, Jacob, Scott, and two deputies returned to the office inside the courthouse. Scott and Jacob were soaking wet. Leaves and mud covered their uniforms. Only their duty belts and service weapons were clean and free of debris. Maribeth glanced at the two other deputies, who didn't seem to be wet or dirty, and wondered what had happened. Maribeth asked, "Did you two pull someone out of the water?"

With sarcasm in his voice, Scott looked down and said, "Ya, Momma, we got him out alright!"

Maribeth was overwhelmed with anxiety and excitement. Her voice was higher than usual as she asked, "Well, was he alive? You boys never radioed or called me to send an ambulance or anything."

Jacob smiled mischievously and held out his hand in a comforting gesture to calm the excited woman as he said, "He was just as alive when we got there as when he went in, Ms. Travers." The four men in the room began to snicker at the comment.

Being filled with apprehension, Maribeth's personality changed into what the young men on the force called her 'mommy mode' as she stood straighter and demanded, "You boys straighten up and tell me what happened right now!" Maribeth knew by the look of the four men that there had to be a story to follow.

"You're not going to believe this, Momma," Scott began as he looked down and shook his head. He started the story by holding his arm out as if he was involved in a dramatic act of heroism, "We were the first ones to arrive." Scott looked into the distance. "We saw the body floating in the middle of the water." Scott became more animated as the story continued, "Me and Jake stripped off our duty belts and service weapons and handed them to Brad and Duncan to be safe while we ran down to the beach like two madmen. We headed straight into that cold water to save the drowning victim or, at least, stop a body before it floated any farther downstream."

Scott changed his dramatic storytelling voice into a more flattened tone and ended the story, "About the time we got to the dead center of that muddy water, ol' man Puckett pulled up to the beach in his truck and yelled, 'Thank y'all for saving my scarecrow! The dang thing blew into the creek last night during the windstorm.'"

Maribeth covered a grin with her hand.

Scott continued, "We had just reached the scarecrow when we heard the ol' feller hollering at us from the riverbank. So we decided that we'd bring it back to him since we were already out there."

Jacob concluded, "Yes, we jumped into the Russell Fork River this morning to save a drowning scarecrow that had floated down the McClure River all the way to Haysi."

"I'm still trying to figure out how that old man was planning on getting that monstrous thing in the back of his truck by himself! And what in the world was that thing stuffed with?!" Scott interjected, still frustrated by the event.

Maribeth still looked confused and asked, "How did you two end up covered in dirt and mud?"

Scott answered, "Momma, there's one thing you can say about ol' man Puckett, he doesn't half-ass anything. That damn scarecrow is taller than I am! And the rocks on the bottom of the Russell Fork are as slick as snot on a doorknob! It was hell getting it out of that river after it was waterlogged!"

Even though everyone else was laughing at Scott's frustration, Maribeth heard what she deemed profanities out of her baby boy's mouth and immediately disciplined him, "Scott Anthony Travers, don't you be using language like that around your momma! Now you boys go get cleaned up. You can't do your jobs looking like that!"

As the sheriff and deputies left the room, Maribeth overheard Jacob telling Scott, "Buddy, you know I love you like a brother, but don't you ever drown, or we'll wait until you stop somewhere in Kentucky. As tough as a scarecrow was to get out of that water, we'll have to get a tow truck to drag your big butt out of there!"

Scott replied in his usual, quick-witted fashion by saying, "If I drown, you'd better be there to drag my ass out before I'm waterlogged, or I'm coming back to haunt you!" Both men laughed as the door closed, leaving Maribeth to clean the mess they'd made in the office.

An hour later, Jacob and Scott walked back into the office. Maribeth was talking with a young woman in her mid-twenties at the desk. The woman had long red hair and green eyes. She was tall and wore a burnt orange colored business suit and black heels. Beneath the suit jacket, you could see glimpses of a black silk tank top trimmed with lace.

"I'm glad you boys are back." Maribeth said smiling, "This is Gloria Winters. She stopped by to meet us."

Without missing a beat, Scott leaned against the desk, flashing his beautiful smile and dimples, "We'd have come back faster if you had told us we had such a beautiful guest, Momma." Scott reached out to take the woman's hand and lifted it to his lips to kiss the back of her hand in an outdated way of charming the beautiful woman. "I'm Scott… and I'm here for anything you will ever need," Scott emphasized the last few words as his eyes moved from her feet to her face.

Ms. Winters withdrew her extended hand gracefully but ignored the obvious flirtations. She replied professionally, "I'm with the Federal Bureau of Justice Statistics. It's nice to meet you, Mr. Travers, but I'm here to speak with Sheriff McKinney. Your mother was nice enough to warn me about you before you arrived." Gloria Winters smiled mischievously when speaking the last sentence but did not return the flirtatious gestures.

Undaunted, Scott continued the flirtations by flashing his smile and dimples again and saying, "Well, have it your way, but I know that you'd be much more satisfied having a conversation with me." Scott emphasized the word satisfied while speaking to the beautiful woman.

Jacob decided it would be a good time to prevent his friend from being further embarrassed by the rejection of the beautiful woman. He placed his hand out to shake the woman's hand and introduced himself, "I'm Jacob McKinney, ma'am. Nice to meet you."

"Sheriff McKinney, I've come by because we have some discrepancies in our data, and I'd like to speak with you privately about it."

"Sure, we can talk in my office." Jacob gestured to the door directly behind Maribeth's desk. Jacob followed her into the office and shut the door. As Jacob hung his campaign hat on the hat rack behind the door, he started the conversation, "I apologize for Scott. He meant no disrespect. I'm starting to wonder if he has a mental problem because I'm not sure he can help himself."

Gloria smiled and said, "I took it as a compliment. But you can tell him I am not interested in any man except my husband."

Jacob laughed and said, "I'll let him know. That'll make him feel better. He won't mope around the office for days if he knows you're married." Jacob gestured to a chair for Mrs. Winters to sit in as he took his place behind the desk.

"So, how can I help you?" Jacob asked.

Gloria began, "As you know, the Federal Bureau of Justice Statistics is the statistical agency of the Department of Justice. We collect, analyze, publish, and disseminate information on crime, criminal offenders, victims of crime, and the operation of justice systems at all levels of government."

Jacob nodded and replied, "Yes, you guys provided some training for us here when we received the new software last year. We appreciate it."

Gloria nodded, smiled, and continued, "Last year, ten staff members were given a project by the director to track all the known pedophiles in the United States. We would keep track of their locations, the severity of their crimes, and if they moved between states. I was given the states of North Carolina, Virginia, Kentucky, Tennessee, and West Virginia."

Jacob shook his head as he replied, "Ma'am, I do not envy you. It sounds like you have a pretty rough job."
Gloria nodded and said, "I'm here because we've noticed something odd about the statistics in Dickenson County."

Jacob looked confused for a moment, then smiled and said, "Well, it wouldn't be the first thing odd in this county. I had to jump in the river to save a drowning scarecrow this morning."

Gloria laughed and said, "Maribeth told me about that, and I thought it was quite endearing. It gives new meaning to serve and protect, doesn't it?" They both laughed for a moment.

Returning to the conversation, Jacob asked, "So, what did you find in the research?"

Gloria became somber, "To be honest, we're not sure. But, according to our research, there have been no reported cases of child molestation or child sexual abuse over the last twenty-five years in Dickenson County."

Jacob was stunned. Searching through his memories from his time as a deputy and as sheriff, he couldn't remember a single time he had to investigate any type of sexual child abuse. He had taken the sheriff's office a little over a year ago and hadn't recognized the anomaly. Jacob couldn't understand why that would happen and felt guilty that he had never noticed it. Child molestation had even occurred on some of the Army bases where he had served, but he had not investigated one case since returning home. Dickenson was a small county but couldn't be excluded because of its size. The anomaly was strange.

Gloria allowed the first statistical anomaly to sink in before continuing. "And even more astounding was that when an individual on the sexual registry list moves into this county, they die within three months."

The shock of her statement made Jacob lose his ability to speak. After thinking for a moment, he replied in an almost defensive tone and asked, "Are you saying that we're killing convicted pedophiles that move into this county?"

The young woman apologetically replied, "Sheriff McKinney, please don't be offended. We're not saying that at all. In fact, in every case, it was ruled as an accident by investigating county officers, the state police, and the state coroner in some cases. All we're saying is that it is quite extraordinary that both events are happening, and we want you to be aware of it."

Jacob calmed slightly. "Well, I have to admit that it's strange. I'm also worried that, for some reason, abuse is just not getting reported."

"Child abuse sometimes isn't reported for years. The statistics say that twenty percent of adult females do not report it, and it's higher for adult males. I'd like to offer some help if I may," Mrs. Winters said kindly.

"What do you have in mind?" Jacob asked.

"There are nonprofits that visit schools and put on plays and hand out coloring books dealing with child abuse. With your blessing, I'd like to introduce your school superintendent to a few of these organizations. I hope the kids learn to talk to teachers and police officers if necessary."

"Yes, let's make that happen, and I'm going to start keeping an eye out. I'm having breakfast with Tom Linkard, our former sheriff, tomorrow morning in Haysi. I think he'll want to hear about your statistics."

Jacob and Ms. Winters exchanged information, shook hands, and she left the office. It was getting late in the day, and he had promised Katie he would have dinner with her and Aunt Helen this evening. Scott and Maribeth had already left for the day when he walked through the office, shut off the lights, and locked the office door.

Fifteen minutes later, Jacob was pulling into the crowded driveway of his Aunt Helen's home. He recognized every vehicle. His parents must have also been invited. Jacob heard laughter and talking through the door. There was no need to knock. It was Aunt Helen's house. He'd grown up walking back and forth between his parents and her home. Katie was the first one to greet him. "Hi, Cuz!" she shouted as he wrapped his arms around her, lifting her tall but thin body off the floor in a big hug. Jacob first noticed that her accent had changed a bit while she was in college. Jacob used his finest southern dialect to tell her, "You ain't talkin' right!"

Katie laughed and said, "You did the same thing when you were away, and it's coming back. Give it time. I'll be able to talk more wronger every day!"

The rest of the evening was wonderful. Jacob loved spending time with his entire family. He was glad Katie was back home because now he wouldn't be the only one being accosted for not getting married and creating grandchildren. They were both accustomed to receiving the traditional "Christmas guilt trip," but now, it would be a year-round occasion until someone had a child. He was quietly hoping it would be Katie.

Apparently, it was Aunt Helen's turn to begin the guilt trip. "Katie, have you met anyone since you've been home?"

This was how the guilt trip started on every occasion. Katie and Jacob believed that their parents took turns starting the conversation. The newest problem was that the usual answers were no longer any good. Katie and Jacob had no excuses to fall back on like school or career. They were now both settled, except that Katie lived with Aunt Helen until she could find her own place.

Jacob couldn't use the excuse of not having his own place. He bought a farm on Rose Ridge about three miles from Ridgeview High School. He had bought it after becoming Sheriff. An older widow with grandchildren attending the high school had sold it to him for a steal because she wanted the sheriff to be close to the school in case of an emergency. Jacob's little brother Isaac was at Quantico training for the FBI since he finished four years in the Navy, so he had the perfect excuse.

"Not yet, Mom. But I'm guessing Jake's got them lined up." Katie looked at Jacob with a menacing smile.

Feeling kind, Jacob said, "Yes, I met a wonderful woman today from the Federal Bureau of Justice Statistics." Those words sparked the attention of everyone at the dinner table, and everyone sat up straighter with excitement lighting their eyes. Jacob purposely took a bite of food so he couldn't be harassed for not speaking. They all stared at him and waited in apprehensive silence. He swallowed his food and said, "Yeah, too bad she was married."

Everyone at the table sighed in disappointment and exasperation. His father, Jack, broke the silence afterward, "How did you meet someone from the Federal something or another?"

Jacob laughed and said, "It's pretty cool. Katie, you're gonna love this because you're such a nerd." Jacob smiled when using the juvenile language of their youth. "The woman was from the Federal Bureau of Justice Statistics. She's doing some research and found something strange in Dickenson County."

Katie perked up and excitedly said, "What did she find?"

"Well, it seems that we have no child sex abuse or child molestation in Dickenson County. In fact, we haven't for nearly twenty-five years." Jacob stated.

You could see the wheels turning inside Katie's mind. "That's strange. During our pediatric rotation, we were taught that twenty percent of girls and five percent of boys are sexually molested in the United States before the age of eighteen. They specifically showed us what to look for because we're mandated reporters. Dickenson County is small, but that's still very unusual."

Jacob continued, "Oh, the weird stuff doesn't end there, Katie! Every time someone on the sexual offender registry moves into Dickenson County, they die within three months."

The entire family stared at Jacob in silence.

"What?" Jacob asked defensively.

Jacob's mother, Sara, broke the silence, "Good job, son, now let's not talk about it anymore."

Jacob was shocked and started to speak but was interrupted by his father, who put his hand on Jacob's hand and said with pride bursting from him, "Son, I've never been so proud of you."

"I didn't do anything!!" Jacob stated, still shocked by the reaction of his family.

Katie laughed and said, "Well, it looks like you'd have support from this family if you did!"

Jacob smiled and said, "Well, there's something going on, but I'm still not sure what it is. I'm going to talk to Sheriff Linkard tomorrow morning and see if he ever noticed it."

Helen chimed into the conversation as she reached for the bowl of fresh mustard greens from her garden and said, "Well, in my opinion, people who hurt children are not really human. We kill animals for hurting children. Why don't we kill people who hurt children? Especially when it comes to sexual abuse."

Jacob was shocked by his aunt's statement. She had always been such a loving and forgiving person. Helen was in church eight days a week, but he also knew that she loved children and had seen the repercussions too many times as a pediatric nurse. "There are laws we must follow, Aunt Helen," Jacob stated.

"Those laws are made by man, Jacob." Aunt Helen retorted.

"The good book also says we're supposed to follow man's laws and God's laws." Jacob smiled because he was able to defend himself. Many times, religious discussions with Aunt Helen were a never-ending subject.

Jack interrupted the potential argument by smiling and saying, "Well, I think if weird accidents are happening that make kids safer, and it has nothing to do with Jake ignoring murders, it's God who's doing it, so we all just need to be thankful."

The conversation changed with Jack's statement, and they all began to talk about Isaac and what he had been doing at Quantico. The evening finished with Aunt Helen's homemade jelly doughnuts, coffee, and laughter.

As everyone was leaving, Helen said, "Katie, I know Jacob will probably say he's working as an excuse for not being in church, but I'll wake you up early in the morning since you're not at the hospital tomorrow," in a matter-of-fact voice.

"Yes, ma'am. I'm looking forward to seeing everyone." Katie replied as she hugged her Aunt Sara and Uncle Jack good-bye.

The next morning Jacob and Tom Linkard were sitting at a table in Haysi, eating biscuits and homemade sausage gravy. "Don't be telling Dianne I'm eating this. She's been on me about my cholesterol for two weeks now and won't give me anything but rabbit food at home."

Jacob laughed and said, "Your secret is safe with me. But you're not doing much on promoting marriage to a single guy."

Tom laughed and said, "You mentioned something that happened yesterday. What's going on?"

"I had a visitor from the Federal Bureau of Justice Statistics. She told me that Dickenson County has had no sexual child abuse cases for almost twenty-five years." Jacob waited for a response.

"Hmm..." was the only reply as Tom bit into a sausage.

Jacob looked at Tom questioningly and continued, "In fact, if someone moves here that is listed on the sexual registry, they usually die of an accident within three months." Jacob again waited for a response.

"Really," Tom said.

Jacob wondered if the word was a question or a statement. After a few moments, Jacob said, "Tom, have you noticed anything?"

Tom looked at Jacob solemnly and said, "Jacob, I spent nearly thirty years as the sheriff of this county. If there's one thing I have learned, it's don't look a gift horse in the mouth."

"So, you're saying you noticed it?" Jacob asked. Tom's response was a shock to the young Sheriff.

"I'm saying that this county is not perfect. We have a lot of domestic violence, too much drug use, and way too many other problems to be looking for more." The older sheriff paused momentarily and finished, "But I have noticed the strange accidents."

"So, you noticed that people were dying from strange accidents, and you didn't do anything?" Jacob was shocked.

Defensively, Tom answered, "What was I supposed to do? Should I warn everyone on the registry that moved here? That would sound like a threat. Was I supposed to follow them around to protect them? That would be harassment." Tom's voice calmed, "Did I investigate to the best of my ability? Of course, I did. But every accident was plausible, and even the coroner deemed the deaths accidental. Yes, I noticed it. I did everything within my power and couldn't figure out what was happening." Tom began speaking as if defending himself, but, in the end, he sounded defeated.

"I'm going back and looking at a few old cases to see if they had anything in common. If this is happening, there will have to be some pattern to it. Maybe someone saw something or heard something."

"I hope you have more luck than I did, and you know I'm always willing to help if I can," Tom said approvingly.

Jacob's cell phone vibrated. He reached down to answer the call. After a few moments, Jacob told Tom, "I don't have to tell you I gotta run. I'll catch ya later, Tom." Jacob patted Tom on the shoulder as he walked by the retired sheriff. Jacob was in his car and driving away within seconds.

Jacob was heading to the John Flannigan Dam. The dam offers residents and visitors a wide range of outdoor recreation that includes picnicking, camping, swimming, fishing, water-skiing, hunting, whitewater rafting, tennis courts, and playgrounds.

Growing up in Dickenson County, Jacob had heard the story about how the dam had come to be. In 1957, a flood hit Southeast Kentucky. The rain had fallen for sixty hours straight, and the water rose so fast that the Kentucky residents had to evacuate without their belongings. It knocked out phone lines and electricity and contaminated the water supply. There were food shortages because of the damage to grocery stores and no gas for cooking. Floodwaters and mudslides blocked state and federal highways. Nine people died, and almost six hundred homes were destroyed.

To protect Southeast Kentucky, the John Flannagan Dam was constructed. The dam is almost two hundred and fifty feet high and nearly a thousand feet long. Engineers filled the center with rock over a central clay core that would prevent the water from passing through the dam. It created an almost twelve-hundred-acre lake nearly forty miles around.

Jacob had heard older men in the county talk about working to build the dam with the Army Corps of Engineers between 1960 and 1964. The spillway is an area that contains six massive gates that are used to control the water levels and prevent the lake from flowing over the top of the dam. As Jacob drove by the structure, he wondered how much rain it would take to overflow the two-hundred-and-fifty-foot structure. He turned down the hill towards the spillway area as he thought of the Biblical flood Noah had survived.

Driving by the Army Corps of Engineering building, Jacob made a mental note that once he was down at the spillway, he was out of contact with anyone unless they were standing in front of him. There was no cell phone or radio coverage. Even the booster set up in the patrol car didn't provide coverage in the area below the spillway. Outside contact couldn't be made until he returned to the top of the hill near the Army Corps of Engineering headquarters. He hoped the ambulance was close behind him because if the person were alive, Jacob would need immediate help.

Pulling into the parking area, he saw that the grass had been freshly mowed and the trees throughout the area had been carefully manicured. As he walked through the dew-covered grass, memories of playing on the playground with his friends during church events, birthdays, and social gatherings flashed through Jacob's mind. In the distance, Jacob noticed several people standing beside the wooden fence that guarded the spillway area.

Standing beside the wooden fence were three men with tackle and gear for fishing. The morning air was chilled, and fog covered the area. It was evident that the men had decided to spend the entire day fishing, as Jacob noted that they all had small coolers. Fishermen used these coolers for two reasons: One was to carry their lunch. Then after lunch, they would use the empty cooler to take home their catch for the day. They all looked relieved to see him approach as they pointed to what they could see near the water's edge. He looked toward the area and could see what looked like a body.

Jacob ran towards the body as he heard additional sirens behind him. Several other deputies, a state trooper, and an ambulance, were making the distance down the mountain toward the spillway. Jacob arrived at the body lying face down among the rocks. The body was small, and Jacob pulled it out of the water and onto the rocks near the spillway. Jacob pulled back a thick strand of long red hair to uncover the victim's face. It was a female in her late twenties with a deep gash on her forehead. The body was blue/grey, but Jacob was hopeful and knew paramedics were close. Jacob started CPR but stopped once the paramedics arrived. One paramedic continued the compressions while the second paramedic was opening a defibrillator. The paramedic that had continued Jacob's compressions noted the body temperature was already cold and rigor mortis had begun and decided that the young woman was dead on arrival.

Jacob called for officers to interview the three men fishing. A deputy was told to drive to the top of the hill near the engineering headquarters, block the road with his cruiser, and redirect people who wanted to visit the spillway. Another deputy was asked to photograph the scene. The paramedics removed the body, but Jacob and other officers stayed to investigate the area further.

The rocky area beneath the spillway was relatively clean, with the exception of fishing paraphernalia and a few small pieces of paper. At first glance, it looked as if the woman had been walking on the slippery rocks and had lost her footing. She could have fallen forward, hit her head on a rock, and drowned.

A larger stone protruded from the water directly beside where the body had been found. The waves from the flowing river rhythmically washed over the rock. The scene would have been peaceful had Jacob not realized that the water flowing over the stone would have washed the blood away. With steady steps, he walked closer to the rock. The naturally occurring algae made the rocks incredibly slick at the bottom of the river. He bent over the larger rock to find what he was looking for. A solid line had broken the algae on the side of the stone near the base. When the victim fell, she had placed her hand out to stop her fall, but the algae broke loose, and her hand slipped, causing her forehead to hit the rock. It was the proof Jacob needed to feel more comfortable with a ruling of accidental death. Jacob would have to wait on the coroner's report for anything further.

The following day Scott walked into the office holding a file. "Our accidental death was Marlene Shriver. Her neighbor called this morning to report her missing. She had three kids that the neighbor was watching while she went out with friends. When she didn't return to get the kids, the neighbor called us."

Jacob raised his eyebrows in a questioning look. "That was nice of her. When was she supposed to pick up the kids?"

"About the time we found her body at the spillway," Scott explained.

"Did we locate any family yet?" Jacob asked with concern for the children.

"Yes, she had moved here to stay with a boyfriend that lived up on Caney Ridge. She's from Coeburn. We've contacted her parents, so the kids don't have to go into state custody." Scott was solemn but continued. "There's something you should know. The neighbor agreed to watch the kids because she was worried about what would happen to the kids if she didn't. The neighbor suspected that Ms. Shriver was using methamphetamines."

Jacob groaned and rolled his eyes. With frustration in his voice, he said, "That shit is everywhere."

"The kids are always the ones who pay. We have three kids with no mother now. It's awful," Scott said as he handed the folder containing the coroner's report to Jacob. "The report showed high blood alcohol and methamphetamine use. Cause of death was drowning."

No one enjoyed working at the Sheriff's office on days like today. A gloom and sadness followed when anything happened to a child. Today, because of an epidemic that seemed to be out of control, three children had lost their mother. Scott left the room without his usual joyful expressions or smile and quietly closed the door.

Jacob sat the folder to the side of his desk and continued the research he had started the previous day. He had a list created now. Gloria Winters had been right. There was a list of fifteen names. Fifteen people had been on the sexual offender registry list, moved to Dickenson County, and died within three months. Eleven deaths had been ruled accidental. There were three from the sexual offender registry that had been labeled as suicides, and one ruled as a heart attack. Every death had been within three months of arriving in Dickenson County.

Jacob knew that this was only a start, and to gain a complete understanding, he would have to research every accidental death over the last twenty-five years. While studying, he began to narrow down suspects. It still didn't seem real. Could all of these accidents actually be incredibly well-planned murders? He realized he was looking for someone over forty if the accidents were murders. He asked himself, how many other accidents would never be recognized as murders if they were not on the registry?

Chapter 3

Jacob decided to do his research chronologically from oldest to newest, depending on the date. Harley Brant was the oldest case. It happened in 1999. It was the same year that Jacob's uncle Calvin died. Jacob would have been six years old when the accident occurred. He hoped he'd be able to stir up a few of the old memories for new information.

Harley had moved to Dickenson County after being placed on the sexual offender registry in California. He hoped to start a new life where no one knew anything about him. Harley had bought a garage with a loft apartment upstairs in Trammel at the county's edge. He started a small auto repair business for income and stayed alone. Three months later, a faulty jack collapsed and pinned him beneath the car he was repairing. He was found the next morning. There had been a class action lawsuit concerning the car jack, but Harley had no family to file the claim.

The old police report listed three people who had been seen with Harley the day before he died: Happy Kilgore, Lyle Branham, and Jessie Hatman. Since Lyle's office was close to the sheriff's, Jacob decided to start with him. He called Lyle and offered to buy him lunch so they could talk. Lyle accepted the offer, and Jacob returned to the everyday tasks surrounding the sheriff's office.

For privacy, Jacob ordered lunch to be delivered to his office. While waiting for the delivery, Jacob thought of Lyle. He had known him most of his life. Lyle was a good man and a loving father. He always wore a button-up shirt and tie. He worked as a public accountant and attended church every Sunday with his beautiful wife and two daughters. His demeanor was kind and professional. Jacob had never heard anyone speak a harsh word concerning the man. He had a way of making everyone feel calm and at ease while speaking with him. Lyle would have been about seventeen years old at the time of the accident. It was his car that had fallen on Harley Brant.

As promised, Lyle arrived promptly at noon. "What's going on, Jacob?" Lyle asked.

Jacob replied, "I'm just going over a few old files and wanted to hear about some of the old happenings in the county. Call it nostalgia."

"What do you mean?" Lyle asked and took a bite of the burger delivered only moments before his arrival.

"I want to hear about the day you dropped off your car at Harley Brant's place." Jacob drank from his soda.

"You mean Christine?!" Lyle asked, shocked.

In shock, Jacob nearly choked on the drink and asked, "Christine?"

"Yeah, the kids at school called that old Ford Pinto 'Christine' since the car killed Harley." Lyle laughed.

"Do you mean you continued to drive it after that happened?" Jacob asked with a shocked expression.

"Yes, I did." Lyle said proudly. "I was raised poor, Jacob. I had worked after school and all summer for two years to buy that car. I bought it used and fixed it up. It was all I had. I drove that car back and forth to UVA-Wise every weekday for four years, and it lasted through college. That was until it backfired through the carburetor and burned to the ground two months after I finished my Bachelor's." Lyle laughed at the memory. "It may have been old and involved in killing someone, but it got me through my early years."

"So, can you tell me about that day? I know it's been a while but tell me what you can remember." Jacob asked.

"Well, it needed a catalytic converter. That old Pinto was a '77 model; that was only the second year Ford put those on cars. I could do some mechanic work but didn't know how to put a catalytic converter on a 22-year-old Pinto. Besides, I couldn't weld, and I knew that Harley had the skills and tools to do it. So, I took it to him." Lyle replied.

"Tell me one step at a time and try to remember as if you're there again," Jacob asked. "Just like you did for the cops the day they first talked to you."

"Well," Lyle began, "after school, I drove down to Harley's garage in Trammel. It was around 3:30 that evening when I pulled in. Harley walked out of the little office beside the garage. Harley must have been working that day because he was covered in grease and wiped his hands on an old towel before he shook my hand. He told me to pull the car into the bay. I asked him if he wanted me to pull it into the bay with the inspection pit, and he laughed. He said he'd just jack it up since it was so small." Lyle thought back to the time and continued.

"I pulled the car into the bay and handed him the keys. I spoke to him for a few moments and told him that the new converter was in the hatchback of the car. He told me he liked to work at night and that it would be ready in the morning. That made me happy because I could drive to school the next day if I could get someone to drop me off early to pick it up." Lyle paused for a moment.

"Did you see anyone else while you were there dropping it off?" Jacob asked.

"Yes, I did. Jessie Hatman pulled in while I was there."

"Jessie knows how to work on cars. Why did he pull in?" Jacob prodded.

"When Jessie pulled in, I didn't ask questions. I was glad my dad pulled in to drive me home when he did. Jessie used to have his hands in a lot of illegal stuff, and I wasn't sure why he was there and didn't want to know." Lyle said.

"So, when you left, Jessie and Harley were alone, and the next morning Happy Kilgore found him dead under the car?" Jacob asked.

"Wish someone had called me before I left that morning. I got there about half after seven, and there were cops everywhere. My first thought was that Harley had been arrested for whatever was going on between him and Jessie, but when I asked for my car, Tom Linkard looked at me like I was nuts and pointed at Harley's legs sticking out from under it." Lyle gave a quick look of disgust. "I was late for school that morning, but the principal overlooked it when one of the deputies dropped me off on the way back to the courthouse," Lyle laughed.

Lyle continued, "For a while, everyone thought Jessie might have murdered him. The neighbors on the hill above the garage didn't trust Harley. You know the Kilgores. They've always had dogs, and Happy doesn't like people hanging around. They were always watching and told Sheriff Linkard they had seen and heard Harley working on his old truck in the driveway after Jessie had left. Where Harley liked working at night, they always complained that the dogs barked at the noise all night long."

"Did you know about Harley being on the sexual offender registry list?"

"Yes, but I was seventeen and didn't have kids or a wife." Lyle smiled and said, "I also didn't have much money."

Jacob took a bite of burger, and Lyle picked up a fry. Using the food to point at the sheriff, he asked and laughed, "Jacob, are you getting bored at work?"

Jacob had food in his mouth but expressed his question with his eyes.

"You're researching an accidental death from over twenty years ago? Is there not enough work for you in this small county?" Lyle laughed.

Jacob swallowed the bite in his mouth and replied, "I can't really talk about it right now. Let's just say I'm trying to learn something from some of the old cases."

"You planning on talking to Happy and Jessie, too?" Lyle asked.

Jacob nodded in response while chewing the last bite.

"I don't know where Jessie is, but don't go visiting Happy after seven tonight. That man goes to bed with the chickens and is awake every morning at four a.m., and watch out for those dogs," Lyle laughed as he shook his head.

Jacob laughed and said, "Jessie is easier to find than you were. He's in the holding cell downstairs. Happy and his dogs! I don't know how Penelope does it."

"When his favorite dog died, Happy decided to keep all of the offspring from that dog. The dogs he has now are the children, grandchildren, and great-grandchildren of the old hunting dog. As Happy's family grew, so did the dogs! At one time, he had to buy a kennel license and was really angry when someone called the SPCA. Penelope nearly left him over it. The rumor is that there's only a dozen or so left because Penelope forces him to get them fixed before they are six months old, or she's leaving," Lyle laughed.

"Is that the dog he tells the story about? The one that saved him from a bear once?" Jacob knew everyone in the county had heard that story at least three times.

"Same one. I swear, I think he loved that dog more than he loved his own children. They actually built a box for a casket and called in a preacher when that dog died." Lyle and Jacob laughed as Lyle continued. "There were rumors that he had thought about having it stuffed and didn't speak to his wife for nearly a year because she wouldn't let him keep a large stuffed dog in the living room."

Both men were laughing when Jacob commented, "I'd bet that if we asked her, she'd say it was the happiest year of their marriage!"

The lunch hour was over. Lyle thanked Jacob for lunch and returned to work as Jacob headed downstairs to the holding cell. Approaching the locked cell, Jacob leaned towards the bars and said, "Jessie, you awake?"

A muffled sound came from a half-conscious pile lying on the cot in the holding cell. "Jessie, you remember when Harley Brant died?" A mumble from under the sheet sounded like Russell County, and no more responses.

Jacob decided to make a quick check of the report. He had missed it the first time, but a report showed that an hour after Lyle had seen Jessie Hatman at the garage, Jessie had been arrested for possession with intent to distribute in Russell County. Jessie had served three years for the crime. The report said that he had purchased the drugs from Harley Brant. Jessie had the perfect alibi if a murder was committed. Jacob realized that Harley died at the perfect time because he would have had an arrest warrant from Russell County for selling to Jessie if he had lived.

On his way home that afternoon, Jacob pulled his car off the main road into Happy Kilgore's driveway. Happy lived on a small hill that had a clear overlook to the main road and what was once Harley Brant's garage. The county had taken the property where the garage was located, and it was currently for sale due to back taxes, but no offers had been made on the abandoned garage. Jacob understood why no offers had been made. The property was in disrepair and needed a new roof and additional remodeling if it was ever to reopen. The investment wouldn't be small. Jacob noted that the only two homes within view were the garage loft and the Kilgore residence. Jacob wondered if anyone had stepped foot inside the building since finding Harley's body that morning long ago.

Jacob began the drive up the dirt road that led to Happy Kilgore's home. Happy Kilgore was a collector. Some might have called him a hoarder except for the fact that his collection items were neatly stored and stacked. Happy owned over fifty acres, and behind Happy's home were sheds, buildings, barns, cargo crates, and even a few old box trailers. Each building was filled to the brim with everything you could imagine from days long past. His collection ranged from items like old cigarette machines from the 1950s, old car parts, and satellite dishes to tires and a few old bicycles. The outside of every building was decorated with antique advertising signs and automobile tags from nearly every year and every state. Everyone in the county knew that if you needed something rare, you could depend on Happy to have it.

Jacob pulled into the gravel parking area beside Happy's old truck. The yard was beautifully manicured. Happy's wife, Penelope, was always neat and orderly. She took pride in being a mother and wife, and the only arguments between her and Happy concerned his love for the dogs. Jacob exited his vehicle and saw a pack of large dogs enclosed in the fence surrounding Happy's best collection pieces. The dogs had gathered near the fence to bark at the stranger. Jacob attempted to do a quick count, but the barking and excitement of the dogs prevented knowing the exact number. None of the dogs acted aggressively enough to bite an intruder but were an excellent alarm system to let Happy and Penelope know there was someone in their yard. Jacob smiled as he thought about the old adage, 'loud enough to wake the dead.' The barking dogs might not have been enough to wake the dead, but they were giving it their best shot.

As Jacob approached the home, he stopped at the gate. Inside the neatly manicured fenced-in yard lay one older dog covered in gray hairs. The dog only raised its head to look at Jacob as he approached the gate. The front door opened, and Jacob looked up to see Penelope step onto the front porch of the home.

"Good evening, Sheriff! What brings you out this evening?" Penelope smiled as she wiped her hands on the dish towel she was holding. It was apparent to Jacob that the two had just finished dinner, and he had interrupted Penelope while she had been washing the dishes. The sound of the barking dogs must have notified her of his presence as he pulled into the driveway.

Jacob removed his campaign hat and held it in his hands. "Good evening, Mrs. Kilgore. I wanted to talk to Happy if he had the time."

"He ain't done nothing, has he, Jacob?" Mrs. Kilgore had an expression on her face that made Jacob glad to report that Happy was behaving himself. Jacob imagined a violent argument would have ensued had he been there to report anything to the contrary.

"Oh no, Mrs. Kilgore. I am looking into a few older accidents in the county, and I wanted to ask Happy about when Harley Brant died down there." Jacob pointed at the garage across the road from the house.

"Jacob, that's been nearly twenty-five years ago. Our grandchildren are grown now. I'm not sure how much Happy can remember, but I'll holler at him." Mrs. Kilgore opened the screen door behind her and yelled loudly into the house, "Happy, come out here! Sheriff's here wanting to talk to you."

From inside the house, Jacob heard an older male reply, "Tell him to hold on a second. I have to get my boots on!"

Mrs. Kilgore gently smiled, "He's getting his boots on. Please have a seat." Penelope kindly gestured toward one of the rocking chairs on the porch. "Can I get you some cake, Sheriff?" she offered.

Jacob hadn't eaten dinner, so he declined. He knew a slice of Mrs. Penelope's cake would lead to taking one home because she was one of the finest cooks in the county.

They both sat in awkward silence for a moment when Mrs. Kilgore said, "I remember that morning almost like yesterday."

"So you were here?" replied Jacob. He was shocked that no report had been taken from Mrs. Kilgore for the file at the time.

"Oh yes! Happy never admitted it because he was mad at me, but I was why he was down there that morning," she stated.

"Why don't you tell me your side of the story while we wait for Happy?" Jacob asked.

"Well, I guess I would have to say it started two nights before the accident. We didn't sleep a wink that night. Harley would work in that garage all night long with the radio playing, tools clanking, machines running, and enough lights to make it look like it was daytime every night. Night after night, we would be kept awake by the sound of those stupid dogs barking!" With an angry and disgusted look, Penelope pointed at the lot, which sat at an angle to the garage across the road. From that angle, the dogs had a clear view of the garage and the Kilgore home.

"I was grouchy that morning, but Happy was outraged. We had a registered sex offender living across the road with a full view of the house. The kids wouldn't bring the grandchildren to see us. Now, we're not getting any sleep because of his work habits, and we had dealt with enough. Happy went out the door with the shotgun that morning and marched across the street. I almost called Sheriff Linkard to stop him because he wasn't listening to me," Penelope stated.

Jacob wondered why all of this had been left out of the original report but sat quietly as Penelope told the story concerning the morning before the accident.

Penelope continued, "I was scared to death. I thought Happy was going to shoot the man in cold blood."

The loud squeak of rusty hinges distracted Jacob for a moment as a man in his late eighties stepped through the screen door and onto the porch. "Thank God Harley didn't die of a gunshot! Penelope would have testified against me!" Happy laughed as he put his old gray hat atop his head.

Happy stood at the doorway for a moment. He wore a plaid shirt, overalls, and that old gray hat. His work boots were on his feet but had not been tied. Jacob stood up as the older man walked towards him to shake hands. "How you been doing, Happy?" Jacob asked in a friendly voice.

"Even if I complained, ain't nobody listening anymore." The older man smiled.
Mrs. Penelope interjected with a snide remark, "But that won't stop you from complaining now, will it, Happy?"

Happy shot a disdainful look at his wife and then looked at Jacob, "So, what's got you interested in Harley Brant, Jacob?"

"I'm just looking through the old files and making sure nothing got missed," Jacob replied. "So, what happened when Harley saw you with the gun, Happy?" Jacob smiled.

"I just walked over there with that old shotgun of mine and knocked at his door. He was already asleep that morning, and I had woke him up. I didn't point it at him or fire a shot. I banged at the door to wake him up, and when he answered the door, I told him that I'd had enough and if I didn't get sleep from now on, I'd take further steps to correct the problem."

"How did he react?" Jacob asked.

"He just stared at me. He never said a word. I think the man was half asleep standing there. But I guess my point got across because the next night, me and the wife slept like babies," laughed the older gentlemen.

Penelope interrupted the conversation by saying, "That's why he was mad at me the morning he found the body."

Jacob looked confused, and Penelope continued as Happy folded his arms in front of his chest. His body language said he was still angry with her. "Well, the dogs didn't make a sound that night. It was the best night of rest we'd had in weeks. I got up and made breakfast at five and told Happy that I wanted him to take a few sausage biscuits down to Mr. Brant and thank him for not disturbing the dogs."

With his arms still folded, Happy angrily interjected, "Why in the hell would I thank someone for doing what I had to threaten the man to do? That crazy woman is always forcing me to do stuff that don't make no sense."

Jacob couldn't help but hide a grin while watching the couple, who'd been married over forty years, in an argument.

Penelope continued, "Happy, I'll tell you now, like I told you then, it's the Christian thing to do!" She directed her words to Jacob and said, "So, I made Happy take Harley some sausage biscuits down, and that's when he found the body."

Jacob laughed and said, "That's what you get when you do something nice, right, Happy?"

"You've got that right, Sheriff. That woman's gotten me into more trouble doing something nice than I could have trying to do something bad." Both men smiled and laughed.

"Well, I promised Momma I'd stop by on the way home this evening, so I'd better head out. I'm gonna take a quick look at that old garage before it's sold and then head over there. Thank y'all. I appreciate the help." Jacob shook hands and walked to his car. This time the old dog beside the gate didn't even raise his head to look at Jacob as he approached the gate, and Jacob silently wondered if the dog hadn't died while they were talking on the porch.

Jacob pulled his patrol car into the parking lot of the old garage. He was unlikely to see any clues twenty-five years later but wanted to stop for good measure. From the outside, the dilapidated concrete and cinder block building was still salvageable. He stood for a moment, looking at the area. The accident happened sometime during the night. Jacob stood in the parking lot, looking at the plain view of the Kilgore home. The dog lot was bigger than Jacob had calculated. He could barely see the fence behind the tall grass from where he stood. Cars were traveling the main road, and a few cars either honked or waved at Jacob as he walked around the front of the garage towards the main door. It was unlocked and was owned by the county, so Jacob opened the door. He stepped into a small office with papers still on the counter, a cash register, and the old check register from the former business still sitting on the counter. A door to Jacob's right was the entryway to the main garage from the office. It was also unlocked, so Jacob decided to look at the site of the accident.

Twenty-five years later and you could still smell oil and grease. If you closed your eyes, you could still imagine a working garage if it wasn't for the thick layer of dust that covered everything when you reopened your eyes. The jack that was the culprit of the accident still sat near a work counter in the bay of the garage. There was a stain about five feet away that Jacob assumed had once been hydraulic fluid from the failed jack. Jacob walked towards the jack and knew someone would have checked it twenty-five years ago. He couldn't find the handle and used a screwdriver lying on the table to raise the jack. His efforts did not cause the jack to move upward as he expected. The accident report read that it would have been sometime after midnight, and the call had come in at ten minutes after seven the next morning. If Happy was taking sausage biscuits down to Harley, the call time made sense.

As Jacob drove to his mother's home, his mind whirled with the new information he had received from Penelope Kilgore. Happy was known to have a bad temper in the past. The rumor was that Happy was known for fighting and bar brawls before he married Penelope. In all honesty, Happy Kilgore could have slipped something in his wife's food that would have made her sleep, and he could have easily walked down to the garage and released the jack. But Jacob also knew that Happy would tell people he did it, why he did it, and give you a detailed explanation of how he did it.

Murdering someone using a jack and making it look like an accident wouldn't have been his style.

Pulling up at his parent's house, he saw Aunt Helen's baby blue Datsun in the driveway and noticed his mother and Aunt Helen on the porch. "Look what Mr. Anderson brought us!" Sara yelled excitedly to her son from the porch. Stepping onto the porch, Jacob looked to see the two women sitting in rockers on each side of what seemed to be a mountain of green beans piled onto a white sheet. His mother wore an old pair of jeans and a tee shirt while his Aunt Helen wore a bulky, bright yellow ankle-length skirt embroidered with different colored flowers and a red, yellow, and blue striped long-sleeved shirt. Helen wasn't known for being able to match her clothes, and she never wore blue jeans. The women had bowls on their laps and a trash can between them. Jacob remembered his grandmother doing this type of work with his mother and aunt when he was a child. As they sat and talked, they would gather a handful of beans from the pile and place them onto a kitchen towel on their laps. Each bean was carefully manipulated to remove the strings, then snapped into several pieces and thrown into the bowl at their feet. When their lap was empty of beans and replaced with a large pile of strings from the green beans, the kitchen towel was emptied into the trash can between them, and the process began again.

As when he was a child, Jacob reached down into the pile and gathered several raw green beans in his hand and began chewing on them. He loved the taste of raw green beans right out of the garden. "Jacob, you know you're gonna make yourself sick," Helen said.

"You two said that me, Katie, and Isaac would get sick from eating raw green beans for years, and it's never happened. Heck, maybe I'll eat so many, I do get sick. I'm just still trying to prove you right." Jacob grabbed another handful and laughed.

Jacob sat down in a rocker across from the two women. "What do you two know about Happy Kilgore's younger years?" Jacob asked unexpectedly.

Sara was the first to reply. "Jacob, Happy is about thirty years older than us. All we know are rumors passed down through the years."

"Well, tell me about the rumors." Jacob continued.

Helen perked up and said, "Well, we all know about the dog that saved him from a bear attack. That's become part of history now." The three laughed.

"I want to know about rumors involving his temper," Jacob stated.

"I know he used to fight, curse, and be arrested from time to time. He used to drink back in the day. Penelope put a stop to all of that from day one," Helen said.

"Did he ever hit her?" Jacob asked.

"Dear Lord, no!" replied Sara. "In Happy's view, raising his hand to Penelope would be like striking God Himself in the face. When that man met Penelope, the whole world changed for him."

Helen laughed and said, "I once heard that he punched a man in the face for whistling at Penelope, and that was before they were even dating. Your Uncle Calvin heard the story from Tom Linkard and came home laughing about it. When

Tom Linkard was a young deputy, he was sent to arrest Happy Kilgore." Helen smiled as she recalled the story.

"You see, up on the mountain between Haysi and the dam, there used to be a bar. They called it 'The Pink Room.' People used to go in to dance, drink, and have a good time. It was well known, and many people visited for the dancing and music even if they didn't drink. Happy was there one night when Penelope walked in. Penelope didn't drink but was there with friends to listen to music and dance. Another man noticed Penelope and whistled at her. Happy had broken the man's nose in three places." They all laughed.

Helen continued, "Since Tom Linkard was a new deputy at the time, he asked Happy if he had hit the man out of jealousy. Happy would only say, 'No one is going to disrespect Ms. Penelope while I'm alive.' He was in jail for thirty days over that!" Helen laughed. "We all found out later that the man he had punched was the judge's nephew!" Helen laughed again. During the conversation, the women worked diligently, stringing and snapping the green beans in front of them. Their hands worked with a rhythmic pattern that looked involuntary as the conversation continued.

Sara continued, "Apparently, he always thought of her as an angel on Earth. I heard that if she hadn't been the one to ask him out, they wouldn't be together now. He thought she was too good for him."

Helen asked, "Jacob, why all these questions?"

Jacob said, "Well, honestly, I'm wondering if Happy might have killed Harley Brant all those years ago."

Both women sat silently with their mouths open in shock. Helen was the first to respond. "Wasn't that declared an accident? I mean, the man was a mechanic; accidents happen."

"Well, I'm taking a fresh look at all the old cases that Gloria Winters mentioned. I've found fifteen people on the sexual offender registry list who moved into the county and died within three months. Eleven were ruled accidental deaths, one was a heart attack, and three more were suicides."

After a moment of shock, Sara broke the silence by saying, "Jacob, do you not have enough to do? How are you supposed to do your regular work and still find a wife to have my grandbabies with while working on cases almost as old as you are?"

Jacob wanted to roll his eyes but immediately stopped because he knew there would be repercussions. Then he realized he was nearly thirty years old and was still afraid of his mother. His next thought was that not settling down and getting married might be an act of rebellion in his subconscious mind, but he immediately put away the idea for a later time. "Mom, there's something wrong here, and I can't put my finger on it, and someone has to figure out what is going on. It just happens that it's my job to figure it out."

"And while you're beating a dead horse, I'm just going to have to wait for grandchildren. Jacob McKinney, you're just like your father, a dog after a bone." Sara shook her head in exasperation. "I'm going to call Isaac tonight and see if he's met anyone special yet."

Jacob shook his head but refused to break his mother's heart by telling her that Isaac was probably too busy with training at Quantico to get serious with anyone.

"I have an idea," Helen abruptly stated. "I'm having a friend from New York visit tomorrow. Why don't you have dinner tomorrow evening with us, Jacob?"

"Oh Lord, I'm getting set up again, aren't I?" Jacob asked flatly. His expression changed to confusion as he asked, "And who do you know from New York?"

"No, I'm not setting you up. She's not from here." Helen had always made it a priority to encourage Katie, Jacob, and Isaac to date and marry from the local area. She didn't like the idea of a city slicker stealing future grandchildren away. "It's just a nice dinner where you can meet her. She's flying home the next day. She works for a publisher in New York. I sent some of my old fiction stories to them about a year ago. The publishing company rejected my manuscript, but she called because she wanted to meet me in person. She said she loved the stories and knows I'll be published even if it's not her company that does it. Besides, I wrote about the Appalachian Mountains, and she wants to see them herself. Isn't that sweet of her?"

"Aunt Helen, you know I love you, but..." Jacob began to reply but was interrupted.

"Her name is Leanne Conoway. I'm going to take her to the Breaks Park for the day, and then she's planning on having dinner with me and Katie. So, you have no worries about being set up because your cousin will be there to protect you when your crazy old aunt is about to embarrass you." Helen smiled.

"Tomorrow is Scott's birthday, and I've already told Maribeth I'd be there. So, I'm sorry, I'll have to decline." Jacob smiled and popped another green bean into his mouth. "Well, I'm heading home to eat dinner and relax with a movie before bed."

Jacob leaned over, kissed his mother on the cheek, and then leaned forward to grab another handful of raw green beans from the pile. The two women glared at him for stealing the green beans as he shoved them into his pants pockets and said, "These are for Katie." They all smiled at the memory of Jacob being a child and doing the same thing. He'd take green beans, candy, or other food items, stick them in his pockets, and claim they were for Katie. They all knew that Katie would never receive the stolen items.

While walking to his vehicle, his cell phone vibrated. The simple text read: House fire on Matthews Street in Clinchco—Jessie Hatman's residence. Jacob sighed and shook his head. He knew Jessie would have been released from custody after sleeping it off in holding. The fire could have been purposely set to remove some kind of evidence. Jacob's next thought was that the rumor of Jessie having a meth lab could be true, and the lab had blown up. At the end of the driveway, Jacob turned in the opposite direction and headed toward Clinchco as he turned on his lights and sirens.

Jacob was proud to see that three of his deputies had beaten him to the scene, and the Clinchco and Haysi Fire Departments were already working to put out the fire before it could reach the other homes in the small town. The Clintwood fire department pulled off the main road to the side street as Jacob stepped out of his cruiser.

Ronnie, the Clinchco Chief of Police, met him at his car. "Jake, don't go any closer. Ricky will take your head off."

Ronnie Thane was a Dickenson County native. He had graduated high school and went to college for law enforcement. Over the years, people had grown to love the man for his sense of community. Ronnie was always helping with events or food giveaways to help the people in the small town. He worked with the county police for several years in his youth as a full-time deputy. In his fifties, he could have retired, but instead, he decided to work as the Chief of Police in the small town and work part-time as the county-wide emergency management contact with the State of Virginia. Jacob respected Ronnie's experience and intelligence and was proud to have good men helping him protect and serve the county.

Jacob reached out to shake Ronnie's hand and said, "Where's Ricky at?"

"He's in full suit." Ronnie pointed at a firefighter dressed in a flame-retardant suit with an oxygen tank on the back. If Ronnie hadn't pointed, Jacob would have still known it was Ricky because he was the only one directing others using hand signals.

As Jacob looked toward Ricky, Ronnie continued, "He won't let anyone go in and told the other departments to stand aside and let it burn, but to protect the houses on each side and try to make sure no one is out here huffing fumes." Ronnie laughed as he spoke the last of the sentence.

"Ricky must be thinking the same thing I am, huh?" Jacob asked. Ricky and Jacob had both heard the rumors that Jessie had started a meth lab in the basement of his old house.

Jacob was glad Ricky was out there. No one else in the county was as capable as Ricky when it came to extinguishing fires. Ricky Plank was another Dickenson County native. He had attended Haysi High School before the schools were consolidated. After school, he went to college for a short time and then married his high school sweetheart. He had been blessed with two beautiful children and had cared for many more. He was not only respected in the county but loved. He was quieter than expected and reserved in his thoughts and actions. It gave Jacob a sense of peace that Ricky was there. Jacob knew that if Ricky hadn't been there already, he'd have called him to the fire himself. With Ricky leading, Jacob knew no one would get hurt fighting the fire.

"Jake, Jessie was let out of holding two hours ago. At this point, we just hope he's not in there." Ronnie said in a somber tone.

Jessie Hatman had been picked up many times for public drunkenness but never a charge that would have required a search of his property. If Jessie was released no more than two hours ago, there was time for him to come home and start making a batch that exploded.

"Well, I'm going to walk down to the backstreet and see who's watching from across the creek. Hopefully, one of them saw him come home and leave again," Jacob said as he began walking towards the backstreet that was separated from Matthews Street by only a small creek. The sun was steadily sinking, and the town was now in the shadows of the majestic mountains surrounding it. The orange hue of the sunset was a sharp contrast to the flames engulfing the home and shooting toward the sky.

As Jacob approached the crowd, several citizens walked towards him, asking questions and passing the rumors that it could have been a meth lab explosion. One resident was Mrs. Bessie, an older woman who had lived in Clinchco most of her life. "Jake, you make sure no one gets hurt. That dang thing might explode again!"

"Yes, Ma'am. Ricky's over there, so everything is under control. He knows what he's doing. He done jumped onto

Ronnie for getting too close, and Ronnie told me that Ricky'd bite my head off for going near it," Jacob said and laughed.

"That's good. The first explosion nearly scared me to death. I was on my front porch knittin' a shawl when it started."

"Mrs. Bessie, did you see Jessie Hatman today?"

"Lord, yes, that crazy youngin' left last night at about six, and I knew he would be looking for trouble. Got all dressed up like it was Sunday morning. He had on a nice shirt and what looked like a brand-new pair of blue jeans. Apparently, he had a date." The older woman nodded her head and gave Jacob a knowing look. "It must have gone well because I didn't see him again until a few hours ago. He must have lost his front door key and had to walk around back and go in through the basement door." The older woman pointed across the street to the burning home. Jacob could see a direct view of where the back door had once stood. Now there was only a hole in the concrete base of the house where the entryway had been located.

Never short for words, the older woman pulled a few loose gray hairs back into the bun resting on the back of her head and continued, "When he came back this evening, it looked like he'd been in a wrestling match in a pig sty. He was dirty from head to toe, his shirt was torn, and his belt was gone off his pants. I don't know what happened in the last twenty-four hours, but it weren't nothing good." The older woman shook her head in dismay at the young man's behavior.

Jacob laughed at the wrestling match in a pig sty analogy. "Well, Mrs. Bessie, he was in holding since about eleven last night. We had to arrest him for being drunk in public again. He looked like that because he'd been drinking and got into a fight with one of the Dooley boys. We just released him two hours ago."

"Well, that makes sense." Mrs. Bessie replied in quiet reserve. "He must have been really drunk to get into a fight with one of the Dooley boys. That takes nerve. I'm guessing that he was so drunk that the other two didn't step in when the fight started and just stood back and laughed. Probably why Jessie made it out alive. Those boys always fight with each other, but they'll defend each other, too," Ms. Bessie said with a nod.

"Did you see him come out of his house?" Jacob asked.

"No, Sheriff, I didn't." The older woman shook her head somberly.

"Well, just in case, I'm going to walk down to the creek and check his backyard as much as possible. If I get too close, Ricky's gonna run me off. But I want to make sure he's not back there somewhere."

The older woman nodded, and Jacob walked carefully down the steep embankment towards the creek. The ground beneath him was still wet from the rain two nights previous. Jacob was thankful because the damp ground and shrubbery would help to stop the fire from spreading.

As Jacob stepped across the small creek, he could see a large square piece of wood in the taller shrubs at the edge of the backyard. Jacob recognized the wood as the basement door. The corner of the door was charred from the explosion, and the hinges were gone. Jacob thought it odd that the doorknob was still connected. He looked around the backyard as much as he could while staying out of the direct path of the smoke cloud emanating from the home. Standing nearly a hundred feet away, you could still feel the heat of the blaze. Jacob couldn't have imagined the original blast that had scared Mrs. Bessie. The door was an old, heavy, solid-wood door that weighed over a hundred pounds. It must have been quite the sight if the original explosion blew the basement door that far.

Jacob stayed around until the fire was under control but left before the fire departments. On the drive home, he thought about seeing Jessie that same morning and hoped Jessie wasn't inside the house.

Chapter 4

The following day Jacob arrived at the office at his usual time. A lack of sleep from the previous day was showing on his face. Jacob expected decorations and gifts in the office from people who could not attend the party planned for that evening but found none. Maribeth and Aunt Helen were sitting at the main desk.

"Glad you could drag yourself into work, young man. Heard you were out late last night!" Maribeth smiled.

"Late? Did you not go home after visiting your momma, Jake?" asked Helen. It was clear she had not heard about the fire in Clinchco the previous evening yet.

"No, Aunt Helen, there was a fire in Clinchco. Everybody thinks Jessie Hatman's meth lab blew up." Jacob sighed. "Any news on where Jessie might be?" he asked Maribeth.

Maribeth handed him a file and replied solemnly, "They found a body at five a.m. this morning, Sheriff. They've sent it out for an autopsy and runnin' some tests to make sure it's Jessie."

Jacob opened the file, sighed, and shook his head. He placed the file back on the desk. To change the subject, he asked, "Aunt Helen, why are you here?"

"I just stopped by to ask Maribeth if she wanted to have lunch with me and Leanne, but she's too busy decorating for Scott's birthday party," Helen replied disappointedly. "Instead of flying, she drove in last night, and I'm taking her to the Breaks. We'll be having lunch at the Rhododendron Restaurant, and I wanted Maribeth to come, too. Leanne is taking a shower and changing at the hotel right now."

"Where is Scott? I thought he'd be here already, and there'd be stacks of presents," Jacob asked.

"That big baby is too busy moping," Maribeth stated.

"What's he moping about? He's usually excited about his birthday," Jacob smiled.

"Oh, every birthday except his fortieth birthday. Heck, I've hidden all the gifts in the closet. I'll be taking them over to the Community Center during lunch. We have cake, ice cream, and hot dogs with all the fixin's," smiled Maribeth. "We've invited everyone. You coming this evening?"

"Not to change the subject, but is that smell coming from the closet?" Jacob asked.

"That's my poultice." She pulled up the hem of her skirt and showed Jacob a wrap around her knee, emulating a smell offensive to the senses.

"Aunt Helen, an x-ray can't hurt, and those poultices are awful!" Jacob grimaced and put his hand over his face.

"I'm holistic, Jacob," replied Helen with an air of pretentiousness that would have made Jacob roll his eyes, but he knew that his aunt would have told his mother about it, and he'd be chastised later.

"Yes, I'll be at the party," Jacob replied. Then with a quieter voice stated, "Mainly to follow Scott around and provide an alibi." Maribeth laughed, but Jacob retorted, "It's an important job! Last year, the deputies felt so sorry for me that a few of them volunteered to take turns and help follow him around tonight."

"Oh, it can't be that bad, Jake," Maribeth replied.

"Oh, it is Mrs. Travers. When your son drinks, he gets…" Jacob stammered, trying to figure out how to be politically correct while in the presence of two Christian ladies. "He gets very personal and overly friendly to all females when he's drinking."

"Well, that's not too bad, Jacob," Helen gently replied.

"Oh, it is. The normal sexual overtones and flirtatious gestures magnify to the point that it becomes vulgar. It's embarrassing! The man gets downright filthy mouthed," Jacob stated.

"Well, I'm sure the young ladies would say something and make him behave himself, Jacob," Maribeth responded.

"The problem is that they don't seem to mind. Scott's an attractive man, and they don't stop him. I think a few of them like it. I even had a few female deputies volunteer to help me watch him tonight, and I was smart enough to shut them down. His flirting becomes what I would consider solicitation when he's drinking!" Jacob laughed.

Helen interrupted, "Jacob, alcohol isn't allowed inside the Community Center!"

"Oh no, Aunt Helen, I said I was following him around and providing an alibi. Last year the party moved from location to location. First, we were at the Community Center, but you two didn't know that we went to three other houses and finally ended up out on a strip mine on top of Dante Mountain building a bonfire that lasted until daylight! God knows where we'll end up after we leave tonight." Jacob shook his head and smiled as if exasperated at the thought.

"Well, I didn't make your job any easier," Maribeth announced. "I invited every unmarried woman in the state. I even tried to get Helen to convince Katie and Leanne to go," Maribeth laughed.

"Oh, I'd bet the single ladies come out in droves, except for my cousin!" Jacob glanced toward Aunt Helen and whispered to Maribeth as if it were a secret, "Scott has a bit of a reputation."

"Well, I'm focused on getting him to settle down finally. He needs to meet a few young ladies. Heck, at this time, I wouldn't mind him getting married to anyone as long as they're breeding age!" Maribeth laughed.

Jacob laughed with the two women, "Mrs. Travers, you're as bad as Mom and Aunt Helen. Our generation wants to do a few things with our careers before kids. It'll happen, just relax and be patient."

"Patient? That man turned forty today, and I'm almost sixty with no grandkids to show for it! A parent needs grandbabies to spoil! That's our reward for not killing our children in their sleep during their teen years!" If it was not apparent that Maribeth was quite distraught at the idea of not having grandchildren, her last statement was the proof needed when she stated, "I'm about to take a sewing needle to those little packages he keeps in the glove box of his truck!"

Helen and Jacob burst into boisterous laughter as they heard a voice from the doorway, "Momma! Don't you dare! And stop snooping through my truck!" No one had noticed Scott at the office doorway. Helen and Jacob burst into laughter a second time.

Jacob walked over to Scott, grabbed him by the shoulders, and turned him around, "Come on, bud, let's go to work before your mom starts donating cells to a cloning company to get a grandchild. Sounds like she's getting pretty desperate!"

As they walked down the hall, Scott looked at Jacob and asked, "We get a call I didn't hear about?"

"Nah, we're just going to go check out something I'm working on."

"What might that be?" Scott said with a disdained tone in his voice.

"You would have been a teenager when John Pober died of a heart attack in 2001, right?" Jacob asked.

"Heck, I was like nineteen years old then. I was in college and working with the sheriff's office part-time. I remember the call coming in, but that's about it. It wasn't a big deal. John Pober was an older man with too much weight."

"Well, I'm not certain he died of a heart attack." Jake bluntly stated.

"Jake, I'm starting to worry about you. Why are you looking at a heart attack that happened when you were three years old?"

"Remember Gloria Winters?"

"Who could forget a woman like that?" Scott said with a lustful look on his face. "Man, I hope her husband gets fat and ugly."

Jacob laughed, "Well, Mrs. Winters shared something with me, and I've been looking into it. Apparently, for almost twenty-five years, every person on the sexual offender registry list that moves into this county has died from an accident within three months."

Scott sat for a moment and thought solemnly. He broke the silence after a few moments by saying, "Have you talked to Tom Linkard?"

"Of course."

"Did he not notice it?"

"Yes, he did, but he asked me what he could have done about it. If he watched them, it was harassment; if he warned them, it was a threat. He was stuck." Jacob replied.

"How many are there?"

"I've found eleven deaths ruled as accidental deaths. There were three from the sexual offender registry that had been labeled as a suicide, and one ruled as a heart attack." Jacob was solemn.

"So, we're going to take a second look at the heart attack victim, right?"

"Yep. Starting with hospital records. Katie's working today."

"Well, I'll let you talk to your little cuz while I talk up a few of the nurses." Scott smiled mischievously. "Maybe they need a personal invitation to my birthday party tonight."

"You never stop, do you?" Jacob asked as he pulled into the emergency room parking.

"Stop what?" Scott asked with a sneaky grin on his face as he stepped out of the car.

"Heck, I don't know if you've ever even met Katie, and you're trolling for women when you've got at least fifty at your beck and call tonight! I don't blame Maribeth for being mad at you," Jake replied.

"Not to insult you, but I'm not interested in your family members. Even though your mom and Aunt Helen are beautiful, they're also too involved in the church for me to even raise an eyebrow at your cousin. I'm not looking to become a priest to keep a woman happy! I love your family, and they're good people. But I like my women...." Scott paused to think of how to explain the women he liked and then continued, "without boundaries." Scott flashed a mischievous smile, and Jacob was thankful that Scott wasn't interested in his cousin, so he dropped the subject.

Both men walked in through the emergency entrance, and as planned, Scott stopped walking once they arrived at the nurse's station in the emergency room. Jacob continued down the hall to Katie's office, where he stood silently watching her from the door for a moment. He was proud of what his little cousin had become but seeing her in a lab coat with Dr. McKinney written below the left collarbone felt strange.

Katie looked up from her computer, "Hey Jake, what are you doing here?"

"I need a favor," Jacob replied with a begging connotation. "I'm not breaking any laws for you," Katie answered suspiciously.

"I'm not asking you to break laws. I just want you to use that computer and look up a body that was brought into the hospital in 2001 and tell me what you think he died of."

"I see no warrant, and you're probably not a family member that can sign a release," answered Katie.

"I'm not asking for anything except your opinion. I don't need any paperwork," Jacob pleaded.

"Fine. What's the name? And I hope you know that I'm doing this so you'll leave me alone. I know if I don't, you'll be here every day for at least an hour until I do."

"Katie, you know me well," Jacob mischievously laughed. "The name is John Pober. Thank you. Besides, all the time I'm in here, Scott's outside stopping all the nurses from working. People are probably dying in your ER right now while the nurses fall all over themselves because of that dang nut!" Jacob laughed.

"I've never met Scott in person, but you keep talking like that, and I'm going to think you have a crush on him." Jacob stopped laughing as Katie's laughter began.

Katie typed and almost immediately said, "Found him. John Pober. It looks like he was a DOA. The physician on duty called it a heart attack. There was pulmonary edema and frothing in the lungs, so I have no reason to suspect anything different."

"Did anyone check his blood?" Jacob asked.

Katie clicked and scrolled over the computer screen. "There's nothing strange. His potassium was a little high, but he was on potassium pills for low potassium and could have eaten something that raised it right before death or forgotten and taken a second one. I don't see anything strange, Jacob. I would have diagnosed it as a heart attack, too. The man was fifty-six years old with a heart condition," Katie said bluntly.

Jacob was a little disappointed but understood what Gloria Winters had said about everything being investigated and seemingly above board concerning the deaths. "Well, I'll try to drag Scott out of here and let the nurses get back to work. I'll holler if I need a tranquilizer to get him back to the car." Jacob laughed, and Katie shook her head.

Jacob and Scott returned to the office to find Cat at the front desk. "Where's momma, Cat?"

"Oh, I came in half a day to let her run down and decorate for her 'itty bitty baby boy's birthday party'." The last of the sentence was spoken in a high-pitched tone as if speaking to a baby, and Cat laughed at her long-time friend.

Cat was dressed in her regular attire. She had come straight from her salon. Jacob was always amazed at how she could type with her fingernails. They were long and beautifully manicured. Her makeup was exceptional, and her hair was set to perfection. Cat could look like a superstar wearing blue jeans and an old Hendrix tee shirt. Yet, she was the only woman at the precinct that he knew he didn't have to worry about concerning Scott's ongoing flirtations.

She and Scott had gone to high school together and were great friends. Scott saw her as the sister he never had. They had laughed together for years about pretending to date so that Scott wouldn't have to go steady with any one girl. He would go out with the other girls once and tell them he was cheating on Cat. He would tell the girls he dated that it added a sense of mystery and excitement to his life when he cheated on Cat.

Scott usually didn't date a girl more than once or twice. Cat and Scott were close. Cat understood that Scott only wanted one thing from the girls he dated. She helped him until she met her first husband in her junior year of high school. Scott always laughed and said that his junior and senior years of high school were the worst dating years of his life because of Cat's first husband.

When Cat had been put in the hospital by her second husband, it had been Scott that sat by her bed day and night. The nurses witnessed his softer side and those who weren't in love with him before Cat's hospital stay fell in love during the time he sat by his long-time friend's bed. He temporarily moved into the basement of her mom's house when she came home. When her second husband was arrested, Scott was glad they found him in another state. Scott wasn't sure what he would have done to the piece of trash that hurt his friend. It was only after he was behind bars that Scott moved back to his own house.

"So, I've heard that you and Deputy Duncan Fuller have been seen around town quite a bit lately," Scott goaded.

"Yes, we have," Cat replied with a sheepish grin that was against her true nature.

"I'm not going to ask if it's going well. I know Jake's keeping an eye out. You two gonna be at my party?"

"Of course! We wouldn't miss the first three hours." Cat laughed.

"First three?" Scott replied.

"Yes, we figure that'll be enough time to find some party where you can drink and blow off steam with women of, oh, let's say, ill repute," Cat laughed.

"Dang! Jake, you hear that? She thinks it'll take me three hours. I told you I'm getting old!" Scott laughed, and Cat shook her head in disbelief.

A call came into the office, and Cat stifled her laughter as she answered it. Jacob returned to his office and hung his campaign hat behind the door. A few minutes later, Scott entered the door to announce that Cat had received a call about several car alarms going off at the Food City parking lot. Figuring it was a joke, Scott was going to check on it since other deputies were scattered throughout the county. Jacob sat at his desk to consider the two suicides on the list. Jacob was happy to find that Cat had been working on uploading the hard files to the new digital ones. He quickly found what he was looking for. The name of another person on the sexual offender registry that had passed away within ninety days was Julia Fernsby. She was from Michigan. She had lost her three children to child protective services because when she and her boyfriend would use drugs, she had been allowing her children to watch her commit what the record referred to as "lewd acts." She had also invited them to participate in sex acts with her and her boyfriend. The file sickened Jacob.

She had committed suicide by jumping off the ledge at the John Flannigan dam in 2002. There had been no witnesses because it had happened late at night. There was a torn note in her handwriting that said, "I'm sorry for everything I've done. Please forgive me." A copy of the note had been placed in the digital file. One of the Corps of Engineer employees had seen the body floating in the waves as the wind blew across the lake. In his report, he said the body was about a hundred and fifty feet from the cliff, and he had seen it as he drove to work that morning. The statement made sense to Jacob. If the body hadn't floated that far out, it would have been hidden by the cliffs from the road. There was no one to ask about the death. So, Jacob closed the file and went to the next name.

Jacob had been only nine years old when Brad Temple's body was found. It was back in 2002, and Jacob remembered people talking about it all over the county for months. Jacob pulled the digital file and immediately remembered why everyone in the county had been discussing it. The suicide had happened at the United Methodist Church that sat in the center of Clintwood. The pastor, Mark Huffine, discovered the body when he opened the church doors early Sunday morning. Brad was shot and lying in front of the communion table below the pulpit. There were photos in the digital file.

Jacob didn't attend the church regularly but had visited on several occasions. The church served regular lunches and dinners every week as an outreach to people in the county. Jacob remembered being there with his mother and aunt Helen during funerals and weddings and helping to feed anyone who might need a meal. Most of his memories were of him and Katie playing between the pews upstairs and investigating every room of the three-story stone building as children.

Brad Temple had moved into the county from West Virginia and was on the sexual offender registry list because he had been found guilty of sexually assaulting his eight-year-old stepdaughter. The file stated that Brad Temple was in recovery for substance use disorder but was still listed as unstable in his recovery process. The record also stated that he had recently been diagnosed with acute bipolar disorder. Brad couldn't find work and was homeless.

Jacob realized that it was the first time he had heard the word suicide and remembered asking Cat what the word meant. Using child-like terminology, Cat had told him it was when someone does something to themself, and they die. Jacob's child mind had a difficult time understanding how anyone could hurt themselves like that. Jacob still didn't understand how someone could take their own life, but as an adult, he recognized that mental health was nothing to scoff at and was thankful for the Dickenson County Behavioral Health Services.

The photos showed a broken doorknob on the side door of the church that led into the kitchen from the side of the building. From that access point, it would be doubtful that someone would be seen breaking into the structure. The screen door was still intact and had not been locked. No deadbolt on the door made access to the building simple once the doorknob had been broken.

Several other photos showed the body leaning up against the leg of the communion table. One photo showed a small entry wound above the right ear. Jacob knew it was the entry wound because he could plainly see the black-gray coloring surrounding the injury where the gunpowder had burned the skin.
.

A large portion of the left side of the head was missing. The exit wound was larger than the entry wound, confirming the use of the .45mm handgun in the photos. The left eye had dislodged from the socket and was still connected to tissue by nerve fibers and was lying on the dead man's cheek. The images showed clumps of scattered brain tissue dried into the thick carpet. The last photo showed the right hand lying beside the body and a .45mm handgun that had fallen aimlessly onto the floor on the right side of the victim's thigh.

The report said the handgun belonged to the pastor and had been stolen from his car two weeks before. A copy of the missing weapon report had been included in the file. The case looked pretty open and shut, but Jacob still needed to talk to Mark and grabbed his campaign hat behind the door as he walked out of his office.

"Cat, do you know where Mark Huffine would be right now?" Jacob asked.

Cat never spoke but, nonchalantly, leaned over and turned up the radio. An announcer came on, and she replied, "Well if I was to guess, he's on his way to the church. They're having a dinner at the church this evening."

Mark was a familiar voice at the local radio station, WDIC. It was the only radio station in the county, and Mark had a fantastic radio voice. Every Friday night and Sunday morning, he had his own shows. He played rock music from the 60s and 70s on the Friday night shows. On Sunday morning, you'd find him there playing what he referred to as music for getting ready for church starting at seven a.m. This was a Friday, so Jacob assumed someone was off from work, and Mark had been covering the station since Cat had been listening to WDIC that morning.

Jacob thought about walking to the church since it was down the street, but he changed his mind when he realized he might get an emergency call. Jacob didn't want to take the chance of having to run the quarter of a mile up the street to the courthouse. Jacob made the short drive to the empty parking lot and waited for Mark to arrive.

While waiting for Mark to arrive, Jacob decided to get out and look around the building. The Methodist church had been initially constructed in the 1860s, but the building before him was completed in 1911. It was three stories and was constructed of the native sandstone found in the county. Beautiful stained-glass windows had been shipped from England during the church's construction and had stood the test of time. The windows had even survived a church fire that had happened years ago.

The stained-glass pieces held together by lead strips and the large sections of sandstone made a beautiful and historic centerpiece of the town. At the front corners of the building were two towers. The taller tower encased windows at the very top. The shorter of the two towers held crenellations at the top as if meant for battle.

Jacob admired both the architecture and the history of the building. The county had nothing like it, and the structure stood as a historic landmark. Jacob was still admiring the beautiful structure when Pastor Mark pulled in beside him. Jacob stepped out of his vehicle to say hello and was immediately greeted with a large, friendly smile and a handshake.

"Morning, Sheriff! How have you been?" Mark asked as he shook Jake's hand.

"No complaints from me, Pastor. I've been doing well" Jake replied.

"Your momma and Aunt Helen gonna be out this weekend? We're having an ice cream social for the kids." Mark's voice exuded excitement at the thought of having more kids in the church.

"I haven't asked, but you know how those two are. Mr. Anderson has loaded them down with green beans, and they've been stringing and canning this week, but I have no doubt it's in the plans."

"Them, too? Mr. Anderson brought some down to the church, and the women's group has been working them up for the needy. I swear, if everyone could grow a garden like Shelby Anderson, there would be no world hunger!" Mark laughed. "So, what brings you down? Are you hungry? We're getting started on lunch."

"No, thank you. I'm saving my appetite for Scott's party this evening. Are you going to make it?"

"I'll stop by and grab a hotdog before the show. Your Aunt Helen was insistent that I stop by. She said she's going to have all the pastors in the county pray for her a grandbaby." Mark laughed a hearty laugh. "I'm guessing I should pray for a few of those young ladies, too. They'll need church by Sunday if I'm guessing right." Mark emphasized the word need in the sentence, and they both laughed as Jacob nodded.

"So, what do you need, Sheriff?"

"I hate to bring up old memories, but do you remember when you found Brad Temple's body?"

Mark became solemn. The memory was still fresh in his mind, even though it had happened so many years ago. "I remember it too well," was Mark's reply.

"Can we go over it one more time?" Jacob asked.

"It's strange that you ask, but okay," Mark replied. "Has new evidence of something come up?"

"No, I'm just looking into some older cases," Jacob replied.

"Well, I had finished the radio show and drove down to the church. It was around nine a.m. I opened the door, and there was the body."

"You didn't notice the doorway?"

"Jacob, I didn't even look. The screen door was shut as usual, and I don't usually walk over to check the doors before walking in."

Jacob nodded. "So, there was no sign of anyone else here?"

"Not that I saw. The police checked everything out and dusted for fingerprints, but it's a church. People are in and out all the time. Plus, they found residue on his right hand from the gun. We didn't have security cameras back then."

"Did you ever question why Brad chose to commit suicide at the church?"

"I thought about it for months. It still haunts me today. He had come here once or twice to get himself right with God. He had expressed to me that he could never be forgiven for what he had done. I tried to explain to him that God could and would forgive anything and everything. We had several long conversations about God's love and forgiveness." Mark's voice broke as he said, "I've always felt like I failed that young man." Jacob noticed tears welling up in the pastor's eyes as Mark lowered his face and rubbed his eyes.

"I'm sorry I had to bring it up, Pastor."

"It's alright. God understands mental illness, and the young man had problems. God has given me peace with what happened, and I trust that, even though I wasn't here when the young man needed me, Jesus was right beside him as it happened."

Jacob nodded and gave a half-hearted smile to the pastor as his cell phone rang. It was Maribeth calling from the town hall. "Jacob, can you drive up and help us move this cake? We can't get it in the door without help."

"I'll be right there," Jacob replied.

Mark smiled and said, "That must be one heck of a cake!"

"You know how this party is… every year it's like this, we might as well ask the board of supervisors to make it a county holiday," Jacob smiled.

"Well, you be careful tonight, and I'll see you later if I can get through the crowd," Mark laughed.

Jacob drove to the town hall and helped with the cake but then returned to his office. Cat and Scott were at the desk. "Anything happen while I was away?"

"Anna George called," Cat replied.
Jacob's face immediately became solemn. "Please don't tell me we had to send someone down to arrest Stanley again."

Stanley George was married to Anna and had been known to be abusive. He had been arrested multiple times for domestic violence against Anna. Every time he was arrested, Anna would refuse to leave him. Many times she explained to police officers that she couldn't leave Stanley because she could not support herself and her children with nothing more than a high school education. She would also explain that Stanley didn't mean to hit her every single time officers had to become involved.

Jacob was exasperated with the man, but he never showed it, mainly because Scott needed him to be the calm one in the situation. Scott had once said that he wished Stanley would swing at him during an arrest just so he could hit him back. But Stanely was a very small man and would never attempt to strike a man, especially a man the size of Scott Travers.

Cat replied, "No, she wanted to let us know that Stanley had gone deer hunting this morning at about three a.m. and was supposed to be back home right after sunrise. He didn't come home, and she can't reach him on his cell phone. I told her to give him a few more hours because he probably had to field dress the deer he shot and carry it back home."

Jacob nodded and thought about how a sweet person like Anna didn't deserve to be mistreated by a person who claimed to love her. "Well, I'll be in my office if you guys need me. Scott, do you want to take a half day off and take a nap before tonight? I know how you old guys need your naps."

"OLD?! I'm not the one who has volunteers to help watch over one old guy tonight, now am I?" Scott emphasized the words one old guy. Jacob laughed as he walked into his office.

Jacob sat down at his computer. Connor Stolley was the next name on the list of suicides. It happened in 2005. Jacob noticed that it had occurred on October 31st. Multiple drivers traveling through Clinchco on their way to work that morning reported seeing something that looked like a body hanging from the train trestle. Several had seen the body and thought it was a Halloween prank set up the night before. Ronnie Thane, who was only a deputy with the Clinchco town police at the time, had been the first one on the scene and realized it was no prank.

The report was incredibly thorough. Jacob could see how Ronnie had become the chief of police in such a short time. Connor Stolley had moved here from California. He had spent eight years in prison for raping his fourteen-year-old neighbor when he was twenty-one. Connor couldn't find work or a place to live. There had been rumors of him sleeping in the woods near the train trestle. He was only thirty years old when he died. He had been released from incarceration and moved across the country.

Everything in the file was exemplary. There were autopsy reports, witness statements, and everything pointed toward suicide. Jacob could find no reason to question anything or anyone in the report. He was happy that there was no one to question because he still felt sorry that he had to question Pastor Mark that morning. He didn't want to have to bring up bad memories to anyone else today.

Chapter 5

Scott's birthday party was supposed to start at the Clintwood Community Center at four o'clock. Maribeth had invited everyone in the county. Many stopped by just to make appearances and grab a hot dog and wouldn't stay the entire time. It was fifteen till four when Jacob left his office and drove his car the short distance to the Community Center. Jacob found a place to park on the street so that he could easily be called out if needed.

His mother and Maribeth had already arrived and were working to make hot dogs for everyone who stopped by. Scott sat at a table across the room. The table was already filled with women sitting in every chair. The men would walk over to the table, speak a few words and shake hands with Scott, but the women took a seat somewhere around the table.

The side of the room where Scott sat at the table was surrounded by giggling and laughter. In contrast, the other side of the room had food, drinks, and adult conversations concerning county government and other, more conservative discussions. Jacob decided it was better that he stay on the conservative side of the room. He walked toward his mother.

"Where's Katie and Aunt Helen?" Jacob asked.

"Katie's at the hospital until seven tonight, and Aunt Helen had taken Leanne to tour the Breaks. Helen texted and said she will be here after dropping Leanne off at the hotel," Sara answered.

"I wonder where we're going to end up tonight." Jacob laughed.

"Lord, it's untelling," Sara said. She glanced at the table where Scott was seated and said solemnly, "Jake, I'm not happy you're single, but I have to say, I am glad you have good taste in women." Sara glanced over her shoulder to the women surrounding Scott at the table. Jacob laughed in reply.

"Didn't Shirley Jacobs get married last month?" Sara questioned.

Jacob looked toward Scott's table and noticed Shirley sitting at the end seat. She was smiling and laughing with the single ladies at the table. "She sure did, Mom." Jacob turned toward his mother and whispered, "Maybe it's one of those new 'open marriages' they talk about on tv." Jacob grinned mischievously.

"Jacob McKinney! Don't you be saying stuff like that! It's not right for us to even talk like that. She may be waiting with Scott until her husband arrives. It's not right to be judging!" Sara snapped.

Jacob knew that mentioning an open marriage would set his mother into one of her moods, but he couldn't help himself. He loved playing pranks and jokes and watching her get mad. He knew it was childish, but he couldn't stop. "You're right, Mom. She's probably waiting on her husband to meet her for a Friday church service, and she thinks he'll find her quickly if she's sitting with the other young ladies around Scott." Jacob smiled mischievously.

His mother shot a look of dismay over her shoulder at her son but didn't say a word.

Jacob turned toward the door just as his Aunt Helen walked in. She was wearing one of the ugliest outfits he'd ever seen her wear. She wore a baggy Hawaiian shirt and a long flowing skirt that reminded Jacob of the few times he'd witnessed baby poop. To top it off, she was wearing a pair of black tennis shoes.

She walked over to hug Jacob, and he immediately covered his mouth and nose. "Aunt Helen! I thought you were going to wash that off before the party!" Jacob grimaced under his hand as he asked.

"But my new poultice is working wonderfully!" Helen smiled.

"Well, I can think of a million better smells! Is that skunk weed?!"

"Oh no! It's called Skunk Cabbage. It grows in swampy areas near lakes and streams. I had looked and looked for some. I am so glad I found it," Helen said excitedly.

"I think you may be the only one happy that you found it. How did you hurt yourself?" Jacob covered his mouth and nose.

"I lifted a child onto the examination table at Dr. Reynolds' office and somehow hurt my knee."

"Aunt Helen, I know you don't like going to the doctor, but would an x-ray and normal painkillers really be that bad?"

"Hurt my knee and then subject myself to radiation and God knows what kind of chemicals? You know that doesn't make sense, don't you?"

Jacob knew there was no arguing with her. She'd been that way for as long as he could remember. "Aunt Helen, can you, at least, take that off until the party is over? You're gonna run people out of here."

"Fine. But, if my knee starts hurting again, it's going back on," Aunt Helen defiantly replied.

People ushered into and out of the building until nearly eight o'clock that evening. That's when someone mentioned going out to Blaine Kiser's house. Within ten minutes, the building was empty except for Maribeth, Helen, and Jacob's mother, Sara, who were left to clean up. As Jacob was pulling out, he waved at his father, Jack, who was pulling in with his pickup to load the trash. Jacob knew that his father would take all the wrapping paper, decorations, and discarded food to the transfer station in the morning.

Jacob's past experiences at Scott's birthday parties showed him that the party was not a formal affair after they left the community center. Earlier that morning, he had chosen comfortable jeans and an old tee shirt from his closet and threw them in the front seat of his patrol car. He wasn't thinking about impressing anyone, and on the off chance that someone threw up on him, he could easily throw the outfit away. Jacob arrived at Blaine's house and immediately changed out of his uniform. As he tied his shoelaces, he made a mental note that the tennis shoes were relatively new, and he'd try to dodge if someone vomited toward his feet.

Jacob took his uniform back out to his car and left it in the front seat for safekeeping. He walked back into the house, where Scott was seated on Blaine's couch. Six women were sitting on the couch with Scott, and they had positioned themselves beside Scott and also on the arms and back of the sofa, each one attempting to grab Scott's attention. The only thing that drew Scott's attention more was the brown liquid inside the cup he was holding. Scott maneuvered his arm and hand to prevent the cup from spilling like he was an Olympic gold medal acrobat.

Jacob knew that Blaine was an outdoorsman but had never been inside Blaine's house. As Jacob entered the living room, his first thought was to wish someone had warned him. The entire living room was coated in hunting decor. The couch that Scott and the ladies adorned was camouflage colored and matched the two other chairs in the living room suite. There was a deer head on every wall, and deer horn chandeliers adorned the ceilings of the living and dining rooms. Stuffed and mounted ducks, fish, raccoons, and squirrels were on every table. One of the strangest things Jacob noticed was an ashtray made from a deer leg and hoof.

Blaine was about thirty-five and had never been married. Blaine had dated several women over the years, but none had left their impression. It was common knowledge to all women that hunting was more important to him than a girlfriend. His house was a shrine to his love of hunting, and Jacob realized why there had been so many different girlfriends over the years.

Duncan and Cat had come to the party, but Cat was already looking like she was encouraging Duncan to leave. Jacob understood Cat's hesitancy to come to the house. Not only were the dead animals visually offensive to Cat's personality, but it was loud and incredibly crowded.

"JAKE!!" Scott yelled from across the room. He walked over and threw his arm around his friend. "I've not seen you all evening!" Scott was starting to speak loudly, and Jacob knew that it was the first stage of the evening. The second stage of drunkenness would begin when Scott began to speak in a thick Southern accent.

"I've been around since four o'clock, just like I promised," Jacob replied flatly.

"NAAAAHH!!! REALLY???" Scott replied while leaning toward his friend's face and blowing hot whiskey breath in Jacob's direction.

"Sure have." Jacob grimaced at the smell of alcohol on Scott's breath.

"No wonder yur Sheruff! You got Ninja skills!" slurred Scott as he took another drink.

"Well, maybe it's all the beautiful women catching your attention." Jacob pointed toward the couch, making a half-hearted attempt to distract Scott away from his face.

Smiling, Scott said, "I'd bet yur right. They all look so purty tonight... don't they?" Scott was looking toward Blaine's couch. Stage two of the drunkenness had happened quicker than Jake expected. Jake was thankful when a pretty blonde wearing a low-cut shirt and daisy dukes walked over to help Scott back to the couch while holding another drink.

Jacob was standing near the corner of the room when Blaine walked over. Blaine was in his signature color, camouflage. If Blaine had been outside or sat down on his living room suite, he'd be invisible. From his hat to his feet, he was covered in camouflage. "Hi, Blaine," Jacob spoke.

"Hey, man!" Blaine replied. Jacob immediately knew that Scott was not drinking alone. Blaine walked over and gave Jacob a bear hug, lifting him off the floor. "Has anyone told you that you are the best sheriff we've ever had?"

"Well, thank you, Blaine. And thank you for letting the party come to your house."

"Man, I love Scott, and I love you…you guys are the greatest." Blaine wrapped his arms around Jacob for another hug. "Besides, I've never seen this many women in my house at one time! It's awesome!!" Blaine hugged Jacob a third time and then walked away as if in a trance, following a tall brunette in a mini skirt. Jacob sighed in relief, not wanting another hug.

It was known that Scott flirted with women. It was also well known that his flirting was magnified when he drank. It was also well-known that Blaine became an incredibly loving person when he drank. There was only one person in town that shouldn't drink. That was Linda Lankle. She was a hot-headed redhead that usually wore daisy dukes and tee shirts with graphics from old rock bands. Linda was beautiful but couldn't keep a boyfriend because of her jealous streak. Tonight, she had her eyes on Scott, and she was drinking. Jacob knew that it was not a good combination.

From the moment Linda walked in, Jacob kept his eye on her. She moved across the room with one purpose on her mind and a drink in her hand. She sat down directly on Scott's lap, and Scott didn't seem to mind. He placed his arm around her waist, and four women sitting on the couch left immediately. They knew trouble when they saw it.

"Hey, Jake!" A familiar female voice startled Jacob out of his train of thought. Jacob immediately turned to see his cousin.

"Katie?! What are you doing here?" Jake was shocked to see Katie standing there in blue jeans and a vintage Pink Floyd tee shirt.

"I got off from work, and Leanne and I decided to stop by."

"Who's Leanne?" Jacob had forgotten about Aunt Helen having company from New York.

"Mom invited an editor from New York who wanted to see the mountains and its people. She told you, remember?" Katie laughed. "You can be so absent-minded."

"Where is she?"

"Oh, she wanted to drive some mountain roads, so I let her drive my jeep. She's never driven a four-wheel drive and has thoroughly enjoyed muddin'." Katie gestured toward the door. "She dropped me off and is looking for a parking spot now."

The thought of Scott with Linda on his lap popped into Jacob's mind. He couldn't help but think there would be trouble if those two got together, especially when they were both drinking heavily. Everyone knew that Linda was a jealous person and a tough fighter. She'd been charged with assault on more than one occasion. Everyone also knew that Scott had a wandering eye. Jacob wasn't worried about stopping a fight among the men in the room anymore, but now he had to think of how to handle a fight when it started among the women.

Jacob turned back to where Scott was sitting. Scott must have had a sixth sense that someone was watching him because he looked up to see Jacob. His eyes wandered to the beautiful woman standing beside his best friend. Jacob watched as Scott seemed to become sober instantly. Scott, ignoring the redhead on his lap, stood up. Linda dropped to the floor with a thud, and a curse escaped from her lips. Scott walked slowly and purposely across the floor to his friend. He stood motionless, staring at the woman he'd never met.

Jacob broke the awkward silence. "Having fun, Scott?"

"Ye.. uh... Yes.." came the stuttered words from his lips, but his eyes never left Katie.

Jacob had never seen anything like this from his friend. Hoping to break another awkward silence, Jacob said, "This is Katie."

Katie politely put her hand out to shake in friendship. "Hello."

Scott's face immediately became flush, and he stammered as he said hello and shook her hand. He looked down and seemed to be shy at the moment. Jacob was shocked. He'd never seen anything like that from Scott, and he was beginning to worry that someone had put a hallucinogenic into Scott's drink.

Katie had just begun to speak again when a loud thump happened directly behind her, causing her to jump forward into Scott's arms and Jacob to turn instantly. A beautiful dark-haired woman had pinned Linda to the floor on her back. The dark-haired stranger held Linda to the floor with her right knee planted on the center of Linda's chest. In Linda's right hand was a full bottle of whiskey.

When Linda was dropped to the floor from Scott's lap, she became enraged. Linda walked over behind Katie, intending to hit her in the head with the bottle of whiskey. The dark-haired woman had grabbed Linda's right arm, put her leg behind Linda, thrown her backward to the ground, and pinned her with a knee on the chest.

Jacob reached down to take the whiskey bottle. Scott held Katie in his arms defensively for a moment. Then, as if coming out of a dream, Scott looked down uncomfortably and dropped his arms to his sides. Scott stammered and said, "I'm so sorry, ma'am. I didn't mean to be disrespectful." Katie smiled and said, "You weren't. Thank you for catching me."

Jacob looked around for a deputy and saw Cat. With a smile, Cat immediately volunteered Duncan and said, "Duncan wouldn't mind taking Ms. Linda to the holding cell until she sobers up for you, Jake." Cat had finally found a way to leave the party and was happy to help.

Duncan handcuffed Linda's wrists and escorted her out while Cat smiled.

Jacob looked at the brunette that had taken down Linda and said, "Thank you for your help, ma'am."

"Katie, you were right. The Boy Scout over here just called me ma'am." The woman laughed.

Katie walked over and said, "Leanne Conoway, I'd like to introduce you to Jacob McKenny. Now you have to name any future children after me. I prefer Cathrinus if it's a boy." Katie broke into laughter as Jacob and Leanne's faces reddened with embarrassment.

Attempting to recover from the embarrassment, Jacob laughed and replied, "Katie, I thought you were smart. Do you realize you embarrassed the woman who took down Linda Lankle? Have you been drinking? That's the dumbest thing I've ever seen you do. Most of the men in this room couldn't have taken Linda down like that!"

Katie, Leanne, and Jacob all laughed at the snide remark, but Scott stood utterly silent and still. Jacob looked over at his friend, who was apparently entranced by Katie. Jacob was still amazed at how quickly his friend had become sober.

"So how did you learn that move?" asked Jacob.

"Remember, I'm from New York. We're born with that ability," replied Leanne with a sarcastic smile.

Jacob smiled and looked back over to Scott. With a confused look, he turned to Leanne and asked, "Do you think the four of us should go grab a bite to eat? I think Scott might have gotten a hold of some bad liquor or something."

Leanne looked at Scott and realized that Jacob was probably trying to get Scott out of the party early. Besides, a crowd had been gathering around them because of the fight. Leanne nodded and said, "That sounds like a great idea."

The ringing of the phone awakened Jacob early the next morning. The caller ID said it was Maribeth Travers, and Jacob wondered why she would be calling so early. "Hello?" Jacob answered the call.

"Sheriff, I'd like to know what happened. Around eleven last night, Scott stopped by the house, gave me a dozen roses, told me he loved me, and kissed my cheek. When he left my house, he was smiling like a 'possum. That was the shortest birthday party Scott has had since he was twelve years old. Yet he was happier than I'd ever seen him. What happened?" Maribeth asked.

"Well, we went to Blaine's, there was a scuffle, and then the four of us went to have pizza."

"The four of you?" asked Maribeth.

"Yeah, Me, Katie, Scott, and Leanne. You remember the editor lady coming down from New York to meet Aunt Helen."

"Oh no! He didn't like the lady from New York, did he?!" Maribeth's mind raced, and she began to panic about her grandbabies being so far away. In her mind, she was already thinking about packing everything up and moving to be closer.

Jacob laughed and said, "No, actually, that's the funny part. He met Katie for the first-time last night."

"Really? I thought they would have met by now."

"Nope, last night was the first time he ever laid eyes on her, and honestly, I think he went sober instantly! I've never seen anything like it. He even had a hard time speaking to her." Jacob laughed.

"You're kidding!" Maribeth seemed happy but uneasy.

"Why do you sound disappointed, Mrs. Travers?"

"I'm not disappointed. I'm worried. She's much younger than him, and she's a doctor. I'm just afraid he'll get his heart broken."

"Well, she's twenty-nine, and he just turned forty last night. But, on a good note, she's much older than him if we count maturity into it," Jacob laughed.

"I know. I just worry about him. He loves so hard. I knew that when he actually fell in love with a woman that he would fall hard, and that sounds like what you just explained."

Jacob attempted to calm Scott's worried mother, "Let's just not talk about it and see what happens. You know I've got his back. I'll keep an eye out for him."

"Okay. Well, while I have you on the phone, Anna George called again this morning. Stanley still hasn't come home. Remember, she called yesterday around two o'clock. She's really worried. Can you run by her house?" Maribeth asked.

"Sounds like I need to. That's strange for Stanley. I know he likes to hunt, but it's odd for him to be gone this long."

Jacob got dressed and headed toward the George family home. He was glad he had a four-wheel drive as he started down the dirt road leading off Sutherland Ridge. The house sat nearly a mile off the main road. Fences lined each side of the dirt road. A few goats and cows were grazing in the early morning dew-covered grass. Turning one last curve, the house came into view. It was an old-style wood frame home that had been built in the 1930s as a part of the increase of the coal industry in Dickenson County. The house was in need of painting and the roof had a tarp over one section. Pulling into the driveway, he noticed Anna standing on the front porch.

"Thank you for coming, Sheriff," Anna yelled towards the driveway as she stepped off the porch. The young woman was using a cane and was walking with a limp. Anna looked as if she hadn't slept. Worry lines showed on her face, and she wrung her hands as she spoke.

Jacob walked toward the house and asked, "What happened to your leg, Mrs. George?"

"I fell, and Dr. McKinney said that it was sprung. I have to use a cane, and it hurts pretty bad." Anna replied. "That's why I couldn't go searching for him. Besides, the kids are too young to leave alone."

"So, he left to go hunting Friday morning at three a.m.?"

"Yes."

"Did he tell you where he'd be hunting before he left?"

Anna pointed to the top of the ridge located directly behind her house. "He said he was going after deer, but a bear lives up on that ridge. It's been getting into our garbage and eating corn out of our garden. He had tracked it toward the mountain and assumed it lived up that way."

As Jacob looked toward the mountain, three children emerged from the house. The children were still in their night clothes. The oldest looked no older than eleven or twelve years old. It started to make sense why Anna would stay with George even though he had beaten her on several occasions.

Jacob pulled out his phone, "I'm going to call Maribeth and get some more help looking, but I'm heading up toward that point on the ridge. I'm guessing he was thinking about getting the high ground."

Anna nodded. Her face had a tired and worried look. Jacob dialed as he began to walk toward the bottom of the mountain. In the distance, he could see what he could barely make out to be an opening in the trees that could be the start of a path.

The call to Maribeth was short. He informed her to reach out to every deputy as well as the fire departments and rescue squads. He also informed her about the direction he was headed in case Anna got confused. He had his radio as well as his cell phone on him. Sutherland Ridge had good reception, so he knew he could be reached as he climbed the mountain to the point of the ridge.

The Appalachian Mountains were home to Jacob. Jacob had been in the Rocky Mountains, the Blue Ridge Mountains, and visited the Smoky Mountains, but there was something different about the Appalachians. The mountains protected the area from natural events like tornadoes, and if you lived on top of the mountain, you weren't affected by flooding. The wildlife was abundant, and the air was cleaner than in the cities.

If there's one thing that Jacob loved about the mountains, it was that they never stayed the same. Some places on the earth stayed the same. The same temperatures and the same colors in the dirt and vegetation. The deserts were always hot and dry. The badlands of New Mexico were always windy and gold-colored year-round. In the Appalachian Mountains, it was always different. Every day was different in the mountains: different colors, different seasons, different animals, and different vegetation. There was always something new and wonderful to find in your surroundings and, sometimes, within yourself, in these mountains.

The mountains changed from season to season and sometimes month to month based on the weather. The mountains would also vary based on the elevation where you were located. Ferns and moss grew near the bottom of the mountain where they could take in the largest amount of water flowing down from the mountaintop. Hardwood trees loved the center elevation, and pines loved the top of the mountain. In the morning, rays of sunlight cascaded across the hills, shining the hope of a new day. In the evening, the sunset caused the mountains to be beautifully romantic in the spring and summer. In the fall, the sunset over the mountains could cast feelings of foreboding. Jacob had traveled often during his time in the military and had always missed these mountains.

He remembered camping with Katie and Isaac when he was younger. At night, the trees would glow mysteriously under the moon's light. Katie had always said it was spooky to her, but the sight always felt calming and soothing to Jacob. It was as if he was sleeping in a haunted forest but had nothing to fear. He was quite comfortable and at home in the Appalachian Mountains.

Jacob often felt he had forgotten something at home when he visited cities. One night, outside Charleston, West Virginia, he realized what he had forgotten. It was the stars. The nighttime sky in Dickenson County was covered with stars. The lack of large towns and bright lights allowed the stars to shine with fantastic clarity.

The economy was the only negative aspect of living in the mountains of Southwest Virginia. Dickenson County had no four-lane roads or interstates, which was a deterrent to manufacturing in the county. The people of Dickenson County were poor. The county itself was poor. The mountains that lovingly protected its occupants from natural disasters also stopped progress. Jacob had always wondered if stopping progress was a positive or negative because the small, hometown aspect of the county was a blessing you couldn't find anywhere else in the world.

Jacob stepped onto the path and was surrounded by trees. As he made his way up the mountain, he looked around for signs that someone else had been there. He hoped to find a footprint or other indication that Stanley had traveled that way. There was nothing out of place. Spider webs crisscrossed the path. Jacob was thankful that the early morning dew was still connected to the spider webs because it illuminated the webbing. He could wave his arms to remove them before walking into them face first. Jacob smiled as he thought to himself, *Do spiders want to catch a human face, or is it that we just notice them more when they hit you in the face?*

Jacob had traveled about a mile when he noticed something off the side of the path. It looked like a pile of clothing. Jacob made his way through the bushes toward the mound. Lying in tall grass, he found the body of Stanley George. The right side of his chest was covered in blood, and an arrow was protruding from his rib cage.

Jacob grabbed his cell and called Ricky Plank. He knew that Ricky would be part of the fire department that had already arrived at Anna's home to tell him where he was and that he had found Stanley without putting it across the radio.

The phone only rang once when Ricky picked up, and he answered, "Yeah, Sheriff."

"I found him, Ricky. He's dead. It looks like he wasn't the only one hunting in these woods. He's got an arrow sticking out of his right side. It looks like it punctured his lung. I called because I'd rather tell Anna myself."

"Well, Pastor Mark, Maribeth, and your mom are here already, and a few ladies from the church are coming up. So, she has some support. Tell me where you are located, and a few of us will come up with a gurney."

Jacob explained his location and waited for the firefighters and rescue squad members to arrive. Once they were on the scene, he walked back toward the home to give the news to Anna. Jacob dreaded this part of his job. He thought of the adorable kids he had seen on the porch that morning. On the walk, he wondered what they would do. How would they make it without a father? Stanley may have beat on his wife, but she had no education, no other family, and no way to support her kids.

Jacob stepped onto the porch and was met at the front door by his mother. One look in Jacob's eyes and Sara knew the news wasn't good. She followed her son as he walked into the living room and sat beside Anna George on the couch. Mark and Maribeth sat in chairs adjacent to the sofa. Jacob held her hand and told her he had found Stanley's body. The sobbing was heartbreaking. Jacob wondered if Anna was crying because she feared how she would take care of her children or if she was genuinely heartbroken by losing the husband that had been violent with her so many times.

Jacob left Pastor Mark and the ladies from the church to care for the bereaving wife and headed back to the office. After hearing what happened, Cat took Maribeth's place in the office. Cat knew that Maribeth would want to be there for the grieving woman, so she had come to work with Duncan that morning.

On the drive back to the office, something kept bothering Jacob. That wasn't the first time someone had been shot with an arrow in Dickenson County. He couldn't remember the specifics like the name or the date, but he knew in the recesses of his mind that this had happened before.

Jacob sat at his desk and checked the names that had once been on the sexual offender registry list but had passed away after moving to Dickenson County. The list contained the names, the dates, and the cause of death. Scrolling down the list with his finger, he found what he had been looking for. Andrew Calcraft had been found with an arrow protruding from his back in 2006. It was deemed a hunting accident, but no one had ever found the other hunter.

Jacob decided to focus on the 2006 accident first. This would allow time for evidence to be worked on concerning Stanley George's death. Andrew Calcraft was originally from Idaho and had been convicted of the sexual molestation of a fifteen-year-old. He had spent ten years in prison, and when he was released, he came to Dickenson County. He had picked up work at a local trailer park. He lived in one of the trailers and worked on the others in the park. The park owner was a local woman named Beverly Burke. Beverly was the last one to see him alive. Her statement was in the file, but Jacob felt he should speak with her in person. He decided to drive to her home on Caney Ridge.

Arriving at the trailer park, Jacob immediately saw an older woman working in a raised flower garden. A walker stood beside her as she worked. He hadn't seen her in a long time but was confident that the woman planting flowers was Mrs. Burke. She had been an elementary school math teacher and had retired after teaching for nearly thirty years. She had been Jacob's sixth-grade math teacher. While Jacob was in the Army, he had heard about her husband passing away from a heart attack. She had focused on their grandchildren and babysat as often as possible.

The older woman lit up with a bright smile upon seeing the sheriff exit his patrol car. "Well, if it isn't the young Sheriff McKinney!" The woman walked over and threw her arms around Jacob's neck. "I haven't seen you since you were knee-high to a grasshopper! How have you been, Jacob?"

"I'm doing well, Mrs. Burke. You planting bulbs today?"

"I sure am. Have to plant them in the fall before the first frost, you know. What brings you out here? Have you finally decided to ask my great niece on a date and need me to give my blessing?" The older woman laughed, but Jacob knew that she was quite serious.

"Mrs. Burke, you know that I could never keep up with Nadine. That girl doesn't need to marry a Sheriff but some kind of wild animal trainer!" They both laughed because they knew Nadine's reputation and there was truth in the statement.

"I have to admit, my brother was overprotective of her when her mother died. She wholeheartedly rebelled against it. I'm just glad you're not coming to tell me that you've got her locked up." Mrs. Burke shook her head.

"Nah, she's not that bad yet. I just came up to ask you about Andrew Calcraft. Do you remember him?"

"How can I forget? My, that was a long time ago. Harvey had just bought this land and a bunch of run-down trailers." She smiled at the memory of her dead husband. "Oh, he had the biggest plans! He was going to fix all of them up and make it really nice. We were going to live on the rent money in our retirement years and travel around the States together. When he had the heart attack, it left those dreams just sitting and rotting. He was the one who hired and worked with Andrew. Andrew told us that he wasn't from here. He was honest and told us about being in prison and the reason. He had no place to stay because no one would rent to him. Harvey and I didn't have any kids of our own, and the trailer park was just empty trailers that needed fixing back then. So, we let him stay in whatever trailer he chose if he would fix up the others. He worked seven days a week on them. He'd get started at sunup and work until it was too dark to see. He was a hard worker and did a great job." The older woman finished with a sense of pride as she said, "He finished two before he died."

"He finished two in three months? That is impressive," Jacob replied.

"It was so sad. Andrew asked Harvey and me if he could have a day off to go bow hunting. He was poor and said that if he got a deer, he'd dress it and clean it, and we could store it in my freezer and share it. I thought that was so sweet of him. I hadn't had deer meat since Harvey's nephew moved out west. I told him he didn't need my permission for a day off, and I hoped he got a deer. He told me he was leaving early the next morning, and Harvey loaned him one of his old bows and a few arrows. That was the last time I saw him." Mrs. Burke looked down in sadness, and Jacob noticed the bluish streaks in her silver hair for the first time.

"He was found on Clinchfield land, wasn't he?"

"Yes, everyone hunts up there. I showed him the path behind my house."

"Did anyone else know he was going?"

"Anyone else? Jacob, what has gotten you into asking about an accident that happened so long ago?"

"Well, I'm just looking into a few old cases. It's kind of a rule. One last look before we close them for good. You know?"

The old woman looked confused momentarily and said, "Well, I guess it's good you're doing your job. That's what the citizens pay you for. I'd say the whole church knew."

"The whole church? What happened that the whole church knew?"

"Well, they always ask if we have any prayer requests during service. I requested that we pray that Andrew got a deer and mentioned that he was leaving out the next morning to go bow hunting."

Jacob laughed, and Mrs. Burke commented, "I didn't get deer meat from Andrew but hit one with a car two weeks later. Nadine and her daddy came up and cleaned it, and I still got what I asked for. The Lord always answers prayers!" The older woman smiled.

Jacob and Mrs. Burke laughed together for a moment, and he asked, "Did anyone dislike Andrew or threaten him?"
"Oh yes! Lots of people. That's why he stayed here in the park for the entire three months. He couldn't go anywhere without people yelling or calling him names. He even had eggs thrown at him once. It got to the point that I told him that I'd go get what he needed, or we'd have it delivered if he needed supplies for the trailers. Andrew was a small man, and I feared he'd get hurt if he left the park. It turned out I was right."

"So, no one ever admitted hunting up there that day or was investigated?"

"Tom Linkard talked to every bow hunter in the county. No one saw Andrew that day or anyone else. That Clinchfield property is pretty big, and there's all kinds of ways in and out."

"Did you see anyone go in?"

"No, I'm in bed by nine and don't get up until six. That's been my sleeping schedule since I was a young teacher. But I told Sheriff Linkard that I knew Andrew had left early that morning. I had a little dog named Rowdy at the time, and Rowdy started barking at about two in the morning. His barking had woke me up, and I yelled at Rowdy and went back to sleep."

Jacob's cell phone vibrated, and he looked down to see a text from Cat. "Well, I'd better head back to the office. Cat's messaging me. It was so good to see you, Mrs. Burke, and if there's anything you need, you just call me, okay?" Jacob hugged his old friend and retired teacher.

"Oh, I will. And remember, Nadine's single if you ever get the notion," the older woman yelled out. Jacob waved and smiled as he stepped into his cruiser.

Arriving at the office, Cat asked, "So, you didn't reply, and I ordered lunch. I got you a sandwich."

"I forgot. I used your text to say there was an emergency and had to come back. I was talking to Beverly Burke up on Caney Ridge. You know she can get into conversations that last for hours." Jacob smiled.

"Yes, she can. Why were you up there? Changed your mind about Nadine?" Cat asked in jest while stifling back laughter.

"I was just talking about something that happened years ago. Back in 06, there was a man shot the same way Stanley George was this morning. You haven't had time to put it into the system yet, so I'll pull the hard file."

"Really?" asked Cat. "I don't remember it."

"It was just on the chance that I realized it. I don't think it's related, but I just wanted to ask a few questions."

Cat nodded, and Jacob walked toward the file room. Andrew Calcraft's file was quickly located, and he returned to his desk. Everything Jacob was looking for was in the file. Interviews with hunters that may have been on the property that day, photographs, and the autopsy report from Richmond were all included in the file.

Jacob sat down and began to read. Jacob compared what he had witnessed that morning to the photos in the file. It was strange how much alike the two victims were. Both were smaller-sized men who had been bow hunting. Andrew had an injury to his back, and the photos showed the arrow sticking out of a blood-stained shirt. Stanley had been shot in the side. Could it be that Stanley heard something and was turning around when the arrow caught him on the right side? Jacob looked harder at the photos. There was something strange about both arrows, but Jacob wasn't a bow hunter and couldn't put his finger on it.

The autopsy showed that the arrow removed from Andrew Calcraft was only twenty-four inches long. It was made of fiberglass with a razor tip. Jacob picked up his phone and called Grant Mullins. Grant owned the local outfitter's store and was an avid bowhunter.

"Hey, Grant, quick question." Jacob began.

"Sure, but before you ask, I should ask you, since I know what happened this morning, is this confidential?" Grant laughed.

"Actually, yes, just keep it between us. Okay?"

Grant became serious. "Will do, Jake. What's up?"

Jacob continued, "What would you think if I said I needed a twenty-four-inch arrow with a razor tip?"

Grant laughed and said, "What kid are you teaching to hunt, Jake? And wouldn't it be better to bring the little girl or guy down here and let me teach them? You don't bow hunt."

"A kid?!" Jacob asked, surprised.

"Yeah, man, that's a kid-sized arrow. The length of the arrow is based on the length of your arms from tip to tip with your arms spread. Then, the length is divided by two and a half. That's your draw length and the size that your arrow should be. I also know that measuring your arm span like that usually equals how tall you are. When you say twenty-four inches, I know the person is around five feet tall. Do you need any? I have plenty in stock. Even have the kid-sized compound bows down here."

"Let me guess, there's no background check, and you can even buy them with cash, right?" Jacob asked sarcastically.

"Well, yes," Grant answered cautiously. "I sold a crap load last Christmas."

Jacob sighed. "Let's keep this conversation between us, okay, Grant?"

"Sure thing, man. Catch ya later. I have customers coming in."

Jacob sat back in his chair. His mind whirled. A kid? That made sense. A kid wouldn't have had a hunting license and might have snuck out to hunt and accidentally killed Andrew. A kid might not have known the arrow hit anything when fired. Jacob wondered how long the arrow that killed Stanley was and if there were any other similarities.

Chapter 6

"The party was on Friday. You would think that everyone would be sober and
 ready to work by Monday, wouldn't you?" Jacob asked as he stood in front of the conference desk at the police station looking disappointed in the men and women around the table. "I'm not going to ask how many in here were relieved when Stanley George's body was found so quickly. I'm not going to ask how many didn't reply to Maribeth's call or text when we started looking for him. I swear, guys, you have to stop being so happy that Scott is getting older. He does it a little bit every day!" Jacob sighed and ended his early morning rant with, "I guess I should be happy that it's only celebrated once a year!"

The officers surrounding the table were sober, but you could tell that headaches and nausea from the celebration were still prominent among the group. The room was silent, so Jacob shook his head and continued. "I'm handing out arrest warrants and notices for you guys. I'm also handing out patrol assignments and…" Jacob looked around and noticed the absence of a familiar face… "Where's Scott?"

"Sorry I'm late, everybody!" a voice boomed behind Jacob. "Isn't this a beautiful day! Just listen to those birds singing, and the fall decorations look beautiful around the building. It even smells better, and I swear, do you think the sky is actually bluer today?" Scott pointed towards the window. Moans of grief came from many sitting at the table due to the headaches and nausea.

"I know you were off this weekend, but would you mind telling me why you're late?" asked Jacob.

"I want everyone to know how much I love and appreciate them. It's important to show love to people every chance we get," Scott replied.

Jacob looked at the deputies and solemnly said, "Is he running for office, or has he lost his mind?"

"I need to know if there's a difference," an officer replied from the back of the room as the others stifled laughter.

Another officer replied, "My money is on the mind thing…." The officers laughed again.

The expression on Jacob's face was one of confusion and curiosity. He knew his friend was serious but also wondered if he hadn't been diagnosed with a terminal illness or been saved during a church service since he saw him last. The drastic change of personality was unsettling.

"O…K..." Jacob replied slowly, unsure what to add and noting that he needed to question Scott about his actions privately.

"How about I buy everyone coffee to go this morning?!" Scott happily announced. "Any takers?"

"Scott, we need to talk, so why don't you just call down to Legend's for a tab, and everyone can grab it to go?" Jacob replied, not wanting Scott to take over the meeting.

"That's a great idea! Coffee on me!" He shouted as he walked out the door to call Legend's Coffee and set up a running tab.

The look on Jacob's face after Scott left the room made many of the deputies giggle. He was shocked by the changes in

Scott's attitude and could not hide his emotions. After a few minutes, he said, "Dismissed." The deputies all went to grab their coffee and report to their duty assignments.

Walking into the office, Jacob saw Maribeth at the desk. Scott was on his phone with his back turned. Jacob, not wanting to interrupt Scott or let him know he was asking about him, signed to Maribeth with hand gestures. He first pointed at Scott and then twirled a finger at his head as if placing circles around his ears with his fingers. His face was questioning. Maribeth replied by putting both hands at shoulder height, palms up, and shrugging her shoulders. She also looked confused. She then mouthed the words, "All weekend."

Before Jacob could return to his office, Donna Carpenter, a supply sales associate from a local tactical store, walked into the main office. Donna Carpenter was a beauty. She stood five foot nine and had wavy blonde hair midway down her back. She wore a red miniskirt, a black low-cut blouse, and high heels. "Good morning," she said, smiling seductively in Scott's direction.

Scott said, "Thank you so much! Good-bye." Scott hung up the phone and looked at the lovely woman before him. "Good morning, Ms. Carpenter. Hate to miss our conversation, but I have to run over to Haysi. Have a lovely day!" Scott left the station in a hurry.

Maribeth, Jacob, and Donna all looked at each other shocked. "Do I look okay?" asked Donna.

"You look lovely, sweetheart. We think it's just him." Maribeth replied as Jacob nodded.

"He always hits on me and asks me out while he does the order for the police station. This time, he treated me like I was his cousin." Donna seemed disappointed.

Maribeth gently consoled the young woman. "Honey, don't let it bother you. None of us know what happened, but he's acted like that all weekend. I'll do the order today."

Jacob walked into his office and sat down at his desk. About thirty minutes later, an exuberant Scott entered the room. "Sorry, I had to take my debit card down there so they knew I meant business about the coffee. So, what you need, Jake?'

Being professional and compassionate, Jacob asked, "Scott, are you alright?"

"I'm doing great. I'm happier than I've ever been! Isn't life wonderful?" Scott completed the reply with a relaxed sigh.

"If you say so," was all Jacob could say before a knock came from his door.

It was Katie. She was in khaki pants and a blue, long-sleeved, button-up shirt. Her lab coat was hanging over her arm. "Jake, I have the info you needed. I was on my way to the hospital when the coroner called, so instead of calling, I decided to stop by. Hi, Scott."

Scott immediately stood but didn't reach out his hand or reply to her acknowledgment of him in the room.

"The arrow from Stanley George was twenty-four inches. It's the same size I used as a kid."

"Dang. Two kids, over twenty years apart. I'm beginning to think we need some hunter's safety courses in this county! How tall is Stanley's oldest kid?"

"Not tall enough. Besides, that would mean a kid, accidentally or on purpose, killed their father. The kids probably weren't even out of bed yet. Besides, you're missing something, you idiot." Katie replied with a cocky attitude.

"What am I missing?!" replied Jacob defensively.

"Well, sometimes adults only grow to five feet tall." Katie sarcastically retorted.

"Well, most of the men are over five feet tall in the county, so it sure does lower the suspect list."

Katie rolled her eyes in frustration and said sarcastically, "Oh yes, we women are saints and would never, ever hurt another human being!"

You could see the shock on Jacob's face. "You think it could have been a woman?"

Katie looked at her cousin with a flat expression on her face. "I wonder how we're related sometimes, you know that?" Katie answered. "Yes, it could have been a woman who shot the arrow."

"Anna George is around five feet tall and pretty small built," Jacob replied.

"It wasn't her," Katie replied.

"How do you know?" Jacob asked.

"Because last week she came into the emergency room. She has a partial disruption of the ACL. She's not supposed to be even walking around on that cane. I warned her about it." Katie replied.

"Okay. You don't have to prove that you're smarter. We know you are… now please speak English."

"Well, putting it bluntly, she wouldn't have been able to walk up there and do it. Her x-ray showed a pretty bad injury. She couldn't have walked up there. But I'm in a rush. I gotta get to the hospital. What are you doing for lunch?"

"I'll probably be headed up to the George's and see if there's anything left to do. But Scott might be interested."

Scott's head darted toward Jacob in shock.

"What do you say, Scott? Mexican sound good?" Katie asked.

Scott stammered… "Um, um. Okay," were the only words formed.

"Great, meet you there at noon." Katie smiled as she turned and walked out of the office.

Jacob looked at Scott in surprise, "Holy Shit!"

"What?" asked Scott.

"It's Katie. That's the change we all see. It's Katie."

"Katie said you were an idiot." Scott paused for a dramatic effect and continued, "Now, I am inclined to agree." Scott stoically replied.

Scott turned as he walked out the door, "Did you seriously not think about a woman committing murder, Jake?"

"Scott, I've known my cousin all my life. If I had mentioned the possibility of the shooter being female before she did, she'd have yelled at me for being too critical of women and not trusting females. That would have led to a bunch of psycho-babble that none of us want to hear. If I don't, I just look like an idiot. Trust me; sometimes it's better to be an idiot. Besides, I love messing with her head." Jacob laughed mischievously.

Scott shook his head in disbelief and left the room. Jacob laughed and picked up the Calcraft file from his desk. He thought to himself. If the two events were murders and were connected, a small female over forty could have committed both murders. Then again, why would someone who had killed someone on the sexual registry go after Stanley George? Stanley was known to hit his wife, but his kids were never reported as being abused.

Jacob thought of the times he had been called to the house because of Stanley's temper. He had witnessed Anna crying and bruised. Was it possible that the kids were being abused as well? A quick call could answer that question.

Jacob picked up his phone. The answer came quickly. "Dr. Reynolds' Office, how can I help you?"

"Aunt Helen? Are you working today?" Jacob asked.

"Yes, I still work part-time when they need help. You okay?" Helen asked.

"I just needed some inside information. Can you tell me anything about the George family's children? Were there any signs of abuse?"

"Jake, I'm not going to tell you how to do your job. But you're not getting anything out of me. It's against HIPPA regulations, and you know it. Besides, you know we're mandated reporters of abuse. If you want information, you're going to have to ask a judge to get it for you. And don't ask Katie, or I'll be very angry," Helen replied flatly.

"I love you, Aunt Helen." Jacob laughed as he hung up the phone. Barbara, the regular nurse, would have told him anything he needed to know, and he knew that. But his Aunt Helen was by the book.

A trip to Ridgeview Elementary School was now Jacob's next stop. Walking out the door, he yelled, "Hey Scott, wanna go with me to the elementary school?"

Maribeth called back, "He's not here. On a call."

Jacob arrived at the school right before lunch. He went directly to the principal's office. Theresa Barton, the school secretary, was at the desk. She was an older woman who had been at the school for years. She also knew more about the kids at the school and the families than anyone else.

Jacob smiled, "Hi, Theresa," he said.

"Sheriff! It's great to see you! How have you been?"

"Not bad. Can I ask you a private question?"

"Sheriff! I never knew you felt that way." Theresa smiled and laughed. "You know, older women are an excellent way for a younger man to learn."

Theresa was a good person. She was a faithful wife and devoted mother, but she loved to flirt and make younger men uncomfortable, and Jacob knew it. It was her way of being mischievous.

It was a rare occasion that Jacob blushed, but this was one of those occasions. "Theresa! You're a married woman." Jacob laughed.

"It's okay. My husband likes you really well, Jacob." Theresa laughed a boisterous laugh.

Jacob laughed again, and Theresa asked, "So, what you need, Sheriff?"

"Do you know if any of the George children have been hurt or injured lately?"

"Do you mean the man who died this weekend? Stanley and Anna George's kids?"

"Yeah, I'm just looking into something."

"Well, their oldest son is in sixth grade. He's eleven now, and he had a bad bruise on his side about two weeks ago. I saw it when he went to the nurse's office about it, and I honestly thought it was shaped like a fist. I asked him what made the bruise, and he said he had wrecked on his bicycle, and the handlebar hit his rib cage."

"Did you believe him?"

"Actually, he showed us the other scratches and scrapes from where he had landed in a briar patch, so I had no reason not to believe him."

"Okay. Thanks, Theresa."

"No problem, Sheriff, and if you change your mind about older women, you just give me a call!" Theresa laughed mischievously.

As Jacob drove back to the office, he felt saddened at not having any connection between the two men except the size of an arrow, yet he was glad that the kids had not suffered the abuse of their father. He had seen their mother beaten too many times.

Marlene Branham was at the office chatting with Maribeth when he walked in. "Hi, Sheriff." Marlene smiled. Marlene was in her thirties and worked for the insurance agency down the street. She was dressed professionally in black slacks and a beige button-up shirt. She was holding a folder under her arm.

"Hi, Marlene. What brings you down here?"

"I have good news, but I am also getting prepared to be questioned about a few things," Marlene answered indirectly.

"Should we talk in my office?"

Marlene nodded shyly. "We probably should."

Walking into the office, Jake sat down and waved to the chair on the other side of the desk, "Have a seat."

Marlene sat down and handed the file across the desk. Jacob opened the file and stared briefly before replying, "Please excuse my language, but holy shit."

"I thought you'd think that."

"Is this real?"

"For the family's sake, I sure hope it is."

"What do you mean, you hope?" Jacob asked.
"Well, the application was done online. The signatures were electronic, and there was cash in an envelope put into the agency's drop box for the payments to the policy paid up for the next year." Marlene replied.

"The policy is paid for the next year? It looks like someone is getting a partial refund." Jacob stated flatly.

"We sent letters to the address on the application, which is the George family's address explaining the policy. No one ever contacted us to say they didn't purchase a policy. Of course, the way it looks, Stanley was the one who purchased the policy for himself, and he made Anna the beneficiary. The thing is, it was done electronically, and the adjuster will ask me about the possibility of Stanley doing this. I've never seen Stanley with a cell phone, much less a computer. Plus, as poor as they are, how did they get the cash for the entire first year of the payments?"

"So, they're going to question you about a life insurance policy with a double indemnity for an accident. What is this, a half a million?"

"They're going to ask me about it. Especially now that Stanley is dead."

"Well, I have to say, there's no way that Anna could have killed him. I talked to Katie this morning, and she used big words to explain something about Anna's knee. She couldn't have made the walk. The kids were asleep, and no one saw anyone else out there. It looks like a hunting accident that no one is admitting to."

"What about the possibility of Stanley completing the paperwork online?" Marlene asked.

"Well, was all the information accurate?"

"It was. We checked the birth dates and social security numbers of both parties, and both were correct. If it wasn't Stanley, it was someone that knew a lot about both of them."

"I don't see the problem. A librarian, a teenager, a teacher, nearly anyone could have helped him." Jacob smiled.

"Well, how did they afford to pay over two thousand dollars on the premiums? I'll have to explain that, too." Marlene acted nervous.

"I have no idea. Maybe they sold something, or he's growing weed on the mountain. Heck, he might have even borrowed it from someone. If we can't explain it, will it stop Anna and the kids from getting the insurance money?"

"I'm not sure. When it's large amounts, insurance companies sometimes like to look into it."

Jacob decided that calming Marlene would be his priority, "Well, then let me know what I can do if they send someone out to look at it, okay? For the time being, all we can do is help her file the claim and wait to see what the insurance company does."

Marlene stood to shake the sheriff's hand. Jacob responded in kind and shook her hand as she smiled and said, "You're right. I'm just overstressing about it. I just wanted to let you know in case they need to speak with you."

Jacob handed her the file as he walked Marlene toward the door and said, "Yeah, I worry about stuff too much, too. I am trying to worry about things when they happen and not if they happen."

"Good advice." Marlene smiled and left.

Jacob shut the door to the office and then looked toward Maribeth and asked, "Have you heard from Scott?"

"Yes, I couldn't say anything in front of Marlene, but the call he took before you went to the school was a doozy. The Haysi Town Police called up here because there was an accident. Phil Yandell was riding a four-wheeler up on Spearhead Trail. He had just come down from the Haysi section and drove down the hill from the Kiwanis Park. He sped up at the edge of town once he hit the paved road. Phil lost control and hit the old Rockhouse right before the bridge. He hit one of the lower platforms of a window, flipped the four-wheeler through the window, and fell to the bottom. The four-wheeler fell nearly eight feet and landed on top of him."

"You have got to be kidding me." Jacob looked stunned. "Was Phil drinking?"

"According to the people riding with him, he wasn't drinking but was laughing and showing off a bit. I've never heard of Phil even drinking a beer."

"Does Scott need any help?"

"No, he said he was fine and that the State Police and ambulance were already there. The fire department used a winch to pull the four-wheeler back out."

"Ambulance? Is Phil okay?"

"No. They did everything they could. There was a stick at the bottom that severed an artery when he fell. According to the chief down in Haysi, he bled out pretty fast."

Jacob shook his head in sadness as he walked into his office and closed the door. He sat down and returned to the list. Robert Gagnon was next on the list. He died in a dirt bike accident in 2010. Robert Gagnon's grandparents were born and raised in Dickenson County. They owned fifty acres up on Brushy Ridge. They had passed away in the 70s, and his mother had inherited the property but had not lived on it since she was a child. She had been married to Robert's father, an Air Force pilot, and moved to Massachusetts when she was eighteen.

Robert was incarcerated for only five years for the kidnapping and rape of a twelve-year-old girl. He was released in late February 2010. He couldn't find work or housing in Massachusetts, so Robert decided to live on his grandparents' old farm in Dickenson County. He moved to the county in May of the same year.

Robert lived in his grandparents' old house. It was a wood frame house that had been built in the 1930s. Thankfully, his grandfather had wired the old house with electricity when Robert's mother was born in the 1970s. But, due to the property being so remote, the water came from a cistern located beside the home that caught rainwater. The old house had no insulation, and the only heat source in the old place was an old wood stove in the living room. The taxes on the property were paid every year, and Robert's mother signed the fifty acres over to Robert.

Robert had started a garden and bought chickens. He wasn't allowed to own a weapon but was allowed to use a bow to hunt. He planned on using his grandparents' old smokehouse to create his own smoked venison. It was a quiet existence away from almost everyone in the county.

Robert owned an old dirt bike. Since he only rode the dirt bike a short distance on the main road once or twice a month, local police ignored it. The dirt bike was his only source of transportation. Robert lived a quiet and solitary existence and stayed out of everyone's way.

Once or twice a month, he would ride his dirt bike down to a local store to buy milk and bread. It was during that time that he'd made contact with a few people about purchasing marijuana seeds. He guessed he could grow marijuana on the land his grandparents had left him to make money. If other growers hadn't completed police reports, no one would have known much about Robert.

The month of August in southwest Virginia is hot and dry. The temperature usually stays around ninety degrees. The report in front of Jacob said that the original call was made to dispatch on August twenty-eighth. Charlie Kiser, Blaine Kiser's father, had made the call. He had been hunting on the property across from Robert's and caught the scent of a rotting animal.

Charlie had walked down the mountainside, into a small valley, and up the adjoining mountain. The odor became worse. He assumed he would find the carcass of a deer, a bear, or a coyote. He walked up the mountainside, watching carefully for prey animals that might also be looking for the decaying smell. At his feet, he noticed tire marks in the dirt in front of him. He visually followed the tread marks on the path, raising his head and looking into the distance as far as he could see. In the distance, Charlie could see a tire sticking out of a bush and what looked to be a person lying in the path. He began walking quickly toward what he hoped was not a person and yelling, "Hey, hey, you okay?"

In his quick, uphill movement, Charlie stumbled. It was then he noticed the human head lying under a bush beside him. Jacob smiled at the generalized words in the statement because, in his written statement, Charlie said it was the fastest he'd ever come out of those woods.

Jacob leaned back in his chair to think. Jacob was sixteen years old at that time. He remembered Charlie teaching Blaine to hunt. Blaine was still an avid sportsman and seeing his house at the previous weekend's party had proven it. Until now, Jacob had never realized why Charlie had given up hunting. That year, Blaine would have been about fourteen, and Charlie had given all of his guns and bows to his son.

Jacob returned to the report in front of him. A single line of barbed wire had been stretched taut across the path, and no one knew why. No one was allowed on Robert's property. There were no trespassing signs posted every twenty feet. Robert didn't want anyone hunting on the property or trespassing. Robert had decided it was best for everyone if he stayed away from people.

Everyone knew about Robert's conviction, so no one questioned why he wanted to be alone. Most of the county was glad to stay away from him. The mystery of how the line came to be across the path his dirt bike took was never solved.

Robert had been traveling at a fast speed down the hill. The barbed wire had caught him beneath his chin, causing decapitation. The body fell directly beneath the wire, and the dirt bike rolled aimlessly into the weeds near the road. The head of the rider had rolled down the dirt bike trail and into the ditch, where it was found six days later by Charlie Kiser.

Jacob knew Charlie would be home, so he decided to visit him. Charlie still lived out on Highland Road, and Jacob knew that it would be about a thirty-minute drive through narrow and curvy roads to get to the house. Jacob had told people that Dickenson County had roads that never ended because a five-mile drive could take over twenty minutes, depending on the road.

Maribeth wasn't at her desk, so he called out as he picked up his police radio, "Mrs. Travers, I'm heading up on Brushy Ridge for a few minutes."

"Take your radio!" Maribeth answered from the back of the supply closet. "You don't have a cell signal up there!"

Jacob smiled. "Already got it! Be back in a while!"

Jacob had a love-hate relationship with Brushy Ridge. He hated it because it was so far away from the county seat, and car accidents happened up there quite often. In the winter, the ridge was especially treacherous. Brushy Ridge was so high up that some said it had its own climate. In the winter, there would be flurries at the bottom of the mountain, and the top would be covered with two feet of ice and snow.

The love part of Brushy Ridge came from its beauty. From on top of the mountain, you could look across fields of green and see straight into the heavens. From the top of the mountain, the rest of the world seemed to vanish. The stress, the hustle and bustle of the world just melted away into nothing beyond the edge of the fields. From the top of Brushy Ridge, staring into the sky at night was like looking into the abyss and having the ability to see the past, present, and future in the same moment.

Jacob turned onto Highland Road and immediately saw the small brick home. Charlie was beside his house working on what looked like would become a garage in the near future. Charlie wore old blue jeans, work boots, and a plaid shirt with a pocket on the front. He wore an old bill cap nearly all of the time. He loved bill caps and was always excited during election years to get new hats from candidates. Jacob had noticed that Charlie would accept a hat from all the candidates, but he only wore the cap if he wanted the candidate to win the election. As Jacob stepped out of the patrol car, he noticed a car hidden under a car cover, and his suspicions were confirmed. Charlie was building a garage.
"Hey, Sheriff!" called out Charlie as he looked over his shoulder before hammering another nail into place.

"Looks like you're building a garage, Charlie."

Charlie looked over his shoulder again and smiled. He put down the hammer and walked toward the car cover. "You're not going to believe what I found last weekend, Sheriff!" Charlie pulled back the car cover to reveal something that looked like an extremely large pile of rust.

Not being able to recognize the automobile and not wanting to admit it, Jacob said, "Boy! Ain't she a beauty! What year is she?"

Charlie laughed and said, "I knew you'd recognize a '69 Maverick! The wife keeps calling it a pile of rust, but she's my new lady! I bought her from a guy over in Dungannon for two hundred bucks! She sold new in '69 for two thousand dollars, and when she's fixed up, I'll be able to get about thirteen grand out of her!"

"Nice job, Charlie! I never knew you worked on cars!"

"Oh, she's my first. I learned how to use that Google machine and have been watching other people do it." The older man smiled with pride as he spit into a bottle sitting nearby. Charlie had always used chewing tobacco.

Jacob smiled and said, "Well, ain't that something! What's Mrs. Kiser think of all this?"

Charlie smiled a toothless grin and said with a laugh, "She said it's worth the money to keep me out of the house!"

They both laughed, and the older man continued, "You'll learn once you're old and married a long time; old men drive old women nuts just to get toys like they did when they were young."

"I'm going to remember that advice and use it one day, Charlie!" Jacob laughed.

"So, what you doing all the way up here, Sheriff?" asked Charlie.

"Well, I wanted to ask you about finding Robert Gagnon. I hate bringing up old stuff, but I wanted to hear more about the story."

The old man stopped smiling and sighed, "Jacob, that case closed over ten years ago, and I try not to think about it. It gave me nightmares for years after. Even now, every time I smell a rotten animal or see something dead, it makes me sick. Why do you want to know about that stuff now?"

"I'm just trying to do my job, Charlie. Making sure that everything is wrapped up from the past."

Charlie's eyes and mouth narrowed. "Jacob McKinney, that better be the last time you judge me as being stupid. You and I both know that Gagnon's case is closed, and there's no reason for you to ask me about it. Now you'd better tell me the truth about why you're asking."

Jacob immediately recognized his error and felt guilty for thinking he would be able to cover up the truth from someone like Charlie. "I can't tell you everything, but I can tell you that, for some reason, when people on the sexual offender registry list move into the county, they die within ninety days."

Charlie immediately laughed and said, "And there's a problem with that?!"

"Well, Charlie, it's against the law!"

"Dying is against the law now? I need to start voting more!" Charlie laughed.

"No, murder is against the law, Charlie." Jacob remained professional.

"You said people died within ninety days, were they murdered?" Charlie asked.

Jacob stammered and said, "Well, I can't prove it yet. That's why I've been looking at them."

"Them? How many we talking about, Jake?" Charlie became more serious.

"There's a total of fifteen people over a twenty-five-year period. Eleven were ruled as accidental deaths, three were ruled as suicides, and one a heart attack." Jacob was being straightforward with the older man.

"So, you're saying that if all these accidents and suicides are linked, there's a serial killer here?"

"It seems far-fetched right now." Jacob seemed embarrassed making the statement.

Charlie nodded. "Jacob, we voted you in because we believe in you. We believe that you'll do what's right. Now, spending time researching all these old cases may not be the best way to use your time. It may be that all these cases are just coincidental. If they are linked, and someone is killing off pedophiles that move into our county, I honestly don't see the harm, and if I knew someone was doing that, I wouldn't be telling you nothing about it because I believe they're protecting our children."

The older man paused for a moment and said, "Now, I can either tell you what's already in the statement that I wrote that day for the police, or I can tell you something good that happened yesterday, your choice."

Jacob smiled and relaxed a bit, "I think it's time I heard something good."

The men laughed, and Charlie spit in the bottle once more before he continued. "Me and Blaine had planned on going up to Spearhead Trails in Clintwood and do some skeet shooting all week. Yesterday morning around eleven, he called and asked if he could bring a friend. I asked him who it was, and he told me the story of what happened with Scott Travers dumping Linda Lankle off of his lap and onto the floor over a woman that Blaine said was out of Scott's league. I don't know who he was talking about. But, anyhow, Blaine had felt bad for Linda and picked her up from the jail yesterday morning. She was feeling a little depressed, and he invited her to go skeet shooting with us."

Jacob smiled and laughed, "What happened?"

The older man's eyes lit up. "What happened? That cute little girl can shoot! She whipped me and Blaine good out on that range, and when we got back home, she drank us both under the table! We found out that there's nothing more she loves to do than hunt and fish! Heck, I think my son finally met his match!" Both of the men laughed.

"Well, better tell him he'd better walk the line with Linda. She has a jealous streak, and I don't want any women in town getting whipped. She doesn't fight fair either," Jacob warned.

"I don't think another woman could stand a chance anymore. My Blaine was ready to ask for his grandma's wedding ring last night! I could see it in his eyes." The old man laughed and continued, "Heck, it's got his momma so riled up that she's in there working on a wedding quilt and singing lullabies for her grandbabies that ain't even here yet!"

The men laughed for a moment, and Charlie asked, "You want a beer, Jake?"

"It's a little early for a lightweight like me, Charlie, but thank you anyhow. I have to be heading back to the station."

Charlie put out his hand and said, "Well, thanks for stopping by, Sheriff."

Jacob shook his hand and said, "Charlie, thank you. I think you're right. I'm going to slow down a bit and focus on what's happening now and slack off working on these past cases. You're right. There's a lot to be done, and I've already worked on half of them with no ties at all. I appreciate the advice."

On the drive back to his office, Jacob had time to think. He'd already looked at seven of the fifteen deaths. There was nothing. The only thing he had that looked suspicious at all was a short arrow. There was work piling up, and Stanley George's case was still fresh on his desk.

As Jacob walked into the building, he could hear laughter coming down the hall from his office. Walking into the office, he saw Maribeth, Katie, and Scott standing around Maribeth's desk. Maribeth had a white box filled with Mexican food in front of her. The office smelled wonderful, and Jacob realized he hadn't eaten lunch.

"Hey, Cuz, where you been?" asked Katie.

"Apparently, wasting time. But it's over now." Jacob smiled. "Heard you had a rough start to the day."

"Yes, but lunch made my day." Scott smiled a genuine, friendly smile at Katie. "How were you wasting time? Doing what?"

"Been going through those old sexual offender registry cases. I've gone through seven with no luck at all. I'm going to back off of them for a while. I've got other things to do. Like, wonder why you didn't bring me food, too."

"We didn't know what you were doing, but we knew Maribeth was here not eating. So, Scott and I bought lunch for her." Katie verbally scolded him for not making sure Maribeth had taken lunch.

Jacob stuck his tongue out as if he were eight years old again, and Katie replied with the same facial expression and added a squinched-up nose.

"Well, back to the hospital. Thanks for having lunch with me, Scott. I had fun." Katie smiled.

Maribeth interrupted, "Hey, before you leave, I bought tickets to the Jetti this Friday and can't go. Do you want to go with Scott and use my tickets? I hate for them to go to waste. The Barter Players are coming over and performing *My Fair Lady*."

Katie replied, "You know, I've not been to the Jetti since before I left to go to school. That would be fun. I love that movie."

Jacob smiled and said, "Yeah, Scott, take Katie to see a movie about a tall, skinny woman who can't talk right."

Katie gave Jacob a piercing look, understanding that the reference was supposed to insult her.

"I'd love to, Mrs. Travers." Katie stammered. "Well, that's if Scott is willing to go. He might not want to be seen with a tall, skinny woman that don't talk right," shooting a scowling look at her cousin a second time.

"I think it would be great," Scott replied.

"See you then," Katie replied as she left the office.

After Katie was out of earshot, Jacob immediately turned to Scott. "What happened to lines like, 'We'll start with dinner and end with breakfast'... or, one of my favorites," he glanced toward Maribeth, 'I'm not sure they'll let me into the Jetti with a cute little snack like you on my arm.'" As Jacob spoke the words, he imitated Scott's usual masculine behaviors of leaning toward a woman, winking, or touching her face. Jacob and Maribeth started laughing as they remembered the bad pickup lines Scott had used over the years.

"Hey, it's not like that. We're friends." Scott retorted.
Jacob and Maribeth looked at each other and laughed.

"Seriously, she'd never date someone like me. I'm not that stupid. She's beautiful, kind, funny, smart, a Harvard graduate, and an E.R. doctor. I'm just a cop, and we're friends. That's it." Scott shrugged his shoulders and left the office.

Shocked, Jacob looked at Maribeth. Maribeth had the same confused look on her face and said, "I don't know if that was funny or sad. It's funny he doesn't realize what's going on, but it's sad that he thinks she's not interested."

"Yeah, I liked seeing Katie laugh like that. She's happy." Jake solemnly replied.

After a moment of silence between them, Jacob asked, "By the way, when did you get those tickets to the Jetti?"

"When they go on sale tomorrow morning, why?" Maribeth smiled.

Jacob laughed and was happy to be in on the secret that Maribeth was creating dates for Scott and Katie.

Chapter 7

Jacob was late getting to the office the next morning. Cat's smile greeted him as he walked in the door. "Where have you been?"

"I came in late because I went to Stanley George's funeral last night. They're burying him today. Why are you here instead of Maribeth?"

"Maribeth is taking the day off to go somewhere in Tennessee to buy cloth."

"Cloth?" asked Jacob.

"Something about a wedding quilt." Cat looked confused.

Jacob laughed. "What is it with the women and their superstitions around here?"

"I'm confused. Who's Maribeth making a wedding quilt for?" Cat asked.

"She's just hoping Scott and Katie work out," Jacob casually replied.

Cat looked shocked. "Scott and Katie! That would be wonderful! They're perfect for each other!" Cat was getting tears of joy in her eyes.

"Not you, too! I'm still trying to figure out what this wedding quilt is!"

"It's a quilt that has a bunch of rings on it. It symbolizes love and romance. Apparently, you only get one of them because I only got one for my first wedding." Cat laughed and then stopped almost immediately and became serious, "Wait, do you think that's why the second two didn't work out? Because trust me, I'll be having a wedding quilt if I have to make one for myself if I ever get married again. I'm not going to risk it!"

Cat was visibly shaken by the superstition. Jacob just shook his head in disbelief and walked into his office. From his office, he heard her yell, "Jake, there's a message on your desk."

Picking up the small piece of paper, he dialed the number. "This is Sheriff Jacob McKinney calling for Donald Staff."

After a short pause, a man picked up the line. "Sheriff McKinney, I am an adjuster for the insurance agency of Stanley George. I've already contacted the coroner's office and the Virginia State Police. I'm just interested in knowing if there have been any other developments on the George case."

"I agree with the report filed by the Virginia State Police. It looks like an accidental death. We've exhausted our resources and have not found anyone who had a motive to purposely hurt Mr. George in any way."

"Was Mrs. George questioned concerning the death of her husband?"

"Yes, she was, but it was determined by her medical doctor that she would have been unable to walk the distance from the home required due to an injury in her left anterior cruciate ligament that may require surgery to repair in the future." Jacob smiled to himself. He didn't mind using Katie's smart words once in a while to sound professional.

"Thank you, Sheriff. I'll send this to our underwriters so that we can get everything handled as soon as possible."

Jacob hung up the phone thinking about all the donations the area churches had gathered to help with expenses. He wondered if the donations would last the family long enough for the insurance company to make a decision.

The rest of the week slowed for Jacob. Without the additional work of researching the list of accidental deaths, Jacob found time to help give away food at the food bank and help around the county. Jacob loved people, and it showed. Children were especially important to him, and this week, he even had time to visit Ridgeview High School. He had been thinking about spending more time there because a few teenagers could be thinking about careers in law enforcement or the military, and he could help them decide by answering a few questions.

When Friday rolled around, Jacob decided to watch the Ridgeview Wolfpack football game. He had posted deputies at the game but never gave himself a post so that he would be available for all emergencies. Scott had the night off and, according to Maribeth, was taking Katie to the play they had discussed earlier that week.

During the football game, Jacob was constantly standing and cheering. The team was exceptional. Several people stopped to shake Jacob's hand and say a few words. Two older women walked by, and Jacob overheard one woman tell the other, "We always have a good team because we know how to raise up good, corn-fed boys!" Jacob laughed and remembered back to when he played. He was one of the smaller players. Most of the Ridgeview Wolfpack were over a hundred and eighty pounds and averaged six feet tall. Jacob had been five foot ten since he was in the ninth grade. Aunt

Helen and his mother had worried that Katie would be taller than Jacob. They were both thankful that Katie had failed the task by only one inch. At five foot nine, Katie was the tallest woman in the family.

Jacob had always found the terminology of corn-fed to be funny. The term referred to how farmers fattened up a hog before slaughter. Then he thought back to when he played football on the Ridgeview team. It didn't seem difficult in his youth, but now, watching as an adult, he could see how the terminology fit. It was a tight game that could have been associated with a slaughter, but thankfully, no one was hurt.

Jacob was enjoying the game, and when it came to the fourth quarter, the teams were tied. Everyone in the stands were standing up during every play. It looked like the game was heading into overtime. The excitement was incredible. Jacob thoroughly enjoyed himself as he watched the team play when he felt his phone receive a text.

The text was from Katie. Come to Jetti now, appeared on his phone. Jacob felt his heart jump. The text alarm went off again. It was Scott. The text simply read 10-82 Jetti. The Virginia State Police codes weren't used on a county level anymore, but in this instant, Scott had probably used the code because he knew Jacob would understand immediately. Scott rarely sent notices like that over text. Jacob hated to leave the game, but he knew that he was needed at the Jetti. He was thankful that his cousin and best friend were safe, but the message from Scott told him that there was a dead body at the Jetti Baker Center.

Jacob arrived at the Jetti Baker ten minutes later. He was thankful he had parked where he could easily maneuver out of the Ridgeview High School parking lot. Pulling in at the Jetti, he noticed that the play had ended, and most of the vehicles were already gone. He walked into the building and met Stephanie Parker. Stephanie had taken the position with the town to help increase sales at the Jetti Baker Center only three years ago. She had done exceptionally well and brought shows and music into the county on a regular basis.

The old theater had been remodeled when Jacob was a child. From the outside, the Jetti Baker Center was marked by an old-style, vertical marquee that proudly displayed its name. Beneath the vertical sign was a beautiful, antique movie theater marquee facing the main street of Clintwood. A group of artists had painted a mural on the side of the building that was a testimony to the county's history. The beautiful mural was starting to wear after years of weathering. Jacob always loved the mural, and it seemed that you could find something new every time you took the time to look. The beautiful artwork commemorated our Native American culture, the coal industry that was once the centerpiece of the economy, the railroad trestles, the music, the wildlife, and the people of the community. The mural was a beautiful addition to the town.

The front doors were beautiful, hardwood French doors with brass handles that opened to an old-style movie theater setting. The walls to the right were decorated with local artwork, and to the left was the concession booth. The inside of the Jetti was made warm and welcoming by the hardwood trim around the walls and doors. The floor was tile at the front and became carpeting throughout the building as you entered the foyer. Two hardwood doors marked the entrance to the theater that held seats for over three hundred people.

To most, the theater would seem small, but in Dickenson County, it held most of the community events. If an event needed more space, such as a play or music, the Jetti would schedule a second, third, or fourth show depending on the number of visitors on the first night. The Jetti Baker Center added a sense of class that wasn't overbearing but gave an impression of sophistication not found everywhere in the county.

Stephanie was small with sandy blonde hair. Her husband, Kaiden Parker, stood beside her with one arm wrapped around her shoulder in a compassionate gesture. Stephanie was distraught and holding back tears.

Jacob began, "Hey, Stephanie, I got a text to come down. What's going on?"

Stephanie regained her composure and said, "After the show closed, everyone was leaving, and one person didn't get up. I walked down the aisle to wake him because I assumed he had fallen asleep. He didn't wake up. I caught Katie in the parking lot, and she and Scott ran back in to check, and he's dead."

"Where are they?" Jacob asked.

"They're still in the auditorium with the body," Stephanie said, pointing toward the entryway.

Jacob opened the door to find the Jetti theater brightly lit. It was a sharp contrast to the times he had visited the Jetti before. During showtimes, the lights were dimmed, and only the aisles had walkway lighting. Scott and Katie stood beside an overweight male lying in the aisle that looked to be in his late forties.

"What happened?" Jacob asked.

Katie began, "Stephanie came out to get us when we were leaving. We ran back in and found him unconscious, sitting in the aisle seat right there." Katie pointed at an empty seat that had popcorn spilled onto the floor in front of it. A drink was still sitting on the floor beside the seat. Even though comfortable, the seats at the Jetti Baker Center did not have cup holders, and visitors would usually sit their cups in the seat or floor.

Katie continued, "I checked for a pulse, and then Scott helped me get him onto the floor. We took turns doing chest compressions since we had no PPE gear. After ten minutes, I called it myself. The ambulance is on its way, but they aren't here yet. We've heard that they're having a difficult time getting through the traffic at the ballgame."

"Isn't that Clark Lewis?" Jacob asked.

"It sure is," replied Scott. "He graduated a year after I did. He taught the shop class at the high school."

"Any idea what caused it?" Jacob asked.

"Well, considering he was in my emergency room last week because of his diabetes, and he is diaphoretic, I'm guessing he died of something relating to his diabetes," Katie answered.

Scott smiled. His dimples and beautiful smile had a boyish charm when he said, "Diaphoretic means he was sweating."

Jacob smiled and said, "She's teaching you the big words, is she?"

Scott laughed and said, "I'm picking up the language."

The ambulance sirens could be heard outside. Jacob and Scott walked into the foyer while Katie gave directions to the EMTs that had responded.

Jacob looked at Scott, "I think you have something on your mind, and considering that you're not smiling, it's not Katie."

Scott chuckled. "Am I that transparent?"

"Only to everyone."

"We need to look into this, Jacob. You know how you mentioned that people from the sexual offender registry list move here and die within ninety days?"

"Yes, but that guy didn't just move here. Clark's lived here all his life," Jacob replied.

"Here's the thing, this week I got a call from Doris at the high school. She asked me to come in and talk privately with a few of the boys next week. The students have said a few things that made her worry that Clark may have been touching a few of the boys at the school. She said that she thought I'd be able to get more out of them if I spoke with them man to man."

"Did she have an actual complaint from a child or parent?" asked Jacob.

"No, she had just overheard some conversations that made her worry. She heard something about Mr. Lewis letting favorite students come to the shop room outside class hours and after school. Doris is a good woman, and she cares about the kids. She's also one that doesn't jump to conclusions."

"I think we should go see her on Monday. Maybe talk to a few of the guys in shop class," Jacob replied.

"I think we need to work this up by the book." After a short pause, Scott continued, and placing an emphasis each time he said the word 'if,' he said, "If there is a person that's killing people on the sexual offender list that move here, and if that person got wind of what was going on at school, that person could have handled the situation before we even knew about it," Scott replied.

"You do realize how many 'ifs' you just had in one sentence, right?" Jacob smiled.

"You know the old saying, better safe than sorry."

"I'll call Duncan. He's good with collecting evidence, and that man loves a crime scene. I'll have him gather the popcorn, drink, and anything left behind," Jacob stated as the body of Clark Lewis was rolled by them into the waiting ambulance.

Stephanie and Kaiden walked over to Jacob and Scott as the conversation ended. Stephanie seemed calmer, and Kaiden no longer had to console her.

"What a night, huh?" asked Scott looking toward Stephanie.

"Well, I'll never forget it," Stephanie replied with a half-hearted smile.
"I'm ready, Scott." Katie walked up behind them, holding her purse in her hand. Her jacket was gently draped across her arm.

"Are you sure? Shouldn't you go to the hospital?" asked Scott.

"You're not getting out of buying me dinner because of a dead body. Besides, I usually like to work on people who are alive," Katie smiled. Katie thought of how he had known Mr. Lewis and corrected herself. "But I'll understand if you don't want to go. You knew Mr. Lewis better than I did."

"No. I mean, I knew him. But," Scott stammered but then relaxed with a sigh, "I think dinner would be great," Scott smiled.

"No reference to dessert, Scott?" Jacob questioned. "It's so strange hearing you speak to a woman without your words dripping sexual overtones. It's like you grew a vocabulary."

Without warning, Katie became angry, "Jake! I'm telling you right now. If I want dessert, I'll have dessert." Katie's eyes pierced in a glaring look. "And no one is going to stop me from enjoying my dessert. Do you get me?"

The last time Katie looked at him like that, she had been in the process of throwing him off of a mound of dirt while playing King of the Mountain in the backyard when they were less than ten years old. Jacob knew that look, and he knew he would get in big trouble if he didn't listen.

"Scott, I think she just threatened me," Jacob joked.

Leaning toward Jacob and tugging his ear, Scott loudly replied, "What? I didn't hear anything. Gosh, that play was loud, wasn't it, Katie? Ready to eat?"

Katie grabbed Scott's arm, and he formally escorted her out of the Jetti to his car as they laughed at Jake.

Kaiden looked at Jacob and said, "Thank God she's family, Jake. I think she could whip you if she took a notion."

"I've been on her bad side, and I'll tell you, don't underestimate her because of her size. She fights dirty," Jacob confirmed.

Stephanie interrupted with a thought. "If you make her mad, please let me know. I want to sell those tickets! I'd bet you could fund the Jetti for ten years on those ticket sales!" They all laughed at the thought.

Duncan arrived a few minutes later carrying a tote bag loaded with evidence bags, gloves, and other tools he would need. "Where did it happen, Sheriff?" Duncan asked.

"Check the third row from the top. It's an aisle seat. There's popcorn spilled on the floor in front of the seat, so it's easy to find." Jacob pointed toward the entryway located on the left of the building.

Duncan disappeared through the door only to return in a few moments. "Sheriff, your text said to bring something to hold a liquid drink. What drink?"

Jacob looked confused. "The drink was sitting on the floor in the aisle. It was a white styrofoam cup with a lid and straw. I wanted to know what was in it."

"Sheriff, there's nothing but popcorn on the floor," Duncan replied.

Jacob seemed frustrated but returned to the theater seat. There was no sign of a cup. Jacob questioned himself. Had he imagined it? No. He remembered it in his mind's eye very clearly. It was one of those objects that stuck out in his mind because it was strange for some reason, yet, Jacob had no idea why.

"A styrofoam cup, Jacob?" asked Stephanie.

"Yes, it was a white styrofoam cup with a lid and a straw sitting right beside the seat he was found in." Jacob looked up and down the aisle, under the seat, and was about to start checking the trash cans when Stephanie interrupted.

"He must have snuck it in."

"What?" asked Jacob.

"We only sell twenty-ounce bottles. Lewis would have had to sneak it in," Stephanie clarified.

"Nice. So, we don't know where it came from, and now, we don't know where it went." Jacob sighed with discontentment but now understood why it had stuck out in his mind. The Jetti Baker didn't sell fountain drinks.

"Think one of the EMTs picked it up?" Stephanie asked.

"I'm gonna radio out to check," Jacob replied.

After a few moments, Jacob reached the EMTs that had picked up the body on the radio. They remembered seeing the cup because it was between the body and the seat. No one had touched the cup, and they had been last to leave the auditorium.

"How does something like that disappear?" Jacob was thinking to himself but speaking out loud. "No one else was here."

Stephanie interrupted his thoughts again, "Well, the Barter Players were backstage packing up. Maybe one of them came into the auditorium?"

Jacob's eyes shot toward her. His first thought was that the cup might have evidence. His second thought was, what if it was poison? Jacob immediately turned, ran down the aisle, and through the doors leading to the backstage area. He didn't want anyone accidentally taking a drink if it was poison. If it wasn't poison, it still may be evidence of what had happened.

"Can I have everyone's attention, please?" Jacob called out over the performers and stagehands. "In the aisle of the auditorium was a white styrofoam cup with a white lid and straw. Has anyone seen it because it could be evidence?"

The director walked over to Jacob and asked, "Evidence of what? We've been packing up and taking down the stage for the last hour. We didn't even have the curtains open, and no one left."

Jacob was exasperated. His hands fell to his sides, and he said, "I'll let Stephanie explain." Stephanie brought the director to the side to inform him of the death in the audience.

Jacob returned to the auditorium and found Kaiden looking through the trash cans. "I appreciate the help," Jacob said.

"It's no big deal. I was just hoping someone wasn't thinking and trashed it." Kaiden shrugged.

Jacob bent over a trash bag lying nearby and started sifting through it. "Is there any way someone could have gotten in and got by us?"

"Someone could have come in the back door. We were all in the foyer when the EMTs left with the body. Someone could have walked in, grabbed the cup, and left." Kaiden looked toward the rear of the building as he spoke.

"I'll ask the Barter Players if anyone saw anything." Jacob walked toward the rear of the building.

Everyone was still packing up. "Can I have everyone's attention one more time, please?" The crowd stilled. "Did anyone see someone they didn't recognize backstage this evening?" The group was quiet and looked confused.

The director grasped Jacob's arm. "Sheriff, they've seen lots of people they didn't recognize. We travel around the area, and many of our actors aren't even from this state. They won't be able to point out someone who doesn't belong because they're not from here. Plus, several audience members left when the play ended using the stage entrance in the back."

Jacob turned to Stephanie, "Are there cameras set up anywhere?"

"No. We don't keep money in the building, and we're on a shoestring budget."

Kaiden walked up behind them. "I couldn't find anything that even looks like a styrofoam cup. I checked every trash can."

"Well, guess we're at a dead end. I'll find out what the hospital says in a day or two."
Stephanie placed her hand on Jacob's arm. "Jake, go home and rest. You worked last weekend because of Scott's birthday, so it's your weekend off. Go get some rest."

Jacob patted her hand comfortingly. "I think I'll take your advice, Stephanie."

Jacob turned toward the doorway and heard Kaiden say, "Be careful, Jake." Jake waved his appreciation and left. He tried to enjoy the evening drive back home, but he couldn't shake the feeling that he had lost evidence. He felt empty and guilty. He kept thinking he should have never left that room. He wondered what could have happened to that styrofoam cup. As Jacob obsessed over the loss, he realized that until he had a cause of death, he couldn't be certain that the cup was evidence at all. He decided that tomorrow he'd spend time with his dad.

It was ten the next morning before Jacob arrived at his parents' house. Spending the day with his dad was the break that Jacob needed. He dressed to work and wore an old pair of blue jeans and an old, dark blue tee shirt with paint on the sleeve and chest. He remembered helping Katie paint Aunt Helen's kitchen during one of her spring breaks from college and smiled as he remembered the paint fight. Katie had started it by putting paint on his chest and sleeve with her paintbrush, but it was one fight that Jacob had won because he remembered her running from the house screaming, "Not my hair!" She didn't say that he couldn't paint her arms, clothing, or face, though.

For a moment, he questioned whether to wear tennis shoes or work boots. Ultimately, he chose the work boots because he didn't know what he'd be doing that day, and he'd rather be prepared than comfortable.

"Half the day done gone, boy, where you been?" his dad yelled from the backyard. "I already made your mom breakfast, winterized the camper, cleaned the yard, and am working on taking down that tree your mom hates."

"I was out late last night digging through the trash," Jacob laughed.

"Trash? Son, you need a new hobby," Jack laughed.

"We had a death at the Jetti last night. Clark Lewis died."

"The shop teacher?"

"Yep," Jacob replied.

"How did he die? He was young. Wasn't even fifty yet." Jack kept talking, and Jacob waited to reply. "Hate to hear that. I knew his dad. That'll be a big funeral. It was a big family, and everyone in the county knew them. You didn't answer me."

"Heck, Dad, you were processing everything, and I didn't want to interrupt the conversation you were having," Jacob laughed.

"Jake! Stop it. What happened to that poor kid?"

"Well, Dad, we're not sure yet. Katie thinks it was his diabetes that got him."

"She doing the autopsy?"

"No, she and Scott were the first ones on the scene."

"What was she doing there?"

"She's been hanging around with Scott. They claim they're just friends, but when I teased Scott a little last night, she darn near bit my head off!" Jacob laughed.

"That's my girl!" Jack laughed. "Scott knows I have to kill him if he treats her like he has other women, right?"

"Yes, sir."

"Well, come on, we still gotta cut this tree up and stack it to dry out. Somebody's gonna need firewood this winter. I don't want anyone cold because we can't do some work, and I definitely don't wanna hear your mamma grouch at me because we have an ugly tree on the property anymore."

They quietly walked over to the tree, and for the next two hours, Jacob's ears rang with the sound of the chainsaw. His father cut, and Jake would stack. As many times before, the men worked in silence. Jacob had helped his father cut and stack wood for neighbors many times over the years.

Jacob thought back to when it was the three of them. His dad would be using the chainsaw while Jacob, being six years older, would be helping by keeping his little brother out of the way by challenging him to move the cut logs. At twelve years old, Jacob was entertained by the grunting, groaning, and struggling of his six-year-old brother. But, when his brother moved the cut log to the stack, Jacob wasn't sure who of the three was the proudest. Isaac would smile from ear to ear with every accomplishment. Isaac never quit, and he never complained. Jacob knew that was what would make him a great FBI agent.

The chainsaw quieted. "What you grinning about?" Jack asked.

"Just remembering Isaac pushing those logs when he was six. Remembering him grunt, groan, and sweat is still funny to me."

"It was funny until you two got into a wrestling match when he was twelve. I think that's why you ran off to the Army," Jack laughed.

"No wonder he beat me. I played a football game the night before and was half-dead. I don't think that should count," Jacob replied defensively.

"Twelve." was his father's only response.

"He was a big twelve."

"Twelve," came the response again. "Now, let's go eat lunch. I'm starved."

Sara had made sandwiches and had two beers sitting on the table when they walked in the door. Sara loved being a wife and mother and took her job seriously. She was always cooking, cleaning, and helping people in the community. She and Helen loved helping give food away at the food bank or helping the churches with community events.

It was strange to Jacob. Only Aunt Helen went to church regularly, and when Jacob thought regularly, he meant that she went to a different church every Wednesday and every Sunday. His parents only went on special occasions like Easter and Christmas. They may have been sisters, but his mother and Aunt Helen were exact opposites. Jacob realized that it was probably because of his Uncle Calvin's death. The changes in his Aunt Helen had been instant and permanent.

All three sat down on the back porch to eat the sandwiches. The two men drank a beer, but Sara opted for sweet tea. Beer wasn't typical in his parent's home, and Jacob knew that when Sara had a list of chores for her husband, she would buy a six-pack of beer to reward him for completing the list.

"Guess who called this morning?" Sara said with an excited tone.

"I don't know, Mom. Who?" asked Jacob.

"Leanne Conoway." Sara sounded too excited. "Well, she didn't call me; she called Katie, and Katie said she's coming back into town in a month or so. She said she loved it here."

Jacob rolled his eyes. He knew where this was headed. "Mom, I've met Leanne; she is beautiful and intelligent." As Jacob started to speak, Sara's smile grew. "But Mom, I don't think she needs a man in her life. She's quite capable of taking care of herself. In fact, she whipped Linda Lankle at Scott's birthday party. I don't think I'd ever be able to be more of a man than she is," Jacob laughed.

Jack placed his hand on his son's shoulder and solemnly said, "Jacob, I understand. I've heard about Linda's ability to fight in a brawl, and I'd have to say, I'd probably be afraid to date the woman that whipped her, too."

Jack and Sara began to laugh together while Jacob rolled his eyes.

"Well, she'll be staying with Aunt Helen for a week now, and then she's coming down a few days during the Thanksgiving break. She has an appointment to speak with a few school board members and is thinking about teaching. She has a

Master's in English, and she'd be a great teacher," Sara smiled.

Sara loved teaching and spending time with the kids. She had thought about retirement several times but had only managed to convince herself to stay at the elementary school year after year. Every child in third grade loved Mrs. McKinney.

"Mom, please don't start sewing." Jacob had recalled the wedding quilts that were now becoming more of a tradition than a superstition.

"Jacob, I can't sew! What are you talking about?"

"Nothing… but please don't expect anything to come from the visit."

"I'm just telling you to be nice because she may end up being one of our teachers," Sara said with a hopeful look.

"Well, we still have the gutters to clean, and I think we'll be done early, Honey," Jack called Sara by her pet name for her most of the time. "Having Jake here to help saved some time."

"Well, I could think of some more chores, but I'll let you guys do what you want today, Sara laughed.

"I think we should probably clean Helen's gutters while at it. I don't want her climbing that ladder like she did last year. That's the most stubborn woman I've ever met." Jack shook his head.

"You know she hates asking you to do things for her, Jack," Sara said sympathetically. "She once said that she never wanted you to feel like you had to take care of her since Calvin died."

"I know my big brother. If the situations were reversed, he would have taken care of you and the boys like they were his own. I'm just doing what I know he'd do." Jack's face was stoic and solemn when he talked about his brother.

"Then you two be careful. No falling off of anything. Oh! And I noticed a loose step on her porch when I went up there last week. Please fix that, too," Sara smiled.

Jack smiled and kissed his wife on the cheek. "Anything for you, beautiful!" as they walked off the porch toward the garage to get the ladder.

"Dad," Jacob began, "Do you think it's good to do something bad for the right reasons?"

"Well, Jacob, that sounds like something you should have asked yourself about ten years ago," Jack laughed. "Why you asking now?"

"Remember when I mentioned that the Bureau of Justice Statistics found that when people on the sexual offender registry list moved here, they died within ninety days?"

"Yeah, why?"

"Well, this stays between us, but Scott said he had a report last week that Clark Lewis might have been inappropriate with some kids. Now, he's dead. What if it's not just people on the sexual offender registry list?"

Jack stopped for a moment and looked at his son. "So, you're saying that we might have someone killing people that hurt children in the county?"

"Dad, I have no proof of anything. I have investigated seven of the deaths that happened from the sexual offender registry list and found nothing except the arrow that killed Stanley George was the same length that killed Andrew Calcraft back in 2006. Remember, he was the guy on the registry that helped Mr. and Mrs. Burke and died in the hunting accident. Last night, I wouldn't have thought twice about a diabetic dying during a play, except that Scott mentioned a rumor the guidance counselor overheard. Also, last night, a cup went missing."

Jack leaned the ladder against the house. "A cup?"

Jacob steadied the ladder as his dad climbed. "Yeah, there was a styrofoam cup beside the body when Scott and I were there. The EMTs saw it, but when we went back to check for evidence, it was gone. We checked the Jetti inside and out and went through every trash can. We didn't find a thing. It's like it vanished into thin air."

"So, you think it was poison?" asked Jack.

"I don't know what to think because I lost the cup," Jacob replied, infuriated with himself.

"Well, from a personal standpoint. I can tell you that if someone had done that to you boys or Katie, I would be in prison today. So, right or wrong, the person doing this is ultimately protecting children."

"So, you don't think it's wrong to murder someone?" Jacob asked, shocked by his father's response.

"I just thank God I never had to make that decision. But I'm not going to be the judge and jury for someone who did because I understand what they're feeling."

"But it's murder, Dad. It's against the law," Jacob said with stress in his voice.

"That sounds like you. Everything is always black and white, right and wrong, good and evil. There's no gray areas in your mind. There never has been. You also think that the laws that mankind creates are the ultimate measure of morality."

"So, you're saying that if someone had hurt me like that, you'd have murdered that person?"

"I'm saying thank God it didn't happen. Because, in truth, I'm not sure if I'd have been able to stop myself. The minimum they would have received is an ass whipping from hell. Besides, better for me to do it than your momma. If someone had hurt you kids, we'd have been cleaning up the mess for six months. That woman has a temper, and trust me, she'd have chopped someone to pieces." Jack smiled, but then became solemn again. "I believe it takes a sick person to hurt a child that way, and if someone came to me right now who had hurt a pedophile and needed an alibi, I'd give them one."

"Dang, Dad! You always told me to respect the law."

"Sometimes our laws aren't tough enough. Especially when it comes to hurting children, the people that commit those crimes are usually serving minimum sentences for it. That's not right. Those people are predators that are out to destroy the innocence of childhood. It causes the kids to grow up with guilt, anger, and confusion. The lucky kids are the ones who get help from psychologists, but many don't because they never talk about what happened. The kids suffer the rest of their lives, and so should the person who does it."

"What about innocent until proven guilty?"

"No one has to prove a child is innocent, Jacob," Jack replied.

"So, you think if I find out someone is killing pedophiles, I should just ignore it?"

"I think that's a personal and ethical dilemma that you'll have to decide if the time ever comes. I've always stood behind you a hundred percent on anything you tried to do. But, this time, if it's happening, I hope you never find the proof." Jack's solemn face told Jacob how strongly his father felt about the subject.

The two men finished cleaning the gutters of both houses and fixed the step at Helen's house just as she came home from working her Saturday morning shift at Dr. Reynolds' office.

"You two didn't have to do that!" Helen said as she was getting out of the car.

"I didn't want you falling off the ladder," Jack said.

"So, you'd rather you or Jacob fall off a ladder instead?" Helen smiled.

"If I fell, Sara would take care of me, and if Jacob fell, he'd end up with every eligible woman in the county taking care of him. Heck, if he breaks his leg, we might get him married off! You'd be denying me and Sara of potential grandbabies by not letting him break his leg," Jack laughed.

Helen laughed and looked at Jack. "Jacob, honey, you'd better start dating before your daddy breaks your legs." Helen laughed harder and continued by saying, "And don't give my sister that idea… she'll be buying a baseball bat and chasing you down!"

Jacob laughed. "Well, tonight, I plan on seeing a gorgeous woman."

Helen's eyes brightened. "Oh! Who is she?"

"Scarlett Johansson has another movie coming out on Netflix tonight," Jacob smiled mischievously.

Helen's smile vanished. "Jacob, those jokes are getting old. So, you're going to have to pay me back by taking Leanne out to eat when she gets here next month."

"Hey, I just helped clean your gutters and fix your step!" Jacob retaliated.

"I know how this works, young man. You held a ladder and handed your daddy the nails. You're going." Helen was sticking to her guns.

Jack laughed, "Helen, the boy's scared to death of that girl."

"I am not, Dad," Jacob countered.

"You can get Katie and Scott to go with you. They can protect you." Helen laughed. "Besides, do it to make me happy, Jake." She smiled and pinched his cheek like he was eight years old again.

"Okay, Aunt Helen. I'll do it," Jacob reluctantly agreed.

"While we're talking about Katie and Scott, I should ask you. I see Katie after their dates, but I've not met Scott yet. Should I be sewing?" Helen asked.

Jacob thought about the answer for a moment. It would be a great time to be mischievous to Katie or tease Aunt Helen. He couldn't decide who he wanted to mess with at the moment, so he replied, "Let's give it a little more time, Aunt Helen," to which she nodded.

After a few moments, Aunt Helen became excited, "Oh Lord! No wonder she can't land a man! I've not taught her to make homemade gravy yet!"

Jack jokingly replied, "So, it's your fault after all! You know a woman can't get a good man unless she can make gravy and biscuits!"

Jack was laughing and making Jacob want to laugh, but when Jacob saw how distraught his poor Aunt Helen was, he couldn't do it. Helen replied to Jack's laughter by saying, "Well, I'll see you at breakfast tomorrow morning, Jack." She smiled and walked into the house.

Jack stood there momentarily, realizing that he'd have to eat Katie's first attempt at homemade gravy and biscuits, and he no longer found the situation funny.

On the drive home, Jacob thought long and hard about what his father had said concerning the deaths. On the one hand, Dickenson County loved their kids, but on the other hand, he had to follow the letter of the law, and murder was a crime. Could vigilantism be justified? He was bound by the law, but what were his personal views on the subject? He had never stopped to think about how he felt about the subject, only that the law said that no individual could be the judge, jury, and executioner, no matter what crime was committed.

Jacob had worked in law enforcement for only twelve years but had seen more than his fair share of crime in those twelve years. First, he was an auxiliary officer in the county when he turned sixteen. He had left to join the Army after he graduated and came back eight years later to work as a deputy under Sheriff Linkard for two years before being elected into office. Jacob had dealt with child abuse cases in the field, but it also hit him personally.

Whenever he worked on a child abuse case, he would think about a childhood friend. Her name had been Savannah Colton. He had met Savannah when he started middle school. She was a pretty girl with long blonde hair but was quiet and shy. She always walked with her head down and rarely made eye contact. Jacob had tried to be friendly with her several times, but the little girl seemed sad. Jacob remembered a time when a teacher had patted her on the head, and Savannah had immediately pulled away. The expression on her face gave the impression that the girl was terrified. Jacob had thought it was strange.

Jacob also remembered Savannah missed school a lot, but it worsened during their seventh-grade year. After Christmas Break that year, Savannah had not returned to school. When the children asked where she was, the teacher explained that Savannah's father had died in a car accident, but she would be back in a few weeks. The kids in the class liked Savannah and would try to talk with her and be friends, but Savannah would always shy away from people as if she couldn't trust anyone.

After Savannah's father died, Savannah missed school even more, but the teachers didn't seem to mind. In later years,

Jacob learned that Savannah had told her mother about the sexual abuse she had suffered when her father was alive. She had undergone extensive psychiatric treatment due to the abuse. The teachers understood and were just glad to see her getting help.

Jacob's memory of Savannah was probably stronger than it should have been because she had impacted his life. Just after completing ninth grade, Jacob's mother came to his room and gently told him that one of his classmates had died. Savannah had committed suicide.

She and Jacob were only fourteen when she had taken an excessive amount of her mother's sleeping pills. Savannah's mother died less than a year later in a car accident where she had been driving drunk. Jacob had always wondered if the car accident had really been an accident or if the mother had committed suicide, too.

Childhood sexual abuse destroyed the life of a beautiful person and friend. Jacob had thought about it many times as an adult and had always felt sorry that he had not recognized the symptoms of the abuse. He rationalized the emotion by saying it was because he was also a child, but the guilt still lingered.

Jacob's mind was whirling with questions. Was there someone murdering pedophiles in Dickenson County? He had no proof. In fact, there was no proof any murders had occurred at all. But what if someone in Dickenson was killing people that hurt children? Could that be a good thing? What if it wasn't one person but several? If the murders were happening and he could find proof, would it be a bad thing if he sent the murderer to prison?

Jacob pulled into his driveway and decided to take the day to do some fishing tomorrow. He could sit back on the creek bank and let his mind wander. Since he had no proof any murders were committed, he'd just sit back, fish, and thank God for the peace and quiet. Until tomorrow, he and Scarlett Johansson had a movie date.

Chapter 8

Jacob had decided to throw a line into the creek at Frying Pan. As he sat alone, he thought to himself. He had always wondered where the unique names of area locations had come from. Odd names that stood out were Frying Pan, Sandlick, Birchleaf, and the infamous, and usually mispronounced, Haysi. He knew the area well but loved having his GPS on to get a good laugh. Even computers didn't pronounce Haysi with the long 'I' sound. It was comical to Jacob. He was thankful he grew up here because aerial maps would occasionally display mining roads that were not accessible to regular traffic.

More than once, he'd had to call the local towing company to get an out-of-towner unstuck from the dirt roads leading to local strip mines or gas wells because the GPS had led them across a mountain. Jacob always wondered what city people thought when they heard the GPS coordinates leading them down a road that was not just unpaved but usually had no gravel, and the ruts in the road showed that only ATVs had accessed it within the past year or two.

Jacob let his mind wander until it rested on the ethical question his father and Charlie Kiser had asked him. In Jacob's black-and-white world, if someone sexually abused a child, they should face punishment for their crime in the eyes of the law. But Jacob had to admit that was true for any crime. Jacob also knew that the punishment should fit the crime, and he had to admit sometimes the penalty for raping children wasn't enough.

Jacob ended his fishing expedition early that day because he finally realized that thinking about a problem that probably didn't exist was silly. People had accidents. People sometimes died. It didn't mean that it was happening purposely. It just meant that people sometimes died within ninety days of moving to Dickenson County. A very select group of people died within ninety days of moving to Dickenson County.

Jacob sat back and thought for a moment. In his mind, he realized how crazy that would sound if he said it out loud. On the one hand, everyone that moved to Dickenson County on the sexual offender registry list died within ninety days. On the other hand, there was a serial killer in Dickenson County that hadn't been caught or even investigated for over twenty-five years. Jacob wasn't sure which thought was crazier.

Jacob decided something while fishing on Frying Pan that day. He loaded up his tackle and drove toward his office. He was still wearing his old work boots, jeans, and a tee shirt. Jacob knew the question would weigh on his mind until he had an answer. His mother would have called it a dog with a bone.

Cat was sitting at the front desk. "What in tarnation are you doing here? It's your day off and look what you're wearing!"

"I've got something on my mind."

"Well, it's clearly not your choice of attire! Take off your boots! You're spreading mud, and I'm not paid enough to clean up after you," Cat complained.

Jacob sat down in a chair at the front desk. Since he wasn't in uniform, he couldn't complain about walking around the office in his sock feet. In truth, it made him feel more relaxed. He set his shoes beside the door and walked toward his office before Cat spoke again.

"What's on your mind, Jake?" Cat asked.

"I'm going to go through eight more old files and see if there's anything we could have missed."

"Is this about those people on the registry?"

"How did you know?" Jacob looked surprised.

"This is a small county, Jake. I'm sure someone here knows what you had for breakfast," Cat laughed.

"Well, if it's so small, what's the consensus? What should I do about it?" Jacob smiled but was looking for information.

"Most people say we should find the person doing it…" Cat began and made a small pause before continuing, and then flatly, she said, "And give them a medal."

"Cat, I can't prove that anyone's been murdered. It's just an incredibly strange coincidence right now. Besides, let's say there is someone behind these accidents. When does it stop? The law isn't meant for one person to be the judge, jury, and executioner. What's it going to lead to? Is someone going to be shot for running a red light? We may be a little behind the times in these mountains, but it's still not the old West. No shootouts at noon in front of a saloon here!" Jacob laughed.

"I wish we did have a saloon!" Cat smiled. "That would be awesome!"

Jacob laughed and walked into his office and shut the door. He opened the top drawer of his desk and pulled out the list he'd made. The next name was William Henry. Jacob typed the name into his computer. William had moved to Dickenson County from Colorado in 2011. The photo showed an extremely large man with a long and bushy gray beard. The report stated that William was six foot four inches tall and weighed over three hundred pounds. In look and demeanor, William Henry could be called a mountain man.

William Henry had lived in the mountains of Colorado his entire life. He had very little contact with society, and when his parents died, he decided it was time to get a wife. Knowing little of the outside world, William had kidnapped a thirteen-year-old girl and brought her to his cabin. He had been convicted of kidnapping and rape and spent seven years in a Colorado prison.

William never adjusted well and was focused on getting back to the mountains. He decided to move to the Appalachian Mountains and chose Dickenson County. He arrived in late summer and stayed in an abandoned home with no electricity or water about half a mile past Thunder River Campground in Haysi. He did odd jobs when people would allow him and fished or hunted for food. When he needed money, he'd chop wood for the campers and visitors at the campground.

William Henry's body was found lying on top of an old chainsaw behind the shed he had been using for shelter. Jacob looked at the photos. The right side of his abdomen looked like it had been chewed up where the saw had cut into his body. The blood in the photos prevented Jacob from seeing any detail of the wound. There was a stack of wood in the corner of the photo. It looked like he'd been cutting fallen trees and tripped. He landed on top of the chainsaw while it was running.

Even though most of the photos were quite gory, Jacob studied them intently. He magnified the pictures and was thankful that Cat had been able to upload the file. As he studied the photos, something caught his eye. The vintage chainsaw had what looked like initials carved into the orange paint on the side. Jacob stared at the engraving. It was difficult to make out because of the blood, and no one had noticed the carving enough to clean it and snap a photo. Jacob was almost sure the initials left in the orange paint were CK.

Jacob thought back. He had seen those initials recently carved into something. Where was he? He remembered seeing a hammer and a saw with CK scratched into the side. A jolt came over Jacob's body, and he sat more upright when he realized he had been at Charlie Kiser's house to ask him about Robert Gagnon's death. He had noticed the same initials carved on Charlie Kiser's tools.

Jacob's mind began to work things out. How did William Henry get Charlie Kiser's chainsaw? Charlie found Robert Gagnon's body, and his chainsaw was the culprit to William Henry's death. Charlie was over forty. Charlie was around six feet tall, but he knew enough about bow hunting that he could have changed the bow length so that he didn't draw attention to himself.

Jacob knew that Charlie had nothing to do with the suicides or Harley Brant's accident, but he had a common link between the two accidents. If he could somehow link Charlie to the arrows that killed Andrew Calcraft and Stanely George, he'd have links to four of the accidents. The problem was that the link was an old friend Jacob had known his entire life.

Another problem was that Jacob dreaded asking Charlie about the chainsaw that linked him to the second death. The two men had died a little over a year apart. Jacob also knew that Charlie was a tough old man and would fight him if he felt like he was being accused of something he didn't do.

Jacob could be looking at the business end of a shotgun if he accused Charlie the next time he visited.

Jacob heard a knock and a voice. "I'm heading home, and you are, too. It's your weekend off," said Cat.

"Home? What time is it?" Jacob asked while looking at his computer.

"It's six-thirty," replied Cat.

Jacob was so focused that he'd lost track of time. "I've been at this five hours?" Jacob asked.

"Yep, I haven't heard a peep out of you. I thought you were taking a nap," Cat laughed.

"Mom!" Jacob said excitedly and grabbed at his waist, looking for his cell phone. He realized almost immediately that he'd left it in his truck.

"What about your mom?"

"She's going to kill me. I was supposed to be there for dinner thirty minutes ago!" Jacob quickly walked toward the door and grabbed his shoes.

As he tied his shoes, Cat said, "I'll be nice and turn out the lights and lock up. You hurry up, and I'll call your mom and let her know you're on the way."

"Thanks, Cat!" Jacob yelled as he quickly walked down the hall and out the exterior door.

Jumping into his truck, Jacob saw his cell phone lying on the seat beside him. He remembered taking the phone off his side and leaving it in the truck while fishing that morning. Pulling into his parents' house a few moments later, he noticed Aunt Helen and Katie had already arrived.

"You're late, son!" his mother said as he entered the house. Everyone was already sitting at the table. His mother and father were at each end, Aunt Helen sat near her sister, and he and Katie were across from one another. There was an empty chair because Isaac was still in Quantico.

As Jacob sat down, he asked, "Anyone heard from Isaac lately?"

"He calls every Sunday afternoon like clockwork. He's so much better with time and making sure his mother don't worry about him." Sara answered with a sneer at Jacob.

"I got a little busy, Mom," Jacob answered.

"What you been doin, Cuz?" Katie asked. "It couldn't have anything to do with a girl. Dressed the way you are, you're gonna start running them off," Katie laughed.

"I had a day off and tried to get caught up."

Katie knew that when Jacob answered questions in a short and sweet manner, he was hiding something. "Caught up on what?" she asked, probing the truth that Jacob was hiding.

Jacob knew she wouldn't give up, so he finally admitted the truth. "I skipped church and went fishing down on Frying Pan, you nosey little snot."

Sara immediately chastised her son. "We don't use words like that at the table, young man, and you're old enough to know that."

As Katie laughed, Helen, clearly offended, took her turn and said, "You skipped church on purpose without an emergency?"

Katie laughed again, and Jacob lowered his head. "Yes, Aunt Helen, I did. I needed time alone to think."

"Well, maybe you taking Leanne out on two dates would make amends for upsetting me and your mother." Aunt Helen smiled.

Katie burst out with laughter. She knew Jacob was in trouble and was enjoying the moment.

"I wouldn't laugh if I were you, young lady! You and Scott are going with them because he's afraid of her," Helen stated.

"What?!" Katie blurted out. Not even Katie knew what shocked her more, the idea of a double date at her age or that Jacob was afraid of Leanne. "How'd I get wrapped up in this?"

Jack leaned over and whispered to his niece, "Just lose 'em." His failed attempt at whispering led to a smile on Katie's face and a mischievous glance in Jacob's direction.

Jacob, sensing an opportunity to change the conversation, asked, "So, how is Scott now, Katie?"

Katie sat in silence while the family waited for a response. "Jacob, you see him more than I do. Why would you ask me?"

"Well, you've been spending time with him, haven't you?" Jacob grinned.

"We've had lunch a few times and dinner once," Katie answered conservatively and professionally.

"Anything else?" Jacob smiled.

"Jacob! Don't be crude!" Sara admonished.

Katie interrupted in a sad tone and said, "No, Aunt Sara, that's the problem. Scott's a perfect gentleman. He acts like he just wants to be friends. I don't think he's interested in me at all."

"Bom, bom, bom..." Jacob sang. Everyone's attention was now directed at Jacob because of his childish behavior. "Hey, that needed a sound effect!" Jacob stated defensively.

Sara's head shot in Jacob's direction, "And that's why you're not dating. I can't believe you're Sheriff! If people only knew how you acted like a ten-year-old around us, they'd have never elected you," Sara complained.

Jack smiled and gently took Katie's hand. In a concerned and serious voice, Jack asked Katie, "Do you think he heard the rumors about what I'd do to him if he hurt you and he's scared of me?"

Katie smiled and patted her uncle's hand, and said in a serious tone, "He might be, Uncle Jack. Scott's a big guy, but he knows not to mess with you already."

Jacob asked, "Why don't you do something, Cuz?"

"What ya mean?" Katie asked.

"I mean, like, step up onto a concrete block or something and kiss him," Jacob replied.

"Normally, I would do that, Jake. But here's the problem. Scott Travers has had women hanging on him for years now. I don't want to be like them. I shouldn't have to make the first move. I'm different from the other women."

"Well, I'm not sure Scott can do that. I'm guessing he doesn't know you're interested in him, and you wanting to be different is going to lead you to being single." Jacob purposely emphasized the word 'you' both times he said the word.

Jack took another bite of food and spoke with food in his mouth, "You and him both afraid of women, son?"

Jacob looked at his mother and said, "Why don't he ever get in trouble for being crude?"

Sara smiled, winked at her husband, and said, "Because it's sexy when he does it."

Sara knew her son wouldn't ask her any more questions if she related it to sex, and she won the argument instantly. The women laughed at Jacob rolling his eyes.

"No, Dad, we're not afraid of women."

Jack shrugged his shoulders and continued eating.

Aunt Helen lit up. "Oh! I have an idea!" She looked at Sara. "Let's have one last big barbeque before the weather gets cold, Sara! We can invite Scott and Leanne, Maribeth, and everyone else."

Sara lit up with delight. The one thing the two sisters had in common was that they loved to have a party. The subject changed, and now dinner conversation was consumed by the two women planning a barbeque. Jacob and Katie volunteered to put the dishes in the dishwasher.

As Katie brought the final dish from the table, she whispered to Jacob, "Jake, as much as I love watching you in uncomfortable situations, you better make a run for it. Our mothers are in there talking about Leanne, and I heard something about a quilt. Your mom can't sew, and she wondered if it would still have the same power if my mom did it for her. Now, I'm not sure, but I think you just got married." Katie held a serious expression as long as she could and then laughed.

The look on Jacob's face was priceless to Katie. "Tell everyone I got a call."

"I'm not lying for you!" Katie whispered.

"Fine!" Jacob whispered back. With a louder voice, Jacob yelled, "I gotta call, y'all. I'll talk to you this week. Love you, Mom, love you, Aunt Helen, love you, Dad!" Jacob shot out the back door and was in his truck within seconds, afraid the two women would start measuring him for a tuxedo.

The following day, Jacob pulled into the Ridgeview High School parking lot. Scott was in a separate car and pulled up beside him. They walked in together with the single purpose of finding out what Doris knew concerning Clark Lewis. Neither man looked forward to asking the questions they had on their mind.

"Do you have a sick feeling in your stomach?" asked Scott.

"I hate to say it, but yes," replied Jacob.

The school was beautiful, as always. It was a magnificent structure sitting atop Rose Ridge overlooking the beautiful mountains. They stopped by to say hello to the resource officers and then continued down the hall to Doris Deel's office.

Doris was a kind woman in her early fifties. She had been the guidance counselor at Ridgeview since Jacob could remember. Unlike other teachers and staff, she dressed more casually and occasionally rode a motorcycle to work. She liked Southern rock music and had posters of musicians on her office walls. She had a way with the kids, and they opened up and talked casually with her despite the age difference.

"Good morning, Jacob! Scott had mentioned coming, but I didn't know you were. How have you been?" Doris smiled as he walked into the room.

"Well, we had a pretty rough Friday night." Jacob smiled.

"I heard. Clark was a diabetic, but we all thought he had it under control." Doris seemed distraught.

Scott interjected, "Doris, I tried to stop by last week but couldn't. Even if Clark is dead, we still need to talk to you about why you called."

"People would say I was nuts, and it was just kids talking, but kids reveal a lot when they talk. I take them for their word and believe them. Some adults think they just make things up, and they don't. Someone has to believe them." Doris replied.

"What have you heard?" Jacob asked.

"I don't want to speak ill of the dead, but I was told that Clark Lewis had a special group of young men that he allowed to hang around the shop when they didn't have class. I was also told that these young men were hanging out there after school hours."

"That doesn't seem that bad, Ms. Doris. What made you worry?" Scott asked.

"The parents of a male student contacted me. The student had photos of his girlfriend on his phone…." Doris stammered a bit… "they… um… they were… she wasn't completely covered in the photos."

Jacob and Scott weren't oblivious to the teenage concept of sexting, and no one was naïve enough to think it wasn't probably happening at Ridgeview. So, the declaration was not as much of a shock to them as it was to Doris.

"The parents called me because they wanted me to talk with the female involved. They didn't want the police involved because both children are only fourteen. They both just started high school. According to the boy, the girl let him take the photos. The parents deleted the photos and took their son's cell phone. My job was to sit down and talk with the young lady concerning the photos."

"Hope she doesn't make that decision again," Jacob interjected. "I'm glad they'll listen to you."

"I called the young lady into my office the same day of the phone call. She told me that the young man she allowed to take photos of her was a friend since kindergarten. He wanted to get into a new, secret group at school. She told me the boys had to take photos of females every week and show them to everyone else. That was what made you a member of the special group. Naked pictures of adults would allow one week of membership, but photos of young girls that were disrobed would allow the boy to be part of the group for a month. Another rule was that it had to be girls and women you knew. The photos couldn't be downloaded."

"Oh, my God!" Scott stated, shocked by what he had heard.

"That's not all of it. This special group was created by Clark Lewis. He called it the boy's photography club. I found out later that the boys in the group also showed him the photos. He'd let them smoke cigarettes and weed when they hung out in the shop building between classes and after school."

Both men were shocked into a moment of silence and stared at Doris. Jacob broke the silence by asking, "When did you learn about this?"

"I learned about the photos Thursday morning. I learned about Clark being the leader and notified you and the principal Friday evening. By Friday night, Clark was dead."

"So, since the school is handling most of it and informing the teenagers, I need to know if anyone over eighteen, besides Clark Lewis, was involved with the club."

"We've notified parents and staff already. It's an absolute mess, but it's handled outside the courtroom. So far, everyone involved is underage except for Clark. But we will reach out to you if any other adults are involved. I don't think you have to worry about that."

"So, besides you, the principal, and the boys, did anyone else know about Clark being involved?" asked Jacob.

"I don't think so." Doris shook her head.

"Can you write up a statement of everything you've told me, Doris?" asked Jacob.

"I'll be glad to. I'll be as detailed as I can, but I'm leaving out the names of the kids due to privacy. They're all getting counseling because of this."

Jacob nodded. "Thank You, Doris. Come on, Scott, we have some work to do."

The men waited to speak until they were outside the building. "Well, Sheriff, what's your idea?"

"Well, first, I'm going to call the Commonwealth's attorney and ask about getting a search warrant for the home, computers, and cell phone of Clark Lewis. If there were any other adults involved in this, I want to know who it was," replied Jacob with anger and determination in his voice.

"Dang, Jake. I'm glad there were witnesses to where you were Friday night!" Scott laughed. "You sound like you'd rather skip the warrant and get this handled."

"Someone already did half the job for me, Scott," Jacob said dryly.

"Anything you want me to do?" Scott asked before he stepped into his car.

"Yes, find out if Charlie Kiser had tickets to *My Fair Lady*. If he didn't, find out where he was Friday night."

After the Commonwealth's attorney heard about what happened at the school, the judge was notified, and a search warrant was issued. Jacob spent the rest of the day with six other county officers searching through Clark's home, his office at school, the shop building, and Clark's automobiles. All of the computers and cell phones were brought back to the Sheriff's office to be searched for child pornography.

Jacob left the office around eight that night. As he left, he stopped by the office two doors down from his own to speak with Duncan. "How's it going?" Jacob asked.

"Well, it's slower than I thought, but there's a lot to go through. The cell phone had some photos, and I've already looked through the current files, internet histories, logs, cookies, and deleted files. I connected the forensic software to recover the deleted files and am waiting on that now. He had two computers at home and one at work. The one from work was clean, but I'm still looking through the other two."

Duncan looked tired. Several times he rubbed his eyes. "Duncan, let's finish this up in the morning," Jacob suggested.

Duncan looked at Jacob with harsh sincerity in his voice. "Sheriff, sometimes people make bad choices and commit a crime on accident. Sometimes people commit a crime because they're bad people who don't care about others. But, when it comes to hurting children, that's the lowest of the low. In fact, if you ask prison inmates, they'll tell you that a pedophile is the bottom of the barrel of humanity. If someone who has murdered others with their bare hands and is spending the rest of their lives in prison tells you that a pedophile is the bottom of the barrel, you listen. Some people can't be rehabilitated… no matter how long the prison sentence."

Jacob had forgotten that Duncan was a corrections officer at Red Onion State Prison before joining the Sheriff's office. He walked over and put his hand on Duncan's shoulder.

"Listen, man, he's dead. He's never going to hurt a child in any way ever again."

Duncan looked at Jacob. His demeanor was of forced self-control. "How many people did he share those photos with that didn't die with him? I'm angry, Sheriff. I want the FBI to have the name of every single piece of shit he sent those photos to."

Jacob could see Duncan's hands shaking. "Duncan, come with me. We'll hit the punching bag at the Black Diamond Gym before we go home. It's open twenty-four hours, and we need it."

"Sheriff, I have work to do."

Jacob spoke kindly but firmly. "Duncan, I've never given you an order. I don't give you direct orders because you're a great officer, and I respect you. You're always there and willing to help in any way. Please don't make me change that."

Duncan dropped his arms. "You're probably right. Okay, Sheriff."

Jacob drove the short distance and held the punching bag while Duncan wailed on it for nearly an hour. Jacob had never noticed Duncan's strength or stamina. For a small guy, he could really punch when he was angry. When they left, Duncan requested to be dropped off at Cat's house. Jacob understood. Sometimes you just need to be able to talk to someone. The next evening Duncan had completed the work and had the list of emails and IP addresses for the FBI.

"Did you recognize any of them, Duncan?" asked Jacob.

"Not one." Duncan looked defeated.

"You know, I'm glad you didn't. I'd hate for a human to be punched the way that bag was last night." Jacob smiled.

Duncan left the office, but Jacob kept thinking about his last statement. Duncan was stronger than Jacob had thought. He was also shorter than most of the other deputies. Duncan was over forty, and he'd worked at the Sheriff's office for over twenty years. When Duncan first started in the Sheriff's office, he was a dispatcher. As a dispatcher, Duncan would be the first person to be notified if someone reported sexual child abuse.

Jacob decided to categorize Duncan with Charlie Kiser as potential suspects in his mind, although he thought he was crazy for considering either of them. Jacob decided to learn more about each crime before he became suspicious of everyone in the county. Thinking of Duncan as a potential suspect also seemed hypocritical. Twelve hours before he had witnessed Duncan's anger for the crime, he had felt the same anger. He understood Duncan's feelings of rage and would have deemed himself a potential suspect if he'd been older.

Jacob sat back in the chair at his desk. His thoughts were on how to ask Charlie Kiser about the chainsaw. As he mulled it over in his mind, the thought occurred to him to ask Blaine about it instead. Blaine was about two years younger than Jacob and would have been about twelve years old when William Henry had been found. Jacob had to admit it was a long shot, but he'd rather ask Blaine than Charlie.

Jacob drove the short distance to Blaine's house and knocked on the door. From inside, he heard a female voice yell, "I'll get it, honey!"

The door opened, and Linda Lankle stood at the entryway smiling. Linda was wearing an old Kiss tee shirt and daisy dukes. "Well, hidy, Sheriff! Come on in!" Linda said as she stepped aside.

Jacob immediately noticed that the house seemed cleaner and smelled like potpourri. "Hi, Linda. Is Blaine around?"

"He's in the bedroom. I'll go get him. Go ahead and have a seat." Linda pointed to a chair. "My man's staying out of trouble, ain't he, Sheriff?" Linda smiled.

"Linda, you've got one of the best good-ole boys I've ever met. Now don't you be running this one off. He's a good one." Jacob smiled.

Linda smiled and headed down the hallway. As she returned, she asked, "Jacob, I just finished a pie. Would you like some? I made it for my man, but he won't mind you having a slice."

"Well, aren't you quite the little Suzie homemaker? I've never seen you this happy, Linda. I'll take some to go if you have a paper plate. I have to get back to work, but I'm not going to miss a chance to try out your cooking!" Jacob smiled.

Linda seemed excited about getting Jacob a piece of pie and smiled one of the biggest smiles he had ever seen. As she disappeared into the kitchen, Blake appeared from down the hall.

"Hi, Sheriff! What you doing out this morning?"

"I have a strange question, Blaine," Jacob started.

"I have no secrets," Blaine smiled.

"Do you remember an old Craftsman chainsaw your dad had when you were about twelve years old?"

"Oh no!" Blaine became serious and sat straight up in his chair. "Don't tell Dad! He don't know!"

"No secrets, huh?" Jacob laughed. "What happened?"

"Well, it killed old Will Henry!" Blaine blurted out.

"So, you knew?" asked Jacob.

"Of course, I knew. Tom Linkard came up to the house, and Dad was gone, thank God. I'd have had my butt worn clean off from the beatin' had Tom asked him first!"

Jacob knew there was a story to this and had to smile. "Okay. How did William Henry get that chainsaw?"

"Well, I was twelve, and we needed to cut up some firewood. Dad wanted to go hunting that weekend, so he gave me that old chainsaw and told me to cut firewood for the house. Dad had already bought him a new one, so I would get the old chainsaw," Blaine explained.

"Instead of cutting it myself, I took off down to Haysi. I told Will that I'd trade him that old chainsaw for a load he'd already cut up. An older friend loaded the firewood into his truck and dropped it off for me. When Dad got back from his hunting trip, I told him that I'd cut the wood, but lost the old chainsaw."

"And your dad still doesn't know?" asked Jacob.

"It's not like an ass-whoopin' for lying has a time limit, Sheriff," Blaine replied. "He might be old, but he can still pack a walloping."

Jacob laughed at the local colloquialism. There were spankings in most of the United States. Whoopings in Southwest Virginia, but a walloping was a whooping that was much worse, and, to Jacob's knowledge, it was only found in Southwest Virginia.

"So, your dad never knew that it was his old chainsaw that Will Henry fell on?" Jacob continued to laugh.

"Heck no! Sheriff Linkard didn't want two dead bodies!" Blaine laughed. "If you find me dead from a skeet shootin' accident, you know it weren't no accident, and he found out, Sheriff."

Linda walked into the room with a paper plate covered with a napkin. "Oh, Blaine, honey, we both know that if you die from an accidental skeet shooting accident, the Sheriff's gonna question me first," Linda laughed. "All he has to do is find out what woman you looked at twice, and he'll even have motive already!"

Linda handed Jacob the pie and then sat down on Blaine's lap and kissed his cheek. Jacob laughed and then shook his head.

"I'm glad that's straightened out. Thanks for the info, Blaine. I'll make sure it doesn't go past me." Jacob smiled and shook Blaine's hand. Linda opened the door for Jacob and waved as he pulled out of the driveway.

Over the next several weeks, Jacob stayed busy with his usual duties as sheriff and left the list he'd created in the top drawer of his desk. Scott and Katie were going out together more often. Yet, according to Katie, Scott had never even tried to kiss her goodnight, and she was sticking to her guns and not making the first move. Jacob could tell that Katie was becoming frustrated with the situation, which would lead her to dating someone else. Jacob didn't want to see Scott hurt but was desperately trying to stay out of a situation between his best friend and his cousin.

It was now late in September, and Jacob rechecked the October schedule. Jacob had already developed a schedule for the events being held throughout the month of October. Deputies would be stationed throughout the county on several different weekends. Haysi, Clinchco, and Clintwood were organizing their events on different weekends of the month, so Jacob had the list of events and was double-checking to ensure that deputies were scheduled in their hometowns. Everyone worked on Halloween night to prevent anyone from drinking and driving and help watch out for kids. Deputies with children worked the early hours so they could trick or treat with their kids. Any deputy that didn't have kids would work the night shift.

Everything was happening during October, including the barbeque Aunt Helen and his mother were throwing the first weekend of the month. Maribeth decided she wanted to help, and she had a meat smoker. So, all three women were working and planning for the event of the year. The planning had been so exhausting that they decided to have a potluck instead. Everyone was invited and told to bring a side dish, drinks, paper products, or dessert. Helen, Maribeth, and Sara would provide a huge side of beef and smoked pork.

Jacob always loved October. The first two weeks of October in Dickenson County changed the mountains. The leaves would change from green to shades of red, orange, and gold.

Later in the month, the leaves would change from red and gold to brown and then fall from the trees as the weather became colder.

As was his usual habit, Jacob stopped at his mom and dad's to have dinner with the family after work. Walking in the back door, he yelled, "I'm here, Mom."

From the living room, he heard, "We're in here, Jake."

The kitchen smelled like homemade bread and pecan pie. Jacob wondered why his mother was making a dessert. She usually only made a dessert for a family meal when they had company. He walked through the dining room and into the living room, where he immediately noticed Leanne Conoway sitting beside Katie on the couch.

"Hey, Cuz!" Katie smiled. "Glad you made it!"

"Hi, everybody. Hi, Leanne. Glad you made it down from New York safely," Jacob nodded in her direction.
"Dinner's ready, everybody. Let's get to the table," Sara announced.

Jack said grace, which was unusual. On ordinary occasions, he'd pass over saying grace to Helen. It was strange to Jacob, and he wondered what was happening. Then he realized that his mother probably told his father that he had to make a good impression.

Helen started the conversation, "Jake, are you going to take a few days off since you worked so much through September?"

"I doubt it, Aunt Helen. It will be a tough month with everything happening in the towns and the whitewater rafters at the Breaks. There will be more people in this county than you could shake a stick at!" Jacob shook his head.

Leanne interrupted and asked, "White water rafting at the Breaks? I thought it was just hotels and a restaurant."

Helen replied, "Oh no, my dear. It has campgrounds, fishing, boating, horseback riding, swimming, hiking, a zipline, and much more. Every October, some of the best white-water rafters in the world bring their kayaks and try to raft down the Russell Fork River. It's what they call class five rapids." Helen lowered her voice as if it was a secret, "Class five and higher is dangerous, and sometimes people are hurt or killed on them."

Leanne nodded her understanding. "Katie, we need to go back, and you can show me the rest of it."

Sara immediately spoke up, "Jake can do it."

And there it was. Jacob had been waiting for someone to do or say something embarrassing, and it didn't take long at all. He put his elbow on the table, put his forehead in his hand, and shook his head.

"What?" asked Helen. "You promised me that you'd take her out. It's perfect."

Leanne spoke up, "It's okay, Boy Scout, you don't have to be afraid. I won't throw you off an overlook or anything."

Katie and Leanne started to laugh.

"Can you people be more embarrassing?" asked Jacob, blushing.

"I can't believe you asked that... we're your family... of course we can be more embarrassing." Katie retaliated while laughing.

"Leanne, I hope you know that we're going on two dates while you're here," Jacob stated bluntly. "One date is because I held a ladder, and the other date is because I was late for Sunday dinner."

"Oh! So, I'm being used as a punishment, am I?" Leanne laughed.

Helen interrupted and, in a sweet and kind voice, said, "Oh no, dear, think of it more like we're using you to make him not be afraid of women."

Jack was silently nodding, but Katie began laughing hysterically and nearly spit out the drink of pop she'd just put into her mouth.

"Oh, this is going to be the best story when we're old, Jake!"

Jake solemnly looked at his cousin and said, "So, that's your way of telling me that one day I'm going to laugh about the embarrassment I'm feeling right now?"

Katie was laughing so hard she couldn't answer but only nodded.

Sara had been calm and reserved the entire conversation but decided she would point something out to Jacob. "Jacob, honey, you were working on those old cases. I think Leanne could probably help. Being an English major and an editor, she's accustomed to research. Maybe she could help you study the old cases?"

"What old cases?" Leanne asked.

"Oh boy! Can I tell her?" Katie had stopped laughing and was now as excited as a kid at Christmas. She would finally be able to tell someone what Jacob had been investigating.

"Okay," said Jacob. "It's not like the entire county doesn't already know or heard rumors about it."

"Okay, Leanne, long story short. A serial killer has been running loose around our county killing people on the sexual offender registry list for over twenty-five years," Katie announced.

"Seriously?" asked Leanne. Jack, Sara, and Helen continued to eat quietly and allowed Jacob to respond.

"Prove it, Cuz," was Jacob's response.

"The only reason you can't prove it is because whoever it is, is smarter than you. Every time it happens, it looks like an accident," Katie smarted back.

"Well, Boy Scout, two brains are better than one," Leanne replied. "Besides, I love a good mystery," Leanne smiled.

"Well, they're all old cases. It couldn't hurt. Come down to the office tomorrow, and we'll get started," Jacob responded.

Chapter 9

Monday morning, Leanne was in Jacob's office at eight a.m. Knowing that she wouldn't fit into what she had described to Katie as a 'uniformed environment,' she chose a pair of blue jeans, a loose-fitting light blue colored blouse, and tennis shoes. Her black hair was draped around her shoulders and reminded Jacob of the ocean waves at midnight.

"Okay, Boy Scout, where should we start?" Leanne asked.

"Well, you're going to play catchup today. I've gone through eight of the original deaths already. Maybe you can see something I didn't. You're okay with gory stuff, right?"

"If I'm not, I'll just pretend it's a work of fiction or a piece of art that looks very real. I'll be fine. Do you think that there's a killer?"

Jacob shook his head. "Honestly, I don't know what to think. If someone is killing pedophiles, they're good at their job. They're very good. So, I don't know."

"So, how many do we have on the sexual offender registry list that died?"

"There's a total of fifteen. There were eleven that died of an accident, three from suicide, and one heart attack," Jacob handed Leanne a stack of files. "Here's five of them. The list I created is on the top. I've researched the first eight names and questioned a few people. I left the current notes on my progress in the files. The rest we can start tomorrow. For any of the names you don't have files on, you can ask Maribeth, and she'll log you onto a computer and get the file. Sound good?"

"Sure, but where will you be?" Leanne asked.

"I have to give the deputies their orders and stop by the school. They're talking to the students again to make sure nothing like what happened with Clark Lewis ever happens again. They've brought in a psychologist to give a presentation and offer students help. I have to be there in case some of the students bring any more evidence to light."

"Well, I can't promise I won't take over while you're gone. I have excellent leadership qualities, and I may just be Sheriff for the day," Leanne cocked her head to the side and laughed.

Jacob laughed and reached toward the hat rack beside the door. Her smile and laugh made him wonder if she was flirting with him. He grabbed his campaign hat from the top and placed it on her head. "Good, I could use a break." He smiled and left her to catch up.

At the school, Jacob stood in the rear of the auditorium as the students listened to the psychologist talk about grooming techniques predators use and concepts like body safety boundaries. Jacob was impressed at how the psychologist explained it in terms that the younger kids would understand and the older ones would listen. Lastly, the psychologist explained boundaries concerning photographs.

At the end of the program, Jacob was asked to speak. He stepped to the front. "Good morning, everyone. I'll keep this short and sweet. Thank you all for coming down for the presentation. I hope everyone here has listened and understands that if you've been involved with any of this, it's not your fault, and you are not in trouble. You have done nothing wrong." Jacob paused for a moment. "We only want to make sure that every single one of you is safe and gets help if you need it. If anyone wants to talk, please come forward to your guidance counselors, or you can walk into my office anytime. Again, thank you for being here today."

Jacob stayed at the school until nearly noon. He spoke with all the staff and counselors. Several students came up to speak to him, but the conversations with the students tended to be about football, law enforcement careers, or his military experiences. He was disappointed that no new information came from the presentation and decided to eat lunch since he had skipped breakfast that morning. Instead
the High School cafeteria, Jacob opted to drive back to the office and ask Maribeth and Leanne if they wanted to grab a bite to eat.

Jacob walked into the office at twelve-fifteen. "Hey, Maribeth, you want to grab some Mexican food with me?"

"Why Sheriff, thank you for the invitation, but you know I bring my lunch. Besides, Leanne has been studying in your office and hasn't eaten yet. She's been in there quiet as a mouse. I checked on her once, and she was so focused that I startled her when I walked into the room. Besides, I'm not going to be a chaperone for you. You need to go ask her instead," Maribeth smiled mischievously.

"Fine," Jacob replied, rolling his eyes.

"Son, as a favor, I'm not going to tell your mama about that eye roll, but don't let it happen again," Maribeth laughed.

Jacob was laughing at Maribeth's remark as he entered his office. Leanne didn't notice him walk into the room. She was focusing on the computer screen and her work.

Jacob broke the silence, "Have you found anything yet?"

Leanne was startled and screamed a small squeak as she looked up. "Boy Scout! Can you not scare me to death?"

"Sorry, I'll walk louder from now on," Jacob laughed. "Did you find anything?"

"Thanks to your notes on the interviews that you recently did, I found nothing," Leanne seemed disappointed.

"Well, let's go grab some lunch. You like Mexican?"

"Sure."

Leanne grabbed her light jacket as she left the office. The September air was getting colder by the day, but she only needed a light jacket because the climate was still much warmer in Virginia than she had become accustomed to in New York.

While eating, she and Jacob didn't get a chance to talk because county residents kept stopping by the table. Leanne met people from every office in the courthouse, local doctor's offices, and even a few that Jacob had previously arrested. It seemed that everyone knew and liked Jacob. Even the people that Jacob had arrested were incredibly honest and even laughed about Jacob arresting them when they introduced themselves. Leanne felt like she'd shaken hands with half of the county by the time they returned to the office.

"How was lunch?" Maribeth asked as they entered the room.

"Exhausting," Leanne replied.

"I hope you got to eat. It's always like that when Jacob goes over there on a Monday. I think everyone eats there on Mondays," Maribeth shook her head.

"You're not joking!" Leanne agreed.

"Stop your whining and let's get to work," Jacob said with a smile.

"Okay, Boy Scout, let's go catch a killer," Leanne said in an attempt to sound tough and then laughed as she followed him into the office.

Jacob removed the list from the stack of files and read the next name. "Okay, the next name is Craig Nellor."

Jacob sat down at his desk and logged into the computer. Leanne sat beside him as he typed in the name. The record revealed itself on the screen before them. "Craig Nellor moved here from Oklahoma in 2012. He spent three years in prison after his stepdaughter reported sexual abuse that had taken place over several years when she was a child. He died in an explosion in his house. The record says a propane gas explosion in the kitchen caused it."

"Were there any witnesses?"

Jacob laughed. Yes, there was. Cletus Colley lived across the creek from the house. He lives up in the hills off the Left Hand Fork of Lick Creek. "We'd better take a four-wheel drive up there. I'm not sure what the road will look like this time of year. It's a two-mile-long dirt road into nowhere."

Jacob stopped at the front office as they left to tell Maribeth where they were headed.

"Y'all better take a four-wheel drive, Sheriff," Maribeth replied in a worried tone.

"We will, Maribeth." Jacob smiled, and the two walked out the door.

In the hallway, Leann asked, "Everyone takes care of you, don't they, Boy Scout?"

"I guess they do. I never thought about it before," Jacob replied.

"I have made a decision," Leanne stated suddenly.

"And what's that?" Jacob asked.

"From now on, when I go somewhere with you or Katie, I will count wildlife. Not birds but squirrels, deer, elk, bears, and raccoons. You never see animals from a moving vehicle in New York unless it's on a leash or at the zoo." Leanne stepped into the four-wheel drive and shut the door.

"What gave you the idea to count them?" Jacob asked while buckling his seatbelt.

"It's just something to pass the time on these narrow, winding country roads. Besides, it'll keep my mind off the lack of guardrails in this county. I love driving here because it's like a roller coaster ride," Leanne laughed.

"I'm glad you're counting animals instead of counting the potholes or areas that need guardrails and don't have them," Jacob laughed.

"I'm not sure I can count that high, Boy Scout," Leanne smirked.

As Jacob pulled into the driveway, he said, "Don't get out when I stop, okay?"

Leanne was confused but tentatively replied, "Alright…."

"I'm telling you this because Cletus is one of the old-timers. He doesn't get much company up here and stays to himself. He makes moonshine, and we all know it. It's just his way of living. He doesn't bother anyone, but he's always packing his shotgun with him. So, stay in the vehicle until I get out, okay?"

Leanne shot Jacob a shocked look. "So, we're going to have a gun pointed at us?"

"Probably," Jacob calmly stated.

"Boy Scout, if I get shot down here after living in New York my entire life, I'm blaming you." Leanne raised an eyebrow at Jacob.

"Oh, that's another thing. You won't be able to understand half of what he says. I'll try my best to interpret the words quietly to you."

"Does he have a speech impediment?" Leanne asked compassionately.

"No, he just talks like the old-timers. You'll pick up some, but not all of it."
Jacob pulled into a worn section of the yard where people parked and honked the horn.

An older man wearing bib overalls with no undershirt appeared in the doorway, holding a shotgun pointed at the vehicle. "Hey, Cletus! How you been?" yelled Jacob.

"Jake, I pert near fared!"

Jacob whispered to Leanne, "Fired."

"Now, Cletus, we talked about that. You promised not to go shooting anyone until you knew who they were." Jacob got out of the vehicle, and Leanne followed.

"Lordy Jake, ain't she a perty one, she yourn?"

"No, she ain't from here, Cletus. She's one of them city folks from New York. Girl can't even talk right," Jacob flashed Leanne a look and a smile. Leanne simply raised her eyebrow.

"'Ats all right. She just needs some learnin' on how to worsh, cook, and clean up the eatin' table. Can't have your house lookin like a cobbled-up mess of karyn. Who's she out of?"

"Not met her folks. Couldn't tell you, Cletus."

Jacob whispered to Leanne, "He thinks you could learn to be a good wife, and he wants to know who your parents are. Just stand and smile." Leanne shot him a raised eyebrow again.

As they stepped onto the porch, the older man leaned the shotgun onto the wall near the door. "Y'all look tard, ya et yet? Fratmatter, got me a bait of fish and whole mess a tators I was fixin' to cook on that far ovair, yount some?"

"Nah, Cletus, we done ate Mexican for lunch, but thank you kindly, sir."

"Y'all pull up a cheer," Cletus motioned to an old glider on the porch. "You youngins can scooch right close, Jake. I ain't tellin' nobody."

"Cletus, you been talking to my Mama?" Jacob laughed.

"She started sewin', has she? Woman's probly desprit for grand youngins by now," Cletus laughed. "What brings y'all out?"

"Well, Cletus, you remember when that Neller man died over yonder 'cross the crick?"

"Heck yes, nearly rurnt my britches that night. I was watchin' out yonder winder," Cletus pointed toward his kitchen window.

"You saw what happened?" Jacob asked.

"Sure nough," Cletus nodded. "I had me a hankerin' for one of them sody pops. I brought back a poke of 'em. I like em 'r sody pops," Cletus nodded again.

Cletus continued the story. "Seen that no count on his back porch out my winder. It was gettin' dark already, and he started swarpin around at skeeters and thought about how'd I'd like to give him a good wallop." Cletus shook his fist. "He finally got fed up and went in the house. Juice had just been turned on up yonder. He walked in, and boom." The older man said boom with a resounding noise, and his hands flew up into the air, giving a visual demonstration.

"So, he stepped in, and it exploded immediately?"

"Yesum," Cletus nodded.

"Where was the kitchen in that old place?"

"Far side of the house. He woulda had to walk about twenty feet to retch the kitchen. Had me bumfuzzled when Tom said that was wher' it started. Gas musta slipped his mind."

Leanne decided to ask a question, "Did it take long for the fire department to get up here?"

Cletus smiled and said, "Lord yes, little missus. But there came a gully worsher and put most of it out. Then it just smelled like somethin' rottnin. Sure was nasty smellin'. Worse than burnt tars and karyn." Cletus wrinkled his nose and shook his head.

Jacob stood up and held out his hand. "Cletus, it sure was good to see you. You stop by and see me when you can. You know Aunt Helen needs her yearly cough medicine, so you stop by anytime."

The two men shook hands. Leanne shook the older man's hand and said, "It was nice meeting you."

"Young lady, iffin the Sheriff don't steal you up, you come on back, alridy?"

Leanne laughed and said, "I sure will." Jacob laughed because he knew Leanne had no idea what she had agreed to.

On the drive back to the office, Leanne asked, "How many explosions do you guys have around here?"

"Well, it's not an everyday occurrence," replied Jacob.

"Well, that is two I've heard about. Wasn't there an explosion in Clinchco recently?" asked Leanne.

"Yes, but almost everyone agrees that it was probably a meth lab explosion."

"Wasn't it tested to find out?" Leanne asked.
"Well, the owner and culprit died in the explosion. That's a lot of money to spend for a small county when there's no one left to prosecute," Jacob replied.

"I hadn't thought about that." After a moment of silence, Leanne said, "I read about someone making a bomb with a light bulb. When the light was turned on, the bulb exploded. If accelerants were already in the room, it would cause a very large explosion."

"What have you been reading?" asked Jacob, shocked by the statement.

"Do I need to remind you that I'm an editor? I read a lot. I'm asking because I remember the book as fiction, so I honestly don't know if it's possible."

"It is possible," answered Jacob.

"If a light bulb was planted in the back of the house and he turned it on, would it ignite the propane in the kitchen area about twenty feet away?"

"It's a long shot, but if the house had lower ceilings like some of the old houses and it was a larger tank, it might be possible," Jacob stressed the word might.

Jacob continued, "But you still don't have a motive with both cases. One person was a convicted pedophile, and the other had never been accused of that specific crime like the ones from the sexual offender registry list. Jessie was a handful, but he'd never been accused of that."

Leanne sat quietly, thinking.

Arriving at the office, they decided to stay late and look into one more name before eating dinner at Aunt Helen's house. Jacob read from the list. "Number nine, James Lafont." Leanne typed it into the computer.

Leanne began to read. "Looks like he moved here in 2013, and within three months, he was dead from…." Leanne paused, "Boy Scout, it says he fell into a hog trough!"

"Yes, ma'am, it does," Jacob smiled at her shock.

"A pack of pigs killed someone?" Leanne asked, laughing. "Bacon gets its payback, huh?" Leanne couldn't control her laughter. Jacob smiled and shook his head at her amusement.

"It's called a passel or a team of hogs. Around here, most people call them a team. An average hog is between three hundred and seven hundred pounds. They're not the cute little things you see on T.V. They also have a bite force that can produce two or three hundred pounds per square inch."

"Is this all hogs or just hogs found in Dickenson County?"

"Oh, that's all of them," Jacob smiled and nodded.

Leanne turned back to the screen. "It looks like this man was originally from Nevada. He had spent time in prison for the molestation of several young boys. He moved here and found work on a hog farm owned by Joshua Gilbert. The report says he accidentally fell into the hog pen."

"Josh is a local here in Clintwood. He owns a hog farm out on Brush Creek. He has around four hundred hogs most of the time, so I can see that happening. Someone from Nevada wouldn't be as careful as someone who grew up around hogs."

Leanne read the statement that Josh had given the day of the accident. "Mr. Gilbert wrote that he had gone inside the shed to unroll the water hose because the feed was too dry for the hogs. He said that while he was in the shed, he heard a thump, and the hogs started squealing. He ran out and found James dead, and the hogs were still attacking the body."

Leanne scrolled down and saw the photos. "UGH! Hogs can do that?"

"They can and do," Jacob nodded.

"That's awful," Leanne turned a little pale but did not turn away from the photos. "Well, at least I won't feel guilty about eating bacon now." Leanne shrugged as she shook off the feeling of nausea. "Do you think we should talk to Joshua Gilbert about it? See if there's anything else he can tell us?"

Jacob looked at his watch, "Yeah, we should have time to stop by his house on the way to Aunt Helen's." Jacob looked at his watch, "We'd be just in time for dinner."

They both grabbed their jackets and climbed back into the four-wheel drive. They headed toward the west end of Clintwood but turned right at the first light. The road sign read Brush Creek Rd. They traveled several miles before turning left onto a gravel driveway. There were no trespassing signs, and caution signs posted every few feet. Five rows of barbed wire surrounded the fields, with an electric fence lining the top and one near the bottom. Leanne could see a few hogs scattered about within the fence.

"Dear God! What is that smell?" Leanne asked while covering her nose and mouth with her hand.

Jacob began to laugh. "It's a hog farm, Slick."

"Slick?" Leanne asked with a confused expression.

"Short for city slicker. It suits you," Jacob smiled mischievously.

"Well, hog farm or not, it could use an air freshener. Yuck!" Leanne grimaced, and Jacob laughed at her again.

Jacob drove the vehicle into a parking spot in the house's driveway. It was a small but well-kept brick home with a lovely little front porch decorated for visitors. As they stepped onto the porch, Leanne realized it looked rarely used. The smell of the air on the porch confirmed the suspicions. Jacob knocked at the door.

A woman in her late forties answered the door. "Hello, Sheriff, how've you been?" Before Jacob could answer, the woman immediately wrapped her arms around Jacob in a hug. "Oh, look, you've brought me some company! Hello, young lady! I'm Mary Belle Gilbert. Y'all come on in!"

Jacob entered the house, and Leanne followed. The woman was dressed in blue jeans with a floral print shirt. She was wearing an apron. "Y'all excuse how I look. I was just cannin' up some apples. Have y'all a seat. Would you two like something to drink?"

Finding a break in the conversation, Jacob replied, "No, Mary Belle, we've come out to ask Josh about something. He around?"

"He's just getting out of the shower. He'll be here in a second or two. Who's this lovely young woman?"

"This is Leanne Conoway. She came down from New York and is visiting my Aunt Helen and Katie. She's helping me with a few jobs in the office while Katie and Aunt Helen are at work."

"That is right. Have you heard any more news about Tabitha's new baby? She usually works with Dr. Reynolds and had to be off to have a baby. Your Aunt is being so nice and replacing her for a few weeks. How's everything been?"

"Well, to be honest, Mary Belle, I didn't know anything about Tabitha having a baby. I'm just used to Aunt Helen working once in a while when they need help. So, you know more than I do," Jacob smiled.

"Leanne, I'd bet that's strange to you. Being from New York and all. Everything that happens in small counties is big news. Everyone knows everyone else's business around here."

Leanne smiled and nodded, "Yes, it's a big change."

"Have you met with the school board yet?"

"What?" Leanne asked.

"Well, I'm assuming that you're the Ms. Conoway that a few people mentioned was talking about getting your teaching license and moving here," Mary Belle smiled. "I hope you do. We need more teachers, and we have plenty of eligible men, don't we, Sheriff?" Mary Belle winked and smiled in Jacob's direction.

"Well, I haven't put much thought into it...." Leanne stammered.

"Well, I hope you do. We'd love you to come out to the church one Sunday while you're in. I'm sure that Helen will drag you out one weekend. How's Scott and Katie's relationship doing? Are they still together? Those two are the talk of the town right now. Seems like everyone is excited about Scott finally settling down, and we all love Katie." Mary Belle took a moment to stop talking when she heard her husband walking down the hall. "Josh, you need anything?" she shouted over her shoulder.

Josh Gilbert arrived at the end of the hall and smiled at his wife. "Mary Belle, don't you beat them poor youngins to death." Jacob stood from his seated position as Josh entered the room. Josh smiled and shook Jacob's hand before sitting down beside his wife.

Jacob returned to his seated position near Leanne as Mary Belle continued, "It's good just to sit and catch up once in a while, Josh!"

"It's also good to have dinner on time," Josh smiled at his loving wife.

"Lord have mercy, and it's going to be late. Ya'll excuse me. I'm gonna run and finish dinner. Would you like a bite to eat before y'all leave?" asked Mary Belle before making her way hurriedly toward the kitchen.

"We're eating at Aunt Helen's today, and she'd whip us both for spoiling one of her dinners, but thank you for the invitation," Jacob shouted toward the kitchen door.

Josh smiled at the two visitors and said, "So, let me guess. You want to ask me about the day that James LaFont died, right?"

Jacob laughed, glanced toward the kitchen, and said, "Guess there's no reason to ask how you knew."

"You know how these women like to talk around here, and I know you've been asking a few others about things that happened a while back. I was just wondering when you'd get around to me," Josh laughed.

"So, tell us everything from the beginning."

"That was the year that the twins started college. That's the problem with having four girls and no sons. I had to hire someone to help me with the farm when the last two girls left for college. I run an ad in the newspaper. At first, no one seemed interested. The ad was for room and board and a few wages, so most people weren't interested. James LaFont called us first and then came over to meet us. He told us that he had grown up right outside Las Vegas and had spent time in prison out there. He said he was trying to start over."

Leanne's interest was perked, "Did you ask him about his previous crime?"

Josh nodded and replied, "Yes, and we even pulled up his record on the sexual offender registry list. We thought long and hard about the situation. When no one else applied, we hired him because he wouldn't be around any kids out here on this farm, and I was desperate for help."

Leanne nodded. "Did it bother you or Mary Belle?"

Josh nodded again, "Hell, yes, it bothered us, but he claimed he hadn't touched those boys the entire time he was here. It was hard not to believe him. But, according to the record, several boys accused him. No matter what he did, Mary Belle and I needed the help, and if he needed to start his life again, we wanted to make sure it wasn't around children."

Jacob and Leanne nodded in understanding, and Josh continued, "That city boy had never been around one hog, much less over three hundred of them. I was worried about him getting hurt, so I separated about thirty sows into a pen. I had already bred them, and they were all due to have piglets in a few months. I thought it would be a good idea to let him learn by working with just those sows before we separated them into separate pens before they delivered."

Leanne interrupted and said, "I've never been around them before today, too, so I can understand. Jake was telling me how dangerous it was today." It was the first time that Leanne had said Jake's name. She had called him 'Boy Scout' since their first meeting. Jacob thought it was odd to like the sound of her voice as she said his name.

Leanne continued, "So, sows are pregnant females, and they'll deliver in a few months, but why do you need to separate them?"

"Well, a pregnant sow can deliver eight to twelve piglets at one time. If you have thirty pregnant sows, that could lead to over three hundred piglets. We separate them because those little fellers could get stomped on by the other hogs. So, we just leave mommy and her piglets alone until the piglets get bigger."

"That makes sense," Leanne nodded.

Josh continued the story. "We were feeding the hogs that evening. I wet the feed with water because it helps the hogs to gain weight. I think the piglets come out healthier when they're wet-fed too. The feed was too dry. I usually just spray water directly into the trough, so I stepped inside the shed door to unroll the hose hanging inside. James was out of my view for less than three minutes before I heard a thump and then heard the hogs squealing," Josh looked downward. It was clear that he was visibly shaken by the memory.

"I'm sorry I have to ask you to relive this, Josh. But we must go through it one last time. I promise, as long as I'm Sheriff, you'll never have to tell it again."

Josh laughed and joked with Jacob by replying, "Crazy way of getting a vote there, Jake!"

Everyone laughed, and Jacob replied, "You know what I mean, Josh."

The laughter died down, and Leanne asked, "What did you do?"

"We use a shovel to stir the feed, and there was one near the fence. I picked it up and did my best to knock the pigs away from him, but the pigs were frightened and continued to attack his body. I got bit twice that day, and it left a few scars, but I survived. I couldn't get the hogs away from him, so I did the only thing I knew to do. I opened the gate on the back of the corral to let the hogs run into the field, but he was already dead. Mary Belle came out of the house when she heard the ruckus, and I yelled to her to call for an ambulance. She ran back into the house and called 911 while I guarded the body after the hogs had cleared out."

"You heard a thump before the pigs started to squeal?" asked Leanne.

Josh nodded. "Yeah, I did. I figured it was the sound of him falling into the trough."

"It was just you, Mary Belle, and James here that day?" asked Jacob.

"Yes."

"Thank you, Josh. I just wanted to hear the story from you. I appreciate it. I hope it didn't bother you having to relive it," Jacob replied.

"Honestly, Jake, I wish it did. I feel bad not having more sympathy. But it's hard to have sympathy for someone that hurt so many boys."

Jacob and Leanne shook hands with Joshua and left for dinner with Jacob's family.

After getting into the vehicle, Jacob looked at Leanne and said, "Well, you know my family. Tell me about yours."

"How long is the drive?" asked Leanne.

"Is your family that large?" asked Jacob, smiling.

"No, but my family is a long story. We're not as close as your family is. It's nice being around your family. You can see how much they love one another."

"Well, we've had tough times, but we've pulled through because of our love for one another."

"My family broke from tough ties. I guess that's what makes the difference," Leanne solemnly replied.

Jacob could hear the sadness in Leanne's voice and was desperate to change the subject. Without warning, Jacob slammed on the vehicle's brakes, and seatbelts caught both of them as they lurched forward. Leanne screamed, "What the…" but stopped short when she saw what had caused Jacob to hit the brakes so suddenly.

Jacob broke the silence. "I think you might want to count that as more than one animal."

In front of Leanne stood a black bear crossing the road. It was aloof as it leaped over the guardrail. "Holy shit!" was her only response. The look of shock on her face was quite entertaining to Jacob. He liked the way she looked at the bear in wonder and astonishment. Her face seemed to glow, and her eyes lit up like a child's gazing at Christmas lights. Jacob turned his gaze because she was quite beautiful.

"Well, looks like you're getting to meet all the residents in the county. Including some of the larger, four-legged ones," Jacob smiled.

"I've never seen one outside of a zoo. That was amazing. Can they hurt you?" asked Leanne.

"They can, but they don't. They're more scared of humans than humans are of them. A small dog can run them out of the yard," replied Jacob.

"They're beautiful."

Jacob never turned his eyes from her as he said, "Yes, they are."

Leanne smiled, looked away, and said, "We'd better get to Helen's before she starts to worry."

The drive to Aunt Helen's was a little quieter than Jacob had expected. He decided not to make Leanne uncomfortable by complimenting her beauty again.

Before long, they pulled into the driveway, and Katie met them on the front porch. Before she could speak, Leanne blurted out, "We saw a bear! A real, live bear! A live bear, just wandering down the road! It was free!"

Katie began to laugh. "Yes, we have those around here. Come on in. I'm starving, and mom's got dinner ready."

They all walked inside to the smell of freshly baked rolls, green beans that were fresh from the garden, and fried chicken. Several side dishes were sitting on the table, and Aunt Helen had made her famous jelly donuts for dessert.

As they walked into the dining room, Leanne whispered to Jacob, "Thank God Helen didn't make pork. I'm not sure if I could have handled that tonight."

Jack sat at one end of the table with Sara at his right side. Helen sat at the other end of the table with Katie to her right and Leanne in Isaac's usual place on her left. Jacob sat between Katie and his father, across from his mother. As Jacob sat down, he made a mental note to behave himself. He could be kicked under the table from any direction for inappropriate behavior. Jacob didn't mind sitting near his parents because, after the reaction he had received in the vehicle, Jacob was just glad that the family had not purposely worked it out to seat him at Leanne's side.

Conversation surrounded Leanne and the day she had spent with Jacob. "It's different in New York," Leanne stated. "I don't even know the person that lives across the hall from me."

The statement brought facial expressions of sadness from Helen and Sara. Helen asked, "Where do your friends and family live, honey?"

"Well, my mom and dad divorced. My mother remarried and lives upstate with her new husband. He's a psychologist. My dad moved to Georgia several years ago and has a law practice there. I don't hear from him much. Although, I do get friend requests on social media from his new girlfriends. Usually, there's a new friend request every month, and usually, they're younger than me." Leanne shook her head in dismay at the thought of her father's dating habits.

"Do you have any brothers or sisters?" Sara asked compassionately.

"I had a little sister, but she died. So, it's just me now," Leanne replied.

Helen reached out and took Leanne's hand. She smiled and said, "I've heard it said that everyone on the planet is related within fifth cousins. So, don't you worry, you've got a whole pack of cousins now."

"Great, Mom! You just gave Jake another excuse for not asking Leanne out!" Katie replied and laughed.

To lessen Jake's embarrassment, Sara asked Leanne, "Speaking of Jacob, did you two find any new evidence today?"

"I learned a lot, but I don't think we found anything new," replied Leanne.

"Well, Leanne did point out that there weren't too many houses that exploded here. We have house fires, but explosions are few and far between," Jacob commented.

"Explosions?" Sara asked.

"Yes, Matthews Street last week and, before that, Craig Nellor's house."

Katie interjected, "But Matthews Street was a meth lab, not the home of someone on the sexual offender registry list. Has the killer expanded the victim pool?"

"Katie, we don't have proof of a meth lab. Stop listening to rumors," Jacob retorted.

"Well, the last time I checked, Jessie Hatman wasn't a pedophile!" Katie defended herself.

Helen brought jelly donuts and a fresh pot of coffee from the kitchen. As she sat dessert on the table, she said, "Now kids, it don't make sense to get into an argument at the dinner table about something neither one of you can prove."

"It's just strange, Aunt Helen. We have two explosions and two deadly, kid-length arrows. Four accidents that were uniquely similar happening more than twenty years apart," replied Jacob.

"Jacob, what are you talking about?" asked Sara. Jacob's father, Jack, used the distraction of the heated conversation to reach between Jacob and Sara to retrieve his second jelly donut.

Well, we found out that the arrow that killed Stanley George was the same length as the arrow that killed Andrew Calcraft." As Jacob spoke, he put a hand out in front of him, demonstrating the comparison between the two men. "Andrew was on the sexual offender registry list, and Stanley wasn't." Jacob continued, using both of his hands to separate the people he was comparing, "The first explosion killed Craig Nellor, a man on the registry. The second explosion killed Jessie Hatman, and he wasn't on the registry," Jacob placed his hands down. "There's another coincidence that I can't talk about yet."

Katie looked bluntly at Jacob. "Do you seriously believe that we've not heard about Clark Lewis? This is a small county, Jake."

"Does Scott tell you everything, Katie?"

"He doesn't have to. The parents called me. I've even had a few people stop by the emergency room to have talks with their teenage daughters."

"I was at the school this morning… how long have other people known?" Jacob asked.

"I had people stopping by the emergency room for non-emergencies all weekend. Since I was born and raised here and am the only female doctor for miles, they're bringing the girls to see me."

"Well, I guess I should ask you what you learned," Jacob declared.

"Absolutely nothing. Every parent that brought their daughter to me was just nervous. There were no signs of any abuse or photographs that had been taken. The girls were glad their parents had brought them to me. Behind closed doors, the girls admitted that their parents had heard things from other parents and were being overprotective. I calmed the parents and sent everyone home."

Everyone sat at the table quietly for a moment. Helen broke the silence. "I can't blame them. If I thought Katie might have been involved with something like that as a teenager, I'd have probably done the same thing."

Sara nodded, and Jack responded with a grin and said, "Well, we don't have to worry anymore. Clark Lewis will never hurt a child again."

Jacob knew where the conversation was headed and that his entire family would condone the murders. He interjected, "We're not getting into this conversation in front of a guest. I don't want Leanne to think the whole family has mental issues."

Leanne looked around the table and laughed, "So, I'm guessing most of you believe in justifiable homicide?"

"There's no such thing. There are laws for a reason," Jacob interjected.
"Good thing I said most, huh?" Leanne laughed. "We're just having a conversation, Boy Scout. No reason to get your panties twisted. Besides, you're driving me back to the hotel, and I'm not going to get in a vehicle with you in a grumpy mood."

"Oh! I forgot to tell you! I'm working the early shift tomorrow. You got volunteered to drive Leanne to the hotel tonight," Katie smiled.

Jacob laughed and shook his head. If there's one thing he could say for his family, they were relentless!

After doughnuts and coffee, everyone said good-byes and left Helen's house.

Buckling into the vehicle, Jacob asked, "So, can I ask what happened to your little sister?"

"It's not a good story," Leanne replied.

"Well, knowing the ending, I can't imagine that it is. If you don't want to talk about it, you don't have to."

Pausing a moment, Leanne sighed and began. "Her name was Megan. I was fifteen, and she was eight years old. I was babysitting while Mom and Dad were Christmas shopping. A friend stopped by and asked if I wanted to go for coffee downstairs. He was cute, and I said yes. She was alone for only fifteen minutes. I could see the front entrance of our apartment building from across the street. She didn't leave the building."

"She was kidnapped?"

Leanne looked down and said, "Yes."

"How do you know she died?"

"Her body was found a week later. Her body had been thrown into a trash dumpster six blocks from our apartment building. She had been sexually tortured, mutilated, and raped. The coroner couldn't figure out if she had been raped by multiple men or by one man repeatedly. She had died from blood loss. Her body had been thoroughly cleaned, and there was nothing in the dumpster with her, not even her clothes. They never caught the person that did it."

"I'm so sorry," Jacob touched her hand and she pulled away.

"It was never the same after that. My parents divorced, and I was left alone. They always said they didn't blame me for what happened, but they never looked at me the same again."

"Hey, I'm not letting you go back to the hotel alone after telling me a story like that. Let's go get ice cream. Ice cream always makes people feel better," Jacob smiled like a little kid.

"There's an ice cream parlor here? I've not seen one," Leanne stated.
"Oh, there's not. But we have a grocery store that's open until eleven, and we can take a couple of pints and some plastic spoons and hit the walking park. I'll buy the ice cream if you let me count it as a date. Aunt Helen has been on me, and this is a good opportunity to get out of debt with her," Jacob laughed. "You can tell her we fought like cats and dogs, and you refuse to go on another. Sound good?"

"Sounds like a plan!" Leanne laughed.

The walking park in Clintwood had string lights surrounding the fence that provided a romantic illumination. The fountain in the center had not worked for years but added to the park's decor. The grass in the center of the park was still lush and green. Jacob and Leanne sat down on the steps of the gazebo that graced the end of the park near the entry.

"So, what was it like growing up here?" asked Leanne.

"My summers were outside, running barefoot through these mountains. My winters were outside with a sled in these mountains," Jacob laughed.

Leanne smiled, "That sounds pretty great, but weren't you afraid of bears and the other animals living in the woods?"

"The only animal you need to be afraid of here is a snake. We have timber rattlers and copperheads. You can step on one if you're not careful. The bears are usually afraid of humans."

"So, your mom let you do this on your own?" Leanne questioned.

"The rule at my house was to stay within hollering distance and take a dog with you. Rain or shine, you could find me and Katie almost always outside."

"A dog?" asked Leanne.

"The dog would usually find a snake before we would. A snake bite might make a dog sick, but the dog would live. A snake bite could kill me or Katie."

"So, you grew up wild?" Leanne laughed.

"I would say I grew up free as a bird," Jacob responded.

"That's quite the contrast from New York. My parents worked, so Megan and I had a full-time sitter. We were driven to school, picked up at school, and carefully watched when playing at the park or attending school events. We never had the freedom you're talking about."

"So, you've never ridden horses or dirt bikes?" Jacob asked.

"Sometimes, there was a man at the park who had ponies. The Nanny would pay him to lead Megan and me around in a circle, but I don't think that's what you mean," Leanne laughed.

"Dang, I brought you here to cheer you up, and that's the saddest childhood I've ever heard of! You were in prison! How did you survive?" Jacob laughed.

Leanne laughed as she threw her ice cream container into a park trash can. Jacob stepped over and threw his container away. "I guess the date's over now. I'll drop you by the hotel."

"Okay," Leanne replied.

As Leanne stepped from the vehicle, Jacob asked, "Do you need a ride to the office tomorrow?"

"No, as long as it's not raining, I like the walk. See you in the morning." Leanne closed the door and walked toward the hotel. Jacob pulled out of the parking lot towards home, thinking about everything he'd learned about her tonight.

Chapter 10

Leanne slept well for the first time since she'd discovered Dickenson County. It was strange not to hear sirens, honking cars, and moving traffic all night. The quiet was almost disturbing. She had learned to play the sound of rain on her phone so that she could sleep with some kind of noise. She was leaving for the short walk to the Sheriff's office, and just as she reached for the knob of her hotel room door, she received a text. It was from a phone number she did not recognize that simply said, "I'm downstairs."

'That's creepy,' she thought to herself. She decided to play the odds and see who had sent the text. The elevator doors opened, and Jacob stood waiting for her.

"You know I almost didn't come down. I didn't know who was messaging me."

"Oh, sorry. I got your number from Katie. There's been an accident at the Breaks, and we've gotta move." Jacob handed Leanne some papers. "You can try to read those as we drive up but don't get sick in my cruiser. Car sickness is hard enough on these curvy roads, but reading while you're riding in the car could make things worse in a hurry," Jacob laughed.

"So, what's happened?"

"Some kids sneaked out of their hotel room to watch the sun come up at the Tower's overlook. They must have been city kids because, from the Tower's Overlook, you're facing south. They'd have had a hard time watching the sunrise from there," Jacob laughed.

"Did they fall?" asked Leanne.

"Nope, they found a shoe in a tree," Jacob shook his head. "Then, they decided to climb on the banister and could see a leg sticking out from under the rock at the base of the cliff. They reported it to a ranger, and they called us."

"Could someone have survived that fall?"

"I have no idea. My guess is that it would depend on how many trees and rocks they hit on the way down."

Leanne sat buckled into the passenger seat. The papers remained untouched in her lap.

"Check out the papers I brought you," Jacob directed.

Leanne flipped open the file and began to read, "Oh my God! This has happened before! This says the body of Carl Flippant was found at the bottom of the Towers Overlook nearly fifteen years ago! Carl was listed on the sexual offender registry list from Delaware."

"Yep."

"Do you know who's at the bottom now?"

"I don't have a clue. But I called Duncan, and he's on his way with the Matrix 3000. So, we'll know pretty fast. We should also be able to tell if the person is alive."

"You know, I don't know what that is," replied Leanne.

"It's a drone. We're the only county in the state that has one. We received ours through grant funding. The Matrix 3000 has a camera that can see someone from four-hundred feet away and can measure the surface temperature of an object."

"That's impressive."

"Well, in these mountains, it's almost a necessity. We can use it to track people based on body heat through a dense forest or locate an active shooter."

Jacob pulled through the entrance of the Breaks Interstate Park and pulled into a small area used for parking. They walked the short trip to the overlook and were met by Aiden Stoddard. Aiden had been the park superintendent for several years.

"Hated to drag you out, Sheriff, but this calls for more than me."

"It's no problem. This is Leanne Conoway. She's visiting from New York and is helping me with a few things around the office."

Aiden reached out and shook Leanne's hand, "Nice to meet you."

"Duncan is on his way with the Matrix 3000. Where is the shoe you said they found?" Jacob asked.

Aiden walked over to the overlook's edge and leaned against the banister. A white tennis shoe was hanging on a limb about five feet from the cliff. It looked to be a man's shoe, and Jacob estimated it was a size eight or nine because it looked smaller than his own.

"You said they could see a leg?" Jacob asked.

"Stand on the middle rail, lean out, and look down," Aiden directed.

Jacob climbed up on the rail.

"Boy Scout, be careful. We don't need two people down there," Leanne said nervously.

"I see it. It's definitely a human leg. It looks broken."

Duncan walked down the trail to the overlook carrying a large black case. "I got here as quick as I could, Sheriff."

"Thanks, Duncan. Get her flying. There's definitely someone down there. I can see a broken leg sticking out from the bushes."

Within ten minutes, Jacob could hear the soft hum of the blades as the drone took liftoff. Duncan maneuvered the equipment and camera with expert hands. Leanne watched as the drone lifted over their heads and flew with the grace of a predatory bird. Duncan turned on the camera. Within minutes, he had located the body. Duncan used the zoom feature on the camera to recognize the individual and look for signs of life. When he was unable to identify the body, he changed the settings on the camera to register the heat sources.

"Sheriff," Duncan said with sadness, "I'm reading nothing but the ambient temperature."

Jacob sighed. For a moment, he paused and then said, "Thank you, Duncan. Let's get a crew down there before wildlife destroys any evidence."

"Yes, sir," replied Duncan as he maneuvered the drone back to the top of the cliff.

Jacob turned and began to walk toward the parking area. Leanne followed. "Can I ask a question?" asked Leanne.

"Sure," Jacob answered sadly as he continued walking toward the parking area.

"I'm assuming that the person down there is dead since there's no body temperature, but how long has that person been there?"

"At least six hours. The temperature last night was about forty degrees. Based on the body temperature, this happened yesterday afternoon. We'll know more after the body is retrieved," Jacob said with sadness.

Leanne could feel his sadness. Even though Jacob didn't know who was at the bottom of the cliff, he felt a loss. Leanne recognized that he genuinely cared about people, and finding the body this morning was truly bothering him. She sped up her steps and caught up with him. She took his hand in hers as they walked together. Jacob was startled for a moment and looked into her face. She smiled an understanding smile. He gripped her hand and smiled at her display of compassion.

They walked to the parking area holding hands, and he escorted her to the vehicle's passenger side. He released her hand and opened the vehicle door. Jacob reached onto the dashboard and retrieved the paperwork from the last time a body had been found.

"While we wait on the rescue crew, let's take a look at this," Jacob said. Jacob opened the file and placed it on the hood. They stood beside one another as they read through the papers.

"Carl Flippant, Sexual Offender Registry from Delaware, looks like he spent three years in prison for molesting a ten-year-old female that lived two doors down. This man was a biology teacher when he lived in Delaware." Leanne stated with disgust. "How does that happen? How does a person go from someone trusted with children every day to an abuser?" "You know, sometimes I thank God I can't answer some questions. I wouldn't want the ability to think that way," replied Jacob. "There's a report from the park in here. It looks like visitors had reported a smell at the overlook for nearly a week before the body was found."

"It looks like he left Delaware right after he was released," Leanne noted. "Oh my God, Jacob!" Leanne startled. "The little girl he molested committed suicide right before he was released." Leanne covered her mouth with her hand for a moment. With tears in her eyes, she said, "Jacob, she was only thirteen!"

In a display of compassion, Jacob wrapped one arm around Leanne's shoulders. "I wouldn't doubt that he was forced to leave Delaware. There were probably family members that were threatening him," Jacob stated.

Dropping his arm, Jacob returned to the file. "There's nothing about any threats in here."

"What did he do for a living when he moved here?"

Turning to another page, Jacob continued, "It looks like he made money by selling wild herbs and plants."

"What kind of plants?" asked Leanne.

"Mainly wild, mountain plants. He would gather the plants and then sell them online. There's a big following for wild-grown natural herbs in the natural medicine community."

Leanne regained her composure and began flipping through the photographs of the accident. "Want to hear something funny?" Leanne asked.

"Now?" asked Jacob in a confused tone.

Leanne smiled. "Normally, these photos would make me a little nauseous, but knowing what happened to that little girl, it gives me a sense of peace and makes me feel like there's justice in the world."

Jacob leaned over to look at the accident photos. The photos showed a half-eaten body that had swollen to an unrecognizable state. The body had a dark coloring from decomposition, and the intestinal tract was clearly visible. Jacob looked at the coroner's report. "Oh, this is not good," stated Jacob.

Leanne looked around his arm at the report. "What is it?"

"The coroner's report notes that both arms, both legs, and the jaw were broken in the fall. The worst part is that there was a change in hemoglobin and swelling levels in the abdominal area that are different from the other areas. The coroner noted that several bite marks probably happened while he was still alive."

"Wow," remarked Leanne. "He wouldn't have been able to fight back or yell out loud enough for someone to hear him. That's horrifying."

"Does it still feel like justice?" Jacob asked.

"Truthfully?" Leanne paused, "It feels like karma is wonderful," Leanne said with an evil smile.

There was no argument from Jacob this time. He understood Leanne's feelings came from the love she had for her sister. He imagined that she had wished the same type of accident would befall her sister's murderers. For the first time, he allowed himself to think of how he would feel if Katie or Isaac had been murdered in the same manner as her sister. He remembered the anger and hatred he held for the ex-husband who had put Cat in intensive care. He remembered how sad he had been finding out about his friend Savannah. For the first time, he felt like the law was not enough sometimes.

The rescue team pulled into the parking area with no lights or sirens. Jacob was thankful that Duncan had informed them that the person was already deceased. He didn't want to wake the park visitors that were staying at the hotel or camping in the area. If the sirens and lights had been active, it would have woken half the park and drawn a crowd.

The entire process took three hours. Half of the rescue team walked down to the body. Duncan accompanied them with an evidence kit in tow. Duncan took photographs and gathered everything that could have been considered evidence.

Using the radio, Jacob spoke with Duncan. "Do we have an ID?"

Jacob released the radio handle, and Duncan's voice replied, "He looks familiar. Give me a second, and I'll check for a wallet." After a moment, Duncan replied, "Sheriff, this is Johnny Bressett! I knew he looked familiar!"

"Thanks, Duncan. We'll wait for the cause of death before we notify the family."

The rescue team unloaded a litter from the firetruck. The litter was a canoe-shaped safety harness stretcher or basket designed to be used where there are obstacles to movement or other hazards. The team fastened the litter to the winch and lowered it to the bottom of the cliff.

The rescue team then loaded the body onto a litter. The team at the bottom of the cliff connected the litter to straps thrown down by the crew at the top. Using a winch, the body was pulled to the top of the cliff without incident.

Jacob stood at the top of the cliff with Leanne as the litter bumped the side of the rock and was tossed about. The body arrived at the top and was loaded into an ambulance. Katie, or another doctor, would have to decide on the specific cause of death. Jacob and Leanne helped load the rescue equipment while they waited for the team from the bottom of the cliff to make the climb to the top. Forty-five minutes later, the rescue team from the base of the cliff arrived at the top. The team looked exhausted, and everyone was breathing hard from the climb. Jacob laughed when the rescuers told him that 'next time, dangerous or not,' they were going to use the winch and be pulled to the top.

Jacob looked at Leanne and said, "Hospital, next stop."

"Sounds good," replied Leanne.

Strapping into the seatbelt, Leanne sighed.

"Tired?" asked Jacob.

"Not physically. I guess you could explain it as being emotionally and mentally tired."

"I get that. There are some days that I want to go home in the middle of the day and take a nap!" Jacob laughed.

"How do you do this? It seems to me that your job is twenty-four-seven. How do you relax?"

"Well, I have a huge crush on Scarlett Johansson, so her movies help," laughed Jacob.

"Seriously, who doesn't have a crush on her? I'm straight and have a crush on her!" Leanne's laugh would have been infectious had it not had such a calming effect on Jacob. Her laugh was like listening to raindrops on a tin roof during a summer storm. As Jacob listened to her laugh, he only smiled because he didn't want to break the beautiful sound.

"So, anything else? Closet alcoholic because of the stress? Addicted to drugs? Is there a Dickenson County fight club?" Leanne laughed again.

"I go fishing when I need to think. Does that count?" asked Jacob.

"How long do you fish when you go?"

"Until I figure out what I'm thinking about."

"And, on average, how long does it take you to figure things out?" asked Leanne.

"I think my longest fishing trip was thirty minutes," Jacob began to laugh at himself.

Leanne laughed and said, "You could save the life of one worm by staying at home with your cell phone off!"

Arriving at the hospital, they found that Katie was on duty. The body had been removed from the litter and was now lying on a hospital gurney.

Walking into the emergency room, Katie looked up and said, "Hi Leanne, Hi Jake, got it."

"You already have the cause of death?" asked Jacob.

"C2 fracture with spinal cord injury. It was instant. He dropped on his head and broke his neck. Who is he?"

"Johnny Bressett," replied Jacob.

"Not sure I knew him. Did he have a wife or kids?" asked Katie.

"No, he worked quite a bit and kept his mom and dad's old homeplace up." Jacob looked down at the body covered by a sheet. "Do you have a time of death?"

"Based on body temperature and decomposition, within the last twelve hours. It happened sometime yesterday. I'm guessing right at dusk or later."

"I wonder what happened? He wasn't that tall. He couldn't have accidentally fallen from the railing unless he was standing on it for some reason," remarked Leanne.

"He didn't have a camera or cell phone with his personal effects. I watched Duncan retrieve everything he could from the pockets," Katie replied.

Leanne's face darkened. "Could this have been suicide?"

"I can't rule it out, but there wasn't a note, and there are better ways to commit suicide at that location. If I had been thinking of suicide at the Towers Overlook, I'd have brought a rope and anchored myself to the safety rails. The fall only had a fifty-fifty shot at killing him." Jacob responded.

"Scott said the same thing," Katie added.

"I was wondering where he was. Duncan helped all morning at the scene. I guess he waited here all morning, right?" Jacob raised an eyebrow at Katie.

"Not all morning. He arrived at work at nine and found out what happened. The rescue crew was already in transit with the body. He met them here. He said to tell you he was heading out to grab you something to eat because he knows you and Leanne haven't eaten yet, and he'd deliver the news to the family when you gave your approval. He said you're probably starving," Katie smiled.

"Well, he's not all wrong," Jacob pulled out his cell and texted Scott. 'Advise the family.' A text was returned from Scott's phone saying, 'You have lunch at the office. Thanks for not waking me up this morning.'

"Well, me and Leanne will leave you to finish up. We're heading to the office to eat lunch and start looking at the next accident from the sexual offender registry list."

"Hey, before you leave, I have a question," Katie directed the question toward Jacob.

"Okay. What is it?" Jacob asked.

"Dr. Reynold's nephew, you know, the one who's a surgeon now?" Katie began.

Jacob looked warily at Katie, "Yes?"

"He asked me to dinner, and I don't know what to say," Katie concluded quickly.

Jacob had a look of disdain on his face. "I knew you two knuckleheads would have me right in the middle of this. No matter how hard I tried to stay out of it, I knew one of you would drag me in on it!" replied Jacob.

"Jake, I need help. I really like Scott, but he doesn't like me, and I can tell. He hasn't even made a pass at me. I'm just your little cousin to him. Sometimes, I think he's nice to me just because we are cousins," Katie looked sad.

Jacob felt bad for his cousin. He didn't want to see her hurt. But he also knew that Scott had feelings for her that he wouldn't show because Scott felt he wasn't good enough. Jacob remembered the day Maribeth had offered Scott and Katie theater tickets. He remembered the look on his friend's face as Scott said, 'She'd never date someone like me. I'm not that stupid. I'm just a cop, and we're friends. That's it.' Jacob knew that Scott had feelings for Katie and that Katie's feelings were growing for Scott every day. Scott was his best friend, and Katie was his cousin, and Jacob didn't want to get blamed for future children or a breakup.

Breaking his own rules concerning the relationship, Jacob said in an exasperating tone, "Katie, just kiss him."

"No," was the immediate reply. "I won't be turned into those women he's dated before who threw themselves at him."

Jacob laughed and replied, "Katie, it's been almost three months since his birthday. I think we're way past comparing you to those other women."

Katie, being stubborn, said, "No, I've made up my mind. If he has feelings, he'll show it."

Jacob sighed, "Fine. Then at least ask him why he's never kissed you. He deserves to be able to answer the question himself before you go out with another man and leave me to deal with a whiney, brokenhearted, mopey best friend for who knows how long."

Katie cocked her leg and placed her hand on her hip. "Jacob, seriously, why do you have to be such a drama queen sometimes?" Katie walked away, mumbling to herself, 'Brokenhearted, my ass.'

Leanne hugged Katie good-bye. During the hug, Leanne whispered in Katie's ear, "We can trust him, can't we?" Katie released the hug and looked at her cousin questioningly as he walked toward the hospital doorway. "I think we can," and she nodded at Katie.

At the vehicle, Leanne asked, "Next accident? I think we should compare this one to the one from ten years ago. We might find a link."

Within minutes, they arrived at the office. Maribeth called out as they walked through the door, "I'm in the back, be there in a second."

"It's just us, Mrs. Travers," Jacob replied.

"Okay. Scott left you two lunch in your office," Maribeth shouted from the end of the hall.

Jacob opened the door to his office and immediately noticed that the lights were off and two candles were burning on his desk. Everything had been removed from his desk and transformed into a romantic, candlelight dinner. He looked at Leanne and laughed.

Leanne leaned through the doorway and began to giggle while Jacob yelled down the hall, "Maribeth, I had no idea Scott felt this way about me. I'm so flattered."

Maribeth's laughter echoed down the hall, followed by, "I'm not sure he meant it like that, so don't get your hopes up. You might end up heartbroken!"

Playing the part, Jacob bowed and waved his arm toward the open door and said, "Madam, your table awaits."

Playing along, Leanne curtsied and said, "Thank you, kind sir."

They both sat down at the makeshift table and soon realized it was too dark to see the meal prepared for them. Jacob stood from the desk and walked to the door. He flipped on the light switch. Leanne blew out the candles, and they could see cheeseburgers and fries with two drinks in front of them.

"Well, Scott doesn't like me well enough for steak, does he?" Jacob laughed.

"You're right on that! If a man wants to show me that he's interested in me, it takes a steak dinner, red wine, and a cheesecake. All prepared by him!" Leanne laughed. "This isn't a lunch that says, I want a relationship. It's a lunch that says, I want a high five."

"I'm trying to figure out where you're gonna find a man that can make wine!" Jacob laughed. "If you're thinking of a man around here, you're gonna have to settle for ol' man Cletus Colley's Moonshine."

"Speaking of Mr. Colley, what did he mean when he said something about you stealing me and me coming back to his house?"

Jacob burst out with laughter. "You agreed to date him if you didn't marry me." The look of shock on Leanne's face was priceless! Jacob was laughing so hard he was nearly gasping for breath.

"He did not! I did not! Oh my God! Jacob!" Leanne threw a French fry across the table, hitting him in the chest.

Using the thickest southern accent Jacob could reach, he replied, "You'd better eat your food instead of throwing it. You're gonna need your strength to cook, clean, and raise all them youngins!" Jacob continued to laugh until Leanne finally calmed down.

"Well, at least my initials won't change, and I've always loved fish… even though I don't think I've ever tried bait fish." Leanne attempted to regain some dignity.

Jacob laughed again, "A bait of fish is a 'batch or a school' of fish. It's an amount, not a type of fish."

Leanne raised her head high and replied, "Every relationship has communication problems when it first begins, Jacob!" They both laughed.

After lunch, Leanne threw the wrappers away, and Jacob pulled his laptop out of the drawer. Scott had stashed the laptop in the top drawer when they had eaten in the office, so Jacob knew exactly where to locate it.

"Okay, let's compare notes from the two accidents at the Breaks."

Jacob was interrupted by a knock at the door and replied, "Come on in!"

Scott opened the door. It was unique for him to knock. "Why'd you knock?"

"Well, the door was shut, and I thought you might be busy," Scott glanced toward Leanne and smiled his mischievous smile.

"I have one thing to say about our lunch, Scott."

"And what might that be?" Scott was smiling wider.

Jacob raised his hand in a high-five gesture, and Scott replied by slapping his hand to Jacob's. Scott read too deeply into the high five and assumed that Jacob had scored, but when Leanne burst into laughter, Scott became very confused.

"Did you tell the family?" Jacob asked.

"Yes, I also dropped by his house to make sure it was locked up. You ever been there? Man! That guy has one of the biggest flower gardens I've ever seen. You can smell the flowers from down the road! I thought he had a lady living there, or his momma was doing it, but it was him. He loved growing flowers."

Feeling her sarcasm kick in, Leanne replied in her best southern accent, "Yeah, that's just as strange as a man settin' up a candlelight dinner for another man, ain't it?"

Jacob started laughing, but Scott was astonished at the change in Leanne's speech. "You'll fit in just fine 'round here, girl!" Scott smiled and left the office.

Jacob laughed as Scott shut the door and said, "Okay, let's get to work."

Jacob and Leanne sat quietly, comparing everything they had between the files. The two men had nothing in common except the Towers Overlook and flowers. Even the cause of death had been different because Johnny Bressett had died from a broken neck, and Carl Flippant had died of blood loss from trauma.

"Let's look at a different one. I feel like we're getting nowhere," Leanne sighed.

Jacob looked over the list and then tapped the computer. "This one's gonna be fun," he stated in a flat voice.

"What happened?" asked Leanne.

"This one happened when I was in the Army. Looks like ol' man Mullins had decided to hire someone to help him cut a tree off of the property where he has a trailer park on the edge of Clintwood."

"Tree land on him?" asked Leanne.

"No, our victim fell head first into a woodchipper."

"Wow," stated Leanne in a shocked tone.

Jacob continued, "Victor Loughty, sexual offender registry list from Utah. Looks like he found work cutting trees."

"In Utah, he worked as an elementary school janitor. He was convicted of crimes against multiple minors," Leanne stated as she scrolled by, leaning over Jacob.

Normally, Jacob would have complained about someone taking over his computer and hovering over his shoulder. But, this time, Jacob didn't mind. He could feel her face near his and smell the scent of her skin and shampoo. He turned toward her and asked, "Want to go see Mr. Mullins?"

As he turned toward her, their faces were nearly touching. She realized the closeness to him was almost intoxicating. His eyes looked deeply into her own. Leanne drew back and stuttered as she regained her composure, "Good… good idea." She walked over to get her jacket off the coat rack.

The drive was short to Ol' Man Mullins' trailer park. It sat directly on the edge of the town of Clintwood. "Want to know the first thing I found strange about this, Slick?" Jacob asked, referring to Leanne by the nickname he had given her.

"What?" asked Leanne.
"Ol' man Mullins is the cheapest old codger I've ever met. Mom probably never mentioned the death to me because she knew I'd have never believed that he hired anyone to help with anything," Jacob laughed, and Leanne smiled as he spoke.

"Is that him?" asked Leanne, pointing up the driveway.

"That's him. I think he's in his eighties, and he still gets out and does the mowing and weed eating at the trailer park. He also cleans and remodels the trailers and renovates them when people move out. I hope I can still do that when I'm in my eighties." Jacob shook his head in disbelief.

Leanne commented, "I hope I live to see eighty!"

The vehicle came to a stop in the driveway of the home. Mr. Mullins turned off the weed eater and said, "Well if it ain't little Jake! How you been doing?"

"Not too bad, Mr. Mullins. I brought a friend with me so you'd have something pretty to look at while we talked. I thought that would be better than a box of chocolates!"

The old man laughed a toothless laugh and said, "Pretty ladies are always the best company, ain't they, boy?" Mr. Mullins patted Jacob on the back as he shook his hand and then shook Leanne's hand. "Good to meet you, ma'am." Leanne nodded.

"What brings you out? I ain't picked up a bad renter, have I? Ain't nobody cookin' that damn meth out here, are they?" he asked.

"Oh, you'd know if they were Mr. Mullins. I'm sure of that!" Jacob replied. "I'm out here to ask you about that feller you hired to trim a tree when I was in the Army. I just heard about it, and me and Leanne decided to drive over and ask you about it."

"I hadn't thought about that in years, Jake. My pretty Ellie was alive back then. It was her idea for me to hire somebody. It made me mad as hell. I had to pay that feller a fifty-dollar bill to cut down one tree and put it through the chipper."

"What made him fall into the chipper?"

"Hell, if I know. He weren't drunk or anything. He came out and started working that next day. The tree was touching the back of my house. Ellie was inside, and I was helping him. I shouldn't have been helping him because I'd paid him that fifty dollars, and he should have done it alone for that amount of money."

Jacob and Leanne stood silently, listening to the story.

"It was hot that day, and I went in to get Ellie to get us something to drink. When I came in, the chipper was pointed away from the side of the house. Me and Ellie was standing there talking in the kitchen. We could hear the chipper. All of a sudden, that chipper made a loud noise, and it sounded like somebody threw fresh hog slop up against the siding, and the chipper made a grounding sound and stopped."

"Had you seen anyone else around that day?" asked Leanne.

"Not a soul. Me and Vic got started about seven that morning. I thought sure we'd have people complainin' about the noise, but we didn't. We decided to get started early because of the dang heat. It was summer, and it was nearly eighty degrees by that time. Hotter than hell." The older man shook his head as he recalled the memory of that day.

"Who knew that you had plans to cut that tree down?" Jacob asked, realizing he may have a whole park full of suspects.

"Hell, I don't know Jake. I told Vic to rent that woodchipper. I don't know who he told. I didn't bother telling anybody. It's my park, and I do what I want when I want. I don't need nobody's permission."

Jacob nodded. "That's strange. Reckon he just slipped?"

"Tom Linkard thought he might'a had a heat stroke. No way of knowing. Not much of the feller left to test." The older man spit chewing tobacco out on the ground and shifted his old, gray-colored bill cap.

"So, the whole body went through?" asked Leanne.

"Sure did, young lady. I had him rent one of the commercial chippers because I wanted it done in one day. I didn't want to have to pay him another fifty-dollar bill to come out and finish it on another day."

Leanne thought to herself. She estimated that the older man had paid three or four times the amount of Victor's pay on renting the equipment to keep from paying for the help a second day. She thought that was curious but never said it out loud. She made a mental note to tell Jacob later.

Jacob broke her chain of thought. "Mr. Mullins, were you aware that Victor had been in prison?"

"Nope, no one said a damn word about it until he was spread all over my siding." The old man waved his hand as if to demonstrate. "Ellie was mad as hell at me. She was so upset that he'd stain the vinyl. I cleaned it up for her until she was satisfied that you couldn't see anything."

Jacob reached out to shake Mr. Mullins' hand as he said, "Well, I just wanted to hear it from you. I appreciate the time, Mr. Mullins." Jacob shook the older man's hand and looked at Leanne. "Better get the lady back to the office. Thanks again."

Leanne stood silent and a little shocked. The lack of compassion was almost disturbing. Getting into the vehicle, she asked Jacob, "Is he always like that?"

"What do you mean?" asked Jacob.

"Well, he's a little callous about the whole situation. Heck, he's worse than me. He was upset that the man made a mess on his house when he died. And do you realize that he paid three or four times the amount for the woodchipper as he would have spent paying Victor for another day? Jacob, no one can prove to me that the old man didn't come up with the idea, get the commercial woodchipper, and shove Victor into it himself. All he'd have to do is get his wife to lie for him."

"Have you not realized it's that way with almost all these murders? Kilgore could have given his wife a sleeping pill and sneaked down in the middle of the night and killed Harley Brant. Charlie Kiser could have killed two of them with a small arrow because he knew we wouldn't look for a full-grown man. Every single accident has a way of being a murder, and we can't prove anything."

Leanne sat silent for a moment. "This is quite frustrating."

"Yes, it is," agreed Jacob as he started the vehicle to head back to the office.

On the drive back, Jacob was deep in thought. Leanne broke the silence. "Want to know something I noticed about you?"

Jacob looked at Leanne and laughed. "Well, I guess I should consider it a compliment that you noticed me at all."

"Have you ever listened to yourself?" Leanne asked.

"What do you mean?"

"Well, when you speak to me, Scott, Katie, and a few others, you speak more professionally. When speaking to Cletus Colley or Mr. Mullins, you use a more southern dialect. Why do you do that?" asked Leanne.

"Oh, that's simple," replied Jacob. "I realized a long time ago that communication happens best when both people fully understand what the other is saying. If I used a more professional dialect when speaking with Cletus, he wouldn't be as friendly and probably think I was trying to speak 'above my raisin's.' Jacob smiled at Leanne, knowing he had mixed the dialects. "In truth, I speak that way because I would never want anyone to think that I thought I was better than them just because I wear a badge. I'm Dickenson County, born and raised. I'm as much a part of them as they are of me."

Leanne smiled. "That's nice, Boy Scout."

"Hate to tell you, but we're going to have to take a day off from investigating these old accidents. I'm behind on paperwork, but Katie has the day off tomorrow. Why don't you two find something to do?"

"After today, that sounds good. Between the new accidents and the old accidents, I should be able to write my horror novel by now," Leanne laughed.

Jacob pulled the vehicle into the station and was immediately greeted by one of the county newspaper reporters. A camera was in her hand. "Hey Jacob, let me grab a pic of you and the lady. I'm writing a story about the accident at the Breaks." Before Jacob could say one word, the reporter continued, "I know, ongoing investigation, blah blah blah. All I want is a picture," she smiled.

"Okay!" smiled Leanne as she leaned towards Jacob, holding his right arm for the photo. The photograph was snapped. Little did they know that it would be front page news two days later under a headline that read, 'Local Law Enforcement Calls for Reinforcements.'

Chapter 11

It was a Thursday morning when Leanne entered the office. She had dressed comfortably in a dark blue silk blouse and black dress pants and walked the short distance from the hotel and was entering Jacob's office when she heard a loud, masculine voice yell, "ATTENTION!" in a formal military command. Looking around, she saw Duncan, Scott, and several other deputies standing at attention and saluting someone. She looked around. No one was there but her. "What are you all doing?" asked Leanne.

They all burst out laughing. Scott replied, "Well, how should we address the newest officer?"

Duncan handed Leanne the newspaper. She opened it from the folded position and stared at the photo and headline, her mouth gaping. She began to laugh.

"See? This is how rumors get started," Leanne continued to laugh.

Jacob appeared in the doorway. "Glad it's a police station and not a library. What are you guys doing?"

Leanne walked toward Jacob and handed him the newspaper. "Apparently, you didn't pick up the county paper yet."

Jacob opened the newspaper and began laughing. We see why she didn't need a comment. Let's get to work, Slick. You boys need me to find you something to do?"

"No sir," was the comment of the deputies as they dispersed.

Jacob and Leanne walked through the main office and sat at Jacob's desk. "Did you enjoy the day with Katie yesterday?" Jacob asked.

"Oh, it was wonderful. She invited me and a few more friends to ride ATVs to the middle of the world," Leanne smiled.

The middle of the world was formerly a large strip mine that had been reclaimed. Vegetation and wildlife were abundant. Deer, coyotes, and bears were commonly seen there. It was a large, flat, and beautiful open area that rested on the peak of the mountains. The middle of the world was no tourist attraction. Only residents knew of its existence, so it was quite a thrill for Leanne to see it with her own eyes.

"See any more bears?" Jacob asked.

"No, but I did see several coyotes. I'm not sure if I like those or not. I liked seeing the deer, squirrels, rabbits, and let's just say, herbivores much better." Leanne smiled and then laughed.

That laugh. Jacob's thoughts were constantly interrupted by the sound of Leanne's laughter. It was the most inane thing to become a distraction. Leanne was beautiful. So, why was it that her laugh was so pleasing to Jacob's ears? Jacob had thought about her laugh several times as he worked yesterday and had to refocus on the paperwork at hand each time because of it. Most men would think of a woman's eyes, her face, her legs, and other parts. But Jacob was at a loss as to why Leanne's laugh stirred up his emotions.

Leanne interrupted his thoughts by saying, "So, who's our winner today?"

Jacob returned to the list he had made of the fifteen names. There were only three names left. It seemed like a waste of time. But Jacob knew himself well enough to know that if the three names were not investigated, he'd spend the rest of his life thinking that one of those names would have made a connection to the other twelve. Even though only three names were left, Jacob didn't want to make an oversight that would allow a murderer to evade capture. Besides, it would be a few more days with Leanne.

"Marvin Adler," Jacob replied. "I remember this. I was a deputy at the time. I didn't work the case and was patrol back then, but I remember this happening."

"What happened?"

"No one knew until the autopsy came back. Marvin was only twenty-two. He seemed healthy, and people here had seen him jogging and working out. The girl's track team found him on top of Birch Knob. He'd been up there for at least a day because the birds had pecked his eyes out already." Jacob scrolled down to a photograph, and Leanne's nose curled up as if she could smell the photograph.

"So, what killed him?" Leanne asked.

"The coroner found six or eight little white berries with black dots on them inside his stomach. It was Baneberry. The locals know not to eat them. I'm guessing he saw birds eating them and thought he could."

"Baneberry? What's that?"

"It's a little white berry that grows on the baneberry plant. Birds are immune to it, so they eat them, but in humans, it stops the heart. Indians used to use the juice on the tips of their arrows. Southwest Virginia is the only area in the state where it grows. The mountains are covered with them."

Jacob turned to the computer and typed a few words. "Looks like Marvin Adler was on the sexual offender registry list and moved here from California."

Leanne was reading over Jacob's shoulder. She stood behind him, her hair draped beside his face as she read, "Looks like he had a difficult time finding work when he moved here."

Jacob could feel her hair touching his face, the warmth of her body, and smell her perfume. It was distracting to the point that Jacob felt like he was intoxicated. Jacob turned his face away from her to break the trance when he noticed the security camera. "Hey, look, Katie's here," he said.
Leanne looked toward the camera. "She told me she had two days off. She never mentioned visiting the office. I hope nothing's wrong."

In the small, black-and-white screen, you could see Katie walking in the door of the building and moving toward the stairwell. She stopped, looked upwards, and smiled, but Jacob and Leanne couldn't see who or what made her smile.

From the other side of the camera, Scott entered the screen. "Oh!" Jacob and Leanne said in unison while focusing their attention more closely on the small screen across the room. They both moved from behind the desk to get a better view of what was happening on the monitor. Standing in front of several small screens, Jacob and Leanne were mesmerized.

"Too bad we don't have sound," stated Leanne.

Jacob reached over and turned the knob. Katie's voice was heard first. "Hey Scott, I wanted to know if you want to have lunch today, but I have a question to ask first."

Leanne turned to Jacob, "Oh my God, she's going to do it!"

Jacob leaned toward the screen… "or she's going to break up with him."

"I'm not sure we should be listening," Leanne said with a guilty voice.

"Scott knows where that camera is! Heck, he helped hang the dang thing up there!" Jacob responded and turned up the television.

"Oh, then we're good," smiled Leanne.

Jacob and Leanne had a perfect view. They were secretly watching both Scott and Katie have a discussion at the bottom of the stairwell. The camera was at an ideal angle to see their body language as well as their facial expression. Jacob made a mental note to compliment Scott on the camera angle later.

Sometime during the beginning of the conversation, Katie stepped onto the first step and was nearly looking Scott in the eyes. Jacob realized that Katie had taken his advice and had maneuvered herself so that she could stand up on something and kiss Scott if necessary. "Scott, I like being around you. I like being friends, and I'd never want to change that." As Katie began, Scott's expression became more solemn. "I guess I should get straight to the point. Scott, why have you never kissed me?"

Scott's face held a shocked expression for a moment, and then he looked down and sighed. "Katie, you have no idea who you are, do you?" Scott said with a soft smile. He raised his hand and cupped the left side of her face. "You're beautiful, a Harvard-educated doctor, and you're the smartest, sweetest, and kindest person I've ever met."

Katie looked confused for a moment. She shook her head and said, "I don't understand."

Scott lowered his hand from Katie's face. Looking down, he spoke slowly, "Katie, I'm just a poor country cop from Dickenson County. You are perfect, and the man you deserve is a king among men." His face was humble and honest. "You're perfect, and you deserve someone so much better than me. I'm not good enough for you, and I know I'll never be the man a woman like you deserves. You deserve diamonds and gold, and I can't provide anything but a pretty view," Scott paused, then his eyes raised, and he smiled a small half-hearted smile, "But if you ever did give me a chance to try to be that perfect man, I know I'd die trying."

Jacob thought he witnessed a glimpse of anger in Katie's expression. He worried about his friend. Katie stared into Scott's eyes, "So, you've hit on every woman in three states and kissed over half of them, and you're saying I'm too good for you?"

Jacob stood taller at the screen, expecting to have to make a run for the stairwell to protect his best friend and possibly arrest his cousin for assaulting an officer.

Scott's only reply was to shrug his shoulders and say, "They're not like you."

Katie leaned forward, wrapped her arms around Scott's shoulders, and aggressively kissed him. For a moment, Scott stood in complete shock, but as he felt her lips touch his, and her body lean into him, he fell into a feeling of complete serenity he had never felt whole until that moment. He wrapped his strong arms around her in an embrace that felt like he was home for the first time in his life. Katie had accepted him, and he would work his entire life to give her anything to make her happy.

"Awww...." interrupted Leanne.

"Glad that's over," stated Jacob.

"Over?" Leanne asked. "That looks like a beginning to me!"

"Oh!" Jacob laughed. "Not the relationship. I'm glad they're finally done using me as the go-between. I was getting tired of it. Scott and his newly found low self-esteem, and Katie with her growing lack of self-confidence. Good Lord, this relationship has been harder on me than it has them!"

They both laughed. Jacob hit a few buttons on the recording system.

"You're not deleting it, are you?" asked Leanne.

"Heck no! I'm saving it!" Next time I'm in trouble with Aunt Helen, I'll give it to her as a gift, and I'll be her favorite child from then on!" Jacob laughed.

Scott and Katie moved from the screen to walk up the stairs to the office. Jacob and Leanne turned down the audio and sat down at the desk to pretend they had not witnessed anything. After a few moments, Katie and Scott entered the office.

Leanne hurriedly grabbed the paper, "Katie, we made the front page!"

Katie opened the paper and saw the photograph. She read the headline and began to laugh. "That is awesome! You've joined a police force somewhere, and you don't remember doing it!" Katie and Scott were both laughing.

After the laughter subsided, Jacob asked, "What you need, Katie?"

"Scott needs a day off," Katie said bluntly as she turned her eyes back toward the photograph in the newspaper.

"I agree! Go home, Scott... Or somewhere, I don't care... Just don't be here," Jacob agreed immediately and without hesitation.

Scott looked confused. "Seriously? Jake, it's Thursday."

"Do you think I'm going to argue with someone who can make family life difficult and a doctor? I'm not willing to argue with her. Go home."

"Okay," Scott smiled and chuckled.

"Now, Sunday is Leanne's last day here, and I was told I was driving her to the airport, so you'll have to work Sunday evening. So, turn off your phone and leave your radio at the office. Sunday at noon is the next time I want to hear anyone say your name. Got it?" Jacob smiled.

"Yes, sir." Scott laughed.

Katie's eyes had not moved from the photograph in the newspaper. "I've seen this picture before."
"Did someone at the newspaper put it on social media?" Leanne asked.

"No. It's creepy. It's the same photograph, but different people in a different place. This is going to bug me," Katie said with a confused grimace. "It's the strangest feeling I've ever had," Katie replied. After a few more moments of staring at the photo, she tossed the newspaper onto the corner of Jacob's desk and said, "I'll grab a copy and focus on it later. Right now, I'm heading home."

Katie grabbed Scott's hand and led him from the room. Jacob and Leanne turned their focus to the camera and watched them walk out of the building together. Katie stole another kiss just as they walked outside.

"Well, I know what they'll be doing!" stated Leanne.

"That's why I'm not giving Scott his PTO time for the days off! Ain't no way I'm paying him to go where he's going and do what he's doing! Even if he doesn't know that I know anything about it!" Jacob bluntly stated.

Leanne laughed and shook her head, "I wouldn't want anyone saying that you paid Scott for services of your cousin."

"Yuck! That's my cousin you're talking about! I don't want to think about it," Jacob grimaced.

Leanne laughed, "Well, let's get back to Marvin so you can get your mind off it."

Leanne moved a chair to Jacob's side instead of leaning over him. She used the mouse as Jacob typed. "This man was only twenty-two years old, and it says it was a heart attack brought on by an accidental poisoning."

Jacob and Leanne clicked through the photos one at a time.

"This is in Dickenson County?" Leanne asked in a surprising tone.

"Yep," Jacob replied.

"I know I'm looking at photos of a dead man, but that is a beautiful place to die," Leanne said as she stared in awe at the photos on the screen before her.

"I'll be glad to take you up there. It's cold and rainy today, so we'll have to put it off until the weather breaks. You don't want to walk up there in weather like this."

Leanne smiled.

Jacob continued, "For the time being, we can take a trip to the high school. Justine Edwards is the girl's cross-country track coach. They were the ones that discovered the body."

"Sounds good," Leanne replied.

Ridgeview High School was usually only a ten-minute drive from the Sheriff's office, but the weather had made a change for the worse. The rainstorm had turned into a gully washer. Jacob estimated the wind was about thirty miles an hour, and the trees were leaning toward the roadway. Jacob parked as close to the High School doors as possible. He realized he'd have to hit the button and have someone unlock the doors. He and Leanne ran toward the building with their arms over their heads. The secretary at the front desk had noticed the police vehicle in the camera and had immediately unlocked the door. Over the outside intercom, Jacob heard her voice say, "Don't buzz, Jake. Just come on in!"

"Thanks, Missy," Jacob said as he and Leanne walked down the hallway toward the gym. Entering the gym, the door on the left was open. A woman in her forties was sitting at a desk. Her sandy blonde hair was pulled into a ponytail, and she was dressed in a Wolfpack gym suit. "Hi, Mrs. Edwards!" Jacob smiled.

"Hi, Jacob! Now, I told you to call me Justine!" smiled the woman. "Who's this?" she asked, smiling and extending a hand toward Leanne.
"Well, the newspaper said she was my reinforcement, but she's a friend visiting from New York. Aunt Helen invited her down, and Mom insisted she help with some old cases. So, she's been helping at the office this week. Leanne Conoway, meet Justine Edwards, our girl's track coach."

"It's great to meet you!" Justine shook her hand. "It must be pouring outside. I have an extra towel." Justine handed the two a towel to dry off.

"What has you stopping by, Jake?" Justine thought of the reason for Jacob's earlier visits and immediately turned pale. "Oh God, none of my girls have been hurt, have they?"

"Oh, no!" Jacob reassured her. "We're here to ask about Marvin Adler. Your cross-country team found him, didn't they?"

"Yes, and I have to say, that was a run no one will ever forget," Justine shook her head.

"Can you tell us about that day, Justine?" asked Leanne.

"Well, the girls were tired of running the same route and wanted a challenge. We all decided to meet Saturday morning for a run to the top of Birch Knob. I had about eight girls on the team then, so we all piled into two cars and drove to the top. I noticed a parked car. We turned around and drove down the gravel road a little over a mile from the tower and parked at a wide spot in a curve. The goal was to run to the top of the tower and back down. For additional safety, I told them to run in teams of two so that no one would run alone."

"That makes sense," said Jacob.

"I waited in my car. I've been too old to make that run for years. It's not an easy challenge, but the girls thought it would be fun."

"So, what happened?" asked Leanne.

"They started running, and I estimated how long it would take for the first runners to get back. I guessed I'd be waiting about half an hour because of the terrain and the steep climbs. The two fastest arrived at the top of the tower and found a dead body. They were my two oldest, so they made everyone turn around. They were smart to protect the younger runners from seeing the body. They said the eyes had been pecked out, and birds were pecking at the body."

"Did you see anyone else?" asked Jacob.

"No one," Justine shook her head. "It was later that we found out about the autopsy results." Justine shook her head. "I always wondered if that wasn't a suicide. I thought everyone knew that doll's eyes are poisonous! I read online that they taste bitter. I wondered how someone got that information without tasting them, but that's what it said."

"Thing is, the autopsy results showed that the berries were probably eaten whole. It's strange," Jacob concluded.
"I would think that someone wanting to try to eat wild berries would want to taste the berry and not swallow it whole," Leanne questioned.

"That's what I thought, too," answered Jacob.

"Well, the body was found after the crows and vultures had gotten to it. Do you think someone forced him and then left and drove away the day before?" asked Justine.

"That's why we came to talk to you about what the girls saw when they arrived," answered Jacob.

"Well, Tom questioned everyone at length, and there are no security cameras up there. He told me that Mr. Adler had arrived alone and had only taken a water bottle with him for the climb. One of his neighbors said he was a real health nut and wouldn't take a Tylenol for a headache. He was known to take hikes and run, but other than that, no one knew him well at all. He wasn't around long enough. He had just moved here a few months before he died." Justine filled in a few gaps.

"Okay. Thanks, Justine. I appreciate the help." Jacob shook her hand again. "We'd better head back to the office. The rain's slowed down, so we might have a chance to get there before we both drown," Jacob laughed.

Leanne and Justine said their good-byes, and Leanne walked with Jacob toward the door. "Do you realize that we only have two left?"

"I know," replied Jacob solemnly.

"I have to say. This is absolutely miserable!" Leanne said with a twinge of annoyance in her voice.

Jacob laughed, "Miserable, huh?"

"Yes, miserable. We've done all this work this week, we're down to only two names, and we've discovered nothing. I'm not used to failing." Leanne shook her head.

"Well, you can be miserable alone because I'm too hungry to be anything else. Feel like pizza?" Jacob turned left at the Ridgeview High School intersection and started the short drive to Haysi.

"Why not?" Leanne smiled.

During the drive, Leanne enjoyed the views of the mountains. On her first visit, Katie had advised her to take Dramamine non-drowsy to avoid motion sickness. "I wonder what an overdose of Dramamine looks like?" Leanne asked out of context.

"Why? Do you feel bad? Katie told me how you get car sick on these roads. They're great fun on a motorcycle, though," Jacob was trying to remain positive.

"No, I don't feel bad at all. I was just wondering if I would become addicted to Dramamine or grow accustomed to the roads if I moved here. Wonder if I'll get a brain tumor from taking so much Dramamine?" Leanne laughed.

Jacob tried to contain his excitement but had definitely heard Leanne talk about moving to Dickenson County. "You thinking about moving down here?"

"Well, everything is cheaper, but the jobs are limited. I'd like to make the money I make in New York and live down here. That would be nice," smiled Leanne.

"Wouldn't you miss takeout food, grocery delivery, and all your friends?" asked Jacob.

"Not really. Yes, the grocery delivery is great, but I'm closer to Katie than I have been with anyone in a long time. After my sister died, I had problems getting close to people. I feel more comfortable with your family than I do my own."

"I don't know if that's scary or sad. My dad is a quiet, hard-working man. My mom is focused on being the world's greatest matchmaker, and my Aunt Helen just might plunk you in the head with a Bible if you step out of line," Jacob laughed.

"That's what makes them wonderful. I love this place and the people here. The entire county is like a huge, extended family."

"I hate to mention this, Slick, but most of us are extended family here," Jacob said., 'Everybody is a cousin to everyone else. '

"I'll probably never leave my job, though. I'd miss that. I love reading and researching. I learn something new every time I read a new book. Plus, they're looking at me for a VP position right now."

"I thought you were planning on meeting with the school board?"

"I applied, but the money isn't good here. I'd make less than half of what I make in New York."

"Is it good to take so much time off while they're looking at you for a vice president job?"

"I had to. It's a new company policy. They're pushing work/life balance, and they don't want us storing up vacation time. I have to use six weeks of vacation time before the end of the year, or I lose it."

"Six weeks! Do you ever take time off?"

"Not really. I never got sick, and there was nowhere I wanted to go. Plus, I had no one to go with me if I did. So, I just didn't use it," Leanne shrugged.

"How long have you been with them?" asked Jacob.
"Six years. I started there after college and haven't looked anywhere else. I guess I'm what they refer to as 'loyal,'" Leanne laughed. "Honestly, I hate job hunting, so I think it's more lazy than loyal."

"Well, I hope you find your perfect balance."

"Perfect balance?" asked Leanne.

"Yes, it's being happy with what you're doing, who you're with, and where you are at the same time. It's a perfect balance."

"I didn't know you could be philosophical, Boy Scout. Thank you," Leanne smiled.

After a few moments of quiet, Leanne remembered something she had forgotten to tell Jacob. "Oh and speaking of vacation, I'll be flying home Monday, and your aunt and mom want me to return for Thanksgiving. Your brother is coming in for a visit, and they want me to meet Isaac."

"Do you realize that you know more about what's going on with my family than I do?" Jacob laughed.

"I said I love your family," smiled Leanne as Jacob pulled into the Pizza Factory.

"Wonder if they'll stop trying to set us up if I start treating you like a little sister?" Jacob laughed and stepped out of the vehicle.

"Well, they wouldn't be so pushy if you just manned up," Leanne stated as she exited the car.

"Man up? What's that supposed to mean?" Jacob asked. He wanted to sound offended, but he couldn't. Leanne's smile caught him off guard, and for a moment, he allowed himself to hope she was flirting with him.

"You're not the worst catch in the county. Remember, I've met a few single ones. I'm not too impressed. You could have your pick of single ladies. I think you stay single because you're juvenile and rebellious, and I can prove it."

"Oh, you can, can you?" Jacob challenged her.

Leanne stopped walking toward the restaurant door, stood straighter, and looked at Jacob. She then stuck out her tongue like a twelve-year-old child. Jacob could only return the gesture acting as if he, too, were twelve years old.

"See? Katie said that would work," replied Leanne bluntly.

A voice to their right interrupted the argument. "Jake, you testing out a new form of investigation technique or something?" Tom Linkard's voice echoed from only about ten feet from them.

Jacob's only reply was to point at Leanne and say, "She did it first."

Tom shook his head. "Now, don't you tell me this beautiful, classy woman stuck her tongue out at you first. I honestly wouldn't believe it." Tom reached out his hand toward Leanne to shake hands and introduce himself. "Nice to meet you," Tom leaned in and whispered, "You must know Katie to know that trick."

Leanne nodded her head and smiled.

"Katie's been doing that since they were little. I think he has it in his mind that the last one to stick out their tongue wins. I'm just not sure," Tom laughed.

"Jake, when you told me a friend was joining us, you should have told me you had finally suckered a beautiful lady into having lunch with you. I would have dressed up for an occasion like that!"

Jacob rolled his eyes and opened the restaurant door for them. Tom ushered Leanne into the room and pulled out a chair for her.

"Thank you, Sheriff Linkard," Leanne said as she sat down.

"Just call me Tom, young lady."

"See, Boy Scout, maybe if you treated a lady like this, one might go on a date with you," smiled Leanne.

"Slick, Tom's married, so don't be gettin' any ideas."

Tom and Leanne both laughed.

Tom and Jacob sat down on either side of the round table. "So, you're Jacob's reinforcement, huh?" laughed Tom.

Leanne laughed, "Yes, an English Literature degree qualifies you to be law enforcement back up in Virginia."

Tom laughed. "Yes, I saw Jack yesterday, and he told me about the confusion. Everyone has gotten a big kick out of it."

A large, deep-dish pizza covered with meat was delivered to the table.

"Your usual, Tom," said the waitress.

Leanne and Jacob looked at one another, confused because no one had ordered. Tom replied to their expressions by saying, "Don't tell Dianne, and I'll buy."

They both laughed.
"You still on that diet, Tom?" asked Jacob.

"That woman is either trying to keep me on this planet forever or kill me. I guess she figures if I didn't die in the line of duty, she would starve me to death with rabbit food!" Tom said as he used the pie server to remove the pizza from the pan and serve Leanne, Jacob, and himself.

Leanne began to laugh, and Jacob smiled. He loved her laugh. Before he realized it, he was looking at her smile and wavy dark hair. He remembered how she smelled as she leaned over his shoulder, reading files. Breaking the trance, he realized Tom Linkard was watching him look at Leanne. Tom only smiled a knowing smile. Jacob felt nauseous and composed himself. He couldn't feel like that because Leanne wasn't interested in him, and she'd be returning home to New York soon.

"So, what did you two kids want to talk to me about?" asked Tom as he took a bite of the pizza and realized it was hot. He grabbed a drink to cool his mouth.

Leanne began, "I've been helping read through some of the old files that were accidents from the sexual offender registry list. We're working on Marvin Adler's and only have two more left. We spoke to Justine this morning, and it's strange that he picked up six or eight poison berries and swallowed them whole."

"That's what the autopsy said," Tom nodded.

Jacob took a bite of his pizza and began to eat as the two discussed the top of the day.

"This whole thing seems fishy," Leanne responded as she took a bite.

"I know," Tom shook his head.

Leanne sat quietly for a moment until Tom broke the silence. "Young lady, I know it's frustrating," Tom placed his hand on hers. "We all want justice, but we must have evidence to find justice."

"There's no way that fifteen people from the sexual offender registry list died within three months of moving here. There has to be something going on here," Leanne said.

Tom was unsure whether Leanne's last words were a question or a comment. They all continued to enjoy the pizza as they spoke.

"I've thought about it for years, Leanne. It's up to Jacob now. At least he has someone in his life that can understand his frustration. I learned early in my marriage not to bring my work home. Dianne didn't understand why I was quieter than I was before. It almost caused a divorce. I started talking to her and letting her know what was happening in my work life and inside my head. It made us closer. I'm glad Jacob has that in a friend. He'll need one. There will be things he can't even talk to Scott about."

Leanne hadn't thought about that. She looked over at Jacob solemnly. He was sharing a part of his life with her that he had never shared with anyone. It was a side of him that was rarely seen.

Tom continued, "If you think you're frustrated, think about what it's like to be me or Jacob. Finding the person doing this was my job, and I failed. Jacob stepped into my place. Can you imagine his frustration? Heck, we can't even figure out if murders are happening, much less the murderer."

Leanne was humbled.

"Do you think that most of the people are right?"

"What do you mean?" asked Tom.

"Should we even be trying to find and stop the murderer? I can make a case that every county in the United States should have a vigilante, just like Dickenson County's," Leanne smiled.

"Well, in law enforcement, we're taught that the law is the final rule of the day. We're not the judge and jury. We follow what's written in black and white. I did the best job I could.

Jacob's doing the best job he can. That's all we can do. In the end, no one can prove anything."

Leanne smiled at Tom. "Tom, are you planning to run for another office?"

Tom laughed and said, "No, what made you ask that?"

"Because you avoided my question. I asked if we should be trying to find and stop the murderer. I want your answer as a man, not a Sheriff."

"Jacob, I love this young lady! You'd better start working harder at winning this one! She's a spitfire!" Tom laughed and then continued, "Let's just put it this way; I worked hard to find a link, a suspect, even one piece of evidence. I failed," Tom looked at Leanne earnestly and said, "It was the one time I was glad I failed. Because, if there was or is a murderer, they never killed an innocent person."

Leanne swallowed a bite of her pizza and looked at Jacob. "Boy Scout, we only have two left. I think it's time we gave up and just enjoy ourselves the last two days I have here."

Tom interrupted, "Which two?"

Jacob replied, "Tommy Dolivo and Margaret Ginart."

"Jacob, that happened after you won the election and right before you took office. I can tell you about those two. They happened at the same time."

Jacob looked confused. "Are you talking about the overdoses? I knew they found two bodies, but I didn't have the details. I wasn't on the case."

"Yes, remember they lived in an old shack up toward Davenport. They didn't have electricity or water. The house was filthy. Their bodies were found after they had been dead for three or four days. It was awful! Made me glad I was retiring!" Jacob laughed.

"That was the most horrible smell! Two drug addicts on a couch. The autopsy said they'd died of an overdose of Fentanyl. We never found out where they got the other drugs, much less the Fentanyl that killed them." Tom shook his head. "The smell was so bad that the owner of that old shack just tore it down. He didn't even try to clean it up."

"I don't blame him!" interjected Leanne.

"So, no witnesses, of course, and the two died from an accidental drug overdose," Jacob shook his head.

Tom nodded. "Aren't you glad you asked me to lunch?" Tom laughed.

"I'm kind of glad we didn't have to look at the crime scene photos, to be honest. What I'm imagining is bad enough," Leanne grimaced.

"Well, now that your investigation of these old crimes are done, let's talk about the juicy rumors around the county! What's up with Scott and Katie?" Tom asked with a smile.

The rest of the lunch, Jacob and Leanne filled Tom in on all the juicy details of the romance from beginning to end. Tom was so pleased that Scott had finally found love and had settled down.

"So, do Maribeth and Helen know yet?"

Leanne replied, "Well, they know they've been seeing each other, but no one but you knows about us watching the video or Scott taking a few days off."

"Did you save the tape, Jake?" asked Tom.

"You know I did!" Jacob replied.

"That would be a nice wedding present," Tom commented.

"No way! That's my get-out-of-jail-free card for Aunt Helen!" Jacob responded.

Tom and Leanne both laughed at his childish fear of upsetting his family.

"Well, hug Helen for me. She took care of my granddaughter this week, and it was the first time she came back from Dr. Reynolds' office after having a shot and didn't ask me to arrest someone!" Tom laughed. "She's three years old and told me a shot was child abuse."

"How adorable!" Leanne smiled. "Kids are so much fun!"

"Oh, if you think kids are fun, wait until you have grandchildren. Having grandbabies is what kids do to make up for all the times they got on your nerves," Tom laughed. "Do you have any kids, Leanne?"

"Oh no! I'm not ready yet," Leanne answered.

"Well, I ask because you never know. Too many young girls around here get married too early. It's a mistake, but they don't listen."

"No, I've never been married," Leanne replied.

"Dang! I've always thought the Yankees talked funny, but I didn't know they suffered from blindness too!" Tom laughed.

Leanne smiled at the compliment.

Jacob looked down at his hip. "Leanne, we've gotta run. I just received a text from Cat. Looks like there's been a domestic violence call, and I'm the closest person."

Jacob and Leanne stood up and quickly said their good-byes to Tom. Before long, they were en route with the sirens blaring and lights flashing from the roof of the patrol vehicle.

Chapter 12

As they sped around curves leading to the call, Leanne asked, "Where are we going?"

"We're headed to Lake Road. Cat didn't put it on the scanner because I know these two. Brace yourself, Slick. This will probably be a doozy!" Jacob shook his head.

"So, this has happened before?" Leanne asked.

"Jr. is an old friend of my grandfather's. They were in Vietnam together. Jr. came back and developed a drinking problem. He saw a lot of stuff over there. It really messed with his head. Usually, he would get drunk and hit his wife, Eloise. We'd arrest him, she would forgive him, and the cycle would repeat. Lately, I'm not sure what's happening to him. Eloise told me he's been having nightmares and flashbacks of Vietnam. I'm really worried about him. He's not supposed to have a gun, but I know he has an antique, one-shot muzzleloader."

"Why don't you call for backup?"

"Out of respect for a brother," Jacob replied, referencing his time in the military.

Jacob pulled down a gravel driveway to a small mobile home and honked the horn before getting out. "Stay here a second or two. Let me see how things are going."

As the car door slammed, an older woman in a pink robe appeared on the porch. "Jacob, he's got the rifle out!" the older woman yelled.

Immediately Jacob opened the door and climbed back into the vehicle. From the back, he grabbed a bulletproof vest and put it over Leanne. "Put this over you and get down," was the order he gave Leanne before grabbing his radio and calling for backup.

Jacob stepped out of the vehicle and approached the porch. "Eloise, are you okay?" he shouted.

"Yes, but Jr.'s been drinking, and he got mad at me. He tried to hit me, but I locked myself in the bedroom and called y'all. He went to get the gun and ended up shooting his television. Last time I saw him, he was out here in the yard yelling and cursing at the neighbors."

Leanne had her window cracked and could hear every word the older woman was shouting to Jacob. She peeked up and looked around carefully. She wondered what neighbors the woman was referring to. Leanne didn't see anyone living near them.

As Jacob approached the front porch to get Eloise to safety, Leanne noticed an older man holding a shotgun sneak quietly around the house. The older man was clearly in his late seventies. He was wearing an old pair of blue jeans, a blue plaid shirt, and a red bill cap that contrasted with the rest of his clothes and looked rather worn. The older man peeked around the corner and saw Jacob. Leanne could tell by his movement that he hadn't noticed her in the vehicle. The older man, who Leanne assumed was Jr., quietly rounded the corner of the house and walked quickly toward Jacob. Jr. raised the rifle at Jacob's back, and Leanne screamed, "Jake!"

Jacob turned and saw Jr. standing within fifteen feet of him aiming the rifle. Jacob made a quick move and lunged toward the older man. Jacob's body caught the older man at the waist, and the gun tilted upwards as it fired. The sound of the gunfire was loud and echoed through the mountains. Leanne was terrified. There was a loud roaring sound from the hillside above them as both men crashed to the ground. Leanne wondered what had been hit. It sounded like a large animal had been wounded and fallen in the mountains behind them. Leanne could see that Jacob had not been hit, but she was terrified.

Jacob and the older man began to roll around in the front yard fighting for the gun. The ground beneath them was wet. Covered in mud, Jacob let go of the gun and stepped away. "You son of a bitch! You made me shoot my cow! I'll kill you for that!" the old man yelled as he raised the butt of the weapon and attempted to strike Jacob.

Jacob was quick and dodged the blow by leaning to his left. With his right hand, Jacob grabbed the butt of the rifle and pulled it from the older man. The older man charged at Jacob. Jacob, covered in mud, stepped to the side and threw a leg out, causing the older man to trip and land face-first in the mud. Jacob immediately put a knee on the older man's back and reached for the man's arms while simultaneously reaching for his handcuffs.

Leanne breathed a sigh of relief. She heard Jacob's voice saying, "You alright, Jr.? I didn't want to do that, but you've made it tough on yourself now. You'll be going to jail this time."

The older man fought for a moment and then relinquished control to Jacob as backup arrived. Sirens that were once blasting from the main road were turned off once they saw Jacob standing in the yard with Jr. in handcuffs.

Leanne recognized Duncan as he stepped from the first car. She heard Duncan laugh and say, "Dang, Sheriff, you decide to get a little dirty today?"

"I've heard there's nothing like a good mud bath to clean the pores!" Jacob smiled. "Will you take this? I have something to check on."

Duncan took Jr. and escorted him to the cruiser. Jacob walked to the passenger side of his vehicle and opened the door, "You okay?" he asked.

"ME!" shouted Leanne. "I watched you nearly get killed, and you're asking ME if I'M alright!" Leanne couldn't control herself any longer and jumped from the vehicle to wrap her arms around Jacob's neck with a hard thud.

Jacob grunted from bruising, "Let's take it slow, okay?" Jacob smiled and laughed as he wrapped his arms around her. "I'm fine, thanks to you."

Leanne leaned back and glared at Jacob with tears welling in her eyes, "Don't you ever do that again!"

"Why did you let him have the gun when you had him down? You could have been killed!"

"Leanne, it's a muzzleloader. It only has one shot in it," Jacob smiled.

Leanne looked confused for a moment. "Well, he almost hit you with it!"

"Slick, he's seventy-two years old. I think I could outrun him," Jacob laughed.

"It sure didn't look like that when he was fighting with you!" Leanne was clearly upset.

"Dang, if I'd have known you would show me attention for almost getting shot at, I think I might have had Scott do it!" Jacob laughed. "Come on, I'll drop you off at the hotel and go home to change. I'll take you to dinner tonight to apologize for scaring you and thank you for saving me."

"What am I supposed to do at the hotel? I don't want to be alone right now. I need someone to talk to after you scared me to death! Your mom and Aunt Helen are working, and I'm not interrupting Katie right now," Leanne's voice trailed off.

Jacob took her by the shoulders and looked into her eyes, "Okay, tell you what, you can go home with me. My only goal right now is to get a shower as soon as possible because I think Jr. and Eloise have a septic leak that's making their yard muddy!"

Leanne stopped a moment and sniffed the air. Her face grimaced as her nose wrinkled. "Ewwww! I think you're right! Now I need a shower! Got some spare clothes?"

"Well, you're in luck. Katie left a pair of shorts at the house last year at the Fourth of July party. You can wear one of my tee shirts," Jacob smiled.

Leanne had assumed that Jacob lived in a small, one-bedroom house that was perfect for a bachelor that was never home. She was surprised when they rounded the curve on the gravel road to reveal a moderately-sized brick ranch home surrounded by fenced-in fields.

"Boy Scout, I would never have guessed your house would be so pretty," Leanne complimented.

"Thanks. I own what's fenced in, too. There's almost eleven acres here. It's such a waste of space. Dad's thinking about buying some cows to keep down the brush. I don't have time to be a farmer and a Sheriff. Well, that's the excuse. Honestly, I think it would be good for Dad once he retires. It'd give him something to do."

"Why did you buy such a big house for one person?" Leanne asked.

"Well, I hope I won't be alone my entire life, plus I got it for a steal. An older woman had grandchildren going to Ridgeview, and she wanted me close to the school."

"That's sweet," Leanne said.

Jacob wasn't sure if she meant that it was sweet that he didn't want to be alone or if it was sweet that the older woman cared so dearly for her grandchildren, but he didn't ask.

Jacob pulled into the carport. "Come on in. You can shower upstairs, and I'll shower in the basement. I'm a little dirtier than you." Jacob looked down at his shirt and pants. "That is definitely a septic leak."

As Leanne stepped from the vehicle, she noticed what looked like a motorcycle and a four-wheeler in the carport but wasn't sure because they were both hidden with a protective cover. She could see an enclosed porch at the end of the house that was not visible from the main road.

Jacob opened the back door without a key, and Leanne asked, "Do you realize how many people leave their doors unlocked around here? Aunt Helen does that too. I'm amazed there's not a burglary every ten minutes."

"We watch out for one another around here. I guarantee every neighbor I have knows that I'm home and that I have someone with me," Jacob smiled. "There's nothing much to do around here except spy on neighbors." Jacob laughed.

Entering the kitchen, Leanne was shocked to see everything neat and orderly. The smell of lemon was emanating throughout the house. "This does not look like a bachelor pad, Boy Scout."

"Don't blame me! My mom and Aunt Helen decorated everything, and they came by and cleaned up after me every Thursday morning. They probably just left."

"Everyone really does watch out for you, don't they?" said Leanne. Jacob understood that it was more of a statement than a question.

Jacob motioned Leanne down the hall behind him toward the bathroom, "Oh, it's partly because they said a man doesn't know how to clean. I was in the Army for eight years and can't clean well enough to make them happy. They come to my house every Thursday morning. They have coffee together, change the radio station, and clean up. I think they enjoy it. One of my neighbors called me one morning because he had seen them dancing in my living room as they cleaned." Jacob shook his head and laughed as he handed her a towel from the hall closet. "I'll go to Katie's room and get those shorts and grab you a tee shirt from my closet."

Jacob stepped into one of the other rooms as Leanne asked, "Katie's room?"

Jacob stepped into the room across from the hall closet, leaving the door open. "Yes, this is the room Katie calls hers. When I bought this place, she said it was too big for a single person, and if I didn't get married one day, she'd have to come live with me," Jacob laughed. "She decorated this room one weekend but has never slept in it."

Leanne looked into the room, delicately decorated with flowers and lace curtains. It was lovely. "She certainly girled it up in there, didn't she?"

"She said if I got lucky one day, it would be my daughter's bedroom. I think she made it girly for a potential niece," Jacob laughed and shook his head. "You've seen how the women in my family can dream!"

Jacob opened the door at the end of the hall. "I'll grab you that tee shirt." He had left the door open, but Leanne couldn't see inside the room from the angle she was standing. She could only make out some type of workout equipment standing behind the open door.

Handing her the shirt, he said, "So, make yourself at home." Grabbing a towel from the closet, he continued by saying, "I'll be in the basement."

Leanne watched him walk down the hall and out the back door holding the towel and washcloth. She stepped into the bathroom and showered. Katie's shorts were a little smaller than what Leanne expected, and she was glad the tee shirt covered them. Looking at herself in the mirror as she dried her hair with a towel, she realized that the tee shirt completely hid the fact that she was wearing any pants at all.

She stepped from the bathroom and noticed Jacob wasn't back from the basement yet. She looked around the kitchen and living room. Leanne felt uncomfortable being alone in someone else's house. So, she decided to take the opportunity to look at the family photos surrounding the walls and lining the mantlepiece in the living room.

There was an old photo of Jacob in a football uniform. Another old photo showed Jacob in his military uniform. A more recent photo showed him and Scott celebrating something that looked like a win at a sporting event. Another photo showed Jacob in military fatigues surrounded by a group of men and women in matching attire. They were all smiling and happy. Katie's graduation photo was proudly displayed on the center of the mantle above the fireplace, resting directly below the television. Leanne wondered who had given the photo its resting place.

Hand-painted artwork displayed a family tree across the eggshell-colored wall. The branches and leaves were intricately winding up and across the wall and stretched above the window. At the base of the tree were two couples. Leanne assumed that the people were Jacob's grandparents. The beautiful ornate frames read 'Lester' and 'McKinney' at the bottom. Above the Lester grandparents were the two daughters, Helen and Sara. Above the McKinney frame were Calvin and Jack in their younger years. The following line of the artwork was Calvin and Helen's wedding photograph beside Jack and Sara's wedding photo. Above the images, placed at angles, were photos of Jacob and Isaac as small children and one of Katie at about two years old. The ordinarily plain wall had morphed into a beautiful work of art using black, brown, and green paints with ornately detailed frames.

Leanne was startled when she heard a noise behind her and turned to see Jacob.

"I'm so sorry!" Jacob was standing in the kitchen, wearing nothing but a towel. His body language and facial expression showed that he was slightly embarrassed. "I thought I had clothes down there. I'm guessing Mom and Aunt Helen folded them this morning and put them in my room."

Leanne tried to hide the fact that she was actually enjoying the view by covering her eyes, but the scene was already imprinted into her mind. Jacob was usually wearing his uniform and bulletproof vest. No one would have ever imagined the well-toned and tanned stomach hidden beneath. "It's okay. You don't look any worse than I do," Leanne pulled the bottom of the shirt up on the side. "I'm wearing pants, but no one can tell."

Jacob felt a little more comfortable and stood a little straighter. "Well, aren't we the pair?" Jacob smiled.

Leanne laughed, and Jacob immediately felt drawn to her. "I'll go grab some clothes." He left the kitchen uncomfortably aware that Leanne, even wearing an old tee shirt, no makeup, and her hair still wet, was probably the most beautiful thing that had ever been in his living room.

Jacob returned wearing gray jogging pants and a tee shirt . "Where's your clothes? I'll throw them in the washer with mine. We'll probably have to wash them at least three times. That's one heck of a smell," Jacob reasoned.

Leanne walked to the bathroom and returned with her clothes rolled up in front of her. Handing them to Jacob, she washed her hands. "I don't want to know what's on them. I think I'd rather trash them than wash them."

"If two washes don't bring it out. I'm going to agree with you." Jacob laughed and took the clothes from her hands.

Leanne noticed that the tee shirt he wore was tight, and his tanned arm muscles flexed as he reached out to get the clothes. When he turned to walk downstairs, she could see the muscles in his back. "I'll be right back."

Leanne took a deep breath in as the door closed. She walked over to admire the wall once more. Jacob and Isaac were so adorable when they were children. She wondered what Isaac was like. So far, the entire family was so wonderful. She couldn't imagine Isaac being anything less than the perfect baby brother.

"Okay. We'll see how that turns out," Jacob said as he returned. "So, you found the wall of shame, huh?" Jacob laughed.

"This is amazing. I love how this was done."

"Guess who did it."

"The artwork makes me think Aunt Helen," replied Leanne.

"Nope. It was Dad," Jacob answered solemnly.

"It's beautiful."

"Dad said, as a man with a home, I had to remember where I come from. The trials my family had overcome would give me strength to overcome my own trials."

"Is that Katie's dad?" Leanne asked, pointing at the wedding photograph.

"Yep."

"Helen looks so feminine in that picture."

"Oh, she was the girly girl when she and Mom grew up. After Uncle Calvin died, she changed a lot. His death was tough on her. She was young and had to rebuild her entire life. She credits God with helping her through, but I have to say, Aunt Helen has been one tough lady since I can remember."

"What happened to Calvin? Katie didn't say."

"He died of electric shock drowning. He stepped into their flooded basement and was electrocuted. He fell forward and drowned before anyone could reach him."

"That's awful," replied Katie. "I'm so sorry."

"It was a long time ago."

After a moment, Jacob broke the silence that had developed as Leanne studied the painting. "Well, I'd better get started."

"Get started doing what?" Leanne asked.

"I promised you dinner, and dinner you'll get," Jacob smiled and walked into the kitchen.

Leanne followed him. "Need the phone?"

Jacob opened the cabinet, pulled out a few bowls, and placed them on the counter. "Heck no! You saved my life today! That deserves home cooking, so I'm cooking for you." Jacob smiled.

Leanne laughed and said, "Can I help?"

"No way!" Jacob placed his hands on her shoulders and turned her around toward the living room. Leanne did not argue when he sat her on the couch. "In fact, you're going to watch a movie while I cook."

Leanne laughed as Jacob picked up her feet and put them on the couch. He pulled the soft throw off the back of the sofa and covered her legs, taking the time to tuck her in from the hips down and around her feet. He grabbed the remote and turned on the television. After a moment, he found a Scarlett Johansson movie. "That'll keep you occupied," Jacob said proudly.

Jacob returned to the kitchen. After a moment, Leanne shouted, "This would be perfect if I had a glass of wine."

As if Jacob had been waiting for the comment, he appeared in the doorway holding a glass of red wine. He handed it to her and said, "I know," and smiled at her before leaving the room.

Leanne settled in and watched the movie. Halfway through the movie, Jacob returned. He gallantly bowed with his left hand extended and said, "Madam, your dinner awaits."

Leanne laughed and took his hand. Jacob led her to a small dining room set off from the kitchen. The table had been set with flowers. Two places were set, and on the table was a steak dinner for two that included a freshly baked potato and a Caesar salad. A glass of red wine sat beside Leanne's plate while Jacob had chosen to drink Pepsi. Jacob pulled the chair out for Leanne to sit.

"No wine?" Leanne asked.

"I'm on call, remember? Scott's doing chores for Maribeth."

Leanne looked confused. "Scott's not doing chores! He's with Katie."

"Well, we're going to call it chores for Maribeth because I don't want to ruin the evening by thinking about what he's probably doing, okay?"

Leanne laughed.

As Jacob walked around the table, he thought to himself, *If Leanne knew the effect her laughter had on him, she'd never laugh in his presence again.* Jacob sat down and asked, "Do you need anything else?"

"No, this is perfect. When did you learn to cook?"

"Eight years in the Army as a single man. I learned to do a lot of things alone." Jacob blushed because he hadn't realized how that statement sounded before he said it.

Leanne smiled and constrained herself from asking about everything he learned to do alone as a single man.

Jacob solemnly broke the short silence saying, "I wish I had left you with Tom today."

Leanne looked surprised. "Boy Scout! That borders on suicidal ideation!"

Jacob looked down and shook his head, "I was scared to death. I was worried about Eloise but knew you were unprotected in the vehicle. That was probably the most terrified I've ever been as a cop or an Army MP. I don't want to feel that kind of fear again."

Leanne could see the pain in Jacob's eyes and, diverting from her regular use of his nickname, said, "Jacob, if I hadn't been there, you wouldn't be here now. That old man was planning on shooting you in the back."

That was only the second time Jacob had heard Leanne use his real name when speaking with her. Whenever she called him Jacob, his heart would leap because it sounded like a beautiful song when she said his name.

"I was wearing a vest," Jacob replied.

"Well, if a vest protects you that well, I'm glad I had one covering me too," Leanne stared back at Jacob.

"I'm just trying to say I'm sorry for putting you in danger, and I'll never do it again. But I'm glad you were there this time." Jacob touched her hand and smiled.

Leanne returned the smile and said, "What's going to happen to the old man?"

Jacob pulled his hand away and returned to his potato. "He didn't leave me any choice. Duncan has him in lockup while he sobers up, and tomorrow, you and I will write statements. We're charging him with the attempted homicide of a law enforcement officer."

"Good," Leanne replied. "I feel bad because he's old, but that was awful today. It was like he was hunting you," Leanne shivered.

"Jr. was in Vietnam. He drinks and abuses his wife. Several times I've had to arrest him for attacking law enforcement that has come to help Eloise. This time was different. I think he had a flashback or something. He kept calling me Charlie while we were rolling around in the yard. I kept wondering who the hell Charlie was, what did Charlie do to piss him off, and why did he think I was him."

Leanne laughed, and Jacob looked down at his plate to block the intrusive thoughts of Leanne's beautiful eyes and smile.

Jacob continued, "I'll talk to the judge and make sure he has a full psychiatric workup. Instead of prison, he might be able to get treatment. At least Eloise won't have to worry about getting hit if he's locked up getting treatment."

"That's sweet of you."

"I hope if I get old and crazy that someone will give me the same courtesy one day," Jacob laughed.

"You know what I don't get, Slick?" continued Jacob.

"What?" asked Leanne.

Jacob paused for a moment. "I don't want to ask this in a way that makes you uncomfortable."

"Just say it, Boy Scout."

"Well, I can't figure out why you're single. I could understand if you were divorced. I could understand if you had just left a ten-year relationship because he wouldn't commit, but how you're single baffles me."

"So, you're saying that you can't figure out what's wrong with me yet," Leanne smirked.

"Actually, yes," Jacob said definitively.

"Well, I told you that I found it difficult to get close to people after Megan died. My parents had me in therapy for a long time. My parents divorced when I was a senior in high school, and that didn't help. I felt alone in this world. I graduated high school and went to college. I focused on studying and my grades. I started working right after college and stayed focused on making a name for myself." Leanne wasn't sure if she trusted Jacob or the wine during dinner was lowering her inhibitions and allowing her to be open and honest with him.

"So, do you date?"

"Of course. I've met an occasional nice person and had dinner."

"What do they do wrong?" Jacob smiled mischievously.

"Most of the time, they're self-absorbed. I think that happens in cities more than here. People here watch after one another more. In cities, we're trained not to care about the other people around us. No one seems to care what their neighbor is going through in the city. I thought about it a million times after Megan died. I wondered who saw her last, who heard something or saw something and didn't ask her if she needed help or call the police to report something they saw or heard."

"I'm sorry," Jacob's expression showed concern.

"That's what led me here. I read your Aunt Helen's short stories about things happening here and the beautiful mountains. I honestly thought she might be crazy. It turns out she's not the crazy one. I've seen a different side to life coming down here."

"What was your worst date?" Jacob asked, smiling.

"A man down the street asked me out. Every day, at the same time, we would see one another in the coffee shop below my apartment. We had several conversations while waiting for coffee, and soon enough, he asked me out. I agreed, and he brought his mother."
"You're kidding!" Jacob laughed.

"Oh, I'm not. She honestly asked me if I was a good cook and if I was fertile while we ate dinner. She turned a date into a job interview to be her daughter-in-law!"

Jacob laughed boisterously.

"What about you, Boy Scout? What's your worst date?"

"I would have to say it was a girl I asked out, and when I picked her up, she had two suitcases with her."

"Suitcases?"

"Yes, suitcases. I thought I would have to ask for a transfer to another base to get rid of her. I guess she decided that a date meant you were moving in together."

"Okay, I have to ask. How long did you let her stay because of sex?"

Jacob was clearly faking a shocked expression. "I can't believe you'd ask that! Do you think I'd honestly take advantage of a situation like that? I'm offended."

Leanne grinned, "Answer the question, Boy Scout."

Jacob shook his head and smiled, "I was twenty-three at the time, and it was only four days."

Jacob and Leanne both laughed.

"Not really the Boy Scout behavior back then, huh?"

"Well, she didn't have any complaints," Jacob smiled charmingly as laughter erupted around the table again.

"Ready for dessert?" Jacob asked.

"Oh, you made dessert?"

"I made it last night and left it in the fridge. They taste better after setting overnight."

Jacob left the table and returned with a round pan and a pie server. Setting the pan down, Leanne saw that the dessert was a homemade blueberry cheesecake. "You did this yourself?"

"Yep. It's a real New York style cheesecake. I thought I'd better make it New York style or the topping would sink into it. Regular cheesecake can't hold the blueberry topping as well."

Leanne dipped her fork into the mixture and took a bite. "MMM" was the only sound she could make for a moment. "Boy Scout, this is incredible."

"Do you want coffee with it? I'm guessing red wine isn't a good mix with cheesecake."

Leanne nodded with another bite in her mouth, and Jacob left toward the kitchen. Leanne thought to herself, *What a meal. Steak, loaded baked potato, salad, and now cheesecake! All homemade!* Leanne gasped, and her eyes widened. It was the meal she described when Scott had brought them lunch. It's the dinner that says he wants a relationship.

Jacob entered the room with coffee and creamer. "I wasn't sure how you took your coffee."

"Thank you," Leanne said with an uncomfortableness in her voice.

Jacob noticed her silence and expression. "Is something wrong?"

"I have to ask you something," Leanne said nervously.

"What is it?" Jacob asked worriedly.

"Is this a relationship dinner?" Leanne blurted out.

"A what?" Jacob asked, confused.

"The other day, I described this dinner when we were talking about the lunch Scott had brought. I said it was a high-five lunch… this is the 'I want a relationship dinner' that I described." Leanne had panic in her voice.

Jacob began to laugh. "Oh my God, woman! I thought you were allergic to something and would die in a few minutes! You acted like something awful had happened!"

"Well, I don't want to give anyone the wrong idea." Leanne tried redeeming herself.

"Listen, we have to talk about this," Jacob smiled and took her hand. Jacob was forced into saying out loud what he didn't want to admit to himself. He knew he was beginning to develop feelings for the woman before him. He sighed and began. He hoped the pain he felt inside wouldn't show on his face or be revealed in his voice.

"I know you're not interested in me. I'm not going to try to convince you of anything. I'm here, and you're going back to New York. A relationship between us is not in the cards. I just knew this was your favorite foods, and I wanted to thank you for saving me today. So you can relax," Jacob smiled, and Leanne sighed.

Jacob continued, "Now, let's take the dessert into the living room and finish watching the movie," Jacob smiled.

"Sounds good."

Jacob sat on the couch the rest of the evening with Leanne at his side. Her head was nestled into his shoulder. His arm wrapped around her shoulders. The throw from the back of the couch was wrapped around her legs. The two sat quietly as they watched two Scarlett Johansson movies. Jacob was glad to just hold her beside him. He was now certain that she didn't have feelings for him. He would have to block the feelings he was developing for her, but for now, at this moment, he was content to just have her near him.

It was only ten o'clock when the last movie ended. Jacob didn't move to get the remote. Leanne leaned her head back and realized that Jacob was breathing deeply and calmly. He was sound asleep. Her face was within inches of his. Leanne could smell his cologne and the heat from his body beneath her cheek. She leaned upward, kissed his cheek, and whispered, "I'm sorry, Boy Scout."

Leanne stood up and covered him with the throw. She turned off the television and went to the only room she felt comfortable in spending the night. Katie's room would have its first visitor.

Chapter 13

Jacob awoke on his couch the next morning. For a moment, he was confused until the memory of the previous night filled his mind. He woke to find Leanne placing a few biscuits into the oven and holding a cup of coffee in her hand. She picked up a second cup and said, "Good morning, sleepy head."

"Did we both sleep on the couch last night?" asked Jacob.

"No, you were out by ten, and I slept in Katie's room. I turned off the television before I went to bed."

"Oh, so we didn't sleep together," Jacob grinned.

"Not even for a moment. I remember the end of the movie," Leanne laughed.

Jacob took a drink of the hot coffee, "You know I'm going to tease you about staying the night with me. God knows how many rumors I'm going to get started." Jacob smiled around the cup of his second drink.

"You? I walked outside wearing this!" Leanne pointed downward at the tee shirt covering the shorts beneath. "I know one of your distant neighbors saw me! I wouldn't be surprised if someone took photos and posted them on the internet this morning!" Leanne laughed.

"Why did you go outside in that?"

"You won't believe this, but our clothes don't stink anymore. I walked down to the basement and put them in the dryer. They'll be ready in a little bit."

"Darn. I'm going to miss those legs," Jacob took another drink of coffee and smiled as he walked down the hall to the bathroom.

Leanne shook her head and reached into the refrigerator to retrieve a few slices of bacon.

Jacob returned to the kitchen in his uniform. "Are you ready for your last day of work? We have to write up statements today. Jr. should be dried out by now."

"I'll get my clothes on if you finish frying the bacon."

"Okay, but you know Aunt Helen is going to think something is up."

Leanne looked at him puzzled.

"She texted last night and told me she didn't know where Katie was and that you weren't answering your phone. I told her you two were out together, and I'd run by the hotel and bring you to her house for breakfast this morning."
"Okay. Breakfast is now canceled." She quickly turned off the oven and stove, "I'll get dressed and brush my hair. What am I going to do about makeup? She'll know something is up if I wear the same clothes and have no makeup on!"

"Calm down, she didn't see you yesterday, and if you told her you spent the night with me, she wouldn't get mad. She'd start sewing a quilt!"

"Sewing a quilt?" Leanne was confused.

"Go put your clothes on, and I'll explain on the way," Jacob shook his head and sighed.

Thirty minutes later, Jacob and Leanne arrived at Helen's. A full breakfast was prepared and sitting on the table. Feeling at home, Jacob walked in and began to pick food off the table with his fingers.

Helen reached across the table and slapped his hand, causing him to drop the piece of bacon he had stolen. Helen pointed at him angrily and said, "Mister, don't add to it! You're in enough trouble!"

"What did I do?" asked Jacob defensively.

"What in tarnation could have possessed you to shoot Jr.'s cow?"

Leanne burst out with laughter.

Jacob began to defend himself. "Aunt Helen, I didn't shoot Jr.'s cow! He did!"

"Well, that wasn't the story at the ladies' church group meeting last night!"

Jacob sighed and said, "Ask Leanne what happened. She was there."

"You had Leanne with you when you shot Jr.'s cow! Doing stuff like that doesn't impress women! We're never going to get you married off!" Turning to Leanne, Helen placed her hand on Leanne's arm, shook her head, and softly said, "I'm so sorry you had to witness that, honey. I swear, we didn't raise him that way."

Leanne began to laugh harder.

"What's so funny?" asked Helen.

Leanne calmed herself and said, "Come on, Helen, we'll have coffee in the kitchen while we wait for Katie."

Walking into the kitchen, Leanne looked over her shoulder at Jacob, who had again picked up a slice of bacon and was about to stick it in his mouth. "You're welcome," Leanne whispered.

After a few moments, Helen returned to the dining room. "You know you're going to church with me on Sunday, right? I have some praising to do!" Helen hugged Jacob with both arms. She had tears in her eyes. "I hate your job. I know you do good work, and it's needed, but I don't like the thought of losing you. Thank God Leanne was there."

"Aunt Helen, I'm fine."

"Well, at least everything turned out alright. Now, sit down and eat." Helen grabbed a spoon and started heaping food onto Jacob's plate.

Jacob smiled at Leanne. "Thanks," he mouthed silently.

Leanne nodded.

The rear screen door swung open, and Katie walked in.

"Girl! Where did you and Leanne go last night?"

Katie looked confused for a moment and then noticed Jacob waving to her from behind Aunt Helen.

"Oh," Katie's words stumbled from her mouth. "We, um, had a girl's night."

"What time did you two get in last night?" Helen asked.

In unison, both women answered at once but gave two different answers. Katie said two and Leanne said three. Helen's expression was confused as she looked at the three of them. "Why do I feel like you three are hiding something?"

All three shrugged in unison.

Aunt Helen raised an ominous eyebrow. "Katie, if you got home about two or three, where were you up until now? You didn't sleep in your bed last night, and Jacob picked up poor Leanne early this morning. Poor thing didn't even have time to put on makeup. But where were you?"

"Emergency call at the hospital," Katie spouted the words out of her mouth as if they tasted sour.

The phone rang and broke the interrogation. The three stood silent and breathed a sigh of relief as Helen picked up the telephone and said, "Hello?"

She continued to speak into the receiver as Katie and Leanne took their place at the table. "Okay. I'll be right there," they heard Helen reply before she hung up.

"Tabitha's out on maternity leave, and the part-time person decided not to show up, so Dr. Reynolds is short-handed again. I'm going in to help. You three be careful today."

Helen left, and as that old blue Datsun pulled out of the driveway, Katie jumped up and headed toward her bedroom. "Thanks for covering for me, Leanne."

"Not a problem. But you should tell everyone that you're dating Scott," Leanne said in a straightforward tone.

Katie stopped instantly at the end of the hallway and turned around, stunned at the revelation. "How did you know?"

"I have superpowers," replied Jacob as he nodded and chewed on the biscuit he had stolen from the table.

Leanne giggled and rolled her eyes. "You weirdo!"

"No, seriously, how did you know where I was so you could cover for me?" With sarcasm in her voice, she said, "You know, I could have been dead in a ditch, and you two just guessed I was with Scott."

Leanne smiled, "You were on camera at the office yesterday."

"Oh. You saw that, huh?" Katie said shyly.

"The whole thing!" replied Jacob. "Glad you took my advice and stepped on the stair," Jacob smiled.

Ignoring Jacob, Katie looked at Leanne and, with a shy smile, said, "Leanne, I think I'm in love.".

"Think? Hell, I know you are! I know Scott is too!" replied Leanne.

Jacob interrupted and said, "So, tell Aunt Helen and Mom so they get off my back and start sewing for you. Then tell Dad so he can feel the privilege of threatening a man twice his size," Jacob smiled.

"This is good, isn't it?" Katie asked.

"It's excellent. Scott's a good man. Stop worrying." The two women hugged.

"I'm gonna go grab some clothes. I'll shower at Scott's."

"We're going to head out. We have lots to do today," Jacob replied, hinting to Leanne that he was ready to leave.

"We'll have to grab my makeup when we get into town," Leanne said without thinking.

"That is right. I knew I forgot to ask about something. Where's your makeup?" Katie paused for a moment before saying, "Oh my God, you're wearing the same outfit you had on yesterday before I left!" Katie's mind quickly began working overtime, and she replied, "Oh my God! Where were you two last night?"

Leanne placed her hand up. "Don't make assumptions. Nothing happened."

Katie's face began to light up with a large smile.

Leanne continued, "I spent the night at Jacob's last night. He made dinner, and we watched a couple of movies."

"Dinner and a couple of movies don't give you a reason to spend the night," Katie raised an eyebrow at Leanne.

"Boy Scout fell asleep at ten o'clock." Leanne nodded her head in Jacob's direction. "I didn't want to wake him to bring me back to the hotel."

"Besides, our clothes weren't clean yet," interjected Jacob without thinking.

"Oh my God! This is getting even better!" Katie laughed. "So, you're telling me that two single, good-looking people spent the night together with no clothes, and nothing happened."

Jacob was about to explain everything to Katie, but his phone went off. "Okay. That means we're on the clock, Leanne."

"We'll explain everything later," Leanne said as she kissed Katie's cheek and left. As she walked out the door behind Jacob, she yelled, "You and Scott have a good day today!"

In the vehicle, Leanne said, "Do you think she believes us?"

"Not a word. Your reputation is ruined now!" laughed Jacob.

Leanne shot a look at Jacob. "So, what was the call?"

"A dead body in a backyard shed."

"What?"

"We're going to Carol and Arlene Yates' house. They're good people. They have three little kids. This morning, Carol found a dead body in the shed near his pool."

"That's a new one. We ran out of old bodies, and now, we're creating more," Leanne smirked.

Jacob turned onto Caney Ridge and drove only a few miles before he turned into the driveway of a beautiful brick home. Flowers were planted along the drive and in front of the porch. Two police cars were already setting in the driveway. Jacob stopped, and he and Leanne exited the vehicle and was greeted by Duncan Fuller.

"What happened, Duncan?" Jacob asked.

"No one knows. Mrs. Yates said she hired a man from Bristol to clean and close down their pool for the winter. The man came to the house the day before yesterday and walked outside to clean and drain the pool. It looks like he finished the work, but Mrs. Yates said he never returned for his check. She told her husband about it this morning, and he went to make sure the man hadn't stolen any pool cleaning equipment he had stored in the shed. He found the body and called us."

"Well, let's take a look. After you, Duncan." Jacob waved his hand in an outward gesture.

Duncan stopped him and whispered, "Sheriff, this is pretty bad. Are you sure you want Ms. Leanne to come? There's a lot of blood."

Leanne overheard the comment. "It's okay, Duncan. Ms. Leanne can handle anything you guys can." She nodded and smiled as she walked by the two men.

In the backyard, Jacob noticed a small wooden shed approximately four feet wide and eight feet in height and length. As Jacob approached the door, he noticed an old-timey hinged lock made of wood that secured the building from the outside, resting on the top of the door.

"What is that?" asked Leanne.

"It's an old-timey lock. A loose nail holds a piece of wood to the outside of the door. When the piece of wood swings down, it locks the door." Jacob raised his hand to the top of the door to demonstrate. "Mr. Yates probably put it high so the kids couldn't reach it."

Jacob opened the door of the shed. Beneath a pile of wood lie a man in his early thirties. Blood was covering the man's face, neck, and chest. The blood had gathered in a large, thick pool under the body.

"What's on top of him?" Jacob asked.

"It was a shelf that tipped over. We're guessing he went inside, and the door locked behind him accidentally. He was probably trying to get out of the shed when the shelf tipped over on him."

"Who is he?" asked Jacob.

"I had to call the pool company in Bristol to find out. They said his name was Richard Talbert. He's been doing some pool cleanings around Dickenson County as a contractor for them. The owner told me that Talbert was checking out the area and was considering moving here to start his own company."

"Did they have a problem with the competition?"

"Nope, the owner seemed to be happy for him. He said Richard had been in prison and was looking to make a new start. The owner was helping him all he could."

"The shelf is pretty sturdy, but do you think it caused that much bleeding?" asked Jacob with a disgusted and confused look.

Leanne leaned towards the body for a better look and said, "No, Boy Scout, I don't think it did. I don't think it broke a single bone."

"Where did all the blood come from?" asked Jacob.

"There's blood on his nose and mouth, but there are also patches of petechiae on his skin. This man died of asphyxiation."

"So, the cabinet fell, and it was heavy enough to stop him from breathing?" asked Jacob, confused. "And how do you know all that?"

"I told you I like to read and learn. It's my job. And I don't think his death had anything to do with the shelf."

Leanne studied the scene more closely. "I have it!" Leanne abruptly stated. "He died of chlorine gas poisoning!"

"What led you to that?" Duncan asked.

"Pool chlorine has sodium hypochlorite in it. Mr. Yates was storing it inside the shed." Leanne pointed at the buckets lying on the floor of the shed. "These were gallon-sized glass bottles of vinegar," Leanne commented as she picked up a label. "He probably used vinegar to clean the pool filters."

Mr. Yates stood about ten feet behind them and stated, "I bought the vinegar on clearance last year and put it in the shed through the summer. I planned on moving it before winter so that it didn't freeze."

Leanne smiled. The shelf fell over, causing the buckets to tip over and break the glass jars of vinegar on top of the pool chlorine making chlorine gas. It happened the day before yesterday, so there's been time for it to dissipate, and we can't smell it anymore."

Duncan replied, "Sheriff, that makes sense. It's a weird accident, but it makes sense."

"Duncan, will you take the photos?' asked Jacob.

"Sure, boss."

"Leanne, come with me please," Jacob asked, but it was heard as an order to Leanne's ears.

"Did I do something wrong, Jacob?" asked Leanne as they walked toward the vehicle.

"A stranger? A weird accident? Is your spidey sense going off?" Jacob raised an eyebrow.

"Crap! You're right. The man had been released from prison. I wonder what the charges were," Leanne sounded excited.

"That's what we're calling Maribeth to ask."

In the privacy of the vehicle, Jacob and Leanne called Maribeth and confirmed their suspicions. Richard Talbert had spent time in an Oklahoma prison after being convicted of the sexual molestation of several minors in his YMCA swimming class.

"We've gotta get to Duncan!" Jacob said in an almost excited tone.

They both ran to the backyard from the vehicle. Duncan was still photographing the scene as Jacob arrived.

"Duncan, plan change. We need to treat this as a homicide."

"A homicide?" Duncan replied. "Sheriff, I'll do whatever you tell me, but are you sure?"

"No, I'm not sure. But, if there's even a small possibility that this was a murder, I'm not going to miss my chance. It's the closest we've come to finding evidence that someone may be murdering pedophiles in this county."

"Pedophiles?" Duncan asked.

"I just got off the phone with Maribeth. He was convicted and spent time in Oklahoma for the sexual molestation of several minors... He fits the criteria except that he hadn't moved here. You told me that his boss said he was thinking about moving here." Jacob emphasized the word 'thinking' as he spoke.

"Okay, Sheriff, I'll get the guys to collect any evidence we can find."

"You might want to check the tree line, too. Me and Leanne will go speak with Mr. and Mrs. Yates." Jacob looked around and asked an older officer to accompany him and Leanne.

Jacob and Leanne walked toward the house. The parents were keeping the kids entertained in the den. That section of the house prevented the children from witnessing the ongoing events in the backyard. Jacob, Leanne, and the officer walked into the den.

"Carol, will you and Arlene let Officer Baker sit with the kids, and we talk in the living room?" asked Jacob.

Arlene looked anxious. "What's wrong, Sheriff?"

"We just have to sit down and write up statements. It's just procedure, there's no reason to worry," Jacob reassured.

Jacob and Leanne sat in living room chairs while the Yates couple sat on the couch. Mr. Yates was holding his wife's hand tenderly with one hand and his other arm wrapped around her.

"So, start from the beginning. The pool needed to be cleaned. How did you decide to have it cleaned, and who to clean it?" Jacob began.

Carol's face made an aggravated expression. "I could have done it, but Arlene wouldn't let me."

Arlene replied, "You've been working too many hours, and me and the boys would rather have you here spending time with us. That's why I hired a landscaper and a pool man."

Carol pulled his arm from her shoulders to the area behind her and said, "My dad worked from daylight until dark six days a week and did chores on Sunday. That's how he taught me, and that's what I should have been doing. I feel dang lazy having someone else do my work for me."

Carol looked toward Jacob to receive some support for his argument.

Leanne interjected with a disdained expression showing that he would get no relief from Jacob, "Jack mows, and Helen and Sara clean inside."

"Hey, I work a lot of hours!" replied Jacob defensively.

Arlene sat a little taller, and her smile could have illuminated the room as she looked at her husband. It was clear that she had won the argument.

"So, Arlene, why did you call that specific pool cleaning company? They're based out of Bristol, I know there are companies in Wise County that do it," asked Jacob.

"It was the first one that came up on Google and answered the phone," Arlene replied.
"We heard he had been servicing pools and hot tubs around here."

"No one referred him to you?" Leanne asked.

"No," answered Arlene. "I called them in the middle of September. He said it would be around the first week of October before he could come out because he's been pretty booked this year."

"Did anyone else know he was coming to the house today?" asked Jacob.

Carol and Arlene looked at each other curiously and shook their heads. Arlene's expression became excited, "Wait, Carol, did you tell your mother?"

Carol thought about it and said, "No, I've been working so much I haven't even talked to her."

"Did either of you see anyone else at the house yesterday or last night?" asked Jacob.

Both shook their heads.

"Did you hear anything last night or this morning, like barking dogs or anything?" asked Leanne, feeling like she was grasping at straws.

"Bradley is allergic to dogs," stated Arlene referring to her oldest son.

"Carol, with you being away from home so much, did you happen to install any security cameras?"

Carol became excited, "Yes, I did. It's attached to an app on my phone." Carol whipped his phone from his shirt pocket and began to scroll. "It alarms when a car comes up the driveway, and there's one pointing at the front and back door."

Showing the phone to Jacob, he said, "See? No alerts for the last two days except for coming home last night and entering and exiting through the doors last night and this morning."

"Nothing pointing at the pool or shed?" asked Jacob.

"I didn't care about the pool or the shed. I was trying to protect my family. That's why the cameras are set up like that."

"You did good, Carol," smiled Jacob as he patted the man on the shoulder. "Leanne and I will get back to the office and document everything. The boys and I should be done here around noon. After the scene is released, Carol, I'd suggest you drag that shed to the corner of the property and burn it. Arlene and the boys don't need to be anywhere near it, okay?"

"You read my mind, Sheriff. Just let me know when you're done with the entire investigation."

Jacob and Leanne left the house and returned to the pool shed. Duncan had given the camera to a second officer and was walking around with evidence bags and tweezers.

"Anybody call the rescue squad yet?" asked Jacob.

"Not yet, Sheriff. We were waiting to get as much detail and evidence as possible before we added the possibility of someone damaging evidence."

"I'll give Kevin a call and tell him to bring Cap up here, too. Let's all stay away from the tree line until Cap has checked it out."

"Who's Cap?" asked Leanne.

"He's just the finest police dog in the state, probably the country," Jacob smiled proudly.

"How's he going to track something if he doesn't know what he's looking for?" asked Leanne.

"Cap's trained to pick up strange scents, follow the scent, and even recognize the scent later. He's pretty awesome. I love to watch him work." Jacob's voice showed his excitement. "If there's been anything in those trees in the last twenty-four hours, we've got them."

An hour later, a large dog with a long and wrinkled face, loose skin, and huge, drooping ears jumped from the rear of a police vehicle. "Boy Scout, I'm not sure that's a police dog," Leanne said when she first saw Cap standing beside the vehicle wearing a police vest.

"Cap is a bloodhound, Slick." Jacob bent over and put both hands on the side of Cap's head. Jacob was nose-to-nose with the large dog. "Best dang bloodhound in the whole wide world, aren't ya, buddy?" Jacob petted the large dog.

"He doesn't like any of us as much as he likes Cap." A dark-haired older gentleman smiled and put out his hand. "You must be Leanne, I'm Kevin Barton. I'm Cap's trainer."

Leanne shook his hand. "So, how does he work?" asked Leanne.

Kevin laughed and said, "Well, we're going to take him out to the tree line, and I'll say, 'Cap, seek him.'" Kevin stood silent.

"And that's it?" asked Leanne with disappointment echoing in her voice.

"That's it," replied Kevin.

"Kevin, stop downplaying it! Leanne, that's when the most beautiful sound in the world happens, and we all play follow the leader! Ain't that right, old buddy!" Jacob had again sunk to one knee to speak to Cap while looking into his large and warm, deep-set eyes that completed an expression of solemn dignity. The dog let out a moan as Jacob continued to rub the dog's ears.

Kevin shook his head, "He always gets like this. Sure glad Cap doesn't listen to him. I'd have to double his salary," Kevin's expression was somber. "Let's go, Cap," Kevin said as he pulled the lead.

Leanne and Jacob followed Kevin and Cap toward the tree line. The woods were beautiful. The leaves were beginning to turn color. Leanne stopped for a moment to admire the leaves of a large, red maple.

"Cap, seek'em," Kevin spoke with determination in his voice.

Cap walked along in front of the group with his nose to the ground.

"So, this is what you're all excited about... the miracle in action... the greatest dog in the world...." Leanne's voice was thick with sarcasm.

"Give it time, Slick," Jacob said.

The four continued to walk through the trees and shrubbery. Leanne enjoyed the beautiful walk among the trees and was thinking about Cap's salary. Leanne silently wondered to herself if he was paid in dog food, steak, or was actually receiving compensation and was paying federal taxes each week. As absurd as it sounded, it just might happen. Cap was more of a police officer than she was, and somehow, she had found herself following him through the woods, chasing a possible murder suspect. Leanne never thought she would be involved in anything like this until she came to Dickenson County.

A small path through the wooded area became a clear area to travel. Cap was diligently focused as he held his nose to the ground taking short but strong breaths through his nose. The four walked for another ten minutes before, from the base of Cap's lungs, erupted a sound Leanne had never heard before.

"ROOOOO," came a sound from deep within Cap. His head perked up, and he began to run. Every few steps, Cap threw his head back and loudly announced he was on the trail. Jacob, Kevin, and Leanne tried to keep up. After only a few thousand yards, the trail had ended. Cap stood near the edge of a gravel road. He walked in circles and did his best to pick up the scent again but failed. The dog sat down and whined. The sound he made sounded sad to Leanne.

Breathing a little deeper after the run, Leanne commented, "That sounds so sad."

Kevin walked over to Cap and patted him on the head. "It's okay, Cap. We got the scent for later."

"That just means you'll get to show off later, Cap," consoled Jacob.

"Do you mean to say he'll remember the smell?" asked Leanne.

"Cap once caught a guy two weeks after the crime," Kevin said.

"Seriously?" Leanne asked.

There was a jewelry store robbery, and two weeks later, the guy was arrested on a completely different charge. Cap was just walking through the precinct when they were booking him, and all of a sudden, he attacked the guy. Cap grabbed his pants, and they ripped. Jewelry fell out of his pocket!" Kevin smiled.

"That's amazing!" Leanne said.

"Some dogs can remember a smell for nearly a year. It's a small county. Cap's never had to wait a year to find a suspect," laughed Kevin.

"Looks like someone parked up here and drove away," Jacob said. "Let's see if Cap can show us exactly where they walked."

"Hey Cap, track," Kevin commanded. Cap immediately understood and began walking the path in reverse, heading back toward the Yates' home.

Cap kept his nose to the ground and tracked the scent to the rear of the shed. Cap raised his head one last time, and a loud "Roooo" came from deep within. Cap stared toward the top of the rear of the shed. Jacob, Kevin, and Leanne stared in the same direction.

Carefully, Jacob reached up and realized that the edges of the boards were frayed. "This board had been recently removed and replaced."

Leanne examined the board. "This board leads down the back side, and when removed, someone could reach in and knock over the shelf."

"Do you realize this is the closest we've ever come to finding the killer?" Excitement echoed in Leanne's voice.

"We have circumstantial evidence on this one crime, it could have been a murder instead of an accident. That's all we have," Jacob reminded her.

"But, if we've found one, it might lead to connections with the others." Leanne pleaded.

"I'm not counting chickens," Jacob replied.

Leanne looked confused and shook her head, "What are you talking about? This has nothing to do with chickens, Boy Scout!"

Jacob and Kevin laughed, "Slick, it's an old saying. I'm not counting my chickens before they hatch. It means that you shouldn't depend on something until you are certain that it will happen. The only way we'll be certain is if we get a signed confession from the killer."

As the rescue squad removed the body, a song began to play. "Where is that coming from?" asked Leanne.

One EMT reached into the dead man's pocket and handed the phone to Jacob, "I'm not sure who it is, but I'm guessing they'll want to talk to you," the EMT smiled.

Jacob took the phone and answered, "Sheriff McKinney speaking." After listening for a few moments, Jacob hung up the phone, "Dang, telemarketers!" Jacob began tapping the unlocked screen, "Let's see who Mr. Talbert has been speaking to the last few days."

Leanne leaned over Jacob's shoulder. "Jake, do you see the number he dialed the night before he died?"

A confused and nervous look came across his face. "Aunt Helen doesn't own a pool."

"Why did he call your Aunt Helen two nights ago?"
Jacob continued to swipe through the phone, "Wait, there's a note on the contact information. It says 'willing to help in DC.'"

"Well, to be honest, that pretty much defines your Aunt Helen. She's always helping different churches, organizations, and people around the county," Leanne said in a comforting voice.

Jacob picked up his phone and dialed. He placed it on speaker, so Leanne and Kevin could hear the conversation.

"Aunt Helen, did you know a man named Richard Talbert, a pool cleaner from Bristol?"

"I sure do. He cleaned Dr. Reynolds' pool and came to the office to be paid. Dr. Reynolds' daughter, Kim, had dropped off his check on her way to work at the library. Kim said he did a wonderful job, and I thanked him and gave him the check. He said thank you and that if I knew anyone else with a pool, he wanted to do more work in the area. I gave him my number, and he was supposed to bring me some business cards to Arlene's house so I could help him drum up more business. Why are you asking?"

"Well, he won't need you to help. He's dead."

"Lord have mercy! What happened?"

Jacob sighed and said, "Well, it looks like an accident. I have work to do so I'll call you later. I just didn't know why he had your number."

"That poor man! We'll need to send our condolences to the family," Helen said compassionately.

"Do you know if he had a family?" Jacob asked in a surprised tone.

"Everyone has family, Jacob," Helen said knowingly, and Jacob didn't argue.

Jacob laughed, "Okay, Aunt Helen, I'll try to get information on where you can send flowers."

Jacob hung up the phone and shook his head, "Aunt Helen wants to send flowers to the funeral of a man she met once."

"Why did you say it was an accident?" Leanne asked.

"Because we don't normally go around saying murder without any proof that it was a murder, Slick," Jacob's tone was blunt. "Until we have proof it's an accident or suicide. And I can guess it's an accident because that is an awful way to commit suicide."

The rescue squad pulled into the driveway.

"Well, let's go back to the station, we have to write our statements from yesterday, and we'll get the autopsy report back from Richmond in a few days. We've done all we can here," Jacob spoke with a hint of melancholy in his voice.

Walking back into the office, Jacob said, "Cat, will you take a statement from Leanne about the cow shooting we had yesterday?"

"The ladies' church group thinks you did it, Jake." Cat smiled.

"Why don't you make a video statement and put it on social media when you're done? Maybe that'll stop the rumors," Jacob shook his head.

"If I were Leanne, I'd rather them talk about you shooting a cow than her spending the night at your house last night." Cat grinned mischievously.

Leanne's eyes widened. "I knew a neighbor saw me!"

"So, you admit it!!" Cat laughed.

"How did you know?" asked Leanne.

"Remember, Scott's my best friend, and Katie told him," Cat smiled.

Jacob stood at his office door with his arms folded across his chest with a large smile crossing his face. He never said a word while watching the verbal exchange between the two women.

"Nothing happened." Leanne declared.

"Well, the look on Jake's face over there tells a different story," Cat nodded in Jacob's direction.

"Stop it, Boy Scout!" Leanne demanded.

"I wasn't doing anything but standing here and smiling," Jacob laughed.

Leanne rolled her eyes and sighed, "Okay. I'm not going to win this, am I?"

"It sure doesn't look like it," replied Cat.

"Fine, Boy Scout, you leave me no choice; admit the truth, or I'm calling your mom and telling her that I spent the night and we're engaged now, and she can start planning a June wedding."

Jacob's arms and jaw dropped, "You wouldn't!"

Leanne stood up and walked toward him. Her eyes pierced with anger as she looked into his. "Test me, Big Man. I dare you."

"You know, there's a piece of me that wonders if you would marry me on a dare," Jacob returned her stare. "But I'm afraid you'd do it to spite me, so, Cat, nothing happened."

Leanne turned with a smile on her face and returned to the chair at the desk. Cat laughed and gave Leanne a fist bump as she sat down.

Jacob returned to his office to write his statement as Cat took Leanne's statement. After an hour, Jacob heard Cat say, "Jake, you hungry?"

Instantly, Jake felt guilty. The entire morning had been so busy that he had eaten a few bites at Aunt Helen's house but hadn't seen Leanne eat anything all day. "Only if I'm buying!" Jacob replied as he walked from his office.

"What made you so generous?" asked Cat.

"I think I forgot to feed my sleepover guest this morning."

Leanne laughed, "Yes, you did."

"Pizza or Mexican?"

"It's Saturday; Pizza Plus, silly," replied Cat.

During lunch, Cat asked, "You two going to the barbeque this evening?"

"Hmm?" replied Jacob with a mouth full of salad.

"Your mom and Helen have invited half the town over for the last barbeque of the summer. They've been talking about it all week. Where is your head, Jacob?"

"I knew. I was invited," smiled Leanne.

"Now I know why you love my family. They feed you, and I don't," smiled Jacob.

"Your Mom and Dad are stringing up those pretty outdoor light strings in the backyard, and your Aunt Helen has two big sides of beef in the smoker. Everyone else is bringing a covered side dish, buns, plates, and drinks. It's all planned. It starts at seven this evening, so you have time."

"Well, I guess we have dinner plans now," Jacob replied.

"They knew it was Leanne's last night here until the end of November, so they wanted to make it nice," smiled Cat.

"Well, it's Saturday, and I'm on call. Think you and Duncan can keep your hands off each other and get some work done if I take Leanne up to Birch Knob Tower?" Jacob smiled.

"It's pretty up there right now. The leaves are changing. You'll love it, Leanne," smiled Cat.

After lunch, Jacob dropped Cat off at the office. Stepping out of the patrol vehicle, Jacob said, "We'll have to take my old work truck up there, Slick. I don't want to take a county vehicle up that road unless there's an emergency. It's a really rough road."

Jacob and Leanne climbed into Jacob's old work truck and drove toward the west side of Clintwood. Turning right on Brush Creek, Jacob told her about the tower's history, "Back in 1964, the original fire tower was built."

"What's a fire tower?" asked Leanne.

"Well, the mountains around us can catch fire because of lightning strikes or people not being careful with campfires or cigarettes. So, people started building fire towers in the 1900s to spot wildfires. People were hired to stand on the fire tower and watch for fires."

"That sounds like a boring job," smiled Leanne.

"Always did to me, too," Jacob continued, "The old tower was torn down in 1980, and, in 1999, the Forest Service started rebuilding it. It took four years to complete. So, in 2003, we had a recreational viewing area for the public to enjoy the mountains. From the top, you're a little over three thousand feet above sea level, and on a clear day, you can see five states."

Jacob turned left onto Birch Knob Drive onto a graveled road. They passed one house at the base of the mountain. Leanne leaned forward to look through the windshield at the top of the mountain and asked, "How far is it?"

"It's almost five miles, and, the worst part, you usually can't go any faster than ten miles an hour to be safe and not jar yourself to death on the rocks."

As they drove up the mountain, Leanne mentioned her ears popping.

"It's the change in the barometric pressure as we go up the mountain. It'll probably do it several times before we reach the top," Jacob warned her.

The drive was slow but impressive. Leanne watched out the windows as they drove deeper into the mountains. It was beautiful. The forest was so thick it was dark in places where the sun couldn't break through to the ground below. The leaves were changing to beautiful shades of brown, red, and gold.

Leanne recognized the Rhododendrons that were so prominent in the area. Their leaves were not turning, "I didn't know the Rhododendron was an evergreen."

"Yep."

"Do you know what all the trees are?" asked Leanne.

"I know the common names of most of them, but I'm no biologist," smiled Jacob. Over the next thirty minutes, Leanne asked questions about the trees. Pulling over at Mullins Pond, Jacob pulled the truck over. "This won't take long. I just want to show you one of the early homesteads."

"There's nothing here," said Leanne.

"Not anymore, but in the 1930s, a cabin was here," Jacob pointed to a historical marker. Leanne's love of reading immediately drew her to the marker as she passed Jacob and walked a few feet before him to arrive at the marker first.

"Thirteen children?" Leanne commented.

"This husband and wife team saved a lot of lives during the great depression, and you comment on the number of children they had?" Jacob laughed.

Leanne looked at him and said, "But thirteen?"

"Families were huge here. There were no grocery stores and no cars. People had to grow and raise what they ate. In order to survive, they would have children who would grow up and work on the family farm. The children also took care of their parents in their old age."

Leanne looked around her in awe of the wilderness. She couldn't imagine living so far away from other people. It was peaceful and beautiful but also felt recluse and eerie.

Jacob interrupted her thoughts, "Come on, we're almost to the top."

Jacob and Leanne walked back to the truck and continued the drive up the mountain. From the base, it took nearly thirty minutes to arrive at the top. Jacob stopped the truck in a small parking area. A path led up the mountain. "We walk from here," Jacob smiled.

Leanne loved the short hike to the overlook and took the time to mention the poisoning of Marvin Adler. "So, this is the last walk of the health nut, Marvin Adler."

"Yes, it was."

"Do you see any of the berries he died from?"

"No, I've never seen any here. I've always wondered where he got them and why he decided to eat them up here."

"I swear, Boy Scout, it looks more like a suicide every time we talk about it."

"It was deemed an accidental poisoning by the coroner, so that's what we have to go with," Jacob shrugged his shoulders.

"Why didn't the coroner think it was accidental?" Leanne asked.

"He mentioned several reasons in the autopsy. First, there was no note. Second, people knew he was focused on his health and was always running and eating organic. Lastly, the berries weren't chewed. The coroner thought that if you knew you'd be dead quickly, you wouldn't worry about the bitter taste, and you'd want to make sure the poison entered your system."

"I hate to say it, but that makes sense too," Leanne's face seemed disappointed.

Reaching a plateau in their walk, Leanne looked up to see a large, steel staircase in the middle of the forest. It was mounted against a rock that Leanne estimated to be around six or eight stories tall. It was as if Leanne had stepped into a fairy tale.

The stone was intimidating in size and stood at the top of the mountain as a king, overlooking his territory. The staircase to the left reminded her of the opening to a fairytale land. Leanne began climbing the stairwell in an exhilarated rush but soon started to breathe harder, and she slowed her climb. There were over a hundred and eighty stairs, and Leanne wasn't one to exercise regularly. Jacob followed behind her. Watching her experience at the Tower for the first time was a treat. She smiled and seemed so excited to experience a new place on Earth.

Reaching the top, Leanne was breathing more heavily as she looked out across the mountain tops. The air was unlike anything she had ever seen before. The air was cleaner and almost sweet to the taste as she breathed. On each side of the railings were labels, and she went from one to another, reading each state and looking as far as she could see.

"So, that's Kentucky?" she asked as she pointed.

Jacob gently smiled and said, "Yes."

"And that's West Virginia?" she asked as she pointed in a different direction.

Jacob nodded.

"So, you're telling me I'm looking at five states from one location?" Leanne asked excitedly.

"Yes, you're currently looking at Kentucky, West Virginia, Virginia, North Carolina, and Tennessee. Today is clear, so you can see Ohio, too," Jacob said as he pointed North.

Looking across the multicolored trees, Leanne seemed almost humbled, "This is beautiful."

Jacob never turned his eyes away from her and said, "Yes, it is."

Pretending not to notice the flirtation, Leanne said, "I've never been so close to heaven."

Again, Jacob's eyes never left Leanne as he shook his head and said, "Neither have I."

Leanne raised her hand as if to touch the clouds. After a moment, she said, "I have to get pictures!"

She snapped photos of every state and then turned toward Jacob, "Come on, Boy Scout! Give me a pose!"

Leanne laughed, and Jacob couldn't help himself. He folded his arms across his chest, stood proud, and smiled at her. Leanne immediately looked at the photo. Leanne wasn't sure what was more provocative, his broad shoulders or boyish grin. "Okay. I'm ready to go when you are."

Reaching the base of the stairwell, Leanne leaned over and rubbed her legs for a moment.

"You might be a little sore tomorrow," Jacob commented.

"Well, I don't work out like you do," Leanne snipped.

"Glad you noticed," Jacob smiled a cocky smile.

"How could I not, Towel Boy!" Leanne laughed.

As they walked down the mountain towards the parking area, Jacob began the conversation, "So, I have a hypothetical question."

Leanne glanced toward him but focused on the path to ensure she didn't lose her footing, "You can ask anything, but it's my choice whether I answer."

"It's a hypothetical question, and since we're alone, if I ever tell anyone you said it, you can just call me a liar," Jacob smiled.

"Okay, what's the question?"

"If a girl like you knew a guy like me in New York, do you think that girl might go out with him?"

Leanne looked at Jacob and grinned, "She might. You never know."

"Good, because I may have to go to New York to get a date. You got any single friends or work colleagues?" Jacob smiled that mischievous and charming smile again.

"Oh! You want to be set up? I can set you up…" Leanne's expression was menacing.

"Now, I'm afraid to ask with whom…." Jacob laughed.

"Oh, trust me, I'd set you up with dates you'd never forget, and you'd never admit!" Leanne laughed.

Reaching the parking area, Leanne noticed a sign that said Jenny Falls, "Where's that go?" she asked.

"There's a waterfall about two miles out. It's almost time for the barbeque, so I'd better take you back to the hotel. Katie said something about picking you up right after work."

Leanne smiled as she climbed into the passenger seat of his old truck, and they started down the mountain. Jacob still wasn't sure whether she was interested in him or not. So far, it didn't look good, but he might be starting to grow on her.

Chapter 14

Jacob arrived at his mother's house an hour later. His father met him in the driveway with a cold beer, "Glad you changed clothes. We don't want no cops around here tonight!"

Jacob laughed because it was apparent that his father was already drinking. Jack drank a few beers occasionally but was far from an alcoholic. Jacob estimated that it was his father's fourth beer, and by the time he finished the sixth, he would be sitting in a chair somewhere, sound asleep.

"Smells good, Dad," Jacob commented as he breathed in through his nose and walked into the backyard.

"Oh, you know that's not me. Your mama and Aunt Helen have used that smoker to its fullest potential the last two days."

The two men walked into the backyard, and Jack proudly reported, "The lights are my contribution."

Jacob was amazed. The backyard was beautifully lit with what seemed like millions of tiny, hanging lights. "You outdid yourself, Dad." Jacob smiled.

The backyard was already beginning to fill. Jacob noticed Blaine Kiser bringing Linda a Pepsi from a cooler. Charlie Kiser, Ol' man Mullins, Cletus Colley, and Mr. Pucket were all gathered near a tree in the backyard telling stories and laughing. Maribeth, Jacob's mother, Helen, Arlene Yates, and Beverly Burke sat around a picnic table sharing gossip. Richard Thane, Ricky Plank, Mark Huffine, Grant Mullins, and Happy Kilgore sat on the back porch, each holding a guitar, banjo, or fiddle, except for Happy. Happy had a harmonica with a foot drum placed at his feet.

People were everywhere. Tables borrowed from the local churches held more food than Jacob had seen in a long while. Aunt Helen and his mother had outdone themselves, and it seemed like everyone in the county was attending the last event of the year.

Jacob felt a hand on his shoulder and turned to see Scott, "Glad you made it."

"I had to be here. I have to be threatened by your dad tonight," smiled Scott.

"Oh, it's not a threat, old buddy. It's a promise. Dad will kill you, and I'd have to lose the evidence to stay in the family. So, please, treat Katie like a princess."

"You act like she's not one," Scott said as he raised an eyebrow at Jacob.

"She used to compete in fart competitions with me," replied Jacob.

"That doesn't mean she's not a princess. It means you're mad because you lost to a girl," smiled Scott.

"Where is she anyhow?" asked Jacob.

"Katie and Leanne are getting ready at Aunt Helen's house. Leanne kept saying she didn't know what to wear, and Katie said she would loan her some clothes," Scott pointed up the road.

From their right, Jacob and Scott heard the twang of a banjo, and the impromptu band began to play an old tune named *An Unclouded Day*. Scott leaned over toward Jacob and whispered, "It's not just bluegrass. It's gospel bluegrass."

"They're not bad…" retorted Jacob, "especially considering they've never even played together before."

"Did someone bring a speaker for my cell phone?"

"I don't know. Besides, even if you don't like it, it's appropriate," Jacob patted his foot.

"You don't listen to bluegrass."

"No, but it's early. Later, I'll go get a speaker, and you can Bluetooth your phone into it."

"Sounds good," Scott nodded contentedly.

Ronnie Thane and Ricky Plank walked by and stopped to shake hands and say hello to Scott and Jacob on their way to grab drinks from a nearby cooler.

The band began to play *Chief Sitting Bull*, led by Grant Mullins on the banjo. It was more upbeat than the previous song, and Jacob noticed Scott tapping his foot. Several people began to flatfoot.

Not wanting to lose momentum, Happy Kilgore yelled out to Penelope and beckoned her to the porch. Penelope willingly sang the words to *Rocky Top* as the band played. Everyone was clapping to the music or flat footing. The entire crowd enjoyed her singing.

Just as the song ended, Jacob heard Scott's stunned voice say, "God help us!"

Jacob turned his head and saw Katie and Leanne arriving fashionably late. Jacob's jaw dropped as he focused on Leanne, wearing one of Katie's blue jean skirts and a tight, white tank top. Katie was wearing a knee-length blue dress with a floral print.

As the two approached, the band began to play *Lonesome Pine*. Taking Katie's hand, Scott said, "My God, you're beautiful!" and started slow dancing with her as she laughed.

Jacob watched his cousin laugh and was happy she and Scott had found each other. Looking at Leanne, Jacob looked down and said, "Glad to see you two again."

Leanne gave him a confused glance, "Two?"

"I wasn't talking to you. I was talking to your legs," smiled Jacob.

Leanne rolled her eyes and said, "Are you going to ask me to dance before Cletus Colley grabs Pastor Mark off the porch to perform a wedding?"

Jacob laughed and led her to an area where people were dancing.

"What's this song? I've never heard music like this," Leanne asked.

"It's bluegrass. The song is *Lonesome Pine*," replied Jacob.

Jacob tried to focus on the music, but Leanne's body gently moved against him. Her perfume wafted under his nose, and he could feel the warmth of her body. He knew that Leanne was leaving and they would never be a couple, but his body was in an argument with his mind, and Jacob fought hard not to lose his heart during the argument.

As they danced, Jacob looked around the room and tried to keep his mind off how wonderful it felt to hold Leanne in his arms. Arlene and Carol Yates were dancing a few feet away from them, and Jacob looked around to find their children playing on his and Isaac's old swing set with Lyle Brantley's two daughters. Lyle was dancing with his wife, and Jacob was amused to see he wasn't wearing a tie. Jacob noticed that Blaine Kiser was still very happy dating Linda, and they were both slow dancing together, and Kim Reynolds was dancing with her father, Dr. Reynolds.

Theresa Barton and Marlene Branham were standing near a tree holding two babies. Jacob wondered who the babies belonged to. Then, he remembered that Tabitha, who worked with his Aunt Helen at Dr. Reynolds' office had recently given birth, but no one had mentioned she had given birth to twins.

The music stopped, and the band started playing a faster song named *Mountain Dew*. Grant Mullins started the song with his banjo, and Mark Huffine sang the words. Many remained on the makeshift dance floor and began to flatfoot. Leanne stood with Jacob for only a moment watching the people around her. "What are they doing?" she asked.

"It's called flatfooting," Jacob replied and laughed. "That means it's our turn to walk to the side and watch and clap for them."

"I want to try it!" Leanne laughed and stepped beside Aunt Helen.

Jacob returned to Scott's side and watched from the side of the crowd. "What a preacher we got here…" laughed Jacob, "Gospel music on Sunday morning after singing about moonshine on Saturday night."

"He's just singing it because Jesus ain't here to do it himself," laughed Scott, "I recall something about Jesus enjoying a good party, too."

They both stood silent, watching Leanne, until Scott leaned toward Jacob, shook his head, and said, "She ain't from here," in a southern accent.

"She definitely is not," replied Jacob with a smile.

"That looks like she's having a seizure while standing upright," Scott commented.

Both men tried not to laugh as Aunt Helen held her hand and attempted to show her how to move her feet to the rhythm of the music. Everyone was enjoying themselves, and several were whooping and hollering to the music.

Someone announced that dinner was ready, and Leanne was more than happy to sit down and stop making a fool of herself. Scott and Katie had already grabbed a plate and were sitting at a large picnic table across from Maribeth and Helen. Leanne made a plate and sat down beside Katie. Directly across from her, Jack and Sara sat near Maribeth and Helen, leaving one empty seat. After a few moments, Jacob sat down in the open seat beside Leanne.

From the moment Jack sat down, he stared at Scott with a menacing look, "Do you have something you'd like to ask me, son?"

"Actually, yes sir, I do," replied Scott in an almost frail voice.

Jack leaned in to listen more intently to the muscled young man who stood six foot five inches tall, "Well, what is it?"

"Sir, Katie wants to date me, and I'm afraid of you so, I keep telling her no but, she won't leave me alone, and I don't know what to do," Scott spurted out.

Jacob choked on his Pepsi and ended up spitting it out on the ground to keep from choking to death.

"Jacob McKinney! Stop acting foolish!" his mother chastised.

"Sorry, Mom, I got choked," Jacob replied, trying to cover his laughter.

The conversation turned back to Jack McKinney, who looked at his niece, "Katie, honey, do you like this young man?"

"Yes, I do, Uncle Jack. He's very nice, and he's good-looking," Katie nodded.

"Well then, son, you're stuck. Katie gets what Katie wants, and you're going to have to date her whether you like it or not."

Scott pretended to be disappointed for a moment but then smiled at Katie and said, "Well, Sir, if you say I have to, I'll man up about it."

After the main course, Maribeth and Helen began discussing color schemes for the quilt they would be sewing together. Scott and Katie stood up to dance again.

"Aren't you going to have dessert?" asked Jacob.

"Man, don't you know I brought my own dessert?" Scott wrapped his arm around Katie's waist and pulled her closer to his side.

"Dang! It used to be gross before you dated Katie, and now it's worse!" Jacob grimaced, "That's my cousin, dude!"

Leanne and Sara laughed at Jacob's reaction to the flirtation.

Before long, Scott and Katie were missing. Leanne covered by telling everyone they had probably gone to get more ice. Cat and Duncan had arrived late, but there was still plenty left to eat, and as Cat was having dessert, Jacob noticed Duncan speaking with a group of older gentlemen near the porch. The band had taken a break, and a conversation had begun. As Jacob walked over to see what the public discussion was about, he noticed his dad sound asleep in a rocking chair on the porch. Jacob smiled as he thought to himself, 'Sixth beer always does it.'

Jacob walked over to the group of men and listened briefly before Charlie Kiser asked, "You done with that crazy stuff yet, Jake?"

Jacob smiled and said, "What crazy stuff?"

"Researching all those dang accidents! It's time you be our sheriff and stop all the shenanigans from the past." Charlie was never one to mince words.

"Well, Leanne's been helping, and it's done. We can't find anything," Jacob said. "Seems like weird stuff just happens here."

Happy Kilgore broke into the conversation, "Well, accidents or not, I'm glad it happened. Makes me feel safer knowing those people don't last long here."

"Just so I know where I stand with you gentlemen, if I had found evidence that it was murders, what would you have done?" asked Jacob.

"We sure as hell wouldn't have voted you back into the office," Charlie bluntly stated as the men around him nodded their heads.

Cletus Colley spoke up and said, "If you'd a caught somebody, I'd 'a claimed it was me until you let them go!" Charlie Kiser, Grant Mullins, Carol Yates, Happy Kilgore, and even Duncan were all nodding their heads.

"Looks like you'd have a lot of work if you arrested someone for that crime, Sheriff," Duncan said.
From the corner of the porch, a voice was heard with slurred speech, "I did it." Jack had woken during the conversation.

"What you do, Dad?" asked Jacob as he smiled at his father.

"I killed them. I killed every one of them." There was a small, quiet pause, "Who were they again?" Jack asked.

"No one, Dad," Jacob replied as he shook his head, smiled, and continued, "So, no one wants me to catch a serial murderer?"

Cat walked up to stand beside Duncan as the conversation continued. Charlie Kiser spoke first, saying, "If it's not accidents and there's a supposed killer, that person isn't a murderer but the county hero!" All the men were nodding.

"Well, my failure in finding any evidence should make you feel better," Jacob said as he felt a hand on his shoulder. He turned to see Leanne and smiled.

"You're going to have to drive me to the hotel. My ride ran off with your best friend," Leanne smiled at the men.

"I'll be glad to," smiled Jacob. "Are you ready now?"

"Aunt Helen won't let me help clean up, and the party is winding down, so when you're done speaking with these good-looking men, I'm ready." Leanne smiled at the men, and everyone smiled back and stood a little taller.

"Well, gentlemen, I think every one of you would whoop me for leaving this lady waiting, so I'll head out. Good night, everyone." Jacob smiled, and as he and Leanne walked away, he whispered to her, "That's the second time you've saved my ass."

"It looked intense, so I thought I'd help," replied Leanne.

Jacob and Leanne walked to where he was parked. Instead of driving a county vehicle, Jacob had driven his old work truck to his parent's house. The parking area could be seen from the backyard. As Jacob walked around the truck, he heard Leanne's voice, "Boy Scout, I have a problem." Leanne was standing beside the open truck door.

"What is it?" asked Jacob.

"I can't get in."

"What do you mean you can't get in?" asked Jacob, confused.

"Katie's skirt is too tight on me, and I can't lift my leg into the truck without showing my underwear."

"How did you get into Katie's Jeep?"

"We were alone. Everyone in the backyard can see me," Leanne said as she nodded to the right to show Jacob that people could see them. "Besides, I'm not pulling my skirt up in front of you!"

Jacob smiled a large, charming smile. Placing his arm on the head of the truck and his head on his closed hand, he asked mischievously, "So, what you wanna do?"

"Well, my only two choices are to get Helen to drive me in her old blue Datsun, or you lift me into the truck."

Jacob walked around to the side of the truck where Leanne stood. He looked deeply into her eyes and said, "I just needed you to say it."

Leanne couldn't help but notice his strong arms and chest as he bent over slightly and placed one arm beneath her knees as the other wrapped around her back. He lifted her effortlessly into his pickup seat and closed the door. The passenger window was slightly rolled down, and she heard cheering from the backyard. Looking over, all the older gentlemen were cheering Jacob on, and he waved triumphantly at the men.

As Jacob stepped into the truck and pressed the clutch, Leanne said, "That was embarrassing…."

Jacob threw the truck into first gear and said, "Not for me," with a smile.

The next morning, Jacob arrived at the hotel at ten a.m. to pick up Leanne and drive her to the airport. He was met by Katie, Aunt Helen, his parents, Scott, and Cat, all stopping by to wish her safe travels. Aunt Helen was especially upset.

"You'll be back at the end of next month, right?" Aunt Helen asked as she touched Leanne's hair.

"I'll be back for Thanksgiving. I promise," Leanne consoled her.

Jacob hadn't realized how close they had all become until that moment. Leanne had spent a lot of time with him, and he was fond of her, but his family had adopted a new niece and daughter.

After saying good-byes, Leanne picked up her suitcase and said, "Come on, Boy Scout. We can't miss the plane."

The nearest airport was in Blountville, Tennessee, and the drive took nearly two hours. During the drive, Jacob and Leanne made small talk about the Vice President job that Leanne might be offered and her life in New York.

"I hate to tell you this, Slick," began Jacob, "But that seems like a poor life to me."

"What do you mean?"
"Well, I guess it depends on how you define rich and poor. If you own a hundred cars, are you rich?"

"I think you'd have to be."

"What if cars are sold for only a penny?" asked Jacob.

"Well, that means they're not valuable, so you're not rich, right?"

"In that scenario, you're right."

"So, rich and poor are defined by the value of something you own and are not in debt for, right?"

Leanne nodded as she thought, "That's a good definition."

"So, how valuable is friendship, love, kindness, and family?" asked Jacob. "You can't buy those things no matter how much money you make. That's the definition of rich."

Leanne sat quietly for a moment and finished the discussion by saying, "I'll have to think about what kind of rich I want."

Arriving at the airport, Jacob carried Leanne's bags and waited as she checked in for the flight. Leanne turned to walk toward the loading area. Turning toward Jacob, she said, "I'll be back for Thanksgiving."

Jacob's stomach was in knots, and his chest felt like a small horse had made its home on his rib cage, "I know," he said stoically.

"Thank you for letting me help with the investigation. You'll have to call me if more information develops."

"I will. Thank you for saving my life," Jacob responded.

Jacob wanted to kiss her so badly that he was nearly shaking. He wanted to take her into his arms and kiss her so hard that she never wanted to leave. But he thought about it and knew she didn't have feelings like that for him and controlled himself.

From nowhere, Leanne wrapped her arms around his neck and hugged him. Jacob responded by hugging her back, and Leanne kissed his cheek as they released the hug. He had seen her do the same thing to his family before she left them. She considered him to be a brother. Jacob had too much respect for women and wouldn't attempt to change her feelings for him. She wasn't interested in him, which was the end.

Over the next month and a half, Jacob kept himself busy by helping with weekend events. Haysi's Autumn Fest was always a big event in the county, with car shows, food trucks, games, and events. Jacob worked the entire weekend. Clintwood would have townwide events the following week, and Clinchco would be the third week. The last week of the month, the Breaks Park would have Halloween events and trunk or treating.

Jacob worked more hours than usual. Sara and Maribeth became concerned and asked Katie and Scott to check on him when he missed more than one family dinner over the next month. Walking into the office one morning, Katie asked Cat, "Where's Jake?"

"He's delivering subpoenas."

"That's a job he had when he started working at the Sheriff's office. Doesn't he have anyone else to do that job?"

"Only about five others. He sent them out on patrol," Cat answered with a disdained look.

"What's going on with him?" Katie asked.

"I'm beginning to believe he's trying to work himself into an early grave. He was here until two a.m. last night," Cat replied.

"Aunt Sara and Mom sent me to see what was going on. Why is he working so much?" Katie asked.

"I have no idea. All I know is that if someone wants time off right now, Jacob doesn't get someone to cover the shift, he covers it himself. I'm hoping the Board of Supervisors doesn't get wind of how much money he's saving the county in labor and decide to cut back the money going into the Sheriff's office. I can't get him to take a day off," Cat sounded defeated.

"Would you like to hear my theory?" asked Katie.

"You'd be one of the few with a good one," replied Cat.

"I think he's missing Leanne. This didn't start until right after she left. He's always worked long hours, but this is getting ridiculous."

"He doesn't seem depressed or upset. In fact, he's been acting like regular, normal Jake."

"And how long has Jake been hiding his feelings behind his badge?" asked Katie raising an eyebrow.

"Crap, you're right. Have you talked to Leanne?"

"I talk to her almost every night. She said Jake's not called or texted her or anything. She said she tried calling the office three or four times, but Jake was always out on a call when she called."

"So, any ideas on what to do with him?" asked Cat.

"None," Katie replied.

"He's not hurting anyone. Think we should just let this play out until Leanne comes back for Thanksgiving?"

"And then what? Will it end because she visits one time?"

Cat and Katie sat quietly for a moment, and Maribeth walked into the office.

"What's got you two worked up? You two look like you're doing math problems in your heads!"

"We're trying to figure out how to get Jake's mind off of Leanne."

"Well, why on earth would you do that?" Maribeth exclaimed.

"Because he's working himself to death trying to keep his mind off of her," Katie said.

"Child!" The older woman said as she shook her head, "Men are strange creatures. He's battling something in his own mind. Working is his release from that battle. At work, he knows his place; he has goals, and he can focus on what's important to him. Right now, he doesn't know his place in Leanne's life or if he has one. I think he wants a place in her life but doesn't recognize the niche he needs to fill. Taking him away from his work right now could be a bad idea because Jake needs to feel like he has a place."

"Can't he just be happy filling the 'niche' every other man fills?" Cat stated unapologetically.

Maribeth shook her head and said, "Some men love with their hearts first. That's true love."

After a moment of silence while Maribeth's profound words sunk in, Katie said, "Well, Cat, you can tell Jake that if he's not at dinner this evening, I'm sending Scott to retrieve him!"

"That makes me want to not tell him. I'd love to watch Scott come in here and throw him over his shoulder and haul him out!" laughed Cat.

"Well, I've gotta run to work. Let me know when you see him, Cat."

"Sure will, Katie," Cat replied as Katie left.

Cat stood up, and Maribeth took her usual seat, "Thank you for keeping an eye on things this morning. I think I found the perfect material for the wedding quilt this morning," Maribeth smiled.

"You're welcome. I didn't have anyone scheduled this early at the shop anyhow. Have a good day," Cat replied as she headed out the door.

Nearly a month had passed since Leanne had left, and Jacob had not made contact with her. When Jacob received the autopsy report from the state lab on Richard Talbert, he remembered promising to call her once he received the report but decided to call her from home because it was getting late, and he didn't want to call her during work hours. Opening the file, the cause of death was just as Leanne had said. Richard Talbert had died of asphyxiation due to Chlorine Gas poisoning. Jacob thought back to the day before Leanne had left. Jacob fought the urge to think about her. He laid the file at the edge of his desk and focused on creating a work schedule for the department through the next month.

Jacob arrived home around eight p.m. He was tired, but knowing he would be calling Leanne gave him a sense of excitement and fear simultaneously. He wanted to talk to her. He had missed the sound of her voice since the moment he left her at the airport. He missed her smile and missed her laughter. Jacob knew he had feelings for her but also knew it was a recipe for disaster. He wouldn't move to New York, and Leanne wasn't interested in being involved with a small county Sheriff.

He had to give her credit, though. She didn't flirt or make him feel like he had a chance. She had made it quite clear that she wasn't interested. At this point, Jacob was thankful that she treated him like a close friend. He smiled as he remembered her in his living room wearing that long tee shirt, no makeup, and wet hair. He smiled again when he remembered her hugging him while he was covered in what they referred to as mud after wrestling Jr.

To Jacob, Leanne was smart, beautiful, and funny. Jacob cared for her, and he wished he could hate her. He wished he could at least like her less because, maybe, just maybe, it would stop him from feeling the pain he had been feeling since she left. The pain he felt was like someone had removed something, and there was a gaping hole left inside him.

Jacob sat down on the couch where he had fallen asleep beside Leanne and pulled his cell phone from his pocket and scrolled through the contacts. Touching her number, he placed the phone to his ear and waited.

Three rings later, he heard Leanne's voice say, "Hello?"

"Hi, I got the autopsy report today."

Leanne sighed, "About time. I thought you'd forgotten about me."

"No, I just didn't have anything to report," Jacob replied casually.

"So, was I right?"

"I'll probably never hear the end of it, but yes, you were."

"I knew it!" Leanne sounded excited.

"Did Cap ever find anyone to match the scent?" asked Leanne.

"Nope, and Kevin's had him at every Halloween event in the county. That dog's smelled everyone." Jacob laughed and said, "Cap even ran over to Aunt Helen and sniffed her dress pocket. I almost fainted before I watched her pull a dog treat out of her pocket for him. He licked her hand and moved on." Jacob and Leanne both laughed.

There it was. Leanne's laugh always made his heart jump and put butterflies in his stomach.

"So, have they decided on the VP job yet?" Jacob asked her in the hopes that he would have to console her.

"I start on December first," was the unexpected reply.

"Oh, well, I guess I should say congratulations," Jacob stammered.

"I'll still be visiting for Thanksgiving, but it'll probably be a while before I can visit again. I'll have a lot more work and responsibilities now."

Jacob could hear the excitement in Leanne's voice as she spoke, "Well, I'm sure Scott and Katie are planning trips up there to visit."

"I've not told Katie yet. I'm going to tell her when I see her because I want her and Scott to come up and see the New York Christmas lights with me one weekend. Think you'll be able to visit, too?" Leanne asked cheerfully.

"I guess, it's according to the schedule. I've been working a lot lately," Jacob replied, but he knew he'd never go to New York to see Leanne. They were living two different lives. She had lost interest in moving to Dickenson County, and he was responsible for fourteen thousand people. He wouldn't leave, and Leanne was happily climbing the corporate ladder. His heart was breaking, but he remained calm. Leanne had never led him on or shown any interest in him. So, it wasn't her fault that he had fallen for her.

"Katie told me she was worried about you working so much," Leanne replied. "I told her that I hoped it wasn't because spending time with me had put you behind in your work."

Jacob's mind flashed back on the memories of Leanne for a moment, and the pain in his chest became worse, "Oh no, not at all. It was great having you out there with me. I'm just working a lot to give the deputies time off when they need it. Besides, it's good to be with the people."

"I'm glad. I miss it, you know?" Leanne gently said.

"Miss what?" Jacob asked.

"I miss the people, the work we were doing, your family, everything…." Leanne stated sadly.

"Oh, don't worry, you can cuddle up every night with a pillow full of those nice fat paychecks and know you did the right thing," Jacob tried to make the statement sound comforting but had failed. "I'm sorry, I didn't mean it like it sounded. I just meant that you love your work and are now paid what you deserve. I can't speak for your editing skills, but I know you're a great researcher."

"I didn't take offense. I knew exactly what you meant. It's a little lonely up here. I'm glad you called Boy Scout."

"Me, too," Jacob smiled.

"Oh, I was going to tell you, I printed your picture and framed it. It's on my desk at work," Leanne laughed.

"Why on earth would you do something like that?" Jacob laughed.

"Two reasons; first, no one ever asks me out anymore. So, I'm not bothered. The men just look at the eight-by-ten and walk away." Leanne laughed.

"Why do they do that?" Jacob asked, confused.

"They don't make country boys in New York, Boy Scout. You're intimidating," Leanne laughed.

Jacob shook his head and asked, "So, what's the second reason?"

"I am the envy of every woman in the office, and several have asked me if every man in Dickenson County looked like you," Leanne laughed, "Of course, I had to tell them yes, and you were actually one of the ugly ones. So, you might get an influx of female tourists next summer."

Jacob laughed at Leanne's way of advertising the county.

They talked a little while longer about Leanne's new job and events Jacob had attended during Halloween until Jacob couldn't handle hearing her voice and laughter any longer. His heart was aching, and he could no longer tolerate the pain.

"Well, I hate to hop off, but I had a long shift today, and I have one coming up tomorrow, so I'd better hit the sack."

"Okay. Well, be careful, Boy Scout, and I'll talk to you later."

They both said their good-byes, and Jacob put down the cell phone. He entered the kitchen, poured himself a large glass of straight whiskey, and then walked back into the living room. Sitting down on the couch, he pointed the remote toward the television and said, "Well, Scarlett, I guess it's you and me again."

Chapter 15

Jacob's hours didn't slow down at work until Isaac returned home for Thanksgiving. Isaac's flight landed the day before Thanksgiving, and his parents and Aunt Helen had all driven to the airport to pick him up. Jacob was glad not to attend the reunion. He knew that his mother and Aunt Helen would be sobbing and hugging Isaac as if they had nearly lost him forever. He also knew that the almost three-hour car ride would include questions about every facet of Isaac's life, up to and including Isaac's daily flossing routine. Jacob was not in the mood to hear it.

Jacob was thinking about having someone stage a fake dead body that he had to deal with or fake an accident, but he knew that Scott would be attending his first McKinney Thanksgiving, and he would get caught trying to get out of the dinner. He and Isaac were still single, so they would receive the traditional interrogation from their mother and Aunt Helen while everyone talked about Scott and Katie being the perfect couple. Leanne would be there, and he'd have to listen to her laugh, and his chest hurt most of the night. Nothing good would come from tomorrow's dinner, and Jacob was grumpy about it. The only thing that Jacob looked forward to at this year's Thanksgiving was pie.

On Thanksgiving morning, the phone rang early. Checking the screen, he realized it was Katie. "What?" Jacob answered.

"I think I know something that might cheer your grouchy ass up," Katie said in a sing-song voice.

"Seriously?" Jacob's voice was even grouchy.

"Yeah, why don't you drive down and pick up Leanne instead of me and Scott?" Katie waited on a reply. "Jake?" "Jake?" Katie looked at Scott, "He hung up on me!"

Scott laughed and said, "Told ya so," as they walked out the door to get into the car.

Jacob went back to bed, and his mother called around noon, "Why are you not here yet?" was her opening statement as he picked up the phone.

"Because Isaac's staying for a week, and I want to get more sleep," Jacob stated grumpily.

Sara's voice lowered in pitch and tone. It was a sound that Jacob knew not to oppose in any way. "Young man, you'd better consider who you are speaking to! I hear the tone in your voice! You will be in this house in one hour! Do you understand me?"

"Yes, ma'am," was the only reply Jacob was allowed to give and did so compliantly.

An hour later, Jacob was shaking his little brother's hand, wearing an old tee shirt with stains and a hole in it and blue jeans that were old enough to be perfectly comfortable and perfect for the trash can at the same time. Jacob also hadn't shaved since yesterday morning and was beginning to grow a five-o'clock shadow.

Isaac took the opportunity to pull Jacob in for a hug when they shook hands. Isaac was younger than Jacob but had outgrown him by two inches. Isaac's hair was black and cut short. While Jacob followed the McKinney genetics line, Isaac followed the Lesters. Isaac's skin and hair were darker, he was taller, and the McKinney blue eyes showed up on

Isaac more than Jacob because of his skin tones. Where Jacob was tanned, Isaac was olive complexioned.

Sara walked through from the kitchen wearing an apron. She looked at Jacob and sighed. She shouted, "Jack, go get the little rebel one of your button-up shirts!" Sara was accustomed to Jacob's small acts of childish rebellion and was always able to handle them with grace.

"You mad because Scott and Katie just left to get Leanne, and she's been waiting at the airport because they thought you were going to get her?"

Jacob immediately jumped out of his grouchy state and said, "What?" His tone was excited and upset at the same time.

"Thought so," replied Isaac. "I'm b.s.ing you, Leanne's at Aunt Helen's with Scott and Katie already. They're getting a few desserts ready."

"What the hell, Isaac?" Jacob whispered, not wanting to upset his mother again today.

"Katie said you were working all the time since the first of October. Mom said you were grouchy this morning. I just put two and two together. Man, you got it bad!"

"I don't know what you're talking about!" Jacob looked toward the kitchen.

"Mom's not listening, and Dad's outside." Isaac knew what his brother was looking for when he looked toward the kitchen.

"Listen, Isaac, Leanne has made it clear, crystal clear; she's not interested in me."

"Thank God for that! I heard she's hot!" Isaac smiled. "Care if I take a shot?"

"Yes, I care if you take a shot!" Jacob was yelling at his little brother while keeping his voice low enough that it did not disturb his mother.

"Good, I knew you wouldn't care if the younger, smarter McKinney tried to get her into the family," Isaac slapped Jacob on the shoulder and walked into the kitchen to see if Sara needed help.

Jacob sat down in front of the television. Jack walked through the house and threw a button-up shirt on Jacob's lap and sat down in a recliner to watch the football game with Jacob. Neither man spoke for the next two hours, with the exception of grunts and sounds of excitement for touchdowns.

Aunt Helen, Scott, Katie, Leanne, and Maribeth arrived at his mother's house around four that evening. Isaac and Scott helped the ladies carry desserts while Jacob and his father sat on the couch watching the football game. At one point, Jacob looked over at his father and said, "Dad, I want to be just like you when I grow up."

Jack McKinney smiled and replied, "Good job, son."

At five o'clock, Jacob heard his mother say, "Jack, you and Jake come in and sit down. We're saying grace."

"You'd better put that shirt on, or she'll have a fit," Jack warned his son as they stood up.

"Fine, but I'm not buttoning it." Jacob retaliated by putting the brown and gray plaid shirt over his arms.

Jack walked into the dining room first and sat down at one end of the table. The additional company meant that Jacob had nowhere to sit. Jacob said, "I'll just grab a plate and head to the living room."

"No, sir!" demanded Sara. "Isaac, scoot a little closer to Leanne and make room for your brother."

Isaac smiled and moved his chair so close to Leanne that their legs touched. Jacob grabbed a stool from the kitchen and sat beside his brother at the corner of the table.

Jack said grace, and everyone began to fill their plates.

"Leanne, I love your perfume," Isaac commented as he leaned toward her.

No one had moved, but a thud was heard under the table, and a "grmp" noise escaped Isaac's lips.

"Isaac, are you alright?" Sara asked.

"Yes, Mom, I am just excited about eating home cooking. It's been too long."

"Aww, that's my baby boy!" Sara smiled and doted.

Isaac took the lead in the table conversation, "So, Leanne, I've heard most of the story, you came down from New York because of Aunt Helen's short stories, and we've now adopted you. Is that pretty much it?" smiled Isaac charmingly.

"Yes, well, except that I tried to help Jacob solve a mystery," Leanne said, being cordial.

"Really? What mystery?"

Jacob swallowed the bite he had been chewing and said, "No proof, no crime, no mystery," as he shook his head.

"Ignore him. He has no imagination," Isaac smiled and cast a wandering look down Leanne's body and continued, "At least, not one as big as mine." Again, "grmp" came from Isaac's throat, and everyone looked confused. "Sorry, I choked a little. This is delicious, Mom."

Sara smiled.

"So, what's this about a mystery?" asked Isaac.

Katie interrupted and began with the visit from Gloria Winters and ended the story when Leanne visited, and she and Aunt Helen were working and couldn't spend time with her.

Leanne then began to tell her side of the story and concluded with, "And, it's like Jacob said, No proof, no crime, no mystery." Leanne shrugged her shoulders.

Isaac leaned back in his chair and said, "Well, you covered all the bases by re-visiting each crime scene. That was good. But, instead of looking at it from the point of view of each crime and trying to paste scenarios together to find a suspect, did you two try to investigate from the point of view that you are certain there is a serial killer, and you're trying to find suspects?"

Jacob wrinkled his eyebrows and said, "Why would we do that if we have no proof that these are even murders?"

Everyone at the table sat quietly as Isaac and Jacob argued.

"Jake, I just finished Behavioral Analysis at Quantico, and there's some great information that might come into play here," Isaac was trying to be sincere. Still, Jacob took it as him showing off in front of Leanne.

Jacob rolled his eyes as Isaac continued, "First, did you ever think about how old the suspect would have to be?"

Jacob sighed and said, "We estimated that, if there were such a person, they would have to be over forty years old."

"That's great!" said Isaac as he leaned over to Leanne.

"Was there anything that made you think male or female?" asked Isaac.

Katie interrupted and said, "The arrow! It was too short to be a man's arrow."

"Or it was an experienced hunter that knew we'd be looking and chose a short arrow purposely!" retaliated Jacob.

"So, if they were murders, were they planned out and organized or by the seat of their pants?"

Everyone at the table nodded and agreed that the accidents were very well planned.

Isaac continued, "The organized killer is the hardest to identify and catch, which probably explains why all the kills look like accidents. The killer would be extremely intelligent and meticulous. They plan out every detail of the crime in advance, and the killer takes every precaution to ensure they don't leave incriminating evidence behind. It is common for this person to watch their next victim for several days to find someone they consider a good target. It matches the accidents of every victim."

Isaac paused for a moment and then continued, "The thing that makes me wonder about the organization level is that organized serial killers usually hide a body. The organized serial killer takes pride in their work. They listen and watch news stories about their crimes. Stumping law enforcement might even be a motivation. If this is organized killings, it doesn't follow the regular behavioral psychology."

"That's because there's no serial killer. It has to be coincidences," Jacob replied.

"Oh no!" interjected Katie, "I just realized we're all thinking it's just one person. What if it's not?"

"What do you mean, honey?" asked Scott.

"What if it's a team or even a group of people? I have no doubt that the older men in the Clinchco Kiwanis group could pull this off."

Jacob laughed for the first time that evening, "What did they do to tick you off?"

"No, seriously, they all love children and are always doing good things for kids! I know they're smart and hardworking men." Katie whispered, "It could be a group conspiracy!"

Jacob continued to laugh, and Scott hid his amusement with a hand over the grin on his face.

"I think it's the protective hand of God," Aunt Helen chimed into the conversation. "We don't have much in this county, but God cares for our kids!"

Isaac continued, building on the previous statements, "Now, the victims. In this case, victims are people on the sexual offender registry. Who would want to kill people on the registry the most?"

Scott took his part in the conversation, "I'd say someone who had been sexually abused. It might be a revenge thing."

Isaac nodded, "Good point. Research has shown us that revenge might be a more powerful motive for a serial killer than profit or psychosis because serial killers target people who display characteristics of someone they despise."

Jack had been sitting quietly, "What about some kind of religious nut?"

Isaac nodded, "That's a visionary serial killer, Dad. They suffer from psychotic breaks from reality and are compelled to murder by entities like the Devil or God. Many times, these people suffer from religious delusions or hyper religiosity."

Jacob finally began participating in the discussion and said, "So, we're looking for a motive, right?"

"Yes, but it's a motive that affects a specific group of people."

"What if it's about protecting children?" asked Jacob.

"That would open up the possibilities of the killer being a teacher, someone in the medical field, a parent, pretty much anyone who loves children," Isaac added.

"Son, you just pinpointed your entire family and almost ninety-nine percent of the community. I thought we were trying to narrow the search down, not add to it," replied Jack.

"It could be anyone," Leanne stated quietly.

"Is there no way we can narrow this down farther?" asked Katie.

"There are four types of serial killers: visionary, mission-oriented, hedonistic, and power/control-oriented. Based on what you've told me, this one seems to be mission-oriented. Whether it has anything to do with religion is difficult to tell."

"Are we looking for a recluse?" asked Scott.

"A majority are not. They're good at blending in with the community and have families, homes, and jobs. It's 'cause they blend in so effortlessly, that they're often overlooked."

"Do we have any way of knowing? Something strange or unusual we should look for?" asked Katie.

"Well, we have the Hare's Psychopathy Checklist," replied Isaac.

"What's that?" asked Leanne.

"It's a checklist of psychopathic personality traits that many serial killers display. Many times, they have a superficial charm, they are egocentric, prone to boredom, they're pathological liars, and they lack sincerity. They have no guilt, emotional depth, or empathy. They are short-tempered and have early behavior problems. They're impulsive and irresponsible parents."

Jacob laughed, "None of that makes sense. If we have a serial killer, someone needs to tell them that they're doing it wrong. Our killer kills people like that."

"Aunt Helen, is something wrong?" Leanne asked.

Aunt Helen held her hand over her mouth and had tears in her eyes, "Let's not work at the table. It's Thanksgiving. We should be talking about love and happiness, not murder. You three can do that later."

"That's right, you kids need to leave our county hero alone!" Jack smiled, remembering the conversation at the barbeque.

Everyone looked down in silence, "Sorry, Aunt Helen," Isaac said. "Let's change the subject. Leanne, did you know the FBI has a field office in New York?" smiled Isaac.

"That's nice." Leanne did not want to show enthusiasm because she did not want to encourage any further advances from Isaac.

"Leanne has an announcement," Jacob stated nonchalantly.

Everyone immediately became enthralled.

"What is it, honey?" asked Aunt Helen.

Unprepared, Leanne announced, "I think Jacob wants me to tell everyone that I got the Vice President position."

"Oh my goodness!" came the roar from the family. Aunt Helen was thrilled and stood up immediately to hug Leanne. Katie was second in line to tell her how proud she was of her.

Sara hugged her last. During the embrace, Sara whispered, "We've missed out on having a great teacher with us, but at least I know why Jake's been so grouchy." Releasing the embrace, Sara smiled, and Leanne seemed to display a look of guilt.

"I won't be able to visit as often, but I'll do my best. The new job comes with a lot more responsibilities."

"We'll all be here for you whenever you get a chance to visit," replied Sara. "The Lester and McKinney families have only been here for almost a hundred years. I'm not sure we'll be going anywhere soon." Sara smiled.

"You know Scott and I will visit whenever we get a chance," Katie promised.

"When do you start?" asked Isaac.

"Actually, I start on December first," Leanne said with a shrug.

"That means you won't be visiting at Christmas," said Katie. Katie's smile had dwindled from her face.

"No, that means you and Scott will take a weekend before the family Christmas party and visit me to see the Christmas lights. You can bring everyone if they want to…," smiled Leanne.

"I can tell you that I can't at Christmas, but I'll do my best to come up after Easter," Aunt Helen said. "Too many families that need help during Christmas, and I'll be really busy with all the churches."

The rest of Thanksgiving dinner was spent talking about Leanne's promotion and plans as to when everyone would take turns visiting her, except for Jacob. Jacob sat quietly and listened to his family discuss travel plans.

Night fell, and while the family enjoyed dessert and coffee, Jacob walked outside to stand on the porch. The quiet of the night and the cool chill of the evening calmed him. It was a dark and clear night. Jacob stood on the porch, leaning against the railing and looking at the stars.

After dessert and coffee, Leanne walked outside to where Jacob stood on the porch alone. "Everything about this place is beautiful. Even the night is beautiful here. I missed the stars when I went back to New York." Jacob remained silent, and Leanne continued, "Want to drive me to the hotel, Boy Scout?"

"Did Isaac not ask if he could?"

"He offered, but I'd feel better if you drove me," Leanne said. "I think your brother likes me more than as a cousin."

"It's because you're not our cousin," Jacob bluntly replied.

"Are you angry with me?" Leanne asked.

Jacob's head dropped from looking at the sky to look at his feet. Jacob shook his head and said, "No. You've done absolutely nothing wrong. It's me. I'm angry at myself."

"Oh my goodness," Leanne laughed and chided, "What did you do to upset yourself so much?"

"To be honest, I grew feelings for someone I know doesn't think of me as anything but a cousin." Jacob stared intensely into Leanne's eyes.

Feeling nervous, Leanne said, "I really want to joke about how Katie is dating Scott, right?"

Jacob stepped toward her, "I think you know the truth."

The intensity of his stare was making Leanne's heart skip beats. She felt butterflies in her stomach, and she was dizzy and short of breath. Placing her hand on his chest before he could step even closer, she said, "Jacob, I'm flattered…."

Jacob stepped back and said, "I hear a but coming."

"You have no idea how messed up I am. I don't want to go to the hotel, I want to go home with you, but I can't."

Stepping forward again, Jacob asked, "Why not? You're happier here, and I think you are starting to have feelings for me." Jacob was making a convincing argument.

Leanne again placed her hand on his chest. With tears in her eyes, she said, "This hurts me, too, but I can't. I just can't. I'm not asking you for time because I've been like this most of my life. I want you to be happy, so you need to forget about these feelings."

"So, you're not interested in me?" Jacob stepped forward again.

"If that's what you need to think for us to maintain our current relationship, then no, I'm not interested," Leanne said bluntly. Her face was stoic even though Jacob could clearly see the shine of the tears in her eyes reflected by the moon and stars.

Jacob stepped back, "If that's your decision."

Leanne stood taller, "It is."

"Forgive me, but I'll ask Dad if he can drive you to the hotel, and please forgive me, but I'd prefer not to see you again for a few months. I just need some time."

"I'm sorry," Leanne said.

"You have nothing to be sorry for. You've always made yourself clear. I just didn't listen," Jacob gave a half-hearted smile.

They both walked into the house, and Jacob asked his dad to drive Leanne to the hotel and left without saying good-bye to anyone.

Time passed as usual. Jacob worked too many hours to keep his mind off of Leanne. Scott and Katie went to New York the second weekend of December and brought home photos. Out of courtesy, they never mentioned the photos or Leanne to Jacob, only that they had enjoyed seeing all the Christmas lights in New York.

For about a month, every day was mundane and repetitive for Jacob. He seemed to be working on habit. Everyone was thankful that he was no longer grouchy, but now they worried that the melancholy state of his existence would never end. They wanted to see Jacob laugh and enjoy his life once more.

Things started to turn around and get a little better the first week of January. Jacob had attended a New Year's Eve party with Scott and Katie in Bristol. Scott had volunteered to be the designated driver for the evening, so Jacob had several drinks throughout the night. They were happy to see him slow dance with several eligible ladies at the party, even if it was with the assistance of whiskey.

By the fifteenth of January, the dark cloud that had been following Jacob around seemed to dispel, and things were finally getting back to normal.

"Good morning, Maribeth!" Jacob shouted as he walked into the office that morning smiling.

"Sounds like you had a fun weekend. Did you go out with Scott and Katie?"

"Nah, I was getting tired of being a third wheel and asked Brandy Tipton for a date."

"The attorney from Buchanan County?" asked Maribeth.

Jacob smiled, "The one and only."

"That's a good match." Maribeth nodded her approval. "Where did you take her?"

"To Gatlinburg for the weekend." Jacob smiled.

"To Gatlinburg? On a first date?"

Jacob smiled and said, "We left Friday, and we just got back. I've not even been home yet."

"It's a good thing you came straight in. They closed the schools because of the ice, and there's a tree down close to your driveway. The roads are awful. Scott was afraid to let me drive myself, so he got up and drove me to work this morning and went back home."

"It wasn't bad on the interstate or the state roads. It's the back roads and mountains that got hit really hard."

"Don't take me wrong, I'm glad to see you're happy, but this thing with Brandy is moving a little fast, isn't it?"

"Nah, life is short." Jacob smiled as he walked into his office, leaving the door between the two rooms open.

Jacob was working on paperwork over the next hour when he heard the emergency call from Maribeth's desk. The voice on the radio said that there was a car accident involving an older, baby blue Datsun that had slid off the road and was now over the mountainside on Sandy Ridge.

For a moment, Maribeth wasn't sure if Jacob had heard the call, but before she could open her mouth to call for him, he jolted from his office door with his coat in hand and ran to a four-wheel drive patrol vehicle.

There were very few cars on the road that morning, and typically, a drive to the top of Sandy Ridge would have taken about thirty minutes, but this morning, with lights flashing and sirens blaring, the drive to the top of Sandy Ridge took only fifteen minutes. The road grew icier as the elevation increased. Jacob could keep traction using the small amount of snow that had gathered on top of the ice. Rounding a curve, he could see the lights of the Sandy Ridge Volunteer Fire Department and felt a little calmer because they were already on the scene.

Jacob stepped from the vehicle and quickly approached the crash site. Cal Edwards, Fire Chief, caught Jacob first, grabbed him by both shoulders and said, "Jake, don't go down there."

In a panic, Jacob tore loose from the man's grip and headed off the hillside. He felt his knee give way in the ice and snow on the steep embankment but ignored the pain to get to Aunt Helen. Arriving at the car, he was gripped with the knowledge that it was too late. She was gone.

Jacob's head fell as he quietly sobbed, standing beside the car. The firemen on the scene all removed their headgear in respect for his grief. After a short while, Jacob started the climb back to the top of the hill. As he walked, he noticed food boxes from Feed America had been scattered down the hill during the accident. Aunt Helen was always doing something good for the people around her, and he guessed that she knew of a family in need and had made the drive early to pick up supplies.

At the top of the hill, Jacob called his dad. Jacob wanted the news broken to his mother gently. He then called Scott so that he could break the news to Katie that Aunt Helen was gone. After years in the military and law enforcement, those were the most heartbreaking phone calls he'd ever made.

When Jacob returned to the office, Cat noticed Jacob limping and his knee had swollen from jumping off the embankment, so she called and made an appointment for him to see a doctor. She knew that Jacob would ignore his pain to be there for his family and that he wasn't in his right mind to make the call himself.

The next two days were a blur: funeral arrangements, visitors offering condolences, and people bringing food to the family. Jacob felt like he was in shock. It was one of the few funerals held in the county where nearly every denomination spoke a few words at the service. Aunt Helen was loved and was never a member of just one church. She loved everyone, and she had many people who would miss her.

During the evening funeral, Mark Huffine walked over to Jacob and handed him an envelope. Jacob looked down at the familiar handwriting. The envelope was from Aunt Helen. "This is strange to say, but your aunt handed this to me last week. She said if anything happened to her, you should get this letter. She said everything goes to Katie except for the box under her bed. She said that Katie will know to get the box to you."

"Thank you," replied Jacob as he placed the envelope in his jacket pocket for safekeeping.

The evening service lasted until nearly ten that night. Isaac had been allowed bereavement from the FBI for a short period and had made the drive home for the funeral. The front row was filled by Katie, Scott, Sara, Jack, Isaac, and, lastly, Jacob himself. Leanne couldn't leave work to attend, but she sent a huge flower bouquet and spoke with Katie late into the night, nearly every night since the accident.

The morning funeral started at ten a.m. The family looked tired and emotionally drained. At the gravesite, Katie said, "Jake, I have something in my car for you. It's locked, so I hope you have a key. Mom told me a week ago that when she died, it was for your eyes only. It was almost like she knew something would happen to her." Katie's head fell, and she began to cry again. Scott wrapped her in his arms and let her cry into his chest.

Jacob nodded. As everyone left the graveside service, the family headed home, but Jacob went to the office. Sitting down at his desk, he opened the letter.

Chapter 16
The Letter and the Diary

My dearest Jacob,

I never had a son, but I've always loved you as my own. I've wanted to tell you something most of your life and couldn't. I'm so sorry I had to kill your uncle.

The first lines of the letter hit Jacob with an incredible shock. He reread it, thinking he must be dreaming or hallucinating. It was a few moments before he could continue reading.

Three weeks before I murdered Calvin, I had gone to the grocery store while he watched your cousin, Katie. Katie was only five years old at the time. I always loved seeing Calvin with Katie. They loved each other very much. When I arrived home, I peeped in through the partially open blinds of the living room window to see what they were doing. I loved to watch them play or nap together when they thought I wasn't looking. I wasn't prepared for what I saw. I imagine you may not believe me because the story does sound unbelievable. Your uncle was an Army Veteran and worked part-time on the police force. Everyone thought of him as a great man.

Peeping through the window, I saw him and Katie sitting on the couch. Katie was laughing. Then I realized that his pants were unbuttoned and unzipped. He was using Katie's innocent little hand to massage himself to an erection. She was laughing because she thought it was a game. I pulled away from the window. Thinking quickly, I ran to the car with the groceries, tore the bag, spilled the contents onto the ground, and honked the horn. Calvin came outside to help me, which drew him away from Katie. I covered my anxiety by saying I was upset about dropping the groceries.

From that day, Katie was never left alone with him. That night, I told him I couldn't sleep and was going to watch television downstairs. In truth, I was thinking about what to do. No one would believe me, and I knew that. So, that night, the plan was born. The next day, your mother watched Katie, and I borrowed her car to drive into town. I started a life insurance policy on your uncle that required his signature, so I told them I'd bring it to them the next day. No one asked questions when I forged your uncle's signature on the documents. All I had to do now was wait for rain. That was a tough two and a half weeks. I had to continue to live in a home with and protect my daughter from a pedophile while pretending to be the happy little housewife. It was most difficult when I was near your mom. She's always been able to read my emotions like a book. So, for those two and a half weeks, I tried to stay away from her as much as possible.

When the rain started that evening, I carried Katie with me into the basement. I first went to the rear of the basement and unplugged the sump pump. I turned off the breaker and pulled the dryer from the wall. Using a large hand saw file from the garage, I filed the cord at an angle to make it look frayed and not cut. I shoved the dryer into place near the basement door and turned on the breaker. It looked like an accident, and no one asked any questions.

I don't regret my decision or my actions concerning the murder of your uncle. We both know that his funeral shaped your young life. You saw the military men and the Sheriff's officers, and you wanted to be just like your Uncle Calvin. I'll let you know, you are a much greater man than your Uncle Calvin. If his death did one thing that made a better world, it was you and Katie.

Over the years, while working as a nurse in a pediatrician's office, I've seen and heard too many abused children come into that office. I couldn't bear to let a child live like that. I knew something had to be done. Someone had to set things right. Someone could commit murder and get life in prison, but someone sexually hurts a child and gets a slap on the wrist. It's wrong, Jacob. Day and night, I earnestly and wholeheartedly prayed to God to end the suffering of these children. It wasn't long before my prayers were answered in the most unconventional way imaginable. I was reminded that we are the hands and feet of God. I was to assist Him with bringing these people to the throne of the ultimate judge.

To avoid being caught, I'd use a scenario that matched a hobby or an activity they enjoyed against them. I made sure to cover my tracks. God alone would tell me when my work was complete. I always wore gloves from the pediatrician's office, and my hair was pulled tightly in a bun to prevent hairs from being left behind. Sometimes I wore a hat or toboggan just to make sure. Beneath my dress, I sometimes wore weights that would cause someone to think I was forty pounds heavier if I left footprints. I also wore those loud-smelling poultices during or after my jobs. I knew everyone hated them, and I explained them away as natural remedies, but the smell would throw off the scent if anyone ever brought Cap in to investigate a scene. Only once did I appreciate those smelly poultices.

As I write this, I remember the conversation between you and Isaac on Thanksgiving Day. I remember holding back laughter until I had tears in my eyes, and you thought I was upset. I told you that you two shouldn't be talking about things like that at Thanksgiving dinner. I laughed because you two hadn't realized the person committing the crimes might not be illiterate. A quick study of serial killers shows that the person would be organized and possibly obsessive-compulsive. I'm not organized or obsessive.

The profile that you both concocted was entirely incorrect and made me laugh.

Over the past year, I've watched you try to figure out what was happening, and I felt saddened by your attempt. Not because you hadn't caught me, but because I hated that you felt like something was missing and you weren't smart enough to figure it out. I'm here to let you know it wasn't meant for you to figure out. There was planning, purpose, and reason for what I did. God set the plan in motion, and none of us are wiser than our Creator. I worked diligently to make sure that no innocent lives were taken during the process of my work.

Now that I'm gone, don't worry about my afterlife. I believe God has ordained my work, and I am heading toward a beautiful place in Paradise to be with Him. There were too many times that God brought the children to me, and they opened up concerning very private ordeals. There were too many times that killing these men and women was not only easy but too easy. I believe God has been using me to set the atrocities committed against His children right.

I've left my journal for you. What you do with it is your decision.

I will always love you with all my heart,

Aunt Helen

Jacob folded the letter and rested his elbows on his desk. His forehead leaned into his hands. Could this be real? Jacob's heart was beating wildly. He felt waves of nausea from deep within his body. The letter had a small key taped to the bottom. Jacob assumed it was the key to the box in front of him. He gently opened the box and found a leather-bound journal. As he glanced through the handwritten pages, he saw names, dates, and details only a murderer would know about the final moments of each person listed.

Quickly scanning through the journal, he noticed a familiar name near the back of the journal almost immediately. He remembered going to Hunter Raynott's funeral.

Hunter Raynott: poisoning 2023
Hunter had been dating a woman from Buchanan County named Darlene. Darlene had a seven-year-old daughter from a previous relationship named Courtney. Darlene had brought Courtney to Dr. Reynolds' office instead of her usual pediatrician because they were thinking about moving in with Hunter, and our clinic was closer to their new home.

Darlene told us that Courtney might be starting a bladder infection because she had recently started wetting the bed. Courtney was small for her age and sat quietly on the examining table with her arms wrapped around her body. The child never looked up and never spoke.

Dr. Reynolds asked the mother about conducting a visual inspection. Darlene consented, and Dr. Reynolds left the room while Darlene and I changed Courtney into an examination gown. I noticed bruising around the breast area of the small child, but I didn't mention it to Darlene. When Courtney had donned the gown, I retrieved Dr. Reynolds from the hallway.

Darlene asked her daughter to lie back, and the girl complied. The seven-year-old girl, who had before sat quiet and withdrawn with her arms around her body, began to kick, scream, and fight when Dr. Reynolds approached. Dr. Reynolds glanced at me, and I shot a look at him that allowed him to realize my suspicions without alarming the mother.

"I'll tell you what," Dr. Reynolds began, "Helen here has been working with kids for over twenty years. I'm going to let her do the inspection if that's okay with you, Mom?" Dr. Reynolds smiled.

Darlene consented, and Dr. Reynolds left the room. To get the girl to relax, I told her I had to check her poopy hole for rainbows and bubble gum. For a moment, the child looked confused. I said, "You've seen rainbows, right?" The girl quietly nodded. "Well, sometimes, rainbows gather up in buttholes, and when people toot, it's so big that it shoots into the air and makes a rainbow. Have you done that yet?" The little girl laughed and shook her head.

"Lean back and let me take a look, okay?" Courtney nodded, feeling more relaxed. The small child relaxed and allowed me to raise the gown and begin a visual inspection. There were signs of bruising around the vagina.

From the top of the bed, I heard a small voice say, "What about the bubble gum?" It was the first time I had heard the girl's voice.

"Have you ever had bubble gum in your hair?" I asked.

"Yes, Momma had to cut it out," she replied.

"Well, bubble gum and rainbows make a bad mix. Can you imagine cleaning up all that bubble gum when it mixes with the rainbow? It covers the trees and the flowers. That stuff is sticky, and it causes ants all over! So, bubble gum rainbows can be dangerous."

The little girl laughed, knowing that everything I was telling her was fiction. But it kept her mind off of what was happening. During the visual inspection, I asked the mom if I could test a spot using a swab. The mother agreed.

Being careful not to hurt or upset the girl, I picked up two swabs. One swab was to show the girl what would be touching her and ensure she was comfortable with the procedure. Upon the child's approval, I tested the outer labia and placed the swab into a sterile tube for testing.

Darlene and I redressed the child, and I stepped into the hallway with the test tube. I spoke momentarily with Dr. Reynolds. Dr. Reynolds talked to the mother, but she denied knowing anything about it. She said her daughter had wrecked her bicycle the week before, which could have caused the bruising.

The date at the top of the paragraph was the day Hunter's body had been found.

Jacob sat back and thought to himself. He was confused and shocked. His mind whirled. How could a woman who loved humanity become this? She always volunteered at the local churches and helped others in every way she could. Jacob thought back to discussions with his aunt and remembered her saying once that anger could be a great motivator. He also remembered the discussion at the dinner over six months ago when Katie had moved back home. That day, Aunt Helen said, "Well, in my opinion, people who hurt children are not human. We kill animals for hurting children. Why don't we kill people who hurt children? Especially when it comes to sexual abuse." The clues became keys that unlocked the mystery Dickenson County had held for almost twenty-five years.

Jacob returned to the journal. The next paragraph was a note that included a recipe. The recipe was for some kind of jelly, and the most prominent ingredient in the receipt was condensed antifreeze. The note said that before going to drink and party that night, Helen had stopped by Hunter's house to ask him if he knew the recipe for his grandmother's jelly doughnuts because hers had not come out right. Helen had offered a donut to Hunter, and he ate it. He replied that he didn't have his grandmother's recipe, but she should ask his grandmother for it. Helen laughed and said, "I have, and she won't share it." Hunter laughed and bragged that Aunt Helen's was better than his grandmother's recipe anyhow. She left Hunter's house about ten minutes before his friends arrived. Twenty-four hours later, Hunter was found dead, presumed to be from alcohol poisoning. Hunter had a reputation for drinking heavily, and his blood alcohol level was still high when the body was brought to the hospital. An autopsy was never conducted.

Jacob stopped reading again and thought of how often he had eaten his aunt's jelly donuts. Everyone in the county loved those jelly donuts. Aunt Helen was known for it. Churches and nonprofits in the county were always asking her to donate her jelly donuts to sell at fundraising events. Jacob thought to himself, "Thank God she had never confused the recipes. She could have killed half the county with those things!"

Jacob turned to the first page of the journal and began to read chronologically.

> Harley Brant: accident
> Sexual Offender Registry from California.
> I knew the jack that Harley used in his garage had a recall. I tried several times but was afraid because Happy Kilgore's dogs kept barking at me. They didn't bark that night because I fed the dogs hamburger meat laced with Benadryl. I threw a ball of hamburger wrapped around the Benadryl tablet to each of the five dogs and waited an hour. The dogs fell

asleep around one in the morning. I put on my gloves from the clinic to prevent fingerprints. I walked down to the garage and walked in through the office door. Harley heard my footsteps and asked who was there. I did not reply but quickly turned the handle on the floor jack. The death was not instant. I could hear him whispering the word "help" as I poured hydraulic fluid that I had found in the garage across the jack stand. I could hear him gasping for air from beneath the car as I left. Tom Linkard never checked to see if the jack was faulty and deemed it an accident.

Jacob sat back and thought to himself. She planned it. She planned everything perfectly. Jacob continued reading.

John Pober: heart attack
Sexual Offender Registry from Oregon.
I stole some powdered potassium chloride from Lyle Brantley's house. His two daughters have an incredibly large fish aquarium and use it for their fish. Seventy milligrams per pound of body weight of potassium chloride will cause what looks like cardiac arrest when delivered directly into an artery. That seems like a lot, but it equals about two ccs from a needle. I

sneaked into his house after he had fallen asleep in his chair that evening. I had stolen some Sevoflurane from the office and placed it on a cloth and covered his nose and mouth. He wasn't able to move within seconds. I removed the cloth and placed the needle into the artery on his right arm. In less than ten minutes, he was dead. I gently removed my things and left. The physician at the ER didn't even notice the needle mark on his right forearm because he'd been to the hospital a few days before.

Jacob sat back and began to think again. Katie didn't pick it up either. Two different physicians separated by over twenty years had declared it a heart attack.

Julia Fernsby: suicide
Sexual Offender Registry from Michigan.
I met Julie in town and asked if she wanted to come over for lunch. We met at my house. I had her park around back because I didn't want anyone making the connection between the two of us. Sara and Jack were both at work that day. So, there was no one around to make the connection.

I made up a story about a friend named Mary who worked with the child protection services in the county where she once lived. I told her that Mary had asked about her because she felt that Julie had been treated unfairly by the courts and was worried about her. It didn't take long to make friends with Julie, and she began to trust me. After a short time, I mentioned that my friend Mary might be able to slip a very small note to her kids. She was thrilled.

I asked her to meet me at John Flannigan Dam that night because I would be waiting on a friend to go catfishing off the ledge that stuck out over the water. I told her that it was a late-night date, and she shouldn't get there until after nine that night because my date would be arriving at ten. Julie didn't know me well enough to know that I didn't date. She walked down to the edge of the rock and handed me the note. I was wearing my gloves when I took the note and then gave her a slight push. She lost her footing. I placed the note on a tree limb and left.

Jacob had never known the cold, calculating woman that his aunt had hidden so well. He was thankful he didn't. As he read, he began to feel grateful that he didn't catch her. He wasn't sure if she wouldn't have killed him or Leanne in order to complete the mission, she thought God had given her.

Brad Temple: suicide

Sexual Offender Registry from West Virginia.

During one of the free dinners offered at the Methodist Church, I stole a key to the church. I claimed I needed to buy windshield wipers before they closed and walked across the street to Advance Auto. I had them make a copy while I bought windshield wipers. Later that week, I found Brad sleeping on the park bench near the library. He recognized me from the dinners, and I offered him dinner and a place to sleep. I told him that I had a key to the church. My original plan was to poison him. But as we walked toward the church, he told me that he'd been depressed. He admitted to me that he had stolen Mark's gun and that it was in his backpack. Instead of slipping poison into his food, I used the Sevoflurane I had stolen for John Pober. I cleaned up the kitchen and, on the pretense of having blankets and pillows stored upstairs, we walked to the chapel area. I walked up behind him and covered his face with the rag as he walked in front of the communion table. He fell limp into my arms, and I managed to turn him around and lean him against the leg of the table. I found the gun in his satchel. It was exactly where he told me it was, and I checked to make sure the gun was loaded. I put the gun in the hand I had watched him eat with earlier and pulled the trigger. I put the weapon directly above his right ear not only because I didn't want to miss anything important, but I also didn't want to damage the beautiful stained-glass windows or woodwork inside the church. I felt so guilty about the carpet that I donated to the church the next week to cover having the carpet replaced.

Jacob remembered speaking with Pastor Mark. He wondered if Aunt Helen had ever witnessed how the death had affected him. He wondered if Aunt Helen knew about Mark witnessing to the man about forgiveness for what he'd done. Then, Jacob wondered if Aunt Helen would have even cared if Brad had been forgiven or not. So far, Jacob had read through four different murders. Aunt Helen had never felt remorse, as he could tell in her writings. She honestly thought that she was on a mission from God.

Connor Stolley: suicide
Sexual Offender Registry from California.
The rumor was that Connor lived in the
woods near the train tracks. I fashioned
a strong rope into a noose and purchased
a blow-up doll. I waited until around 2
a.m. and walked to the edge of the tracks.
It was cold that night, so Connor was
seated by his fire, and I called out to him
to let him know I was there. He asked
what I was doing up there that time of
night. I told him that I had plans to play
a Halloween joke. I told him I planned to
hang the doll on the train trestle as a
prank. Everyone who drove under it the
next morning would think it was a real
person. I told him I was worried about
the wind. Connor volunteered to help me
tie it off. He bent over to fasten the rope to
one of the upright safety rails. Once he
completed tying the noose to the vertical
bars, I simply threw the loop over his neck
instead of the blow-up doll and kicked
him off the trestle.

Again, no remorse. Jacob could not believe that the woman who had partially raised him, had bothered him every Sunday to attend church, and had dedicated her life to helping people had committed murder.

Andrew Calcraft: shot with an arrow
Sexual Offender Registry from Idaho.
It took a while to figure out when he would be leaving the trailer park. Beverly took care to watch his every move. It answered my prayers when she asked for prayer that Sunday because he was going deer hunting. That evening, I took the bow and arrow set I had bought Katie for Christmas when she was eleven and modified the store-bought kids arrow. I added a razor tip that I purchased separately. I was there an hour before Andrew left to go hunting that morning. I was almost caught when that crazy dog of hers started barking. As he entered the woods, I caught him in the back with an arrow, and he went down. I left a different route than when I came in because I didn't want Rowdy barking again.

Jacob remembered back to his youth. He remembered that he and Katie had received bow and arrow sets that year. His stomach turned a little queasy when he remembered asking his father to teach them. Jack immediately pointed out that he was not the archer in the family, but Helen. Helen didn't play sports, but something about her sister's bow and arrow had aroused her attention when she was young. The once 'girly sister' had loved archery in her youth.

Jacob had always heard that hindsight was 20/20. He now understood the phrase far more than he did before. Aunt Helen was the last person he would have linked to the arrows, and she had taught him to shoot.

Samuel Colton: car accident
Samuel had a daughter named Savannah. She was Dr. Reynolds' patient, and after seeing vaginal bruising, I asked her about it when she was alone with me. Savannah was only nine years old at the time. She admitted that her father had been hurting her 'down there' when he drank.

I used a chainsaw file to wear through his break lines before he left for work one morning. That way, it would look like normal wear and tear. I sat in my car down the road, preparing to hit his car with mine if he had anyone else in the vehicle with him. I was relieved when I saw he was alone. Samuel lived on the top of Big A mountain, and as he drove down the hill to work that morning, he hit the brakes, and nothing happened. The car went through the guardrail, hit a tree, and killed him. I kept driving as if nothing had happened. The investigation showed a faulty brake line had been the culprit.

This time, though, I decided to always think things through. I was terrified someone would be in the car with him. I was also scared he'd hit another vehicle and kill an innocent person. Killing only those who hurt children is my purpose and my calling.

Purpose and calling. That's what she was calling murder? A purpose? For a moment, Jacob was fuming. Then he remembered Savannah. Savannah was afraid to be touched by anyone. She wouldn't play games with the other kids. She always looked so sad. Jacob's heart hurt for her. Savannah had started to cheer up and play with Jacob and the other kids between the ages of ten and twelve. He remembered her acting more normal after her father died. At thirteen, she had given up. None of that would have ever happened if her father hadn't been so evil to his own daughter. Aunt Helen calling it a purpose wasn't as upsetting anymore, and he wondered if she wasn't right.

Robert Gagnon: motorcycle accident
Sexual Offender Registry from Massachusetts
I remember his grandparents. They were good, church-going folk. I can't imagine what caused him to end up like he did. But he did. He kidnapped and raped a fourteen-year-old girl when he was twenty-one.

Each morning, before dawn, I'd walk up to his property and sneak past the no-trespassing signs to learn his routines. Each morning he'd ride that bike to the top of the mountain. I still don't know what he was doing up there. He'd come down the hill in a few hours. He was so accustomed to the bike trail he'd made that he usually moved pretty fast as he rode down the mountain.

I used thick work gloves so that I wouldn't cut myself on the barbed wire. I measured how high it would need to be off the ground. I used a barbed wire stretcher to pull the line as far as I could and restrained it to a tree. I completed the work just in time, and I watched as he came down the mountain. He caught the barbed wire right under the chin. I thought it would only break his neck or cut him, but he was traveling quickly that morning.

I watched as the wire cut through his throat and neck, stopping only momentarily when catching the cervical section of the spine. The barbed wire pulled a little, and the bike traveled into the bushes. His body fell to the ground. As the *barbed wire sprang back into position, his head shot backward, up the hill. After a moment, it stopped and rolled back down the mountain under a blackberry bush.*

Well, that was one thing about Aunt Helen that Jacob always respected. She had a stomach of steel. What would have made an average person gag and vomit, Aunt Helen handled with grace. Jacob always wondered if she had been born with that ability or had developed it from years of being a nurse. He had always assumed that her sound stomach was also the reason she could tolerate the smelly poultices she occasionally wore.

Jacob's mind jumped. *Goodness sake!* He thought to himself. She wore those when she had committed murder and was making sure a dog didn't catch her dang scent! It had nothing to do with all-natural remedies!

William Henry: Chainsaw accident
Registered sex offender from Colorado.
I had been going to the campground every Wednesday morning and Sunday morning at daybreak to invite people to church for almost a month. Everyone was accustomed to seeing me there. I learned Henry's routine and when he would deliver the wood he had cut to the campers. I knew he was cutting the firewood early in the morning hours. One Saturday, I left a little early. He stopped sawing and turned off the chainsaw. I told him I was there

to invite him to church. He stared at me with a cold and menacing stare and said, "No." He restarted the chainsaw, and I turned as if to walk away.

I watched him for a moment, and when he sat down the chainsaw without turning it off, I walked over and picked it up. He turned, and I rammed the chainsaw into his side. I knew a bleed from the renal artery would be a quick death.

I have to think things through better next time. I knew there would be blood, and I'm accustomed to seeing blood. What I never realized was the sheer quantity of blood a man that size held or how far it would spray. I had brought a change of clothes with me, but his blood was in my hair and ears and had even drained into my shoes. I changed my clothes but had to drive home to take a shower, burn my old clothes, and then clean my car. It was everywhere!

You have got to be kidding me. She murdered this man with a chainsaw and is upset because there's blood everywhere. Aunt Helen was clearly off her rocker.

Craig Nellor: Explosion
Sexual Offender Registry from Oklahoma

I waited until Craig had the electricity turned on in that old shack. I had the lightbulb prepped for weeks. I hadn't placed the gasoline in it, but the hole was drilled and waiting. I had to wait. A regular fire would have given him time to escape. I was supposed to kill him, not make him homeless. Once I saw him in the grocery store purchasing milk and other refrigerated items, I knew the electricity had been activated.

I sneaked into the house while he was out. I left my car up the road from the driveway, knowing that the fire department would be turning into the driveway, and I didn't want them to see my car. It was a long walk to the top of that mountain, and I had to be certain I stayed out of old man Colley's view, but I made it. I was happy to see that a hundred-pound propane tank was sitting in the kitchen connected to the stove. I went into the back room and replaced the light bulb, and I heard his old truck pulling into the driveway. I ran to the kitchen, turned on the gas, and shot out the door opposite the driveway.

I walked to the top of the hill without being seen and was able to watch at a safe distance. It was still daylight, so he carried his groceries into the house without turning on the light. Then, I watched as he stepped onto his back porch. I watched him smoke several cigarettes, and as it grew darker, he began to swat at gnats that were attacking him. He threw out the last cigarette and walked into the house. He turned on the light. I was thankful that he hadn't smelled the gas as he put his groceries away and that he had allowed the fumes from the propane tank to accumulate while he was smoking. I was delighted knowing I had done my job well.

The first thing that caught Jacob's attention was the words, 'I was supposed to kill him, not make him homeless.' The second thing was the last sentence. Aunt Helen was delighted knowing she'd done the job well. That was what it was for her. It was a job she was doing for God, and that was why she was 'supposed to kill him.'

James Lafont: Fell into a pig trough
Sexual Offender Registry from Nevada
Again, I hid my car past the Gilbert's driveway and walked through the woods to the house, being careful not to disturb

the pigs. I watched as Joshua explained how to feed the hogs to James. They were using a shovel to stir the hog feed with water. I heard Joshua say it was too dry and that he would get the water hose. I was hiding behind the shed. James was watching the hogs eat when Joshua stepped into the shed to get the hose. I stepped to the fence, picked up the shovel, and hit James Lafont in the back of the head. He toppled forward into the pen, and the rest is history.

James LaFont fell into a pig trough. Jacob looked back through the listings. In every instance, Helen had written what the cause of death was according to everyone else. She had never written, I cut the brake lines or hit him with a shovel, or I murdered him. It was always as the coroner or police had written it.

Carl Flippant: fell off the cliff at the Breaks
Sexual Offender Registry from Delaware
Sometimes, my job is almost too easy. Carl was always out looking for plants to sell. I approached him at the food giveaway and asked if he knew what a large, purple-fringed orchid was. He said he did, but he had never seen one because they were rare. I told him I had seen one, but he would have to keep it a secret because

it was at the Breaks Park, and removing anything from the park came with stiff fines and penalties. Carl was incredibly interested. Carl thought he could sell it for a good price because some thought the orchid root and milk could be used as an aphrodisiac.

We decided to meet that evening at dusk so no one would see us. We walked down to the Towers Overlook. I told him that at the base, near the cliff, was the flower and that he could see it from the top by stepping on the second horizontal fence rail. I demonstrated and pointed to the base of the cliff, saying I could see it. He climbed onto the second pole, and I pushed. It was done.

I made sure I didn't hear anything once he hit the bottom of the cliff. When I didn't, I assumed he was dead. It took over a week for anyone to notice that he was gone or that there was a body at the bottom of the cliff.

Jacob read the words and thought to himself; she couldn't have known if he was alive or dead. She left him with a broken jaw and four broken limbs. He couldn't scream as the wild animals attacked him. It was more grizzly than she could have imagined.

Jacob thought of Leanne. He remembered being with her at the Breaks Park when they researched this death. He remembered her telling him about Megan. He had to admit there is true evil in this world. What happened to the kids that placed these people on the sexual registry list was evil. Jacob remembered reading an article that explained that up to forty percent of people charged with child molestation recidivate. There was no excuse and no cure for pedophilia. Jacob was feeling nauseous from the revelation.

Victor Loughty: Woodchipper
Sexual Offender Registry from Utah
Victor Loughty had moved here from Utah after being released from prison for the sexual molestation of several children in a Utah School where he had worked as the janitor. He had also served additional time because of child pornography and a laundry list of perversions against children.

Everyone in this county knows that the morning conversations at Hardee's are the best way to hear the local news, whether it's a rumor or not. It was by God's grace that I was in line at Hardee's at five that morning. I hadn't been able to sleep well since I heard that Victor had moved into the area. I heard ol man Mullins complaining to a group of other elderly gentlemen as they sat and drank their morning coffee. He mentioned that he was paying Victor fifty dollars to cut up a tree and that Victor was in the next county picking up the commercial grade woodchipper as they spoke.

I picked up my coffee and biscuit and left. Two hours later, I parked my car down the road and walked through the woods so I wouldn't be seen. I hid behind one of the trailers and watched as the men cut down the tree and then began to cut it into sections to place into the chipper. It was excruciatingly hot that morning.

At last, I saw my opportunity. Ol man Mullins walked into the house, yelling to Victor that he'd have Ellie make some sweet tea. He had to shout at Victor because the woodchipper was quite loud, so I heard every word. After he stepped inside, I ran towards Victor as he bent over to pick up another log. I was running as fast as I could, and my body collided with him, forcing him, head first, into the woodchipper.

What I didn't realize is that the angle I would hit him would cause his head to crash into the edge of the woodchipper guard. I was running at such a speed *when I hit him that the woodchipper moved. While Victor was going through the chipper, I landed in the yard. I was stunned. I couldn't believe I'd hit the man with such force that the combination of our two bodies hitting the woodchipper would cause it to move. I felt awful for poor Ellie's siding, but I'll never be able to apologize for making such an awful mess on the side of her house.*

Jacob again thought to himself. What is wrong with these people? Ol' man Mullins was upset about the siding, Mrs. Mullins was upset about the siding, and now, Aunt Helen even wrote about the mess she made on the siding. Doesn't anyone realize that it was a human being on the siding?

Marvin Adler
Sexual Offender registry from California
Marvin had been only nineteen when he was charged with the molestation of an eleven-year-old boy. He had been teaching the neighbor boy how to play baseball. The boy's mother found blood in his underwear and brought him to a local hospital, and the physician called the police. A child psychologist worked with the boy at the police station, and the young boy described the molestation. Marvin was arrested and sentenced to only two years for aggravated sexual abuse of a minor.

He had just turned twenty-two when he moved to Dickenson County, and his registration followed him. I caught Marvin at the grocery store in town. He was scratching a case of poison ivy. I walked over and said, "Oh, bless your heart! You have poison ivy."

The young man smiled and said, "Yes, I think the mountains don't agree with me, which is funny because I'm an herbalist. The only thing I know to put on it is aloe, and it's spreading."

"You know we have a cure, don't you?" I asked.

The young man looked confused. "A cure?"

"You probably already know that Hypericum Berries have been used to treat wounds on the skin, right?"

The young man nodded, and I continued, "Well, we have a white version that grows wild here. If you eat six berries, you're cured within two days. We all use it," I smiled.

The young man was amazed. "Where can I find it?" the young man asked.

"They grow all over the place. Just look around for a white berry with a black dot. It's August, so right now, it'll have a red stem. In the spring, they look like black cohosh plants but don't have any berries. You're in luck because the berries just arrived. You'll see birds eating the berries, too. Although I don't know why. Birds must not have taste buds. They're very bitter and taste bad. I'd suggest you take all six berries at once, don't chew, and just swallow them whole."

"I'll look it up," the young man smiled, genuinely interested. I told him that he'd need to google White Hypericum Berries. White Hypericum berries look incredibly similar to the white baneberries that grow here.

"Thank you so much!" He smiled as he walked away.

The next day he was found dead after eating six baneberries. I never knew why he was on top of Birch Knob when he ate them. I assumed he had found the berries *while walking up the trail and ate them while looking at the view from the top of the tower.*

Well, thought Jacob, at least I know why the autopsy showed that the berries were eaten whole. Jacob shook his head in disbelief.

Tommy Dolivo and Margaret Ginart

Sexual Offender Registry from South Texas

When given the job, I usually keep my professionalism. But this time, it was difficult. These two people were the nastiest and most vile people I have ever had the pleasure of ending. They were convicted of sex trafficking in Texas. Stolen children would be delivered to their home in South Texas and chained to walls in the basement. The children were trained to be sex slaves. Buyers would visit the home, and the children would be sold and shipped to Thailand. They served only ten years in a Texas prison for their crimes.

They moved to Dickenson County and immediately fell into an opioid addiction. That made it easy for me. An old friend had passed away from cancer. Her daughter had asked me to pick up the unused medication after her mother passed because she didn't know what to do with it. It sat in the box under my bed for six months before these two vile monsters moved to Dickenson County. I realized why I had kept it once they became addicted.

After dark one night, I parked down the road. I slipped through their backyard and sat on their back porch. I heard loud music and partying. After a short while, the music played, but no one inside the home was moving. I assumed that they both had passed out. With gloved hands, I opened the back door and walked inside. They were both nearly unconscious. I simply walked over and squirted the Fentanyl spray up their noses and walked out.

Jacob thought his sanity was gone entirely when he thought to himself, *I wonder how much money Aunt Helen saved the taxpayers from the future imprisonment of people like this? If forty percent recidivate, how many recidivate and don't get caught? I think she saved the government enough money to end homelessness.*

Marlene Shriver: Drowning
Mother of three children. Her oldest child,
a daughter, described in detail how her
mother allowed men to touch her and see
her without clothes in exchange for what
the child called 'bags of white candy that
mommy needed to be happy.'

I followed her to a party at the spillway
that evening. I watched as the park
rangers locked the entry gate and
bathrooms at ten. About ten people,
including Marlene, had been hiding to
escape being thrown out or arrested for
being drunk in public. I could hear them
talking about spending the night fishing. I
waited in the dark for several hours.
When almost everyone had left, Marlene
loudly announced she had to pee, and the
bathrooms were closed. I followed her to
the edge of the water. She had moved
upstream into the darkness. I hit her in
the back of the head with a stick I found
nearby. The stick wasn't large enough to do
the job, but the rock she hit her head on
completed the work for me. I watched her
body jerk as her life left. The others at the
party weren't concerned for her and didn't
bother to look for her before they left. Most
of my footprints were erased by the water,
but I stepped on the rocks near the edge

as I left to come home and get a few hours of sleep before church.

Jacob thought, *Aunt Helen went to church two hours after murdering a woman.* I wonder why she kept these journals. If it were to prove insanity, she'd have a good case. But I'm not sure that's why she kept them. She said only God could stop her from doing the work He had set before her. Was Aunt Helen done? Will there never be a person on the sexual registry list to enter Dickenson County again? What does all this mean? Jacob continued to read.

Jessie Hatman: explosion
Reported by the daughter of a friend.
Marlene Shriver told me that her "Uncle Jessie" had watched her undress and had fondled her several times for Mommy's special candy. The job wasn't difficult because the man was producing methamphetamines in his basement. After he left the night before, I waited until dark. I found his spare key under the doormat of his porch and locked his front door and threw the key into the grass. When he came home, he'd be forced to use the back door. I made sure it was him that entered the home and no one else. I replaced the main bulb over his lab with a lightbulb I had injected with gasoline which caused the explosion. The light bulb would only be turned on after he came

home and began work to make another batch.

Jacob thought of Jessie in the holding cell. He had been in trouble with the law since Jacob was a child. He'd never attempted to set his life right. Jessie wasn't known to be a pedophile, and he was never arrested for any crimes against children. Jacob wondered if a video hadn't been destroyed in the fire. He could see Jessie taking a video for money but not for his own pleasure. Then again, Jacob knew he'd been wrong before.

Stanley George: arrow
This was out of my normal range, but the oldest child had bruises. Stanley wasn't just hitting his wife. I took cash from my savings and purchased a life insurance policy in his name that would help raise their children. I completed the paperwork online using the information in the children's medical records. I put cash into an envelope with a printed copy of the insurance papers in the office's drop box.

I knew he would be deer hunting on the opening day of deer season. I decided to use the bow and arrow again. I had hidden it in my basement, wrapped in plastic, but I had to buy new arrows and tips. I hoped it would still fire as true as it did long ago.

I followed him when he left his home. He carried a flashlight which made him easy to locate. I used only the moonlight to follow him. As the sun rose, I fired the arrow. I missed my target but managed to hit him in the side. I wasn't sure if he was dead or not when I left. I didn't know what lengths you boys would take to find out who shot that arrow. So, for safety's sake, I put on one of my poultices to throw the dogs off of my scent before I climbed the mountain. That's why I smelled funny while talking to Maribeth during Scott's party. Stanley George was dead before dawn, and no one knew.

It was later that I found out about the bike accident. I still believe I did my duty because it was only a matter of time before he started hitting the children. But, If I don't have a sign in the next few days that I'm doing the right thing, I'm going to slow down for a bit and spend time in prayer.

So, thought Jacob, Aunt Helen knew we were investigating these murders by the time she accidentally killed an innocent man. Well, innocent of hurting his children. I can see the way she was thinking. Most of the time, if a man hits a woman, it spreads to the rest of his family. Whether he beat his wife or not, this time, it was murder. Yet now, there was no one to prosecute for the crime. Heck, I'm not sure I could have prosecuted her anyhow. She was my Aunt Helen. She raised me. I loved her. I still can't believe she did all of this. It's unimaginable.

> *Phillip Yandall: Not mine*
> *I spent the weekend fasting and in prayer. It truly bothered me that I may have killed an innocent man. Phil Yandell's death was the answer to my prayers and confirmation that I was doing the right thing. Phillip Yandell's neighbor had brought her seven-year-old daughter to Dr. Reynolds' office that week. After playing with dolls for a little while, she opened up and told me about the games she and Uncle Phil would play. His death answered my prayers that I was doing the right thing because he was the next name on the list.*

Jacob chuckled out loud while reading the first sentence. 'Not mine,' she said. Jacob shook his head and thought, *She worried over Stanley George, and the death of Phillip Yandall proved to her that she was doing God's work. There's been a lot of odd coincidences in these murders. She makes it seem incredibly easy and gives God the credit many times.*

Clark Lewis: blood sugar
I hated that. Clark's daddy taught history
to your mom and me. I remember the day
he found out he would be a father. He was
so excited. Since Mr. Lewis was a history
teacher, he thought his first child should
be named after a historical person, so he
called his son Clark Lewis after the
explorers Lewis and Clark. The students
thought it was weird, but we had too much
respect for Mr. Lewis in those days to say
anything. I'm glad Clark was the first and
not the only child. I felt sorry for having
to kill him.

Two boys came to Dr. Reynolds' office at
different times over a month. Dr. Reynolds
had been caring for both boys since they
were infants. They were both thirteen and
were brought in because their parents
thought they were depressed. When the
third boy came in, I triaged the boy myself.
During the regular line of questioning, I
told the boy that two other boys from his
class had come to see us and that we
already knew what was happening. He
acted relieved. He sighed and said, "So, Mr.
Lewis is going to get into trouble, huh?" I
said, "Yes, he is."

He asked what he should tell Dr. Reynolds. I told him that he could tell him anything he wanted or nothing at all. It was up to him. He didn't tell Dr. Reynolds anything.

I found out Clark would be going to the play. After the lights went out, I walked down to the third row, knelt, and whispered to him, "Clark, can you tell one of the boys in the shop class that I'll pay them fifty dollars for a new flower box? Mine is getting old." Clark didn't realize that while I was bent down, my skirt covered the cup he had brought in under his coat. I poured four bottles of Humalog into his drink. That amount may seem extreme, but I was worried that it wouldn't be processed by the body like it would if I had injected it. He was dead before the second act of the play.

When I noticed Scott's car outside, I realized the cup would be left at the scene. Someone might test the liquid. I waited outside until I saw people leaving from the back door. I quietly stepped through the rear entry door when one of the audience members stepped out. If anyone saw me, I'd just say I was helping to clean up after the play or that I had forgotten my cup *there when we set up. I quietly waited in the fold of the stage curtains, where I could not be seen until Katie left with the body and the EMTs. That's when I stole the cup and left. I'm glad I went back and got it. The cup was still half full.*

Jacob's mind whirled as he thought to himself. I knew someone had grabbed that cup!

Johnny Bressett: Breaks accident
I was shocked by this one. I had always thought that Johnny was a good guy. His neighbors, Mr. and Mrs. Barton brought their six-year-old daughter, Tiffany, to Dr. Reynolds' office. During the visit, I gave the little girl a doll. She sat quietly while I spoke with the parents. The parents were concerned because she had talked about kissing with your tongue. I asked the parents if I could speak with her alone for a moment. They agreed. The parents left the examining room, and I sat down with Tiffany and asked her why she had mentioned kissing with your tongue. She said, "It's a secret, and I'm a big girl, not a baby. I can keep a secret," she nodded and smiled a proud and innocent smile.

From speaking with her for only a few moments, I could tell the child was being groomed. The only problem was finding out who was grooming her.

"Let's talk about our girl spots. We're both girls. That's not a secret." The little girl laughed and nodded. "Do you know what girl spots are?" I asked. The little girl nodded and pointed at her chest and bikini area.

"When I was little, my mom, my dad, my sister, and my doctor were the only ones allowed to see my girl spots. How about you? Who can see your girl spots?"

The little girl began to count on her fingers. "My mommy, my daddy, my doctor, and sometimes my uncle Johnny. Johnny watches me if Mommy and Daddy work sometimes."

Sounding excited, I said, "That sounds like fun! What do you and Uncle Johnny do all day? Do you have tea parties?"

The little girl became excited. "We have tea parties, and we go swimming, and we plant flowers, and we watch movies, and we do all kinds of stuff!"

"What's your favorite movie?" I asked her. She said it was Rudolph.

"What's Uncle Johnny's favorite movie?" I asked, showing interest.

The little girl became quiet.

"Do you remember the name?" I asked.

"I don't think it has a name."

"Well, what's it about?"

"Uncle Johnny said it's a movie about how grownups show love."

I had heard enough. I gave Tiffany a lollipop and went into the hall and talked to Dr. Reynolds. Dr. Reynolds referred the family to a psychologist. On my way home that day, I drove by their house and realized Johnny lived two doors down. His home was older but well-kept. He had a beautiful flower garden. I decided to mention the purple-fringed orchid again, and this time, I'd mention that it was said to have aphrodisiac properties. It worked like a charm, but I hate that his shoe got stuck in that tree. Someone is going to notice that soon.

On a side note, I had dinner with you, Leanne, Katie, Jack, and Sara that night. The body hadn't been found yet. It's the last time I'll be able to copy a job from the past.

I'm glad my investigation stopped something, even if it was only a repeat of how she killed people.

Richard Talbert:
Sexual Offender Registry from Oklahoma Richard had been working freelance cleaning pools in the area. I met him when he cleaned Dr. Reynolds' swimming pool. He came to the office for his check. There was something eerie and sickening about him. I may have developed a sixth sense.

I jotted down his name and decided to research him. I discovered he had been a swim coach for the YMCA in Oklahoma and had molested several of his swimming students. He spent six years in jail and was released. He had moved to Bristol and worked as a pool cleaner. While at the office, he had told me he was thinking of moving to Dickenson County because it was cheaper to live here than Bristol. I asked him when he'd be here next because I knew a few people that would probably use him. He told me he'd be working at the Yates' home the next week and would leave me some business cards with Mrs. Yates. I gave him my number and told him that I knew quite a few that would want to meet him and see the work he does, so he should call me the night before so I could come up that evening with friends and show them his work. He thought it was a marvelous idea and thanked me.

That same evening, I stopped by to see Mrs. Yates and invite her to a church social the next day. Her three kids were swimming in the pool. She told me she was having it cleaned and drained the next week and wanted the kids to have one more pool day. It was an unusually warm day for the last week of September, and the pool was heated, so she wasn't too worried about the kids getting cold. She told me about Carol working so many hours and that he didn't have time to clean and drain the pool, so she had hired someone to do it.

I noticed the shed. "Is that your she-shed?" I asked.

"Oh no. Carol built it to store the pool chemicals away from the kids. He has pool chlorine and garden tools in there. He found white vinegar on clearance, and there's a big shelf at the back that's loaded with it," Arlene laughed. "I have to remind him to move that before it gets cold enough to freeze. It'll break every bottle he bought." Arlene laughed again and said, "That would be a smell and probably end up killing my flowers."

Without knowing it, Arlene had given me a plan. The next evening, I used a small flashlight and entered the shed. I moved the twelve or so gallon buckets of vinegar to the right side of the shelf and loosened a board in the rear of the shed that aligned with the bottles. Lastly, as I left the shed, I poured the pool chlorine tablets out of the buckets and onto the floor. As I worked, I realized that Carol must love buying in bulk at the end of the year when it's cheaper. There were over fifteen of the five-gallon buckets of pool chlorine. I carefully opened each tub and tilted it over. I was thankful that Carol was working so many hours that no one would notice the mess I had created until Mr. Talbert arrived to clean the pool.

The next week, Mr. Talbert called as promised the evening before he would be at the Yates' home. He advised me that he would be starting by 10:00 a.m. and probably have the work completed by 2:00 p.m. When he arrived the next morning, I watched him from the tree line behind the house. He opened the shed and found the chemicals in chaos. Instead of cleaning the shed first, he simply chose the articles he would need to clean and drain the pool.

He worked quickly and efficiently. He placed the pool cover over the top. I waited patiently in the woods until almost 2:00 p.m. I waited for the perfect time to lock him inside. I was beginning to worry that he wouldn't return to the shed. In his last moments, I witnessed him pick up a broom and enter the shed.

God must have blessed my work because he walked in the door, and the lock fell closed without my assistance. The accident enabled me to stay hidden. He was trapped. I walked to the rear of the shed and *moved the loosened board to the side. I used a small hammer to break every vinegar bottle and then tipped the shelf to make it look like an accident. I replaced the board and tapped it back into place with the hammer. I heard him gasping from the gas entering his lungs as I walked away.*

Jacob closed the journal. "Twenty-five," he said out loud.

"Twenty-five what?" said a familiar voice from the doorway. It was Cat.

Jacob was confused for a moment, not realizing he had spoken out loud. "Oh, I was just thinking about how old I was when Aunt Helen told me she was writing stories. She left me a few of the stories and her recipes for a few of those stinky poultices." Jacob smiled and held up the journal.

"Jacob, you shouldn't be here. You should be with your family," Cat said compassionately.

"Katie has Scott, Mom has Dad, and I'll be okay. Getting back to work keeps my mind occupied."

"Well, I was just checking on you. I have someone waiting. By the way, did you and Leanne ever figure out the accidents that keep happening?"

"Nope," said Jacob. Usually Jacob didn't lie, but this time he felt the need.

"Well, you might get one last shot to catch the county hero. The man waiting at my desk is on the sexual offender registry list. He came in to change his location from Arizona to Dickenson County."

Jacob looked at Cat, "You probably think I should just let sleeping dogs lie. Don't you?"

"Your Aunt Helen would have said the same thing," smiled Cat. Cat looked down at her watch, "You'd better hurry up. You're going to be late for your doctor's appointment," Cat reminded him.

Jacob placed the journal into the wooden box, closed the lid, and locked it with the key, "You can cancel it. I think I'll just use one of Aunt Helen's poultices."

Visit Dickenson County

https://townofclintwood.com/jettie-baker-center
https://haysivirginia.gov/
https://clinchcova.net/
https://www.breakspark.com/
https://dwr.virginia.gov/waterbody/flannagan-reservoir/
https://www.virginia.org/listing/birch-knob-tower/6195/
https://clintwoodumchurch.org/

www.ingramcontent.com/pod-product-compliance
Lightning Source LLC
Chambersburg PA
CBHW070350260626
47161CB00001B/89